"A thought-provoking blend of action and intrigue, with a competent and ethical heroine in Ang and a fully imagined setting whose atmosphere and cultural cues also play important roles. The result is an unforgettable page-turner built on surprises and full of potential."

—*Publishers Weekly* (starred review)

"This one won't stay on the shelf for long."

—*Booklist* (starred review)

"Hartley's fictional world is dense and rich. . . . Smart political intrigue wrapped in all the twists and turns of a good detective story makes for a rip-roaring series opener."

—*Kirkus Reviews* (starred review)

"A city in crisis, breathtaking rooftop chases, harrowing assaults, blood oaths, love and loyalty, brutal betrayals, and impressive detective work by the intelligent, intuitive Ang unfold in a fascinating, vividly described setting that includes smog and slums, gas lamps and opera houses, baboons and bushbabies. A political, multilayered mystery-thriller with a strong, impressively fierce heroine."

—*Shelf Awareness* (starred review)

"Hartley creates a vivid world with wildlife and landscapes reminiscent of those of South Africa in this alternative nineteenth-century fantasy. . . . A versatile work, appealing to all kinds of readers, especially alternative history and fantasy fans."

—*School Library Journal*

"The best imaginary worlds give readers the opportunity not only to enter a different realm but also to consider how that imaginary world reflects or distorts our actual one. Few novels have tackled this as skillfully as *Steeplejack*, the young-adult debut by bestselling author A. J. Hartley. *Steeplejack* is quietly thoughtful and breathlessly exciting."   —*BookPage* (Teen Top Pick)

"Anglet is a heroine cut from the same cloth as Katniss."   —*Justine*

"Luscious world-building, a tense mystery, and a smart heroine combine to make *Steeplejack* an absolute thrill ride."
                                                      —*YA Books Central*

"What a world Hartley has created! A world of great danger . . . murder . . . [and] suspense on just about every page. And enough twists and surprises to keep the pages turning long into the night."
   —R. L. Stine, author of the Goosebumps and Fear Street series

"With its unique South African–inspired setting, richly drawn and diverse cast of characters, and unstoppable plot, readers of any age won't be able to put *Steeplejack* down!"
                              —Carrie Ryan, *New York Times* bestselling
                                author of the Forest of Hands and Teeth series

"A. J. Hartley has created a gritty, fascinating, and utterly unexpected new fantasy thriller with marvelous drama, characters, and a freshness I haven't seen in a long time."
                              —Kevin J. Anderson, *New York Times*
                                bestselling author of *Clockwork Angels*

"With *Steeplejack*, A. J. Hartley introduces a dynamic, complex, and likable new heroine who combines wits, skill, and courage to face deadly challenges in an exotic world. Teens and adults will love this book and want more, more, more!"
                              —Jonathan Maberry, *New York Times* bestselling
                                author of *Rot & Ruin* and *The Orphan Army*

Tor Teen Books by A. J. Hartley

Steeplejack
Firebrand

STEEPLEJACK

A. J. HARTLEY

**TOR
TEEN**

A TOM DOHERTY ASSOCIATES BOOK
NEW YORK

This is a work of fiction. All of the characters, organizations, and events portrayed in this novel are either products of the author's imagination or are used fictitiously.

STEEPLEJACK

Copyright © 2016 by A. J. Hartley

A Tor Teen Book
Published by Tom Doherty Associates
175 Fifth Avenue
New York, NY 10010

www.tor-forge.com

Tor® is a registered trademark of Macmillan Publishing Group, LLC.

The Library of Congress has cataloged the hardcover edition as follows:

Hartley, A. J. (Andrew James), author.
Steeplejack / A.J. Hartley.—1st ed.
    p. cm.
"A Tom Doherty Associates book."
ISBN 978-0-7653-8342-6 (hardcover)
ISBN 978-1-4668-9169-2 (e-book)
  1. Race relations—Fiction.   2. Murder—Investigation—
Fiction.   3. Conspiracies—Fiction.   4. South Africa—
Fiction.   I. Title.
[Fic]—dc23   2016287108

ISBN 978-0-7653-8343-3 (trade paperback)

Our books may be purchased in bulk for promotional, educational, or business use.
Please contact your local bookseller or the Macmillan Corporate and Premium
Sales Department at 1-800-221-7945, extension 5442, or by e-mail at
MacmillanSpecialMarkets@macmillan.com.

First Edition: June 2016
First Trade Paperback Edition: June 2017

Printed in the United States of America

0 9 8 7 6 5 4 3 2 1

For Finie and Sebastian,
and in celebration of those who discover their value
in spite of what they are told

STEEPLEJACK

CHAPTER

1

THE LAST PERSON UP here never made it down alive, but there was no point thinking about that. Instead, I did what I always did—focused on the work, on the exact effort of muscle, the precise positioning of bone and boot that made it all possible. Right now, that meant pushing hard with my feet against the vertical surface of one wall while my shoulders strained against another, three feet away. I was horizontal, or as near as made no difference, the two brick faces forming an open shaft. If I relaxed even fractionally, I would die on the cobbles eighty feet below.

So don't.

It really was that simple. You figured out what you needed to do to stay alive, and you did it, however your sinews screamed and your head swam, because giving in meant falling, and falling meant death.

I was working the old cement factory on Dyer Street, bypassing a rusted-out portion of the ladder to the roof on my way to rebuilding the chimney itself, the top rim of which had shed bricks till it looked like a broken tooth. I braced myself and inched my way up, brick by brick, till I reached the section of ladder that was still intact and tested it with one cautious hand.

Seems solid enough.

I pivoted and swung my body weight onto the lowest rung. For a moment, I was weightless in empty air, seesawing between life and death, and then I was safe on the ladder and climbing at ten times my previous speed.

I am Anglet Sutonga—Ang to those who think they know me—and I am a steeplejack, one of perhaps six or seven dozen who work the high places of Bar-Selehm. Some say I am the best since the Crane Fly himself, half a century ago. They might be right at that, but boasting—even if it stays in your head—makes you careless, and the one thing you really can't afford up there on the spires and clock towers and chimneys is carelessness. If I was good, it was because at seventeen I'd lived longer than most.

I moved easily over the roof to the point where the great round tower of the chimney reached up into the murky sky, tested the ladder, and began the slow climb to the top. Most of the really tall factory chimneys—the hundred- or two-hundred-footers—taper as they go, but they generally flare at the top, sometimes with an elaborate cap that juts out. These make for interesting climbing. You scale straight up; then you have to kick out and back, hanging half upside down over nothing, till you get over the cap and onto the upper rim.

There are no ladders at the top. If you leave them in place, the anchor holes in the mortar will trap moisture and crack the brick, so after each job, the steeplejack takes the ladders down and fills the holes. In this case, the ladder up to the cap was still there because two months ago, Jaden Saharry—the boy who had been working the chimney—fell, and no one had finished the job.

He was thirteen.

Most steeplejacks are boys. When they are young, it doesn't much matter what sex they are, because the work is just getting up inside the fireplaces of big houses and climbing around in the chimneys with a brush and scraper. It is all about being small and less likely to get stuck. But as the steeplejacks grow too big for domestic chimneys and graduate to the factory stacks, strength and agility become key. Then, since no one is looking for a bride who can outlift him, the girls are gradually given other things to do with their daylight hours. I was the only girl over fourteen in the Seventh Street gang, and I maintained my position there by climbing higher and working harder than the boys. And, of course, by not falling.

A new boy—Berrit—was supposed to be up here, waiting for me to show him the ropes, but there was no sign of him. Not a good start, though in truth, a part of me was relieved.

Today I wanted to be alone with my thoughts as much as possible.

Ten feet below the great brick overhang of the cap, I cleared the last mortared hole with my chisel and hooked one leg over the top of the ladder so I could use both hands. I took a wooden dowel from my pocket and pressed it into the cavity with the heel of my hand, then drew an iron spike—what we call a dog—from the satchel slung across my chest, positioned its tip against the protruding end of the dowel, and drove it in with three sharp blows of my lump hammer. The action meant straightening up and back, and I felt the strain in my belly muscles as I leaned out over the abyss. The ground, which I could see upside down if I craned back far enough, was a good two hundred feet below. Between me and it, a pair of vultures was circling, their black, glossy wings flashing with the pale light of dawn. I'd been higher, but there comes a point when a few more feet doesn't really make any difference. Dead is dead, whether you fall from fifty feet or three hundred.

The dog split the dowel peg and anchored in the brick. I tested it, then ran the rope to pull the last length of ladder into place, ignoring the tremble of fatigue in my arms as I hooked and lashed it firm. I took a breath, then climbed the newly positioned rungs, which leaned backwards over the chimney cap, angling my boots and gripping tightly with my hands. Carefully, like a trapeze artist, I hauled my body up, out, and over. I was used to being up high, but it was only when I had to navigate the chimney caps that I felt truly unnerved.

And thrilled.

I didn't do the job just because I was good at it. I liked it up here by myself, high above the world: no Morlak looking over my shoulder, no boys testing how far they had to go before I threw a punch, no wealthy white folk curling their lips as if I put them off their breakfast.

I clambered over and sat inside the broad curve of the chimney's fractured lip, conscious of my heart slowing to something like normal as I gazed out across the city. From here I could count nearly a hundred chimneys like this one. Some taller, some squat, some square sided or stepped like pyramids, but mostly round like this, pointing up into the sky like great smoking guns, dwarfing the minarets and ornamental roofs that had survived from former ages.

It had once been beautiful, this bright, hot land rolling down to the sea. In places, it still was—wide and open savannahs where the sveld beasts grazed and the clavtar stalked; towering mountains, their topmost crags lost in cloud; and golden, palm-fringed beaches.

And sky. Great swaths of startling, empty blue where the sun burned high during the day, and night brought only blackness and a dense scattering of stars.

That's how it had been, and how it still was, not so very far away. But not here. Not in Bar-Selehm. Here were only iron and brick and a thick, pungent smoke that hung in a perpetual shroud over the pale city, shading its ancient domed temples and stately formal buildings. A couple of miles inland, down by the Etembe market, the air was ripe with animal dung, with the mouthwatering aroma of antelope flesh roasted over charcoal braziers, with cardamom, nutmeg, and pepper and, when the wind blew in from the west, with the dry but fertile fragrance of the tall grass that bent in the breeze all the way to the mountains. In the opposite direction was the ocean, the salt air redolent with fish and seaweed and the special tang of the sea. But here there was only smoke. Even all the way up the chimneys, above the city, and at what should have been the perfect vantage on the minarets of Old Town, and on the courts and monuments of the Finance District, I could see little through the brown fog, and though I wore a ragged kerchief over my mouth and nose, I could still taste it. When I spat, the slime was spotted with black flakes.

"If the work doesn't kill you," Papa used to say, "the air will."

I sat on the dizzying top, my legs hooked over the edge, and below me nothing for two hundred feet but the hard stone cobbles that would break a body like a hundred hammers.

I studied the cracked and blackened bricks around the chimney's rim. Three whole rows were going to have to come out, which meant ferrying hods of new bricks and mortar up and down the ladders. It was a week's work or more. I was faster than the others on the team, and though that generally earned me little but more work, I might make an extra half crown or two. Morlak didn't like me, but he knew what I was worth to him. And if I didn't do the job, if Sarn or Fevel took over, they'd mess it up, or miss half of what needed replacing, and we'd all suffer when the chimney cap crumbled.

I gazed out over the city again, registering . . . something.

For a moment it all felt odd, wrong, and I paused, trying to process the feeling. It wasn't just my mood. It was a tugging at the edge of consciousness, like the dim awareness of an unfamiliar scent or a half memory. I moved into a squat, hands down on the sooty brick, eyes half-closed, but all I got was the fading impression that the world was somehow . . . *off*.

I frowned, then reached back and worked the tip of my chisel into the crumbled mortar. Steeplejacks don't have much time for imagination except, perhaps, when they read, and since I'm the only one I know who does that, I'm not really representative. Three sharp blows with the hammer, and the brick came free, splintering in the process, so that a flake flew out and dropped into the great black eye of the chimney.

I cursed. Morlak would let me know about it if I filled the grate at the bottom with debris. I gathered the other remains and scooped them into my satchel, then repositioned the chisel and got on with the job.

No one chooses to be a steeplejack. A few are poor whites and orphans, some are blacks who fall foul of the city and cannot return to a life among the herds on the savannah, but most are Lani like me: lithe and brown, hazel eyed, and glad of anything that puts food in their mouths. A few men like Morlak—it is always men—make it into adulthood and run the gangs, handing off the real work to the kids while they negotiate the contracts and count the profits.

I didn't mind it so much. The heights didn't bother me, and the alternative was scrubbing toilets, working stalls in the market, or worse. At least I was good at this. And on a clear day, when the wind parted the smog, Bar-Selehm could still be beautiful.

I set the hammer down. The satchel was getting full and I had only just begun. Standing up, I turned my back toward the ladder, and for a moment, I felt the breeze and steadied myself by bending my knees slightly. In that instant it came again, that sense that the world was just a little wrong. And now I knew why.

There was something missing.

Normally, my view of the city from hereabouts would be a gray-brown smear of rooftops and chimney spikes, dark in the gloom, save where a single point of light pricked the skyline, bathing the pale, statuesque structures of the municipal buildings with a glow bright and constant as sunlight. Up close it was brilliant, hard to look at directly, even through the smoke of the chimneys. By night it kept an entire block and a half of Bar-Selehm bright as day, and even in the densest smogs it could be seen miles out to sea, steering sailors better than the cape point lighthouse.

It was known as the Beacon. The light was housed in a crystal case on top of the Trade Exchange, a monument to the mineral on which the city had been built, and a defiantly public use of what was surely the most valuable item in the country. The stone itself was said to be about the size of a man's head, and was therefore the largest piece of luxorite ever quarried. It had been there for eighty years, over which time its light had barely diminished. Its value was incalculable.

And now it was gone. I strained my eyes, disbelieving, but there could be no doubt. The Beacon was not dimmed or obscured by the smoke. It was gone, and with that, the world had shifted on its axis, a minute adjustment that altered everything. Even for someone like me, who was used to standing tall in dangerous places, the thought was unsettling. The Beacon was a constant, a part of the world that was just simply *there*. That it wasn't felt ominous. But it also felt right, as if the day should be commemorated with darkness.

Papa.

I touched the coin I wore laced round my neck, then took a long breath. There was still no sign of Berrit, and my satchel needed emptying.

After moving to the top of the ladder, I reached one leg over, then the other. There was a little spring in the wood, but the dogs I had hammered into the brickwork were tight, and the ladder felt sure under my weight. Even so, I was careful, which was just as well, because I was halfway over the perilous cap when someone called out.

The suddenness of it up there in the silence startled me. One hand, which had been moving to the next rung, missed its mark, and for a moment, I was two-thirds of the way to falling. I righted myself, grabbed hold of the ladder, and stared angrily down, expecting to see Berrit, the new boy, made stupid by lateness.

But it wasn't, and my annoyance softened.

It was Tanish, a Lani boy, about twelve, who had been with the gang since his parents died three years ago. He was scrambling recklessly up, calling my name still, his face open, excited.

"Stop," I commanded. "Wait for me on the roof."

He looked momentarily wounded, then began to climb down.

Tanish was the closest thing I had to an apprentice. He followed me around, learning the tricks of the trade and how to survive in the gang, gazing at me with childish admiration. He was a sweet kid, too sweet for Seventh Street, and sometimes it was my job to toughen him up.

"Never call up to me like that," I spat as soon as we were both at the foot of the chimney. "Idiot. I nearly lost my grip."

"Not you, Ang," the boy answered, flushed and sheepish. "You'll never fall."

"Not till I do," I said bleakly. "What are you doing here? I thought you were working the clock tower on Dock Street."

"Finished last night," said Tanish, pleased with himself. "Super-fast, me."

"And it still tells the right time?"

Tanish beamed. Last time he had been working a clock with Fevel, they had left the timepiece off by three and a half hours. When the owner complained, they climbed back up and reset it twice more, wildly wrong both times, too embarrassed to admit that neither one of them could tell time. Eventually Morlak had done them a diagram and they had had to climb up at double the usual speed to set the mechanism. Even so, they had left the clock four minutes slow, and its chime still tolled the hour after every other clock in the city, so that the gang jokingly referred to Tanish Time, which meant, simply, late.

"Well?" I demanded, releasing the hair I keep tied back while I work. It fell around my shoulders and I ran my fingers roughly through it. "What's so important?"

"It's your sister," said Tanish, unable to suppress his delight that he was the one to bring the news. "The baby. It's time."

I closed my eyes for a moment, my jaw set. "Are they sure?" I asked. "I wasted half of yesterday sitting around out there—"

"The runner said they'd brought the midwife."

Today of all days, I thought. *Of course it would be today.*

"Right," I said, half to myself. "Tell Morlak I'm going."

My pregnant sister, Rahvey, was three years my senior. We did not like each other.

"Morlak says you can't go," said Tanish. "Or—" He thought, try-ing to remember the gang leader's exact words. "—if you do, you better be back by ten and be prepared to work the late shift."

That was a joke. Rahvey and her husband, Sinchon, lived in a shanty on the southwest side of the city, an area traversed by minor tributaries of the river Kalihm and populated by laundries, water haulers, and dyers. It was known as the Drowning, and it would take me an hour to get there on foot.

Well, there was no avoiding it. I would have to deal with Morlak when I got back.

Morlak was more than a gang leader. In other places, he might have been called a crime lord, and crossing him was, as the Lani liked to say, "hazardous to the health." But since he provided Bar-Selehm's more respectable citizens with a variety of services, he was called simply a businessman. That gave him the kind of power he didn't need to reinforce with a stick and brass knuckles, and ordinarily I would not dream of defying him.

But family was family: another infuriating Lani saying.

I had two sisters: Vestris, the eldest and most glamorous, who I barely saw anymore; and Rahvey, who had raised me while Papa worked, a debt she would let me neither pay nor forget.

"Take my tools back for me," I said, unslinging the satchel.

"You're going?" said Tanish.

"Seems so," I answered, walking away. I had taken a few steps before I remembered the strangeness I had felt up there on the chimney and stopped to call back to him. "Tanish?"

The boy looked up from the satchel.

"What happened to the Beacon?" I asked.

The boy shrugged, but he looked uneasy. "Stolen," he said.

"*Stolen?*"

"That's what Sarn said. It was in the paper."

"Who would steal the Beacon?" I asked. "What would be the point? You couldn't sell it."

Tanish shrugged again. "Maybe it was the Grappoli," he said. Everything in Bar-Selehm could be blamed on the Grappoli, our neighbors to the northwest. "I'll go with you."

"Don't you have to get to work?"

"I'm supposed to be cleaning Captain Franzen," he said. "Supplies won't be here till lunchtime."

Captain Franzen was a glorified Feldish pirate who had driven off the dreaded Grappoli three hundred years ago. His statue stood atop a ceremonial pillar overlooking the old Mahweni docks.

"You can come," I said, "but not into the birthing room, so you won't see my sister perform her maternity."

He gave me a quizzical look.

"The stage missed a great talent when my sister opted to stay home and have babies," I said, grinning at him.

He brightened immediately and fell into step beside me, but a few strides later stopped suddenly. "Forgot my stuff," he said. "Wait for me."

I clicked my tongue irritably—Rahvey would complain about how late I was even if I ran all the way—and stood in the street, registering again the void where the glow of the Beacon should be. It was like something was missing from the air itself. I shuddered and turned back to the factory wall.

"Come on, Tanish!" I called.

The boy was standing beneath the great chimney, motionless. In fact, he wasn't so much standing as stooping, frozen in the act of picking up his little duffel of tools. He was staring fixedly down the narrow alley that ran along the wall below the chimney stack. I called his name again, but he didn't respond, and something in his uncanny stillness touched an alarm in my head. I began moving toward him, my pace quickening with each step till I was close enough to seize him by his little shoulders and demand to know what was keeping him.

But by then I could see it. Tanish turned suddenly into my belly, clinging to me, his eyes squeezed shut, his face bloodless. Over his shoulder I saw the body in the alley, knowing—even from this distance—that Berrit, the boy I had been waiting for, had not missed our meeting after all.

CHAPTER

2

BERRIT WAS LANI, LIKE Tanish and me. He had been, maybe, ten. I had met him once over our communal meal at the Seventh Street weavers' shed two nights ago, when Morlak thrust him in front of me, barked his name, and told me he would be shadowing me for a few days. I had just grunted, nodding at the boy, who looked subdued and frightened. I had meant to take him aside later on, introduce myself properly—without Morlak standing over us, ready with his clumsy jokes designed to embarrass me—but I never did. Somehow, when I wasn't looking, he had slunk away to sleep, unnoticed. It was a smart and useful skill to have on Seventh Street, inconspicuousness, and I privately commended him for it, but since I was summoned to Rahvey's bedside the following day, I hadn't set eyes on the boy again until I saw his broken body huddled by the factory wall.

Tanish was distraught. He had spent more time with the new boy and had never seen the result of a long fall before. I sent him to get help, and he fled, eyes streaming. Driven by an inexplicable sense of failure, of guilt, I forced myself to look.

I had seen death before. For someone of my age and background, living in the highest and—figuratively speaking—lowest places of Bar-Selehm, it was impossible not to. That does not mean that I was immune to the horror of death, and if you do not know what a fall from a great height does to a human body, thank whatever god you believe in and hope you never find out. I will not be the one to show you.

He looked so very small. Under the horror of how he had died I felt the stirrings of something deeper and more awful: something like grief, which drained my soul and brought to my eyes the tears that I had not allowed myself to shed in front of Tanish. He needed me to be strong, and I had been, but now I was alone and might crack open the door to my feelings. I felt pressure from the other side, like deep water held in check by a dam, and I squeezed the door shut once more.

I took refuge in thought, in reason, which kept feelings at bay. The drop from the chimney was sheer. There was nothing on which the boy might have cut himself before hitting the cobbled ground, so the sharp, precise incision, no more than an inch across and located directly over his spine, was strange. It would need to be cleaned and studied by people who knew what such things meant, but it raised a possibility.

The fall did not kill him.

The idea came before I could dodge it and hung in my head like the absent Beacon, blazing.

Around his neck he wore a copper pendant on a thong, a pretty thing with a sun rendered in gold enamel on a cobalt blue disk. I removed it carefully and pocketed it. There would be someone who had loved him. They should get it.

"YOU FOUND HIM?" ASKED the uniformed policeman who attended the ambulance orderlies. He was tall, white, with an overly tended mustache that was barely the right side of comic. He spoke to me in Feldish, which I spoke fluently, albeit with a Lani inflection. If you worked in Bar-Selehm, you had to, even the Lani, when we left our own communities. It was the language of the whites, and as such, it had become the language of government, of finance, trade, law, and all things that mattered. Lani like Rahvey's husband, Sinchon, who knew only a few words of it, were virtually unemployable beyond the Drowning. I spoke it and, thanks to Vestris, even read it.

I'm not an eloquent person. I read a lot, but I spend my days up with the roosting flying foxes and the silver-winged night crows, who aren't great conversationalists. At night I'm surrounded by adolescent boys, who are worse. I love words, but mostly they stay in my head, especially in the presence of authority.

"I was with the boy who found him, yes," I said.

"His name is Berrit?"

"Yes."

"Last name?"

"I don't know."

"He's a steeplejack?"

"Apprentice. This was his first day."

"And he was going to work with you?"

"Yes."

"And you are?"

"Anglet Sutonga. I work for Morlak." I frowned, and he gave me a hard look.

"What?" he demanded.

"Nothing, sir," I said.

"You were thinking something," he pressed. "What? I won't ask again."

"Just . . ." I faltered. "I wondered why you weren't writing this down."

"Got a good memory, me," said the policeman, gazing off down the alley. "And the city has other things to think about today. Get it all up, lads!" he called to the ambulance men. "There's a tap on the wall. Hose off the street when you're done."

A vulture had settled in the alley and was watching us, waiting. I shouted at it, and it flapped a few paces away, bobbing its bald head.

"Pictures," I blurted out.

"What?" said the policeman again.

"Photographs," I said, eyes down, abashed. "You've started taking pictures at crime scenes. I saw them in the paper."

"So?"

"They haven't taken any," I said, risking a look into his face.

"Crime scenes," he echoed, as if I were unusually stupid. "This was an accident."

"But . . ." I hesitated.

"But what?"

I took a breath. "The body. There's a knife wound on the back."

"Expert, are you?" said the policeman, giving me a sour look this time. "Steeplejack *and* detective, eh? Impressive. I thought girls like you had other ways of making your money." He smirked, then gazed off down the street again. His eyes were straying to where the Beacon should have been, but wasn't. For all his casualness, he looked troubled.

And that, I thought, was that. There would be no investigation, no real questions asked, not for a Lani street brat, particularly on a day when the city's most recognizable landmark had vanished. I put my hand in my pocket and was surprised to find the copper pendant on its leather thong. I took it out. It was a small thing, and for all the care of the workmanship, it was close to worthless.

The thought sent a shard of pain through my chest, and I had to pause and breathe again before squeezing my eyes—

and the dam

—shut, and I pocketed it once more.

Tanish was waiting for me, sitting in the shade, his knees drawn up tight to his skinny chest. He got to his feet as he saw me push through the huddle of gawkers craning for a glimpse of blood. I elbowed aside a man in fancy shoes and a linen suit, who turned abruptly and walked away. Even in my haste to get to Tanish, I noted the speed with which the man left, the focus, the economy of motion, and found myself wondering how long he had been watching and why.

I didn't have the heart to tell Tanish to go home. Sarn had come, he said. Tanish had given him our tools. He would come back soon with Morlak. I didn't want to be around then, so I set off for my sister's house, Tanish trailing silently at my heels like a lost dog.

Everyone was rattled by the absence of the Beacon. You could see them gazing at the spire on top of the Trade Exchange, and there was a more than usually frantic crowd at the newspaper stand on Winckley Street. I scanned the headlines, which brayed the obvious: that the Beacon was gone. Beyond that, the papers knew nothing, and the report was more hysteria than news.

"You gonna buy that?" demanded the street vendor, a black girl with her hair pulled back so tight that her forehead looked strained.

"With what?" I asked with a hollow smile. The girl glared unsympathetically, and I let go of the paper, backing away from the throng and moving around the corner and into Vine Street.

"My mother taught me to read," said Tanish. It was just something to say, I think, but once he got it out, it sounded forlorn.

"My sister taught me," I answered, trying to sound cheerful. "Not Rahvey. Vestris."

"How come I've never seen her?"

"She's too fancy for the likes of you," I said, unable to suppress a genuine smile now.

"Fancy?"

"Glamorous," I said. "Rich."

"I'd like to see her one day," said Tanish. He had heard me talk of Vestris before and had caught a little of my reverence for her. "What does she do?"

"Do?"

"For, you know, a job?" he asked. "I mean, why is she so rich if she grew up like you?"

"Oh, she's just sort of special," I said airily. "She's not rich because of where she works."

"Why, then?"

I laughed, waving the question away. "She's just different from the rest of us," I concluded.

"Special," he said, uncertain.

"Exactly."

And I felt what I always felt when I thought of Vestris: a kind of vague privilege that I knew her. It was like sitting in a shaft of sunlight on a cool day, a private warming glow that made me the envy of everyone around me.

"One time when we were little," I said, "the mine where Papa worked had been closed, and he had no work, which meant we had no money. Vestris brought food home every night. Rahvey asked her how she was paying for it, and you know what she said?"

"What?"

"She said, 'I just ask nicely. I explain that my sisters are hungry, and people give me food.'"

"So she was begging."

"No," I said. "It wasn't like that. She's just the kind of person people want to please. I can't explain it."

Tanish looked at me for more, but I said nothing.

The city was walled, and though urban sprawl had long since outgrown the old fortifications, the walls still marked the limits of Bar-Selehm proper and they were routinely patrolled. It was clear as we approached the West Gate, however, that something different was going on this morning. One of the ancient iron-bound doors had actually been closed—the first time since the city had quarantined itself during a cattle death outbreak three years ago—and people were being funneled through a gamut of dragoons. The soldiers wore their scarlet jackets and feathered helmets in spite of the mounting heat, and they carried rifles with sword bayonets. Two were mounted on striped orleks—local, zebralike horses—which stamped and tossed their heads restlessly. The troops on the ground were white, but there were members of one of the black regiments up on the walls.

This too was about the Beacon. Not Berrit.

The soldiers checked papers, but the only people they detained were those carrying bags, baskets, or crates. Me and Tanish they practically ignored, though I flinched away when one of the orleks stooped toward me, its nostrils flaring. I'm a city girl, and am not good around large animals. Once through the checkpoint, I increased my pace till Tanish was almost running to keep up.

The residential streets of the Drowning had no official names and did not appear on any map, rather coming and going from season to season as the river dwindled and flooded, shifting its course and turning what had been a bustling tent city to marshland. There were no sewer lines but the river in the Drowning. The street corners sprouted ragged produce stands, huddles of itinerant laborers hoping to be hired for a few hours, and makeshift barbecues fashioned from scrap metal and fueled by homemade charcoal. This was where I had grown up. The hut in which I was born had long since turned to firewood, and no one could remember exactly where it had stood, but this was, I supposed, home.

Once. When Papa was still alive.

The Drowning smelled different from the industrial heart of the city where I lived now, a sour smell of bodies and animals and rotting vegetables. I preferred the bitter tang of the chimneys, even if it left me hacking till my throat burned, and coated my face and arms with soot. The Drowning stank of poverty, ignorance, and despair.

I hated it.

The Lani aren't indigenous to the region. We were brought here almost three hundred years ago from lands to the east by the whites from the north. My ancestors came as indentured servants, manual laborers and field hands, living separate from both the indigenous Mahweni and the whites. They were never slaves and believed they had settled in Feldesland by choice, keeping to themselves as the northerners conquered, bought, and absorbed more and more of the land from the native blacks. The Lani were neither military nor political, and reasoned that as long as they were left to their own devices, they were better staying out of the disputes and skirmishes during the white settlement of the region. By the time they looked up from their cooking fires to find that they had turned into a squalid and itinerant people living peasant lives, it was too late.

Most of Morlak's gang came from here or somewhere similarly ragged and decaying. Some of them, like Tanish, still thought of this place as home, and his mood brightened as we reached the first out-lying huts and tents.

"I see Mrs. Emtiga's ass got out again," he said, amused. "That thing needs an armed guard and a castle wall."

I laughed, then risked a question. "Berrit was a Drowning boy too, right? You must have been almost the same age."

A Drowning boy. That's what they called them, proudly and with no sense of the bitter irony.

Tanish didn't look at me. "I didn't remember him till we spoke a few days ago," he said. "But, yes. I think we played together when we were little. Then he went to the Westside gang and I stayed here till . . ."

Till Tanish's mother died.

"Why did he leave Westside?" I went on quickly.

"Got traded," said Tanish. "Part of a deal involving the Dock Street warehouse and some building supplies."

So Morlak bought him. That wasn't supposed to happen, but it did.

"How did he feel about that?" I asked.

Tanish shrugged. "Didn't seem to care," he said. "Said he was going to be something big in the Seventh Street gang."

"He'd been a steeplejack for the Westside boys?"

"Nah," said Tanish. "He said he'd been a pickpocket, but I think he was really a bootblack. Might have done a bit of thieving on the side, but that wasn't how he earned his keep. He'd never been up a chimney, inside or out. He pretended not to be, but I think he was scared of heights."

"So why did he think he was going to be big in the gang?"

"Optimist," said Tanish bleakly. "Always going on about what he was going to do when his ship came in."

I nodded thoughtfully, and as Tanish's face tightened with the memory, I decided to switch direction. "What about you?" I asked, ruffling his hair affectionately. "What will you do when your ship comes in?"

"Ships don't come in for the likes of us," he said.

"Sure they do," I tried, not believing it.

"Then they'll be rusted-up pieces of *kanti*," he said.

I laughed. "Full of rats," I agreed.

"And holes," he added. "And sharks would swim in through the holes and live in the hold, ready to bite your legs off as soon as you went aboard." He grinned at the idea, and that, for the moment, was as good as things were going to get.

Inside the tent city, a gaggle of local women and their kids had already gathered outside the hut. There was a sense of drama brewing in the air, and they paused in their chatter as we approached, nodding at me with caution and watchfulness. Sinchon's look as I opened the hut's juddering door was, however, loaded with accusation.

No surprise there.

Sinchon shared his wife's disdain for his antisocial sister-in-law. He was a hoglike man who scratched a living panning for luxorite in the river above the Drowning. He had found a couple of grains five years ago, but nothing since, and lived mainly off the scraps of minerals he turned up from time to time. The kids laughed at him because everyone knew there was no luxorite being found anymore, but he still thought I was beneath him.

"Where have you been?" he shot, pausing in the whittling of a stick. "The baby is almost here."

"I'm here now," I said.

"Your sister needed you earlier."

"I was working," I replied, avoiding his eyes.

And Rahvey hasn't needed me a day in her life, I added to myself.

"Who's that?" he asked, gazing past me to where Tanish was loitering on the steps.

"Someone I work with. Used to live here. He'll help you get some water."

There was a snatch of conversation from the room beyond the thin lattice door, a woman's voice. Sinchon looked at the door but did not move. Lani men didn't go into the delivery room until it was over.

"Hope to the gods it's not a girl," he said as I crossed the room.

I said nothing, but I felt the chill grip of the idea inside my chest. Rahvey had had a son who she lost to the damp lung when he was two. She had three girls already. She would not be allowed a fourth.

They dressed it up in other words, but the bald truth was that Lani girls were not considered worth raising. They were married off—expensively—as soon as possible, but the problem wasn't really about cost. Lani culture was made by men. They were the leaders, the lawmakers, the property holders. Women raised the children, cooked, cleaned, and did as they were told. If they worked outside the home, they were paid less than men for the same job by their Lani bosses, and working for anyone else meant turning your back on your people. Though Morlak and most of his gang were Lani, the mere fact of working in the city proper meant that to most of the people I had grown up with, I had abandoned them. At their best, girls were pretty things used to ally families. At their worst, an annoyance.

Poverty and ignorance have a way of clinging to bad ideas. The worst among what were sanctimoniously clustered as "the Lani way" was the rule that said that no family could have more than three daughters. The first daughter, it was said, was a blessing. The second, a trial. The third, a curse. As a third daughter myself, I felt the full weight of that last piece of wisdom, which was why I spent as little time among "my people" as possible. Rahvey had three girls already. If she gave birth to another, the child would be sent to an orphanage. In the old days, if no suitable mother could be found, more drastic steps would be taken—a grim little secret the appalled white settlers had made illegal. Such practices had, supposedly, ended, but there were accidents during the birthing of unwanted daughters, which people did not scrutinize too closely.

"Is it true, what they are saying?" Sinchon asked, his hand on the door handle.

"About what?" I replied, thinking of Berrit.

"The Beacon," said Sinchon. His usually impassive face looked uncertain, hunted. "We can't see it. They are saying someone stole it."

I frowned, feeling again that sense that the earth had wobbled beneath my feet. "I don't know," I said.

"Isn't that where you work?" he demanded, masking his unease with a contempt with which he was more comfortable.

"It's not there," I said. "I don't know what happened to it, but it's gone."

Sinchon's face set, but he said no more and left.

The inner room was just big enough for a bed and a stove, and the latter had been loaded with coal. It was stiflingly hot, and the air was vinegar sour with sweat. The midwife, kneeling between Rahvey's splayed legs, shot me a look as I came in and snapped, "Close the door! You're letting the cold in."

There was no cold, but I did as she asked.

At the head of the bed, Rahvey looked surprisingly placid, but when her eyes flicked to mine, her face fell instantly.

I was not the sister she had been waiting for. I never was.

"Pass me that towel," said Florihn, the midwife. I squatted beside her, but kept my eyes on the wall. "About time you were having one of these yourself," the woman added.

I had seen her around the camps for years, coming and going with bloodstained napkins and buckets of water. She lost no more babies than was usual, and had birthed me seventeen years ago, but I had never taken to her. I suppose I imagined the midwife's disappointed announcement of what I was when I had first emerged bawling from my mother. Another girl. I could not, of course, actually remember the moment, but I was sure it had happened, and a small and spiteful part of me hated her for it.

And there was one thing more: My mother had not survived my birth. She had heard me cry, I was told, had held me for a while, but she had lost too much blood, and nothing Florihn had been able to do could save her.

Third daughter, a curse.

So, yes, though the idea made my stomach writhe with the injustice of it, when I looked at Florihn, I could not stifle a pang of guilt.

"Any word from Vestris?" asked Rahvey.

Our idolized elder sister.

My heart skipped a beat at the thought of seeing her.

"We sent to her," said Florihn, not looking up, "but haven't heard back yet."

"She'll come," said Rahvey, lying back. "For the naming, if not before. She'll come."

It was a statement not of hope, but of faith.

I was not so sure. Vestris was twenty-five, eight years my senior, which was enough to mean that we had barely grown up together at all, though my earliest memories were of her—not Rahvey, and certainly not my devoted but illiterate father—reading to me. She had found work at an ambassador's residence while I was still small. There she had attracted the interest of men far beyond our family's caste or social station. Our mother had been, I was told, a beautiful woman, and while both Rahvey and I had inherited something of her looks, it was Vestris who drew people's eyes. In my childish recollections, our eldest sister had been a figure of exquisite and mysterious appeal, and as her social setting improved, so did the wealth of her clothes. She was a society lady now, and her appearance in the Drowning was greeted with the kind of reverent excitement people normally reserved for comets. Rahvey worshipped her.

"Look at this," said Florihn to me, pointing between Rahvey's legs. I forced myself to look, though I couldn't make sense of what I was seeing.

"Is that right?" I managed.

Florihn gave me a smug smile and seemed to wait on purpose, as if driving home my ignorance. "I guess books don't teach you everything," she said.

The learning my eldest sister had passed on to me had always been something of a local joke, especially considering what I had opted to do with my life.

Florihn was giving me an inquisitorial stare, and eventually I shrugged.

"Yes, it's fine," she said at last. "But there'll be no baby today."

"I came because I thought it was happening *now*."

Rahvey said nothing, but gave me a defiant look.

"This is a time for family," said Florihn piously. "You'd know that if you spent more time here."

I blinked. They didn't want me around. Not really. They just wanted me to feel bad for not being like them. I felt the certainty of it like a stone in my boot that I couldn't shake out, a constant irritant that might one day make me lame.

No wonder I preferred life up on the chimneys, alone in the sky.

"I have to go back to work," I said, rising. "Has anyone . . . ?"

I hesitated, and Rahvey gave me a blank look this time.

"Has anyone been to the cemetery?" I asked, my voice carefully neutral.

Rahvey turned away. "We've been a little busy," she said, her voice managing to suggest an outrage she didn't really feel.

I nodded. "I'll go," I said.

"Of course you will," said Rahvey. And this time the bitterness was real.

CHAPTER

3

ON THE EAST SIDE of the Drowning was an ancient, weather-beaten temple teeming with vervet monkeys and fire-eyed grackles. It was as close to leaving the city as I ever got, a kind of halfway house between the urban sprawl of Bar-Selehm and the wilderness beyond. By day, an elderly priest burned incense and chanted among the weed-choked altars for whoever put a copper coin in his bowl, but by night, the little shrines and funerary markers were haunted by baboons and hyenas. For a city girl like me, it was unnerving, but I had no choice. Two years ago, my father's remains were buried here.

Papa.

He was a good Lani, a good father, a kindly, brown-eyed giant of a man, quick to grin, to play, to tease. I had loved him with all my heart, and I missed him every day.

"I'll always keep you safe, Anglet," he had said. "I'll always be there to look after you."

The only lie he ever told me.

I was already grown up when he died, already working, but till then and in spite of everything I went through in the Seventh Street gang, I had never felt truly alone. Papa had always been there, a buffer between me and my sisters, my work, the world in general, ready with a touch, a word, a smile that calmed my raging blood, dried my tears, and told me that all would yet be well. Always. He was my rock, my consolation, and my joy. When Papa looked at me, the universe made sense, and all the words the others hurled at me fell harmless at my feet or blew away like smoke.

He died in a mining accident with four other Lani men. He was trying to reach two apprentices who had been trapped by a rockfall, but the new passage they opened released a pocket of gas. There was an explosion. It took a week to get to the bodies after the shaft collapsed, and I was not allowed to see him. His remains were burned, as is our custom, and the ash strewn over the river, save for one fragment of bone that was interred in the hard, dusty grounds of the temple.

Two years to the day.

I have been alone ever since. I believe the two apprentices were found unharmed.

Tanish came with me to the grave, eyeing me sidelong and careful not to make noise. Partly he was trying to show respect, but it was also the place that left him subdued. He had seen enough death for one day. I would have told him to leave me to my thoughts, but a family of hippos had taken over the riverbank below the temple, and a Lani woman had been killed by one of them when she went to draw water only a couple of weeks before. I didn't want him wandering alone, so I let him hover awkwardly at my back as I found the marker and knelt down, sitting on my heels.

Someone had placed crimson tsuli flowers on the grave, bound with gold cord. They were fresh and lustrous, hothouse grown at this time of year. Expensive.

Vestris.

It had to be. I felt a quickening of my pulse as I sensed my sister's presence, and my eyes flashed hungrily around the graveyard as if she might still be there. But she was gone, and my disappointment felt suddenly shameful. Deflated, I adjusted the flowers and focused on the stone marker, feeling young and alone.

Family is family.

Except when it's gone.

I said nothing, feeling the coin I wore on a thong around my neck.

All steeplejacks wore something that connected them to their past. It was a claim to a version of yourself that wasn't about the work. Berrit's had been his sun-disk pendant. Mine was an old copper penny Papa gave me. It had been misstamped and bore the last king's head on both sides. The Seventh Street boys thought I kept it for luck, because I could flip the coin and always guess correctly what would come up, but I didn't. I kept it because Papa gave it to me and because when he did, he said, "Because it's rare. Like you, Ang. One of a kind."

He thought I was special. I wasn't, but he believed otherwise, and that almost made it true.

Now I turned the coin over and over in my fingers, and the face embossed on its twin sides became his in my mind so that I pressed it to my lips and closed my eyes like a little kid who thought that wishing might bring him back.

I had never lived in Rahvey's house, but those refuse-blown streets with the sour smell of goats and the stagnant reed beds by the river were all too familiar. Whenever I went back to the Drowning now, all I found was what was gone, the spaces Papa had left behind him. No wonder I hated the place. It was a land of ghosts, of absences.

I had learned long ago not to cry, no matter the hurt in your hands or your heart. Tears in the city gangs meant fear and weakness, and they were punished without mercy. I knew that, and I knew that after this morning, Tanish needed me to be strong.

But this was hard.

Harder than I had expected. It had been, after all, two years. The grief at first, coupled as it was with shock and horror, had been almost unbearable, but over the subsequent weeks and months, it lessened. In my childish imagination, I figured it would continue to fade, like a distant ship sailing beyond the reach of vision until it disappeared entirely. But it hadn't, and I saw now, kneeling on the sandy dirt and staring at the roughly carved stone that bore his name, that it never would. I would always be straining to see him, reaching for him, and he would never be there. I would carry his absence like a hole in my heart forever.

I remembered Berrit, a boy I had not known, who died on Papa's anniversary, and a single tear slid down my nose and fell onto the dusty earth as if I were watering a tiny seedling. I wiped the trace away before turning to Tanish, who was gazing about him, looking glum and a little bored. He had not seen.

I laid a fistful of wild kalla lilies on the grave next to Vestris's tsuli flowers and set my face to meet the world, but as I half turned to Tanish, someone called.

"Anglet!"

I recognized the girl as one of those who did errands for Florihn, the midwife. "What?" I called back, though I knew what was coming.

"It's started!" cried the girl.

I FOLLOWED HER TO Rahvey's house, where Sinchon was sitting on the porch, scowling. As I approached, a roar of agony came from inside, a woman's voice—though one so pressed to the limits of human endurance that I heard no sign of my sister in it. I didn't speak to Sinchon, but yanked the door open and stepped inside.

It was even hotter than it had been earlier, and Florihn, crouching between my sister's legs, shot me an irritated look when I entered, as she had the first time. At the far end of the bed, Rahvey's red, glistening face was a rictus of pain.

As I set my things down, she began to scream again, an unearthly, animal sound like the weancats that prowled the edge of the Drowning when prey in the hinterlands was scarce. I winced, the hair on the back of my neck prickling, but Florihn just grinned.

"That's right," she said to Rahvey. "You cry it out."

As soon as the contraction passed, I said, "I thought there would be no baby today."

From her place between Rahvey's legs, Florihn scowled at me, then refocused on Rahvey and said simply, "Now."

It took no more than five minutes, and I kept my gaze locked on my sister's face for as much of it as possible. When the baby emerged, I did as I was told, but I couldn't stop staring at the child.

It was a girl. The fourth daughter.

For a long moment, no one moved or spoke. The baby wailed over Rahvey's exhausted panting, and I just looked at it, registering the awful truth, so that for a few seconds, it seemed that time had stopped.

At last the midwife seemed to come back to herself. Her face was ashen, but she brought her fluttering hands together and pressed her fingertips, a gesture of composure and resolution, both hard won.

Then she stood up and took a deep, quavering breath. "Where's my knife?" she asked.

"Wait," I said. "What are you doing?"

"Cutting the cord," said Florihn. "What did you think?"

Rahvey gaped, her eyes flicking to the midwife for guidance.

"Then what?" I asked.

There was a moment's stillness, then the baby began to cry again. The midwife wrapped the child in a towel and set her on the floor before turning on me and speaking in a low whisper. "Fourth daughter," she said. "You know what that means. Rahvey can't keep it. It goes to a blood relative or we take it to Pancaris," said Florihn.

Pancaris was an orphanage run by one of the Feldish religious orders—dour-habited, grim-faced white nuns who raised children to be domestic servants.

"Till she runs away and turns beggar or whore," I said, looking at the brown, wriggling infant, so small and powerless.

"There's no other choice," said Florihn dismissively. "And they'll teach her what she needs."

"Like what?" I asked.

Florihn gave me a hard look for my temerity, but she answered.

"They'll teach her to scrub. To cook. To wield a pick or wheel a bar-row. Anything else is just making promises you can't keep. You of all people should know that."

I looked to Rahvey, but she kept her eyes fixed on Florihn, the way Tanish stares at me to avoid looking down from the chimneys.

"Rahvey," I said, dragging her gaze to my face. "Maybe there's another way. Maybe this fourth-daughter business can—"

"Can what?" demanded Florihn.

"I don't know," I said, quailing under the woman's authoritative stare.

My sister gaped some more, at me this time, then looked back to the midwife. She squeezed her eyes shut, and a tear coursed down her cheek. Her grief gave me the courage I needed.

"Maybe we could keep her," I said, feeling the blood rise in my face.

Florihn blinked, but she maintained a rigid calm. Her eyes became two slits as she considered how to respond. " 'We'?" she said, staring me down. "What will your contribution be to raising an unseemly child? Where will you be when your sister has to raise more money to feed another mouth?" When I said nothing, she added, "Yes, that's what I thought."

"Sinchon could look for a different kind of job," I said unsteadily, but Florihn, reading the panic in Rahvey's face, cut me off.

"And you'll tell him that, will you?" she demanded. "You have forgotten everything. This is our way. The Lani way."

Then it's a stupid way! I wanted to shout, an old rage spiking in my chest. *You should change it.*

But faced with Florihn's baleful glare, I couldn't get the words out. Rahvey looked cowed, but her eyes wandered back to the mewl-ing infant. I moved to the child, stooped, and gathered her inex-pertly into my arms.

"Put it down, Anglet," said the midwife. "You are only making things harder. This is not helpful. It is cruel."

I avoided her eyes, crossing to my sister with the child.

Rahvey gazed up at me, and beneath the exhaustion and hesitation, I thought I saw a flicker of something else, a faint but desperate hope.

"She looks like you," I said, finding an unexpected smile.

Rahvey took the baby with trembling hands, moving it to her breast. The crying stopped abruptly. My sister tipped her head back a fraction and closed her eyes.

"Three daughters only," Florihn intoned. "Blessing. Trial. Curse. The fourth is unseemly."

"Florihn?" Rahvey said, gazing at the infant now.

"Look what you are doing to her!" said Florihn, seizing my arm and turning me round. "You don't live here, Anglet. You don't belong here."

Anger flashed in my eyes, and she let go of my arm as if it were hot, but then her face closed, hardened.

"We will give the child up," she said. "That is the end of the matter."

"Florihn?" said Rahvey.

The midwife turned to her reluctantly, her expression softening. "What do you need, hon?" she asked, sugar sweet.

"Maybe," Rahvey began, like a woman inching out over a narrow bridge, "if we explained to Sinchon and the elders that we could raise her, maybe they would listen."

"No," said Florihn, so quick and hard that Rahvey winced, and the midwife had to rebuild her look of simpering benevolence before she could proceed. "I am the elders' representative here. I speak to and for them. We cannot allow our traditions, the beliefs handed down to us from our grandparents and their parents before them, to be trodden underfoot when they do not suit our wishes."

"The world changes, Florihn," I said, amazed at my own audacity. "The things we assume will last forever go away like the Beacon."

"That is the city," said Florihn. "That is not us. The Lani must stand by their ways. No mother can have four daughters."

"Perhaps Vestris would help?" said Rahvey. "She's rich, connected—"

"Do you see her here?" snapped Florihn. "Your precious sister has not come to see you for how long now?"

Rahvey said nothing.

"You should forget her as she has forgotten you and the place where she grew up," said Florihn.

I bristled at this, but kept my mouth shut.

Rahvey, meanwhile, seemed to crumple inwardly and, as she began to weep in silence, nodded.

"But she is still your daughter—," I began.

"The matter is closed," said Florihn. "I suggest you leave us to our ways, Anglet. You aren't Lani anymore."

"*What?*" I exclaimed. She had said it like it had been on the tip of her tongue for years and she had waited for the necessary anger to say it aloud. The accusation awoke a new boldness in me. "Look at me!" I said, sticking out my arms. "Lani through and through. Like the people I have worked with every day since I left the Drowning."

"Steeplejacks!" Florihn sneered. "What kind of work is that for a Lani?"

"Common," I replied.

"Urchin work," she shot back. "City work."

"Compared to what?" I returned, fury sweeping away my usual diffidence. "Growing a few onions on the edge of a swamp? Mending pots and pans? Peddling folk crafts to people who think they're quaint? Panning for gold in a river of filth?"

"I will not defend our customs—our heritage—to a . . . a *kolek!*"

Even in her rage, she had to steel herself to say the word. A kolek is a type of root vegetable. Its skin is brown, but the flesh within is white.

If she had not been three times my age, I would have hit her.

She saw me flinch and a flicker of cruel satisfaction went through her face, spurring her on. "But you are not even a kolek," she said. "If you were, the chalkers would treat you better. You are not one of us. You are not one of them. You are not one of the blacks. You are nothing, and your opinions mean nothing here."

I reeled as if struck, and the sensation was not just anger and outrage. Her words were a match touched to the powder in my heart, and now it blazed with a hot and poisonous flame: a part of me thought she was right.

There was a long, stunned silence while I gathered my thoughts, and when I spoke, it was quietly and with conviction. "I will take the child," I said, thinking suddenly and painfully of Berrit, who the world had already forgotten. "She is beautiful. She has been born on the same day Papa was taken from us. She should not grow up unwanted."

The room fell silent again.

"You?" asked Florihn.

"Yes," I said, sounding more sure than I felt.

"By yourself? With no husband?" Florihn pressed.

"What use has Sinchon ever been in the raising of your family?" I asked my sister. She looked away. "I will come for her tomorrow, but you can tell the elders that you want to keep her. Make them talk about it. If they won't change their minds—" I faltered, but only for a second. "—I will keep her. And if I can't, there is always Pancaris."

Florihn stared, her mind working, and Rahvey watched her, wary and unsure, like a cornered weancat.

"Tomorrow?" my sister repeated.

"Yes."

Rahvey looked pale, uncertain, suspended between feelings, but when she felt Florihn's eyes on her, she nodded.

"This requires a blood oath," said the midwife, picking up the knife. "You must swear by all we hold true and precious. Hold out your hands."

I stared at the knife, and the scale of what I was doing crowded in on me so that for a moment I couldn't breathe. "Not my hands," I said. "I have to be able to work."

"Your face, then," said Florihn, her eyes hard. "There may be scarring."

I blinked but managed to shake my head fractionally. "It doesn't matter," I said.

"Very well," said the midwife with a tiny, satisfied smile. "Kneel down."

I did as I was told, feeling the quickening of my heart, as if the blood that was to be let were rising up in protest.

"Anglet Sutonga," she intoned, "do you swear you will take this child, this fourth daughter, from your sister Rahvey and raise her as your own or, failing that, find suitable accommodation for her, so that she grows up in a manner seemly and fitting for a Lani child?"

I opened my mouth, but the words didn't come out.

Florihn's eyes narrowed. "You have to say it," she said.

"Yes," I managed. "I swear."

And without further warning, Florihn slashed my cheeks with her knife, first the left, then the right.

The edge was scalpel sharp, and I felt the blood run before the pain sang out, bright and hot. With it came shock and a sudden terrible clarity.

What have I done?

Florihn methodically took up one of the towels she had brought and clamped it to my bleeding face, gripping my head tightly and staring searchingly into my eyes for a long minute.

There was a knock at the door.

"Can I come in?"

Sinchon.

"In a moment, sweet," said Rahvey.

"Just tell me," he demanded. "Boy or girl?"

The three of us exchanged bleak and knowing looks.

"A girl," Rahvey answered heavily. "We will keep her for tonight, but Anglet will come for her tomorrow. I'm sorry."

Sinchon said nothing—expressed no sorrow, no commiseration with his grief-stricken wife, nothing—and moments later, we heard the outside door of the hut slam closed as he left.

Florihn was still clamping the towel to my face, pressing hard to stanch the bleeding, and I felt a flare of rage that, for the moment, burned away any doubt that what I was doing was right.

CHAPTER

4

"**WHAT HAPPENED TO YOUR** face?" asked Tanish, ashen.

"Nothing," I said, flustered. "Come on. I need to get back to work."

He looked injured by my evasion, so I hugged him matily and tousled his hair till he fought to get free. He watched me as we walked, not believing my playfulness, but I didn't want to tell him what I had promised. Saying it outside the hot little hut would make it real, and I wasn't ready to face that.

"Think you can get us back into the city without the Beacon to guide you?" I asked. A challenge usually took Tanish's mind off whatever was bothering him.

"Easy," he said, bounding ahead.

The city—which is to say the colonial city, the original native settlement having been co-opted and assimilated almost three centuries ago—sat on a hill above the ancient river crossing, its municipal buildings rising stately and imposing, pale stone tastefully trimmed and fluted. It had been built on the promise of prosperity and power derived from luxorite, the same luxorite Rahvey's deluded husband still panned for in the Kalihm. That promise had long since faded and the city had sprawled in other directions, but it was luxorite that had brought the first white settlers.

Luxorite, when first mined, glows far beyond the shine of other precious gems or metals. It has an inner light so potent that a fragment no larger than a grain of sand is as bright as a candle. A few grains together, or a piece such as you might mount in a finger ring, might light a large room in the dead of night. At its mature best, a piece of luxorite is too bright to look at directly, a hard, white light tending to blue that produces sharp-edged shadows. In time it degrades, its light softening and yellowing to amber, but that takes decades, and a single stone might light a wealthy mansion for generations.

A thin seam of the stuff had been exposed by accident on the edge of the river hundreds of years ago. The Mahweni, the black hunters and herders who lived there, treated the place as magical, but eventually began to trade fragments of it for the ironware being worked in the north. Soon settlers came for the luxorite, not because it was beautiful—though it was—but because it was useful, and for a time, it lit their mines and factories as well as their extravagant homes.

But the seam was soon exhausted, and though tiny pockets of luxorite were found nearby, nothing like the expected quantity ever came to light. Soon what little had been mined took on once more the aura of the magical. It was beyond precious. The mines and factories were plumbed for gaslight, and their luxorite sold for more ostentatious use elsewhere. Now, the discovery of an aged grain whose yellow light might fuel little more than a hand lantern would feed a family for several months, but that happened so rarely that the price of the mineral was one of the most stable of all traded commodities in the region. The piece that had been the Beacon was not just priceless; it was also irreplaceable. There was no new luxorite in Bar-Selehm, and the city's heart now was industry and trade. The Mahweni who had shown the white settlers the first seam now wore overalls and fed coal into the city's steam engines and factories. And so Bar-Selehm evolved.

It took Tanish and me twenty minutes to leave the fetid sourness of the Drowning behind, and as much again to enter the city proper. We didn't have money for the underground so we hopped a ride on the back of an oxcart for a half mile, slipping down when the driver turned toward the Hashti temple on the edge of the shambles. Tanish loved that, and I, pleased by his delight, managed to push away any thoughts of Papa; of the boy called Berrit, who had died exactly two years after him; and of the blood oath I had just taken.

Twenty-four hours from now, you will have a child to take care of. . . .

Beyond a dull dread, the thought meant almost nothing to me, an idea spoken in a foreign tongue.

Well, I thought unhelpfully, *you'll find out.*

We walked another half hour, feeling the city grow up around us till the sky became crowded with offices and shops and the world seemed to constrict. I would take the anonymity of the city over the provincial watchfulness of the Drowning any day, or the savagery of the wilderness beyond it, but its hardness and gloom were undeniable.

"I'm going to go and get my tools," I said. "Maybe get an hour in before it's too dark."

"Morlak will be at the shed," said Tanish warningly. "You might not want to see him today. He was in a bad mood this morning to begin with."

"Why?"

"Out all night drinking, I think. Didn't make it back till after we got up, so he probably slept rough. You know what that does to his mood. And since then, he lost his new apprentice." He looked down as he said it, caught between shame and sadness that this was how Berrit's death would be seen: like misplacing a hammer or a chisel.

I ruffled his hair again. "I can handle Morlak," I said.

He smiled wanly, almost able to believe it, and I pressed a couple of coins into his hand.

"Go get yourself something to eat," I said. "Don't go back to the shed for an hour or two. It will be better when everyone else is coming off shift."

Better meant safer. Morlak was more than capable of punishing my apprentice to spite me for my defiance.

"What did you say to the police?" he asked. The words burst out of him as if he had been saving them up.

"About what?" I asked.

"Berrit," he answered. "You seemed upset. With the police, I mean."

"I just don't think . . . ," I began, but hesitated. Tanish's eyes were wide and apprehensive. "They weren't respectful. To the body."

It was a half truth at best, but I didn't want to worry him further.

He considered me, deciding to accept what I had said at face value, and then he was walking away down Ream Street toward the old flag market, where the remaining fruit would be on sale.

MORLAK WAS A POWERFULLY built man turning to fat around the middle but still strong, and when he lowered his head, he looked like a buffalo. He wore his greasy hair long, tied back into a glossy rattail. I had hoped I could grab my satchel of tools and my water flask, then get back to the chimney unseen, but he was waiting for me.

He was sitting at his desk at the far end of the empty weaving shed so he had a good view of the door, and I caught the ghost of a grin on his face as I slid in and made for the gallery of rooms where the gang slept. Normally he would be upstairs. He had a chamber above the shed, inside the old elevator tower, which doubled as his strong room. Anyone caught on the stairs to the tower was, he liked to remind them, dead meat. There was no reason to think he didn't mean that literally. The fact that he was down here at all at this time should have made me wary, but I didn't think it through, and by the time I was coming out of my room with my satchel, it was too late.

He strode slowly toward me, a swagger in his gait, his bulk blocking the narrow corridor. I was used to his temper, his complaints about my work, his petulance and casual violence, but this was something different. It felt calculated, as if he had been planning it.

"Well, well, well," he said. "If it isn't little Anglet, our stray steeplejack."

I said nothing, but I had my weight carefully distributed, my knees slightly bent, ready to run. Not that there was anywhere to go.

"What time do you call this?" asked Morlak, advancing, pretending to be offended. He grasped my face with one hand and tilted it. "Someone tried to cut a smile onto that sour face of yours?"

I said nothing but peered around him, down the corridor, registering the empty shed. The silence bothered me.

"You owe me a day's work," he snarled with feigned pleasantness, still gripping my face. "I'd let you buy your way out of the debt, but you don't have any money, do you, little Anglet?"

"No," I said. I was frightened now. I was used to being hungry, being scorned, even being beaten, but I was not used to this, whatever this was, and I didn't like it.

"No," Morlak echoed. "I feed you. I pay you. I give you a roof over your head. And how do you repay me?"

I never thought to protest, to mention Berrit or say that my sister had needed me. I said nothing because I knew it would do no good. I was aware of how far away the shed door into the alley was, how stiff it was to open. And then I was aware of the way his hand strayed to his belt buckle and knew, with horrified certainty, that this was not the prelude to a beating. This was something else.

I was and was not surprised. A part of me had known it was coming, had seen the way he watched me. But something had always held him back. Whatever that had been, it was gone. He had been waiting for an excuse, and now he was drunk—not on the reed spirit he stank of every morning, but on the power he had over me. He took a step toward me, and now his legs were splayed a little too, like he was poised to spring.

The corridor dead-ended behind me in a painted brick wall. The only way out was past him, back into the shed's cavernous main workroom and through the street door, but that seemed so far away that I could barely picture it.

I felt in the satchel with an unsteady hand and came out with one of the iron dogs I used to anchor the ladders and ropes to the chimneys.

He hesitated when he saw it, but then his grin spread, as if I had given him the push he needed. He lunged at me, seizing my wrists so that the spike fell clattering to the ground. He shoved and I fell to the concrete floor at the foot of my bedroom door. He was on me then. One of his massive fists slammed into my face, and my head banged hard against the ground so that the world darkened and swam. In that moment, he fumbled with his clothes, but when he reached for mine, I kicked up once, hard, catching him somewhere between groin and stomach.

It wasn't a clean hit, but he shrank away, releasing my hands in the shock of the moment, and in that half second of blind, unthinking instinct, I reached for and found the metal spike.

I stabbed once.

It pierced his side somewhere between the ribs, and he bellowed with pain and astonishment.

I did not pause to judge the severity of the wound but skittered out from under him, caught up the satchel, and bolted down the corridor to the door.

"You'd better hope I die!" he roared after me in his agony, his blood pooling under him, his voice bouncing off the walls. "You'd better hope that. Because if I don't, I'll find you. You hear me? I'll find you!"

CHAPTER
5

I FLED. BREATHLESS AND half-blind with tears, I dashed out of the alley—across Bridge Street and down the back of the Weavers Arms—torn between the terror that Morlak might be coming after me and the terror that he was already dead.

I blundered into the nearest alley. Not even an alley, really, more a ginnel, a mere crack between the backs of buildings, barely wide enough to turn in. I staggered into its darkest recess, mad with fear and fury, and stopped, hands shaking, fighting down the urge to vomit.

For a horrible, desperate second, I considered returning to the shed and cutting his throat where he lay. Just for a moment. I saw it through a red mist in my head, and it made a terrible sense, and not just for what he had tried to do. Morlak was a brute, a terror to the "apprentices" in his charge, and little better than a slave holder.

The world would not mourn him.

But to return, to slit him open in cold blood, to drain the life from him, that was beyond me.

For now, I thought bleakly.

Who knew what horrors I would become capable of now that life as I had known it had ended? I had no work, no means to feed myself or the child I had stupidly promised to care for, and if Morlak survived, I would not be safe in Bar-Selehm. Ever. He had promised to kill me, and in such matters, the gang leader was a man of his word.

I HAD NOWHERE TO go, no one to talk to, so I stayed behind the rubbish bins in the alley, trying to shut the terror and shock inside the iron-braced doors of my heart. Even alone, I could not give way to grief or fear. If I did, I might never get out from under them.

I was hungry, and it was getting cold. It was these that finally drove me out into the evening. I was back at the cement works, where I had begun the day so very long ago. A corner of the alley by the factory was still wet where it had been hosed down, but there was otherwise no sign that a boy had died there. Life had moved on, and insofar as the world had known Berrit existed, it had already forgotten him.

As it will forget me if Morlak finds me. As it forgot Papa.

The iron-braced doors creaked at the thought, but they held, and when I opened my eyes again, feeling my breathing steady and my muscles relax, I knew I had to do something, if only to ease the turmoil in my head.

I studied the wall at the base of the chimney, tied back my hair, then began to climb. There was a ledge ten feet below the cap and several bricks wide. I remembered sitting on it to eat my lunch the last time I had worked this chimney. It circled the stack and jutted out far enough that someone falling from there would hit nothing but the ground 150 feet below. With nerve and poise, it was walkable.

I kept my eyes open for Morlak's men, but there was little danger of me being seen up here at this time. Even so, I had to go slowly. My hands were unsteady, and I paused midway up to wipe a fleck of blood from my left wrist.

Morlak's? Or mine from where Florihn slashed my cheeks?

I squeezed my eyes shut to push the memories away, and began to climb again in earnest. I was losing light.

Hoisting myself carefully off the ladder, I moved onto the ledge. Carefully but not slowly. There was no advantage in being in a dangerous situation longer than you needed to be, and caution itself can be dangerous. For a moment, I got one of those rare vistas on the city as the smog shifted and the dying light of the sun picked out the towers, minarets, and spires in amber and gold.

There was no clue that Berrit had been here, no sign of a struggle, though I didn't know what that would look like, and suddenly coming up here looked like a waste of time, a ruse to get my mind off other things.

If I were him, if I were a boy apprentice on his first day, what would I have done? Why would I have climbed up here before my tutor arrived?

To prove he wasn't afraid? To make the initial ascent alone so he wouldn't be embarrassed by how slow and scared he was?

Or because someone told him to?

But if he were meeting someone on the chimney, he'd see them as soon as he came up. Anyone planning to attack him—for whatever reason—would want the element of surprise up here, where one false move meant death.

So if you were his would-be killer, how would you give yourself an edge?

The side of the chimney with the ladder faced the city. The other side faced the river. Even without the usual smoky haze, anyone waiting around that side would be invisible from here, and almost certainly invisible from below. I put my back to the slow brick round of the chimney barrel and inched my way around the ledge.

At first I saw nothing. But at the halfway point, I paused and squatted. There were two distinct indentations in the mortar between the bricks of the ledge, about a foot and a half apart. They were new, unweathered, and sootless.

Hook marks.

THE POLICE STATION ON Mount Street was a blank-faced structure of pale stone steps and columns, undecorated but somehow outsized. It loomed out of the gathering evening breathing power and stability. Around it, the flying foxes were leaving their roosts in its eaves, and the lamplighters were rigging their ladders.

For a long moment, I sat on the steps of a bank across the street, looking at it. Reporting Morlak would achieve nothing other than getting me arrested for assault or murder, but that was not why I was there. I got to my feet, crossed the street between a pair of horse-drawn cabs, and ascended the long, tall steps to the entrance.

I had expected the lobby to be a bustle of noisy activity, but it was silent, and my feet echoed on the tiled floor of a vast, open chamber with a high counter at the far end. I'm taller than most girls, but I still had to look up to speak to the desk sergeant, though I refused to use the wooden step stool. I took a long steadying breath and tried to find the words.

"Can I help you?" he began, looking up from his evening paper and mug of tea, his smile curdling slightly when he saw me.

"The steeplejack case," I blurted. My heart was beating fast and my mouth was dry. "I want to talk to someone. An officer working the steeplejack case."

"Steeplejack case?" he said. "What steeplejack would that be?"

"The boy," I said. "Fell from a chimney." I was gripping the edge of the wooden counter with both hands, knuckles whitening.

"Oh, that," he said, shaking off his momentary confusion. "There's no case. He fell."

"He didn't," I cut in. "I told the . . . the officer at the scene. He was stabbed."

He frowned. "Saw it, did you?"

"I saw the wound," I said.

"So someone killed him, then hauled his body all the way up one of those chimneys just to throw him off again?"

"No," I said. "They killed him up there. They waited for him on a ledge below the cap. They used a body harness or rubble skip hooked to the edge. Then they attacked him from behind."

The policeman was unmoved. "All that to kill a street kid?" he said.

"He was a steeplejack," I said, defiance bristling. The muscles of my forearms were tight with the pressure of my grip on the counter.

"So?" he said. "Not exactly a rare commodity in Bar-Selehm, are they?" He looked me over pointedly.

I fought back the urge to run. I reached across his desk and tapped the headline of the newspaper he was reading. It blared, BEACON THEFT.

A change came over him then. He put down the mug he had been cradling, and his eyes narrowed. "You know something about the Beacon?" he demanded.

"No," I said. "But whoever took it would need a skilled climber."

He was alert now, his eyes fixed on me as one hand groped for a pencil. "What's your full name?" he began, but I had said all I meant to. "Miss!" he called after me as I crossed the empty vestibule and pushed through the revolving door into the street.

"Miss!"

CHAPTER
6

THE MAHWENI GIRL WITH the tied-back hair who worked the newspaper stand was packing up as I arrived, and she gave me a baleful stare as she loaded unsold copies onto a pallet. The evening edition had added a new wrinkle to the story of the missing Beacon, one with actual content, and in spite of my distraction, I stopped to glance over the front page.

LUXORITE MERCHANT SUICIDE! screamed the headline.

"Not a library, you know," said the girl.

I scowled, my eyes flashing over the text.

> In a shocking development apparently related to the theft of Bar-Selehm's landmark Beacon, authorities revealed that the body of a prominent luxorite dealer was found in the exchange building early this morning. He appears to have taken his own life. Speaking on behalf of the investigation, Detective Sergeant F. L. Andrews of the Bar-Selehm police department said that the identity of the trader was not being released at this time, nor was it clear what connection he might have had to the theft of the Beacon. He went on to say . . .

"Did you not hear what I said?" asked the girl, placing one hand over the print.

"Is there anything about the death of a steeplejack?" I asked. "A Lani boy."

She frowned, considering Florihn's cuts on my cheeks. "Fell from a chimney, right?" she said, flipping the first page, then the second.

She indicated a tiny square of print squeezed in between an advert for corsets and a piece about a garden party.

BOY FALLS FROM CHIMNEY.

The entire story was six short lines, and the only thing it said that I didn't already know was that his last name was Samar.

"Friend of yours?" asked the girl.

I didn't know what to say and took the opportunity of her distraction by a customer to slip away, breaking into a half run as I shed what was left of the evening rush.

I BEGGED A CRUST from the baker on Lean Street as he was closing and wandered for an hour, inquiring at the shops and market stalls that were still open to see if anyone had work I might do. Most of them took one look at my soot-stained clothes and the slash marks on my face and cut me off. Two threatened to set the dogs on me. I tried the domestic agency at Branmoor Steps, hoping I could find an entry-level position as a charlady or scullery maid, but the white lady in charge just nodded toward the door with a sour, disapproving look.

In truth, I had other things on my mind. Each moment I waited, the gang leader's fate became surer.

Will he live or will he die?

Either way, the outcome for me was flight or death, but I needed to know, if only so I could come to terms with what I had done. Surely, by now, Tanish would be able to tell me that.

I closed my eyes at the thought of returning to Seventh Street, but when I opened them, I saw, standing across the road and looking directly at me, a familiar white man.

He was wearing city clothes: a pale linen suit and a brown cravat, the same clothes he had been wearing when—I was almost sure— he watched the police remove Berrit's body this morning.

Coincidence?

It was possible. But if he worked in this neighborhood, his clothes were wrong, and there weren't many gentry or factory owners who would be on the streets close to dawn and still out at dusk.

I guessed he was in his thirties, well built, even athletic under the suit. He turned away when he realized I had seen him, bending as if to tie his shoelace. I ran.

Moving quickly down Pump Street, I took a left by the underground stop, then wound my way through the city's darkest alleys, back to the shed and the tuppeny tavern on the corner, where the boys gathered for an hour before bed. If Tanish had wanted privacy, he may have already turned in, but I was hoping that he wouldn't want to be in the shed any longer than necessary.

I was right.

I scaled the timber-framed back wall and crawled to a sooty skylight through which I could see the gang's usual corner. They were all there—Tanish, Sarn, Fevel, three other boys, and two men, one of whom I didn't know—somber faced, staring at their beer. There was no sign of Morlak.

Tanish looked small and still, like a mouse hoping to go unnoticed. His face was pink on one side.

I watched them for almost a half hour before they began to trickle out. Sarn went first, then some of the younger boys. Tanish seemed to hesitate, and I thought he was looking around. For me, I was almost certain. In daylight I might have been a shadow against the grimy glass, but now I was invisible.

And then he was leaving. I started to go but realized he wasn't making for the front door. He was looking for the outhouse at the back.

I slid quietly across the broken slates of the roof till I could see into the yard behind the tavern. It had once been a coach house, but the outhouses were the only structures that had been maintained. I dropped and eased into the shadows, checking for snakes in the tumbledown masonry and fractured barrels. Even in winter it was wise to check for snakes. A moment later, Tanish emerged from the back of the tavern.

I called his name.

He stopped midstride, head tilted like a dog, trying to locate the sound, and I stepped out. I saw the shock, relief, and anxiety that chased each other through his young face. When he came toward me, it was like a guilty creature, hesitant and fearful.

"You shouldn't be here, Ang," he said.

"I know," I replied. "Morlak is—?"

"Not good," said Tanish. "He lost a lot of blood. They've strapped him up, and he's sleeping in the shed. Can't walk up the tower stairs."

"Will he—?" I couldn't finish the question, but Tanish knew what I meant.

"They say the next few hours are . . . Whether he'll live or not, I mean. Ang, listen to me. He has people looking for you. If they find you—"

I reached out to his cheek, tipping his head slightly so I could see the bruising.

Tanish blushed and looked down. "He had Sarn rough everyone up," he said, "but it wasn't too bad. He can't do much himself right now," he said, grinning wickedly for a moment before panicking as if Morlak might be watching. "But when he's back on his feet . . . I don't know. I'm just going to do my work."

"Smart," I said.

"What about you?" he asked. "You all right?"

"Yeah," I drawled with feigned casualness. "You know me. Always land on my feet."

"Yeah," said Tanish, wanting to believe it. "You going to leave the city?"

"Leave beautiful Bar-Selehm, where I have riches at my fingertips and servants to satisfy my every want?" I said. "Never."

He smiled at that, albeit ruefully, and looked down. "You can't stay," he said. "I've never seen Morlak so angry."

"I'll be all right. What are people saying about the Beacon?"

The boy blinked, then shrugged expansively.

"What about Berrit?" I tried.

"No one's talking," he said, again glancing nervously over his shoulder. He fished in his pocket, and a smile—a real, unanxious smile—broke across his face. "I thought I might see you," he said. "Brought you this." He plucked out a threadbare cloth toy, soft and shapeless and missing one eye.

"My habbit!" I exclaimed, taking it and pressing it to my heart. "Thanks."

It had been a rabbit when Papa first gave it to me, but time and love had made it unrecognizable, though I slept with it to this day. It had once been about comfort. Now it was about habit, hence the name.

"Didn't want to see it get thrown out," said Tanish, pleased by my delight. "I thought you might want it."

"I do. Thank you, Tanish."

"I'll try to save your books too."

"Thanks," I said again.

"Welcome. And Ang?"

"Yes?"

"If you do leave," he said, giving me a heartachingly open look, "take me with you."

For a split second I saw the hope and sorrow in his eyes, the panic and anxiety, and I pulled his frail little body to mine and hugged him quick and hard. Then I turned him around and gave him a little shove. "Go to sleep, Tanish. I'll see you soon. Promise."

He did not look back.

I should have slunk away, climbed the broken stone wall up onto the courtyard roof, and melted into the night, but I didn't. I waited, watching him go, so I was facing Fevel and the other man as they came through the back door, looking for him.

Fevel was a weasel of a boy, fifteen, Lani, and skinny—all bone, sinew, and long muscles. After me—and not by much—he was the best climber in the gang. I'd split his lip for him once when I caught him stealing pennies from my room, but that was over a year ago. He was bigger now. The man he was with was older and black. I had seen him around the shed but did not know his name. He carried a heavy crowbar in arms with biceps that rolled like kegs of brandy.

I took a step backwards, but it was too late. Fevel had seen me. He pointed, eyes and mouth wide, savage, and then they were both coming at me, crossing the courtyard with vengeful purpose.

I dragged myself up just as Fevel reached me, so that for a moment he was snatching at air as I scrambled away. I didn't need to look back to know he was coming after me. I ran along the roof, then dropped softly in the alley, not breaking stride as my boots slipped on the cobbles. My pounding feet echoed, and then I was out the other end and running.

At the corner of Randolph Road I risked a glance over my shoulder. They were gaining on me. I made another turn straight through the bare fruit stalls of Inyoka Court, and a pair of monkeys skipped out of my way, whooping and chattering in alarm. I overturned a garbage crate, but my pursuers vaulted and dodged without slowing.

The Mahweni with the crowbar was closing fast, his massive strides eating up the road between us like some great steam-powered machine. While I was starting to tire, he seemed to have hit a steady rhythm. I had no more than a few seconds.

A wagon sat on the corner of the square, one of the high, four-sided things they used to ferry crates of fruit and vegetables. I ran straight at it, timed my jump off the wheel rim onto the top in a scrambling flurry of fingers and torn nails, and landed in a powerful crouch behind the driver's seat. The black man tried to drag himself up, but I kicked at his hands, and he hesitated, then swung the iron bar murderously at me. I hopped back, but the crowbar splintered a crate inches from my arm. I retreated, using the height of the wagon as a springboard up to the gutter of the drapers' on the corner.

It was a good gutter, sturdy iron, and though it shifted under my weight, it held. I scrabbled with my feet for purchase against the corner wall and shinned up to the roof. The Mahweni tried to follow, but for all his strength, he couldn't copy my leap and fell in a heap against the wall.

I moved quickly up the steep rake of the tiled roof, set one foot on either side of the slope, and ran unevenly along the ridgeline, gathering speed for the vault to the next building at the end of the row. Glancing back, I saw Fevel scrambling up after me. He paused when he saw me look, and even in the thickening darkness, something flashed in his hand. A blade.

I vaulted the gap to the next terrace and kept moving, conscious that the tile was glazed and slippery underfoot.

Careful . . . .

I glanced into the street to get my bearings and saw the big man with the crowbar running along the sidewalk, glaring up at me. For a moment, all the terrible things of the day loomed in my head and I froze, unable to think, the tide of feeling straining to burst out and wash me away.

Think.

I needed somewhere they couldn't follow, and for a second or less, my feet slowed. In my mind, I flew high above the city, looking down on it from the vantage of the steelwork smokestacks I had worked last summer.

I was on Coal Street.

One block over was the South Road fish market: I could smell it through the smog, a sourness on the air, like memory.

Down the side was the Old Dockside theater, whose roof was being repaired. There was scaffolding all over it with access to . . .

The Skevington Arms public house, whose fire escape—with a little enthusiastic persuasion—gave on to . . .

The railway bridge over the canal and in to . . .

The sparrow islands, a tight grid of narrow alleys between warehouses and seedy factory dwellings, where any half-wit could lose himself, even with a pack of bloodhounds on his tail. There were no gas lamps on those streets.

That will do.

I ran and jumped, rolled and ran again, then slid the length of a downspout and was across the road before the man with the crowbar knew I was there. I bolted down the side of the deserted fish market and scaled the iron rungs set into the back wall. In seconds, I was across the roof and clambering out over the scaffolding of the theater.

Fevel was still coming, but I had pulled away from him during that last transition. If I could make it over the pub's fire escape before he had me in sight, I was home free.

Well, not home free, but not dead or dragged back to Morlak, which amounted to the same thing.

My heart was thumping with the exertion of the chase, but I was in my element up here, scrambling, swinging, gripping, and hoisting over iron and brick and stone. And though a mistake might send me to my death, I felt strangely composed, far more than I would have been on the ground. My conscious mind was silent now as other parts of me—arms and legs, fingers and the toes in my boots—took over. I focused on each step, each handhold, each shift of weight, so that the whole escape felt choreographed.

Just the leap from the fire escape to the painted iron girders of the railway bridge to go.

If challenged to attempt it any other night, I might have hesitated. Fatally.

Not tonight.

I touched the two-headed coin around my neck, then broke into a sprint along the gantry of the staircase. At the end, I planted my hands on the rail and vaulted into nothing, turning slowly in space so that for a moment I looked bound to land in a bloody heap in the street, and then I was grasping the metal of the bridge and swinging gracefully up.

I knew before I dropped into the sparrow islands that I had shed my pursuers.

Which is why it was doubly alarming to round the corner, smiling to myself, only to have two white men step out of the shadows before I had even seen them. I feinted right, but one of them deftly seized my wrist, twisted it up between my shoulder blades, and pinned me face forward against the wall.

"Miss Sutonga," said the other in Feldish, the man in the linen suit who had been watching me earlier. "What an exciting life you lead! We'd be obliged, however," he added with polite formality, "if you abandoned your plans for the rest of the evening and came with us."

CHAPTER

7

THE MAN IN THE linen suit blew a shrill whistle, and moments later a black carriage appeared, driven by a man in a top hat. He did not look at me or the two men as they bundled me inside.

They were both big men, but they moved with studied efficiency. One of them—the one in the linen suit—had a long pistol with a flared barrel, the other a slender but heavy-looking truncheon, though neither had felt the need to brandish their weapons when apprehending me. They did not wear uniforms or any kind of insignia, but they were not Morlak's men.

"There, now," said the one with the pistol once the carriage rolled off. "That wasn't so bad now, was it?" He smiled, but his eyes held mine with a chill frankness that kept me in place better than his comrade's vise grip on my arm.

While I had been oddly composed when running from the gang on the rooftops, these two, with their quiet professionalism, scared me. What would happen next, who they were, or what they wanted with me, I had no idea.

My eyes flashed to the door handle.

The man with the revolver inclined his head. In a voice as impassive as his face, he said, "Let's not make things more difficult than they need to be, shall we, Miss Sutonga?"

"How do you know my name?" I asked as the carriage slowed, then turned and resumed its former rattling pace.

"All that will become clear," said the man evenly.

"Where are we going?" I asked.

Neither man responded, watching me now as if I had not spoken at all. I had no choice but to sit and wait.

I wasn't sure how long we drove. Ten minutes? Twenty? Once a woman laughed—a high keening that sounded like a shout of pain until the end—and once I thought I heard the driver talking as the carriage stopped, but none of it gave me a sense of where we were. I used my free hand to release my hair and tipped my head forward so that it fell about my face like a veil.

When we finally stopped, the one with the truncheon produced from his pocket a black velvet bag with a drawstring. "Put this on, please," he said, tossing it to me.

I looked at it, feeling stupid and afraid. "Put it on?" I echoed.

"Over your head," said the man with the truncheon. "It's a blind-fold."

I hesitated, suddenly so frightened that I could barely move.

"Put it on," said the man, his voice still low and uninflected. "Or we will put it on for you." He said it matter-of-factly. If there was any emotion beneath the words it was boredom, and somehow this scared me more than if he had threatened.

I pulled the bag over my head and lost the world entirely.

In the confusion that followed, I was manhandled firmly but without obvious cruelty out into the night, then into somewhere more confined, where the soles of my boots rang on hard floors. My hands were held behind my back, but I was not bound, and I was guided expertly, so that only once did I jar my shoulder against a door-jamb as I was steered through. Then I was pushed into a chair and re-leased. I snatched the blindfold from my head as the door behind me closed heavily, and I heard it lock as I swiveled to see if I was alone.

I was.

The room was unlike anywhere I had ever been, and I rose from the chair with a new sense of strangeness. It was pristine, the floor matted with expensive grass braid, the furnishings fashioned from lustrous, striped timber. Most of the decoration was elegantly northern, and the books that lined the walls were in Feldish, but there were tribal masks in red and black that looked Mahweni, and there was a statue of an elephant god in black stone. There were Lani paintings on the wall, showing the story of the young god Semtaleen, who stole light from the stars to bring fire to man—as Papa had told me when I was very young.

A candelabrum suspended from a plaster rose in the center of the ceiling was lit by a dozen tiny glass globes. I stared, barely able to believe it: Each globe contained a grain of luxorite. The light was clear and strong and only very slightly yellow. It would take a Lani day laborer the better part of a year to earn enough to purchase one of those little lights.

There were two doors into the room, but the only windows were set near the high ceiling and showed only the night sky. I would need to stack at least one chair onto the desk to reach the ledge. I moved to it and took hold of its exquisitely inlaid top, hoping to drag it under the window, but it was too heavy. I was around the other side, bent at the waist, and pushing when I heard the door behind me click open.

I braced for the impact of an attack, but nothing happened.

I turned to find a young white man in gold-rimmed spectacles and a crisp suit moving toward the desk as if nothing could be more normal. I say he was white, but as soon as I had made the assessment, I was less sure. He was tanned, though his skin was still several shades lighter than my own, and his hair was black and glossy as the wing of a starling, but when he looked at me through his wire-rimmed spectacles his eyes were a bright and unnerving green. Still more striking, however, was a cruel, sickle-shaped scar, which traced a pale and puckered line right down his left cheek to the corner of his mouth and then back toward his ear. It hollowed that side of his face and twisted his lip alarmingly.

"Please have a seat, Miss Sutonga," he said in Lani, as if I had come for a job interview.

I stared at him, but when he said nothing else, I drifted back to the chair, though I remained standing, trying to look defiant rather than confused and afraid.

"I apologize for the manner in which you were brought here," he said. "It was necessary."

He was peering over his glasses at a notebook, turning the pages absently as if he were only half aware of my presence. When he looked up, snatching the glasses from his head and flinging them onto the desk, his green eyes were bright and amused. He had thin lips and a lean, intent face that looked sculpted out of something hard, but the scar made beauty impossible. His body was long and rangy, fit beneath his slightly mannered formal wear, and he gave the impression of wanting to sprawl and stretch, even as he perched on his chair behind the desk.

He nodded to the chair. "I'm sure you would be more comfortable if you sat," he said.

Heart racing, I shook my head.

"As you wish," he answered.

He had a northern, cultured voice, and he spoke with the air of one used to being in authority, but his Lani was impeccable, and he was no more than ten years older than I was. Perhaps less.

He considered my face. "You seem to have cut yourself," he said.

"Where am I?" I managed.

"My home," he said, as if I should be happy about it.

I could think of nothing to say.

"Tell me about Mr. Ansveld," said the young man.

I frowned. "Who?" I asked.

"Mr. Ansveld," he repeated, enunciating the words carefully. His eyes held mine, and his body was perfectly still.

"I don't know who that is," I said.

"Really?" he said. "Come now. This will all be much easier if we are honest with each other." He smiled. It was a thoughtful, knowing smile, and I wondered if I would live longer if I humored him.

"Who is he?" I whispered, eyes down.

"He was a merchant in the city," said the young man.

"I don't know any merchants," I said. "He left?"

The smile widened, thinning to a tight crease, and he tipped his head to one side, as if I were playing games with him. "In a sense," he said. "He's dead."

I felt again that strangeness, as if the earth beneath my feet had shifted, changing the world in ways I did not understand. "I didn't know him," I said.

"He was a prominent businessman," he continued, watching me like a mongoose at a snake hole. "A powerful man."

"I don't know powerful people," I said. The young man's probing green eyes were starting to get to me.

"His business was entirely concerned," he said, careful as before, "with the buying and selling of luxorite."

That last word flicked out with the force and precision of a cat's pounce, but then just hung in the air between us. I fought to keep any kind of response out of my face, but he nodded.

"That you know," he said, smiling again his knowing and uneven smile.

"I know what luxorite is," I said.

"But I imagine you have few dealings with the mineral yourself," said the man, considering the little bulbs that lit the room. "Not ordinarily, I mean."

My mouth felt dry. "No," I said. "I don't deal with luxorite."

"Not, as I say, ordinarily."

He waited, watching, and I felt obligated to shake my head and mouth the negative again. What was going on here? The question rose in my mind and then repeated with a telling variation: What did he *think* was going on?

"You are, I am told, the finest steeplejack in the city," he said.

I didn't respond.

"But I hear you left work early today," he continued conversationally.

I nodded.

"Why would that be?" he asked.

"I . . . I lost my job," I said, looking down.

"By choice?"

I wasn't sure how to answer that. "Morlak wasn't happy with my work." I spoke as carefully as he did.

The young man nodded. His fingers, which he had steepled together, were long, the nails manicured. "So unhappy, in fact," he said, "that he sent people to kill you, yes?"

There was no point denying it. His men—the phrase was odd, considering they all seemed older than he was—had obviously seen as much.

I nodded once.

"That's a curious development, wouldn't you say? You must have upset Mr. Morlak a great deal."

"That's not hard," I said before I could stop myself.

His slitlike mouth widened again unreadably, and the scar quavered. "No," he agreed. "I would imagine not. But I am curious as to what inspired his wrath on this particular occasion. A businessman such as Mr. Morlak does not give up his best assets easily. I have heard that there are companies who utilize his services expressly on condition that the actual work is performed by you, and judging by the account of the way you evaded his men this evening, I am not at all surprised."

I blinked at the compliment but kept my eyes lowered, my hair half masking my face.

"What did you do, Miss Sutonga? Did you take something of Mr. Morlak's? Or perhaps, something Mr. Morlak didn't actually own but paid you to acquire for him? I believe you had a conversation with a member of Bar-Selehm's excellent police department this evening."

I looked up then, bafflement like a curtain of fog parting around a distant prick of bright light in my mind.

The Beacon?

I opened my mouth, but no words came out, and at last I sat down to still the trembling of my legs. The chair was soft and comfortable, its timber seemingly molded to my form. It was one of the most perfectly designed objects I had ever touched.

"There, now," said the man. "Isn't that better?"

I managed a nod, feeling young and vulnerable in ways I had not felt for years, not since I lived in the Drowning and Rahvey had used that phrase of hers to make me do the chores.

Third daughter a curse.

I felt it more acutely now, a dragging anxiety edged with the white-hot glow of panic.

"So," said the young man, still pleasant, still apparently oblivious to all that was slicing through my mind, but with that same keen-eyed intensity. "Let us talk business."

Under his gaze I felt a moment of choice, as if I were standing on a narrow line of crumbling brick high above some factory, knowing that I needed to jump to safety or cling to where I was and hope my perch stayed intact. I decided quickly, fighting off the self-conscious paralysis I felt under those curious green eyes.

"I don't know what you think I've done," I said, forcing myself to look up and meet his gaze, "or what you think I know, but you're wrong. Morlak attacked me. Tried to . . . Tried to force himself on me." My lock on his eyes broke only for a second. "I fought back and hurt him. It was self-defense. That is why he fired me. That is why he wants to punish me. Nothing more."

He sat back and his eyes contracted with thought. The knowing quality he had exuded to this point evaporated, and he was all watchful attention. "Is this true?" he asked at last.

"Yes. I know nothing about the Beacon."

He leaned forward again. "Who said anything about the Beacon?" he asked.

"That's why you brought me here," I said.

His silence conceded the point. "A boy died this morning," he said. "Or late last night. His name was—" He scoured his desk for where he had written it down.

"Berrit Samar," I inserted.

"Indeed," he said. "And he was supposed to be working with you today, though you did not know him, correct?"

"We met only once," I said.

"And what makes you think he might have been connected to the theft of the Beacon?"

I said nothing, more than tongue-tied. I had no idea who I was talking to.

"And you believe the boy . . . Berrit," he continued, "was murdered. A wound, you said, in the back, yes? Inflicted by an assailant who had been waiting for the boy on the top of the chimney."

"On a ledge below the cap," I clarified. I fished the loop of cord from my pocket and tied my hair back so I could look him full in the face.

"I think you are right," he said. "The body has been examined, which—without your report—would not have happened, and the coroner concurs. Death resulted from a single, narrow incision just right of the spine, penetrating the heart."

I closed my eyes for a second.

"You know the spire above the exchange?" he said. "Where the Beacon was housed?"

"Yes."

"Could you have climbed it?"

"Yes."

"You sound very sure," he said.

"With the right equipment I could scale any tower, chimney, or spire in Bar-Selehm," I said. It wasn't a boast. It was simply true.

"Could any steeplejack have made that climb?" he asked.

"No," I said. "The steeple is stone clad. Tight grout lines. There's nothing to fasten to."

"And, other than yourself, do you know any such person in Bar-Selehm?"

I frowned and shrugged noncommittally.

"Berrit?" he asked.

I shook my head.

"As a helper?" he asked.

"Only in the most basic way. For anything involving actual climbing, he would have been a liability." I felt disloyal saying it, but it was true.

"But you think he was involved," said the young man with the shrewd green eyes.

"He could have been bullied into helping," I said, choosing my words as if I were selecting from a range of tools, "by someone he looked up to who didn't trust his more experienced workers with something illegal."

The man's lip twitched knowingly. I forced myself to stop looking at the scar, the way it produced that strange, slanted quality when he smiled. "Mr. Morlak," he said.

"It's possible."

"And your mentioning his name has nothing to do with any personal hostility you may have toward the gentleman in question, of course."

"Are we still talking about Morlak?" I asked, my face suddenly hot. "Only I don't think I've ever heard his name in the same sentence as the word 'gentleman.'"

He nodded so fractionally that his head barely moved, but he let the remark stand.

He watched me, saying nothing, and my next question emerged without thought, some of my former panic spiking and driving it out. "What are you going to do with me?" I asked.

"Well, I think you should have something to eat, don't you?"

I blinked again, and as I did, the door behind the desk opened and one of the men from the street appeared, the one who had carried the truncheon, though he didn't have it now. The young man craned his neck slightly and the other leaned down to hear his whisper before nodding and leaving as quietly as he had come in. It struck me once more as strange that someone who seemed to have so much wealth and authority should be so close to my own age.

"So," said the young man as soon as we were alone again. "What can I tempt you with? The chef makes an excellent Rasnarian goat curry. I can have him tone it down a little if you don't like it spicy, but I prefer to let the man follow his heart. There's also a very fine sterrel and onion chutney. . . ."

This was all very strange.

"I'd like to go home," I said.

I didn't believe it was an option, but if I was going to be kept prisoner, I would prefer he were honest about it, rather than pretending I was a guest.

The young man sat back in his chair, regarding me with a thoughtful frown that softened his predatory intensity. "Home," he intoned. "A warm, comforting word. But what does it really mean to you? The Drowning, where you are despised; or the weavers' shed, where you have been a slave to the odious Mr. Morlak? I don't think either of those places is terribly . . . secure," he concluded. "I think you are better here with us."

I swallowed, trying to gauge how close to a threat this was, but I floundered, thinking not just of Morlak and his gang, but also of Rahvey's baby, who I had promised to take care of. "Who is *us*, exactly?" I asked.

He smiled again, that same thin smile, then tapped his fingertips on the desktop. "Let's just say," he said musingly, as if making an important decision on impulse, "that you can trust us."

I made a scoffing noise without thinking. "I'm sorry," I said, "but I don't trust people who kidnap me."

He chuckled. "Very well," he said. "My name is Josiah Willing-house, and I work for the government housed in the fair city of Bar-Selehm."

"You are a civil servant?" I returned, not troubling to mask my skepticism.

"A politician," he said. "Albeit a junior one."

"This is not a government building," I said. "It's a town house. Your men drove me around for a while, but I'm guessing from the sound of the cobbles that we're still east of Old Town, close to Ruetta Park."

He smiled again. "Very good!" he exclaimed. "I like that you pay attention. That will prove most useful."

"Useful?" I shot back, bridling at the sense of being patted on the head.

"Not all government work—good work," he said delicately, "work for the benefit of the nation and its people—is done at official build-ings where there are reporters and assessment committees and battles over public opinion. Some of it must be done more . . . quietly. In the shadows, as it were. Things are happening in Bar-Selehm, Miss Sutonga. Troubling things. Occurrences that must be stopped before the situation overwhelms us all."

I said nothing, but he read my skepticism.

"If you are dissatisfied with this simple truth after you have begun work," said the man who called himself Willinghouse, "you will be permitted to leave. No questions asked."

"Work?" I echoed blankly.

"Oh, I'm sorry," he said, smiling once more. "I thought I had made that clear. I mean to hire you."

I stared at him. "As a steeplejack?" I asked.

"Oh, dear me, no," Willinghouse answered, beaming with genu-ine pleasure. "I want you to investigate the murder of Berrit Samar."

CHAPTER

8

IT WAS, OF COURSE, absurd. I was to be a private detective? I couldn't even say the words without smirking. Did such people really exist? If so, they were not stray Lani girls who spent their days dangling from chimneys in the hope of a decent meal.

And yet. . . .

All my life I had been told that anything significant was beyond me, that I was no more than a tool, an implement like a spade or a pick, useful to wealthier, more powerful people—useful, that is, until I fell and broke, when I would be replaced by another implement with a different face, as Papa had been replaced by another man with a pick. I was nothing—like Berrit, like all Lani street brats—except that I was less even in the eyes of my own people because I was the cursed third daughter.

But here was this sophisticated and powerful man telling me I was special, remarkable as a two-headed coin. . . .

And then there was what he had said about how the death of Berrit heralded crimes yet to come, troubling occurrences that would overwhelm us all if not prevented.

"Your friend Berrit is the lion's tail," Willinghouse said. "A detail you spot but think is part of the bush until the beast pounces. There are larger things afoot here, Miss Sutonga. We stand on the very brink of disaster."

The goat curry was, as promised, remarkably good. It was served with tea in translucent china cups and saucers by a silent, elderly white man who I could only describe as butlerish, and I wolfed it all down as if I hadn't eaten for days.

Willinghouse watched me, fascinated, as hunger stripped me of pride.

The door opened and another white man leaned in. He was tall, about Willinghouse's age, and dressed in a slightly old-fashioned suit. He had sandy hair, no mustache, and freckles that emphasized his youth, as did the smile that lit his face when he saw me. "Ah!" he exclaimed. "Our new employee! The steeplejack, yes?"

I blinked at him and checked Willinghouse, who frowned with disapproval.

"We are still working out the details," he said.

"Nonsense!" said the newcomer, striding over to me.

I rose, flustered, wishing I had left my hair down.

He took my hand and shook it vigorously. "Charmed and delighted," he said, beaming. "I am Stefan Von Strahden. Call me Stefan. I'm a colleague of Willinghouse's." He had pale blue eyes and an infectious manner, but his familiar frankness was unnerving.

"A colleague?" I managed.

"In Parliament," he said, adding in response to my chastened look, "Oh, it's not so grand as all that. Shuffling papers and making dull speeches most of the time. Powerfully tedious compared to what you do up there in the clouds! That must be extraordinary!"

"Shouldn't you be at dinner, Stefan?" said Willinghouse icily, the scar contracting into a thin pink line.

"I should," he said, "but I just had to meet this talented young lady. And now I seem incapable of leaving her company."

"Find a way," said Willinghouse.

"Really, Josiah!" exclaimed Von Strahden. "So churlish in front of a lady! Don't you find him churlish?" he asked me. "You'd think a politician would be better at talking to people, wouldn't you?"

"I'm *trying* to talk to her," Willinghouse inserted, sparing me the responsibility of responding. "So if you wouldn't mind—"

He was interrupted by the door opening briskly. A young white woman with hazel eyes and chestnut hair stood in the doorway, her face taut with an exasperation at odds with her elegant formal wear.

"Mr. Von Strahden," she said, somehow managing to sound both bored and irritated, as if the world had let her down, as was to be expected. "Cook says he will not serve dessert until at least one of the male guests is actually at the table, and since I would prefer not to starve to death this evening, I ask that, for the sake of common courtesy, you leave whatever you are doing here immediately."

I was standing right in front of her, but she didn't seem to see me at all.

"Oh," said Von Strahden. "Right. I was just meeting your brother's new associate."

He nodded in my direction, and I, not knowing what else to do, extended my hand toward her. Her eyes found me at last, moved to my hand, and lingered on it, her posture still rigid, her head held high so that she had to peer at me down her perfect nose. Her hands, which were gloved in lace, remained at her side. I lowered my hand, wiping it on my dirty trousers.

"Charmed, I am sure," she said in a brittle voice before turning back to Von Strahden. "Now, Mr. Von Strahden, if you can tear yourself away from my brother's foundlings, I really am rather hungry." She turned on her heel and left.

I lowered my gaze, my face hot with anger and humiliation.

"Ah," said Von Strahden. "Yes. Well, Willinghouse, I will see you shortly. You, my dear steeplejack, I will see when next our paths cross, which will be, I hope, soon." He bowed, smiling at my blushes, and left.

Willinghouse continued to frown. "Stefan is . . . ," he began, but could not conclude the sentence. "I don't know what he is. A force of nature, perhaps, but a good man for all that. I will try to keep him at bay as best I can."

"I'm sure he was just being polite," I said.

"Making up for my sister, you mean," he said as if reading my thoughts. "Indeed. I apologize on her behalf. Believe me when I say that it is not the first time I have done so."

"Is she always that rude?" I asked, made bold by my anger.

"Dahria is rich, and beautiful, and spoiled," he said, "in a world that expects nothing more of her. She is not a bad person, but she has no purpose in life and is therefore lost. One day she will, I hope, find herself. But till then, I would say that her existence is of questionable value."

"She is still your sister," I said, taken aback by his candor.

"Yes," he answered, giving me a frank look. "Which is why I know her worth." He smiled at my shock. "This is not the Drowning, Miss Sutonga," he said. "There are things more important than family, even for one who has recently taken a blood oath." He indicated the slash marks on my face with one finger, and I flinched away.

So he knows more of the Lani way than he has implied. How?

"That is not your business," I said.

"No," he agreed. "Nor do I want it to be. Your private life is of no interest to me, and I would prefer that you keep it to yourself. You may stay here," said Willinghouse, "or I can have my coachman drop you—"

I raised a hand to silence him. "There is something I have to say," I said, marshaling the words. "Whatever else might be going on, Berrit is the reason I am working for you, and his murder will be my primary focus. It may seem like a small thing to you, merely the tail of the lion. It's not. Not to me."

"I thought you didn't know him," said Willinghouse.

"I didn't," I said. "And that doesn't matter. So if you attempt to redirect my investigations, our . . . *understanding* will come to an end. Clear?"

I am not sure why I felt the need to say it, or why—surrounded by such evidence of power and influence—I felt I *could* say it, but I did, and felt better—doubly so when he did not argue or smirk or express incredulity that some street girl should dictate terms to him. He nodded, and I felt some kind of hurdle had been cleared.

It was only later, as I climbed back into the darkness of his carriage, cradling a purse weighted with my "expenses" and surrounded by the hollow, uncertain noises of the night, that I wondered if my righteous bravado had not, in fact, played directly into his hands, committing me to perils I could not yet imagine.

CHAPTER

9

I SLIPPED FROM THE carriage as we rounded the first corner, dropping silently to the cobbles and sprinting off into the night without a word to the driver. It was an empty gesture, but it gave me a feeling of control, even though I didn't know where I was going. I couldn't go to Seventh Street, and I wouldn't go to the Drowning. But one of the few advantages of spending most of your daylight hours hundreds of feet in the air is that you get to see the land laid out like a map, so I know Bar-Selehm as well as anybody.

Most of the streets were empty, enjoying a few hours of quiet before the morning shift dragged workers from their beds, but all along the industrial riverbanks, the factories and dockyards would still be humming with activity. In the insalubrious hinterlands, the pubs and gin houses and opium dens never slept, and I had no desire to stumble through there at this time of night.

I watched a sleek gray mongoose emerge from an alley and pad down the steps of the Flintwick underground station, then picked my way south, toward the Financial District, choosing a series of alleys that emerged into a flagged square surrounded by law offices. The center was dominated by three bashti trees and a bronze statue of some long-dead prime minister. At the east end of the square, atop a flight of broad stone steps, was the Martel Court, a grand structure with a colonnade, a domed hall, and a single clock tower surmounted by a figure of Justice. The statue was gilded and high enough that it provided an orientation point for the city east of the Factory District, almost as conspicuous as the Beacon. At night, it was lit by gas lamps, ignited by a watchman from the observation gallery forty feet below, and they reflected off the eyes of a bushbaby or genet up in one of the bashti trees.

Between the base of the statue and the clock below it was a maintenance room, abandoned since the building was constructed. I stumbled upon it one night last fall, when Morlak had beaten me for breaking one of his substandard hammers. I had fled, roaming the city till I could find somewhere safe from him and his informants. They caught me on the third day, when I went to steal food from the kitchen of the Windmill tavern on Cross Street, and I paid dearly for my truancy, but they never found my bolt-hole. So long as I was careful going up and down, and was quiet when the watchman came to light the lamps, I would be safe there.

I circled the building once and spotted the watchman sitting in a sentry box with an oil lamp, reading a newspaper and smoking a long-stemmed pipe. Awake, in other words, but only just. I made my way to the northeast side and climbed into an ornamental apse with a statue of some ancient judge, setting my boot on his knee and pulling myself up. It was windy out on the balcony beneath the great clock, a chill winter breeze that stirred the smog and made my hair fly. I climbed the ladder to where the globes of the gas lamps sat, then pushed the shutter up and hoisted myself into the space beyond.

I took stock of the room as I released my hair. The blanket I had used last time was still there, as were some of my old books. There was no sign that anyone had been up since. For a few hours, I was safe. I set the "habbit" toy beside me, lay down, and listened to the night, thinking of Berrit, and Morlak, and Willinghouse.

I DREAMED OF SCALING one of the iron foundry chimneys, the tallest in the city. I had a satchel of tools and replacement bricks over my shoulder, which got heavier and heavier with each rung of the ladder I climbed, but I kept going because I thought I would be able to see Papa from the top. When I got there, I opened the satchel, expecting it to contain a baby, but found myself blinded by the light of the Beacon, though I did not remember stealing it. Turning away, I realized that someone was up there with me: Willinghouse, but now he had a terrible gash in his chest that hissed impossibly when he tried to speak. I went to him, used my hand to stop the bleeding, but when I took it away, I was horrified to find that my fist was clutching the bloody spike with which I had stabbed Morlak.

I woke with a start, and the first thought in my head was that today I was supposed to collect Rahvey's baby. I reached for the familiar softness of the habbit and pressed it to my throat as if trying to stanch a wound.

THE SUN WAS NOT yet up, and the night had turned genuinely cold. I was thirsty, but Willinghouse's goat curry was the best meal I had had in months and would sustain me a while longer. I performed the Kathahry in the dusty stone chamber, moving from pose to graceful pose of the balance and agility exercises. They were once a Lani ritual, part martial art, part religious observance, but few people did them now, and I had kept them up only because as a steeplejack, my life had depended on strength and flexibility. Vestris taught me. Rahvey sometimes copied us, but halfheartedly and only because she didn't like being left out. It was one of the things—like reading—that I had felt privileged to share with my beautiful eldest sister.

Long ago.

By the time I was done, the sun was rising over the bay, and Bar-Selehm's ragged industrial skyline was momentarily beautiful again. In an hour, as the day warmed fast, the streets would throng with people, and the Martel Court would be teeming with the anxious and desperate, watched over by dragoons and suited men with sheaves of papers bound with ribbon. It was time to move, but not to

Rahvey's house. Not yet. I had said I would take the child today, but I had not said when, and there were other things I had to do.

I bought a newspaper at the stand on Winckley Street, enjoying the disbelief in the girl's eyes when I put a silver sixpence on the counter and asked if she could make change.

"There's nothing about the boy," she said, watching the way my eyes raked the front page. "The one who fell."

I nodded but didn't speak.

I scaled the water tower on the corner of Old Town, using a combination of access ladder and downspout to reach the roof. Watched by a pair of iridescent bee-eaters, I read the newspapers cover to cover as the light hardened and the temperature rose.

There was no news about the Beacon, although—along with a story about potential land deals between white investors and the unassimilated Mahweni, with the tribal protests that always happened as a result—it still dominated the headlines. The coverage had moved to rabble-rousing. Why had there been no arrests? If the Beacon was still in the city, why had it not been seen? If it wasn't in the city, where was it and how had it been moved? The Parliament had planned a special session to debate the matter, but wasn't that merely a distraction from the lack of progress?

Colonel Archibald Mandel, Secretary of Trade, had made a speech requesting an immediate ban on the sale of luxorite, not just in the city, but nationally and internationally as well. This measure would prevent the Beacon from being broken up and entering the legitimate market. Those whose livelihood depended on the trade had responded angrily, saying that the government should be looking more closely at some of those foreign powers who had no luxorite of their own, particularly the Grappoli.

It was always the Grappoli, our neighbors to the northwest, whose troops, if the papers were to be believed, had been poised to cross vast tracts of bush to lay their hands on Bar-Selehm for close to a hundred years.

The family of Mr. Ansveld, the luxorite trader who had been found dead, issued a statement saying that they had no knowledge of why the "beloved family man" would have taken his own life, and they requested that journalists leave them to their grief in private. A neighbor reported Mr. Ansveld's son saying that had the conditions not made the suicide verdict undeniable, he would not have believed it.

I scowled and rubbed the back of my neck, which had started to burn, then flipped through the large tissuelike pages until I found the continuation of the story.

"Mr. Ansveld's body," I read,

> was found at 8:47 on the morning of the sixteenth by the building's custodian in the company of Messrs. Jacoby Smithe (Under Secretary of Trade) and Hanson Boothes (of the Luxorite Commission), who were scheduled to meet with Mr. Ansveld that morning. The fourth-story room——which is windowless——was locked and bolted from the inside, and tools had to be brought up from stores to effect entry. Mr. Ansveld appeared to have cut his own throat with a razor that was found at the scene.

I rubbed the back of my neck again, but did not move into the shade of the hatch. I combed through the rest of the paper, scanning the pages until I found a grainy halftone picture: a group of stuffy-looking white men in high-collared shirts and sober suits facing unsmilingly forward. The caption called them the Shadow Committee of Trade and Industry. Second and third from the left were two familiar faces, considerably younger than the others, one of them badly scarred: Mr. Josiah Willinghouse and Mr. Stefan Von Strahden.

Shadow Committee.

So my would-be employer had told a half truth. He was who he said he was, but he did not, strictly speaking, work for the government. He was a member of the opposition, the party not currently in power. Yes, he would work on bipartisan projects and initiatives with the current administration, but he was not in a position to make law, determine funding for state projects, or any of the other prerogatives of the ruling party.

A slip of the tongue? I wondered. *A minor embroidery designed to impress? Or a calculated misdirection?*

If it was the latter, it had been a foolish one if it could be dashed by reading a newspaper. Still, it gave me pause, and I felt a tiny disappointment that the circles in which I was moving—albeit secretly—were not quite so elevated as I had thought. It was, I knew, a stupid response, perhaps even a dangerous one, and I found myself thinking about that phrase of his about the troubling occurrences that might overwhelm us all.

Whatever was going on, it was bigger than the death of a Lani boy, or even that of a luxorite merchant.

THE LEADER OF THE Westside boys was called Deveril, a man in his midtwenties with a taste for slim, dusty suits; gold teeth; and a battered top hat with a crow's feather stuck rakishly into the band. His parentage was mixed, largely Lani, but his eyes were the deep, dark brown of the Mahweni, and his hair tended to twist and curl. He wore it in chaotic braids that spilled from under his top hat—half undertaker, half pirate.

He gave me an alarming smile and waved me into his "office," away from the prying eyes of the boys heading out for their day's work. The Westside gang was based in a half-collapsed warehouse, and the standing of the members could be read by how close their quarters were to being structurally intact. Deveril's office doubled as his bedroom, the only room there that had four walls and a ceiling.

He sat in a rickety chair tipped so far back, it seemed about to go over, his feet in hobnailed boots up on a stained desk scattered with paper. "You wannna know about Berrit, eh?" he said musingly. "Poor little bugger. Should never have traded him."

"Why did you?"

"Business," he said. "That's how it goes sometimes."

"Morlak requested him specifically?"

"Berrit? Nah," he sneered, as if the question were idiotic. "To tell you the truth, I was offloading him. The boy was useless for anything but street sweeping and shoe shining, and even, then he was as like to cost me for getting bootblack all over the punters' trousers."

"So Morlak didn't request him?"

"Didn't know he existed till I put the boy in front of him."

"Did he test him, watch him work?"

"Nah," said Deveril, tipping his top hat forward so that the brim shaded his eyes. "Why do you want to know? He was only with Seventh Street ten minutes. You can't have known him."

"He was going to be my apprentice," I said.

He pointed at me, nodding solemnly, as if this explained everything.

"Was he sad to go?" I asked.

"Not so far as you could tell," said Deveril. "Kept himself to himself, you know? Didn't really, as it were, *socialize* with the rest of the chaps. But no, didn't seem sad."

"How long had he been here?"

"Eight months. Maybe nine."

"And he came straight from the Drowning?"

"That's right. His grandmother set it up when his mother died. Tough old bird, she was. Wanted a five-shilling finder's fee for bringing him, if you can believe that. Never even looked at him while she haggled. I gave her two, and she left without another word to him. Just walked out and never looked back." He gave a hard, knowing smile. "No one much cared about Berrit," he said. "Till you. What's that all about?"

"Was anyone else involved in the Morlak trade?" I asked, ignoring his question.

"Like who?"

I shrugged. "Berrit told people he thought he was moving up."

Deveril gave me a shrewd look. "And you reckon that, Mr. Morlak not being everyone's cup of tea, there must have been someone else involved to make little Berrit feel good about the move. Not that I know of, no. Though he said he had friends in high places."

"When did he say that?"

"Last time I saw him. After Morlak had agreed to the trade, Berrit came back for his few bits and bobs. I had a little sit-down with him, make sure he was all right, you know?"

"And he was?"

"Better than," said Deveril. "Quite content, flashing around his advance wages."

"Advance wages?" I parroted. That did not sound like Morlak at all.

"My thoughts exactly," said Deveril. "That's when he said it. I asked him where that had come from, and he gave me this look. Sort of sly, pleased with himself, you know? And he said, 'Friends in high places, Mr. Deveril.' Always very respectful was young Berrit. I appreciated that."

"Did his advance wages include this?" I asked, producing the sun-disk pendant.

Deveril peered at it and grinned. "Nah," he said. "Had that when he first came. It was his mother's, he said. Only time I saw him really angry—and I mean serious, animal angry—was when one of the bigger kids took it from him. Boy went off like a cannon. They left him alone after that, I can tell you."

"And that's all he said. 'Friends in high places'?"

"Not a word more, like it was his little secret," said Deveril. "Like he wanted me to know he was moving up, even if he couldn't say how. Ironical, really, ain't it?" he added.

"What is?"

"Well, he did go up in the world, didn't he?" said Deveril with a bleak smile. "Just came down again right quick."

For a second I just looked at him, then managed to say, "You have his grandmother's name written down somewhere?"

"Written down?" he scoffed. "Nah. Writing is for the slow and clumsy. Me, I like to stay agile."

"Meaning you can't read," I said.

He grinned. "Writing makes people sloppy," he said. "Me, I keep all I need up here." He tapped the side of his jaunty top hat.

"Including the name of Berrit's grandmother?" I prompted.

"Minel," he said proudly. "Minel Samar. Didn't think I'd know that, did ya?"

AS I MADE MY way to the Drowning, I considered what I would say to Florihn and Rahvey. I could not take the child now. That was clear, blood oath or no blood oath. Things had changed in ways I could not have foreseen, and to take the baby would only put it in grave danger.

Surely they will see that?

I wasn't so sure, and the prospect of another confrontation with Florihn and the Lani world she stood for drained all conviction from me. But there was something else I had to do in the Drowning, and I would tackle that first.

Minel Samar was one of those Lani women who was probably only about sixty but looked at least a hundred. She was so hunched over that her toothless, wrinkled face was below her shoulders, but Deveril's assessment of her as a tough old bird was absolutely right. She looked like one of the ancient, scrawny chickens she was feeding with refuse as I arrived, bobbing around the fenceless yard, head twitching on her fleshless neck. I told her who I was and expressed my condolences for the loss of her grandson, but she kept on clucking at the chickens, scattering kernels of grain from the top of her viselike fist so that I began to wonder if she was deaf.

I tried to move into her field of vision, but she turned abruptly. I put a hand on her shoulder and she spun round, not with surprise, but with a baleful stare that made me take a step back, even though she was half my height.

"What?" she snapped. "You got money for me? Whatever Berrit earned is rightly mine now."

"No," I said, taken aback. My hand was in my pocket, fingers closed around the sun-disk pendant, but something stopped me from producing it. "I'm just trying to find out more about—"

"I've got nothing to say," she spat. Her dialect was thick and old-fashioned even for the Drowning. "Useless boy. Always was. Even dead, he's nothing but trouble."

"Trouble?" I said, doing my best to ignore the outrage I felt swelling inside me. "What kind of trouble?"

"People like you," she said, prodding me hard in the chest with a bony finger. "Coming around here, asking questions. Not the first, you know. Bothering me."

"Someone else came to talk to you about Berrit?" I asked. "Who?"

"The chalker with the watch," she said. "Gave me a lousy penny."

"For what?"

"Nothing. Didn't tell him anything, did I?"

"What was his name?"

"Never said. Fancy, though. Old feller. Suit. Gold watch. Came in a rickshaw till they ran out of road. Got his shoes all muddy coming down here, I can tell you." She grinned malevolently, and I had to fight an impulse to get away from her. She was poisonous.

If her visitor had come by rickshaw, I might be able to find whoever brought him.

"What time did he come?" I asked.

"Time? What's it worth to you?"

I fiddled with my purse and produced a sixpence, watching as her eyes got greedy. I held it up, hand closed tight around it. "When?"

"Afternoon," she said, giving it up as if it pained her to part with something she had not yet been paid for.

"When?" I pressed.

She shrugged. "An hour before sundown," she said, palm out for the coin. I gave it to her, catching myself only when she had snatched it away.

"Yesterday?" I said.

"No," she said, her wicked grin returning, her hand reaching out for more money.

I sighed. "What day, then?" I demanded, offering her a single penny.

"Days are bigger than hours," the old woman returned. "You should pay more for them."

I checked my purse reluctantly and produced another sixpence. "That's all I can spare," I said.

She snatched it before I could change my mind.

"Plainsday," she said, already returning to her chickens.

Plainsday?

But that was three days ago. The day *before* Berrit died.

I looked up thoughtfully, my eyes drifting over the tent peaks and tar-papered hut roofs, and I saw up on the rise toward the old monkey temple a young black man with a spear, wearing the plain robes of the Unassimilated Tribes. He was an unusual sight in the Drowning, and my eyes lingered on him.

"He's been around here too," said Berrit's grandmother, spitting another racial slur. "Ought to be a law."

ANGER AT BERRIT'S GRANDMOTHER drove me through the shanty to Rahvey's hut. There was no sign of Sinchon, but then, there almost never was. I knocked once and stepped in, finding Florihn sitting by Rahvey's bedside, the infant slumbering on my sister's breast.

They were surprised to see me. I saw it in their faces. They had talked about me, how I would let them down, break my word, violate the heart of the Lani way. All my reasoned arguments fell away in the need to prove them wrong.

It was the wrong time. The worst time. But I would no longer be judged by these people. I would leave the Drowning with Rahvey's baby and figure out the rest later.

"Is she ready?" I asked.

The two women exchanged looks; then Florihn began fussing with towels and a basket.

"I'll bring her back when it's time for you to feed her," I said to Rahvey. My face was set, but a part of me desperately wanted her to say she'd changed her mind, that she would keep the baby, raise it, love it. . . .

"If you don't, Anglet," she said, "I shan't ask what happened."

I stared at her, and I suppose something of my horror and revulsion showed in my face.

"What?" she said. "Florihn is right. Not everything in life is the way you'd like it to be. Sometimes it's best to accept that and move on."

"Vestris went to Papa's grave," I said. I wasn't sure why I said it except as a way of stabbing at Rahvey, and I immediately wished I hadn't.

"When?"

"Before I did," I said. "She left flowers there."

Rahvey's face closed up.

"It was probably before she got Florihn's message about the baby," I said, trying to cover the cruelty of what I had done.

Rahvey nodded but said, "She still hasn't been, but then, it really was you two who were Papa's girls."

I gazed at her, baffled and upset, then looked away. "I didn't mean to suggest she cared more about the grave than about visiting you," I said.

"No?" she said. "Even if it's true?"

I couldn't answer that, so I looked back at her and responded to her previous remark instead. "Papa loved you, Rahvey. No less than he loved me or Vestris."

She nodded a little too fast, smiling tightly and not meeting my gaze. Her eyes were bright with unshed tears. She passed me the baby, then turned away so I could not read her face as I settled the child into the basket of towels.

"What is her name?" I asked.

"What?"

"The baby. What do you call her?"

Rahvey shrugged. "We only thought about boys' names," she said. "Call her whatever you like."

I picked up the basket. As I did so, the baby stirred, jaws flexing and closing in a yawn. I gazed at her, then looked up, momentarily still.

I felt the eyes of the world as a presence like the rumble of the ocean or the still, insect-singing heat of the savannah. Outside, the Drowning and Bar-Selehm in general were crouched, waiting.

Fourth daughter. Doubly cursed. The child that should not be.

I tried to carry the basket as if it were lighter than it was, as if it held nothing of value. I gave my sister one last look, but Rahvey had closed her eyes.

"Tell no one where she is," I said.

I opened the door and stepped out into the world.

CHAPTER
10

THERE WERE A FEW kids playing out back, and a woman who lived two streets over, a busybody who never actually did anything helpful. The woman rose from her darning as I emerged onto the buckled porch and fixed me with the expectant gaze of one who lives for other people's tragedies.

I felt every muscle tense and had to concentrate to keep my face neutral.

Don't look at the basket, I told myself. *Just walk away.*

So I walked carefully and briskly, face blank, eyes fixed directly ahead, turning toward the crowded industrial skyline. But the city now seemed as different as when I had first noticed that the Beacon was gone. The blown-glass delicacy of the baby changed everything. What had been familiar, even comforting, was now hard edged and dangerous, a walk down a cobbled street suddenly as precarious as scaling a two-hundred-footer. The streets I had known were crowded with skull-cracking brick corners, spear-point railings, and slicing shards of broken glass. The baby's defenseless softness cried out to me every time someone came close, every time the footing felt less than perfect.

I might fall. Not from the sky. Just walking on the uneven sets and cobbles, I might fall, and that would be enough. I braced my arms around the baby, trying to form a cage around its terrible fragility, and my stomach turned.

You can't do this.

At the corner of Old Threadneedle Street, I felt the child stir, and as I passed the entrance to the Northgate underground railway, a noisy belch of smoke burst from the grating in the pavement, and the child began to cry, softly at first, then with real distress. I poked and cooed, but it made no difference. Could she be hungry already? Surely not. We had only just left. I risked taking her out of the basket and holding her against me.

The infant opened its eyes and quieted, seeming to look at me, and when I held it against my chest, I could feel its tiny heart racing so that I felt thrilled, terrified, and so far out of my depth that I could barely see the shore. And then she was crying again, a high cycling wail that closed her eyes and made her face hot.

I'd had her less than an hour and was already failing her.

A white woman in an enormous crinoline-buoyed dress and a pink-bowed bonnet gave me a haughty look as she passed, and as I turned away, I found myself looking up at the implacable stone and high iron railings of the Pancaris Home for Orphaned Children by the canal. It was a hard building, blockish and unornamented save for the thorny rose etched into the stone above the door, which was the emblem of the order.

I knew little of northern religions beyond the fact that for most of them, life was a kind of test, something to be endured before being reunited with the spirit who made the world. They favored self-denial and service, which, for the Pancaris nuns, meant celibacy, teaching, and raising other people's children.

The baby was still crying. I thought of Rahvey saying she wouldn't ask what happened if I never took the child back to her. I wasn't going to abandon the baby, not yet, but I had to see. Perhaps it would be a place of light and happiness. . . .

I climbed the long, steep flight of stone stairs and entered. The building was cold and dark inside, its hallways narrow and echoing. There was no airy lobby, no bustle, no sound of voices to distract from the squawling infant in the basket.

"Can I help you?"

I turned to find an elderly white woman in a black gown and the hair-concealing headdress they called a wimple looking down on me from a high, backless stool at a desk. The stool was inexplicably mounted on a platform accessed by three wooden steps.

"I was just looking around," I answered weakly.

"You were under the impression this was a zoo or a museum?" said the woman, peering at me over her reading glasses.

"No," I said. "A friend of mine has had a baby. I don't think she will be able to keep it. I was wondering, if she were to bring it here, what the place would be like."

"It would probably be better if your *friend* came for herself, wouldn't you say?" said the nun, eyeing my wailing basket. "Show me the child."

I did as I was told, hesitant, but desperate for anything to stop the crying. The nun put the baby on one of the towels over her shoulder and patted her spine till she burped, spewing a dribble of milky vomit onto the cloth, then falling promptly, magically silent. The nun returned the infant to me in superior silence.

"Thank you," I said. "Could I see where the children live? Where they sleep?"

"I fail to see how that is pertinent," said the nun, "but, very well. Come this way."

We descended a narrow staircase into a gaslit, windowless, and whitewashed corridor that smelled of antiseptic. The nun took a ring of keys from her rope belt and unlocked a heavy door, admitting us to a room—also windowless—containing six iron bedsteads, six chairs, six desks, and six small cabinets. There were three children inside. They looked to be about Berrit's age or younger, one black, two Lani, all girls. They were working at their desks, but got to their feet and turned to face the door, standing to something like attention.

They said nothing.

I took a step in, but the nun grasped my wrist.

"I see no reason to disturb their studies," she said.

I hesitated, taking in their blank, hollow faces, the buckets of cleaning supplies and brooms propped beside each cabinet, and asked, "What are they reading?"

"Something improving," said the nun with chill pride. "Devotional texts, moral pamphlets, studies on the value of cleanliness and labor."

Not knowing what to say, I just nodded. I had never thought that hopelessness might have an aroma, but if it did, that was what the still, silent air of the room smelled of: hospital sterility and despair.

The nun showed me out, and I had to resist the impulse to hold the door open, to tell the children to run. But then I was being steered into the nursery, an identical room: white, unadorned, and silent, containing eight cagelike cribs. Another nun sat with a book on one of the curiously high stools. She considered us as we entered, bowing fractionally to her sister before returning her eyes to her reading.

"They are all sleeping," I said, trying to sound impressed.

"It is nap time," said the nun at my elbow, as if this were obvious. "Every day at this time."

"That's very . . . disciplined," I said.

"They need structure in their lives," said the nun. "Most of them are here because their mothers had none of their own—something you might want to pass on to your *friend*."

As I left the room, I thought that it smelled less like a hospital and more like a morgue, as if it were a place where spirit came to die. Clutching the basket to my breast with a new and tortured sense of desperation, I walked quickly down the hallway and out.

PAUSING ONLY TO PICK up a bottle of sheep's milk from the Holymound market, I returned to the Martel Court via the labyrinth that was Old Town, a complex of rough, sand-colored stone and spiraling minarets that had been all there was of Bar-Selehm before the whites came. I pulled my hair back, slipped my arms through the handles of the basket, hitching it up onto my back, and climbed up to the shuttered chamber above the clock mechanism, comfortable in the knowledge that I was invisible up there in the smog. But as I withdraw one arm from the handles to work the louvers, the basket shifted and swung, and for a brief, heart-stopping moment, I glanced down into the face of the sleeping child, suspended by a wicker band over eighty feet of nothing but hard, shattering stone.

I clambered inside, my heart racing as if I had been chased over rooftops by Morlak's gang.

Inside, hanging from a high buttress by its hind legs, was one of the large fox-headed fruit bats that called the city home. It watched me with black, glassy eyes and ruffled its rubbery wings. For a long moment, I just sat there looking at it, and eventually—comfortable that we were no threat to each other—it tucked its head and went to sleep.

What have you done? What are you going to do?

All my excitement about working for Willinghouse, of championing Berrit's memory and serving as an agent of justice, lay exposed as vain and idiotic in the awful frailty of the sleeping child.

I made the place as safe and accommodating as possible: checked for spiders, flushed the roosting bat out of the shuttered hatch, and lay the baby down in her blankets, my worn-out habbit snuggled next to her—horrified by the scale of my own stupidity. For a long minute I watched her, and when she seemed calm, I left.

The child was safer there than on the streets with me. The day was ending, and every footpad in the city would be on the watch for a Lani steeplejack who had offended Mr. Morlak of Seventh Street. . . .

Forcing myself to focus on the investigation, I scaled the back of the public library on Winckley Street, waiting in the shadow of a great stone griffin for the newspaper girl's arrival on the corner below. She dropped from a wagon moments later and set to unloading two pallets of evening papers. I was down, money in hand, in time to be her first customer of the night.

She gave me a curious look but said nothing and handed me the paper. The headline said that the Grappoli ambassador had made a formal protest about the insinuation that his government was in any way associated with the theft of the Beacon. In response, a small crowd had chanted insults outside the embassy till a unit of dragoons dispersed them.

"You can read these as well as sell them?" I asked.

The Mahweni girl bristled. "Every letter," she returned. "You?"

"Ever heard of Josiah Willinghouse?" I asked.

The question seemed to catch her off guard, but she nodded.

I pocketed my change but left a sixpenny bit on her crate.

She eyed it questioningly and, when I inclined my head a fraction, palmed it. "What do you want to know?" the girl asked, still cautious.

"Anything," I said. "I expect you read a lot, selling papers all day. I don't know how much you remember—"

"All of it," she said.

The boast annoyed me. She caught the look on my face and pushed the coin back across the crate toward me.

I sighed and shoved it back. "Fine," I said. "You know anything about Willinghouse or not?"

She considered me for a moment, but she wasn't trying to remember. She was deciding whether to speak. When she did, it came out in an unbroken stream without inflection, and though it was the same voice she always used, her eyes went blank. It felt oddly like someone was speaking through her.

"The Right Honorable Josiah Willinghouse, twenty-four, Brevard party representative for Bar-Selehm Northeast, sits on the Shadow Trade and Industry Committee. Appointed seven months ago. Elected to Parliament three months before that. Currently the youngest serving member. Educated at Ashland University College,

Ntuzu, and Smithfield Preparatory School, like his father before him. Son of the late Jeremiah Willinghouse, also member of Parliament for Bar-Selehm Northeast, mining magnate, and Lady Tabitha Farnsworth, also deceased. Josiah Willinghouse's first parliamentary speech concerned water restrictions at the time of drought and their impact on Mahweni farmers in his district. His motion, which was seconded by Stefan Von Strahden, was denied in a vote along party lines."

A shiver ran down my spine. "How do you do that?" I asked, all my wary hostility swallowed up by awe.

The girl blinked and suddenly was herself again, though she too had shed her hostility. "I don't know," she said, embarrassed by the inadequacy of the remark. "I just remember what I read."

"It's extraordinary," I said.

She flushed and looked away, but there was a flicker of satisfaction in her eyes that she couldn't conceal.

"What's your interest in Willinghouse?" she asked. "Or do you just like handsome politicians?"

"Hardly handsome," I scoffed a little too quickly, so that the girl raised an eyebrow.

"All right," she said. "Anything else you want to know about?"

"Yes," I said on impulse. "Ansveld. The luxorite merchant who died."

"What about him?" she asked, wary again.

"Where did he work?"

"Mr. Thomas Ansveld of Ansveld and Sons Quality Luxorite Emporium, Twenty-two Crommerty Street, Bar-Selehm," she said automatically and without inflection.

I marveled again. "Have you always been able to do that?" I asked.

"As long as I can remember," she said. "My father taught me to read, but it was years before I knew that what I could do was . . . not usual."

"It's a gift," I said, smiling.

The girl looked less sure of that, and a trace of her former stiffness returned. "You'd think so, wouldn't you?" she said.

"I mean it. You shouldn't be selling papers. You should be a reporter."

Something complex flashed through her face, a bright and incandescent joy quickly doused and smothered. "Right," she said. "Now, if you don't mind, I have customers."

I HADN'T LEARNED MUCH, but it felt like a start, and I returned to the Martel Court exhilarated. That feeling was dashed as soon as I climbed up to the louvered shutters of the room above the clock. The baby was crying again. I could hear it like a siren in the air, an awful, accusatory keening.

She calmed a little when I picked her up, but began again when she tried to nuzzle at my breast and found no sustenance. I whispered to her and pushed the habbit into her tiny hands, but nothing helped. She needed her mother, and though she was clearly ravenous, she would not take the milk I had bought earlier.

How often does a newborn feed?

I had no idea.

You can't do this. You don't know where to start.

Reading to her did not help at all, so I put her in the tool satchel along with the habbit and everything I owned, save my books, and made the descent from the clock tower to the street.

On my way to the Atembe underground station, the baby's screaming drawing every eye my way, I thought of the blank high windows and implacable iron gates of the Pancaris orphanage.

Leave her on the steps now, and all this goes away. The nuns will raise her. The nuns know what they are doing.

But I didn't. There was no principled decision, no careful thought process or moral choice. I just didn't because I knew what the place was. I should never have gone. It had wasted time I could have spent doing my new job, and now leaving the child there would be harder. I tried to soothe her, but she wouldn't stop crying. Even without the hostile stares of my fellow passengers, it was a terrible thing to be responsible for that awful, frantic bawling. I let my hair fall in front of my face and kept my eyes down.

At Rahvey's house, I was greeted with outrage and incredulity at my lateness and incompetence, so I fled to the temple graveyard till the feeding was done. The child had quieted the moment Rahvey pressed it to her breast, and the silence bellowed the extent of my failure.

As night fell, however, I grew scared of the cemetery's silence and its deep shadows, and when the hippos began roaring, I couldn't stand it any longer and returned to Rahvey's hut.

Sinchon wasn't pleased. "The baby is feeding," he said, as if I had no other business being there.

"Again?" I asked.

"Babies are always hungry," said Sinchon, staring off toward the river, where a family of warthogs was trotting by, their tails in the air. "Always."

I wrapped myself in a threadbare blanket and slept on their porch for a few hours till Rahvey had performed yet another feeding. I took the child without a word and made my way back into the city, realizing once more that a part of me was hunting for the missing Beacon in the darkness of the rooftops and chimneys.

CHAPTER

11

AT FIRST LIGHT I made the baby as safe and comfortable as possible, then with almost paralyzing reluctance, left her sleeping. She did not cry when I crawled out through the shutter, but her silence rang in my head like an accusation.

I double-checked the address against what the newspaper girl had given me and considered the photograph above Ansveld's obituary. He looked austere and professional, half his face lost in carefully groomed but slightly ridiculous side whiskers.

I had never been inside any of the luxorite vendors' shops on Crommerty Street but I knew the area, having spent a week rigging scaffolding for the roofers on Trimble Avenue the previous summer. A colony of green storks nested along the ridgeline.

It was a wealthy district. Externally, the shops all looked the same—cream-colored stone with formal, expensive trim—and dark inside: all wood paneling and merchandise in glass cases. They were the sort of stores where only certain kinds of people were welcome.

I was not one of them. I brushed the worst of the dirt from my clothes and tried to smooth my hair.

As soon as the bell over the door tinkled, a man looked up from his place behind the counter and gave me an inquisitorial stare. He was perhaps thirty, a pair of the heavily smoked goggles luxorite traders always used pushed back on his forehead. He had a pen in his hand that he held suspended above his notebook, as if caught composing poetry. A vast typewriter sat on the counter, and he had to lean round it to see me.

"We're not hiring, thank you," he said.

"I'm sorry," I said, taking an awkward step into the shop, "I'm not looking for employment."

His brow wrinkled.

I pressed on. "I wondered if you could tell me a little about Mr. Ansveld," I said.

His face darkened, and he got quickly to his feet. "I've told you reporter types before—" he began.

"I'm not press," I said.

"And you're not police," he returned, staring me down.

"I'm here in my capacity as a private investigator serving a prominent client—"

He did not allow me to finish the sentence. "Out!" he said, his voice rising and his face flushing. "You think my family's tragedy is entertainment? You think I want to discuss my father's doings with guttersnipes and vagrants?"

"I am neither a—" I began, but he was coming toward me now, his anger reaching a rapid boil. I moved for the door, but he kept coming, faster now.

"I said get out!" he yelled.

I ducked out of the shop, and he followed, slamming the door shut as soon as I was through it. When I turned, muttering explanations and apologies, he snatched the blind down and stalked back into the dark recesses of the shop. I considered the name above the door, carefully painted in gold cursive on a glossy black background. ANSVELD AND SONS.

My father's doings . . .

I sighed, cursing my clumsiness, and considered the street, with its white ladies in crinolines and its suited men on their way to work. I felt conspicuous, outclassed, and stupid.

Another failure, I thought.

I was almost out of the street when I glimpsed a familiar face. He was white, a boy about my own age, wearing a tweed jacket over a collared shirt with a necktie. The shirt was carefully laundered, and the jacket had been mended several times, but if you didn't look too closely at his boots, he might almost pass for gentry.

He wasn't.

His name was William—Billy—Jennings, a petty thief and pick-pocket who worked for one of Morlak's rivals. He was walking briskly, his eyes flicking around the street, fastening on the women with their little purses and handbags as he moved. I did not think he had seen me.

Falling into step behind him, I timed my approach to a point between two grand terraces where a narrow street ran up under the shade of a tantu tree. He half turned, sensing my presence, but I got a good grip on his left wrist and twisted it. Stifling his cry to avoid attention, he let me propel him a few yards up the street, where we would not be observed.

"What's going on?" he blustered, faltering when he saw my face. "Oh, it's you."

"What are you doing here, Billy?" I demanded.

"Walking. What's it to you?"

"A bit high end for your beat, isn't it?" I said.

"That's rich coming from you," he shot back.

I gave his wrist a twist.

"What do you want? I ain't done nothing."

"Not yet today, perhaps," I said. "But I'll bet you plan to."

"Can't punish a man for what he ain't done yet," said Billy, smirking slightly. "And what's it got to do with you anyway?"

"You work this street a lot?" I asked.

"What do you mean 'work'?" he said, staring me down, though the color in his cheek gave the lie to his defiance.

"*Walk* then," I said. "You walk this street a lot?"

"Sure," he said. "Free country, right? A man has to get around."

"And you see what's going on, don't you, Billy? Always on the watch?"

"What's this about?" he demanded again.

"You see anything odd around here last week?" I asked, relaxing my grip on his wrist.

"Odd? What do you mean odd?"

"Anything out of place—other than you, I mean."

"I don't know what you're talking about," he said.

"Men like you know the routines in a place like this, don't you, Billy? When the streets are busiest, when the ladies do a little shopping after a glass of luncheon wine, which makes them less careful of their belongings, a fraction slower to react when someone dips into their purses—"

"I resent that," he cut in. "I'm a businessman, me."

"So you'll know when people make deliveries, or when there are whispers of important deals. Especially where luxorite is concerned."

"Luxorite?" said Billy. He looked confused and alarmed. "I don't deal in luxorite," he said, smoothing the frayed collar of his over-starched shirt. "Too hard to move, isn't it?"

"No one's accusing you of anything, Billy," I said. "I'm just asking if you've seen or heard anything out of the ordinary."

"Why?" he demanded, reverting to his original tack. "Who wants to know?"

"I do," I said. "I'm curious."

"You can say that again," he sneered.

I made a snatch for his wrist, but he whipped it away. "There's money in it for you," I tried. "If you think of anything."

"How much?" said Billy, giving me a sidelong look. "I mean, if I should remember anything, that is."

"That depends on what you remember, Billy."

"Yeah," he drawled. "That's what I thought. Bloody Seventh Street gang never have any money. What kind of cash can I expect from a Lani steeplejack?"

I wanted to slap him, but something in his last word stirred his memory, and a realization dawned.

"You're the one who had the apprentice what died last week," he said. "What was his name?"

"Berrit," I said.

"Berrit," he echoed. "Right. Sorry to hear it. He fell off a chimney, yeah?"

His manner was different now. People in our social bracket couldn't afford much in the way of sentimentality, but there was a kind of class loyalty that cut across some of the rivalries of race and gang affiliation.

"I don't think he fell," I said.

His eyes narrowed. "And that's connected to this stuff you're asking me?" he said.

"Might be."

He turned away for a moment, thinking. When he looked back at me, there was a frankness in his face that hadn't been there before. "I have a lady friend," he said, "scullery maid for one of the dealers back there." He nodded toward Crommerty Street.

"A luxorite trader?" I asked.

"A bit," he said. "Macinnes. Fancy bits and bobs. Number Twenty-three."

Across the street from Ansveld's.

"And she's legit, this lady friend?" I asked.

"Why wouldn't she be?" Billy demanded, on his dignity again.

"Well, she's with you, for a start," I said.

He frowned at that, then reached into his inside pocket, producing two buttoned pouches jingling with coins.

"I don't want your money," I said.

"Wasn't gonna give you any," he said. He held up first one purse, then the other. "This one," he said, "this is for work. Some of it is, you might say, of questionable origins. This one, though—this one is strictly on the up-and-up. All hard earned and legal-like."

"Why keep them separate?" I asked.

"This one," he said shyly, holding the one he'd said was legit, "that's for the ring I'm saving for. My Bessie will be touched by noth-ing what isn't pure."

I grinned at his earnestness and he blushed.

"Fair enough, lover boy," I said. "Ask your scullery princess what people are saying about the death of Mr. Ansveld." His eyes widened with recognition. "Discreetly," I added. "And keep me out of it."

"Or what?" he said, a little of his former defiance returning.

"Scullery maid for an upmarket merchant, eh?" I said. "And you all honorable and respectable. She might not like to hear that her beau once got his arm broken for trying to sell a pocket watch to the brother of the man he nicked it from the day before."

Billy was famously incompetent. "He didn't break my arm," he sputtered, but the bluster was empty. "Fine," he added. "I'll be dis-creet."

I gave him a friendly pat on the cheek, and he flinched as if I were going to hit him.

"I'll be in touch," I said, checking the clock on the bank across the street. I had to collect the baby and attend a funeral.

CHAPTER
12

BERRIT'S FUNERAL TOOK PLACE at the Lani monkey temple. Anything not wholly burned in the pyre would go into the river—which was once deemed holy—where the crocodiles would take it. Tanish and I had met just outside the West Gate and he had stared openmouthed at the baby while I looked around to make sure none of the other gang members had followed him.

"How long will you keep it?" he asked, frightened for the child and for me.

"Not long," I said, as if I knew some easy, obvious solution that hadn't yet occurred to him. "Does Morlak know where you are?"

"Too busy shouting at people to ask," said Tanish. "And he can't really walk. Moves like a badly made puppet."

He launched into an exaggerated imitation, limping and moaning and cursing my name, so that I laughed for real.

He gave me an uneasy look. "You should get away," Tanish offered.

He said it reluctantly, sadly, knowing he should do so for my sake, but not wanting me to follow the advice. I grinned and ruffled his hair till he pulled free, avoiding my eyes, and skipped away, whooping. The boys in the gang all talked and smoked and drank like adults, coarse and callous, their eyes hard as their hands. But in moments like this, it was like pulling the night shroud from a luxorite lamp, all the boyish rapture he usually kept so carefully locked away bursting out and splashing the world with light.

"Can't catch me, I'm a hummingbird!" he announced, dancing in close, his little hands fluttering on crooked arms, then hopping back and away.

"Here, hummingbird," I said, fishing a piece of succulent spine fruit from my satchel. "Nectar."

He came weaving in again, his hands flickering fast as they could go, and dipped his face to the fruit. He took a bite, still "hovering," and came up with juice running down his chin so that he laughed out loud even as I rapped him on the head with the rolled-up newspaper I was still carrying. For a moment, brief and vibrant and glorious, we forgot we were going to a funeral.

It was clear as Tanish and I drew near the twilit buildings that the service had already begun. I saw torchlight and wondered if the murmur of voices in chanting chorus would wake the swaddled baby asleep in my satchel.

We slipped quietly into the assembly, the hood of my black shirt pulled low over my face. For once my monochromatic wardrobe didn't make me stand out in the Drowning. The huddle of Lani friends, family, and community leaders—including Florihn, the midwife—had put aside their usual riot of colors and looked like a roost of crows. Berrit's hawkish grandmother sat at the front, her face blank save when she fiddled irritably with the mourning veil draped around her shoulders.

She was facing a stack of brushwood doused with oil. A plain pine coffin was wedged into the dry branches, and I watched as the priest's assistant—clad in gray and wearing a chain of bright metal—nudged it gingerly to make sure it wouldn't slide out once the fire took hold. I checked that the sun-disk pendant was under my shirt. I had decided to keep it on me rather than give it to his grandmother and was wearing it on the same chain as the double-headed coin.

She would only sell it, I told myself. *Someone should keep it for Berrit's sake.*

I saw the feathered top hat of Deveril, flanked by a couple of boys from the Westside gang. He looked solemn, and I held my head up long enough for him to catch my eye so that I could give him a nod of acknowledgment. Apart from me and Tanish, no one from the Seventh Street gang had bothered to come, and I found myself wondering again how Berrit could have thought that his move from Westside was a good thing.

Friends in high places . . .

There was, at least, no sign of Morlak. I didn't need telling that he had made a faster and more complete recovery than Tanish had expected or that he was stepping up his attempts to find me. I wouldn't be safe till . . .

Till what? Till the Beacon is found, Berrit's murder is uncovered, and Morlak's body is cut down from the gibbet and thrown to the sharks at Tanuga Point?

Perhaps. I rested my hand on the satchel in which the baby slept silent and unseen.

Berrit's grandmother lit the fire herself, rising just long enough to thrust the priest's brand into the pyre, then returned to her seat, showing no emotion. Once the coffin was aflame, a stick was taken from the blaze and used to start another fire some yards away in a circle of stones. Offerings that had been sacrificed earlier—some chickens and a young pig—were then barbecued for the tribe: life out of death.

It was our way. The same as it had been when Papa died.

Once I might have found it comforting, this circular continuity, but today it felt wrong, or rather *I* felt wrong, as if this were some other people's tradition and I was watching from outside—like one of the white travelers who sometimes came in search of the strange or exotic.

Rahvey was there with Sinchon and their three daughters. I watched her, uneasy, and there was something about her mourning black, her unnatural stillness, and the rare closeness of the family around her that bothered me. She had not known Berrit. None of them had. This was just community support, the rallying around of friends and neighbors, which was the best of what the Lani way had to offer.

But it felt like more than that. I watched the coffin burn, and for a moment I could almost feel the heat, as if I were in there with Berrit and Rahvey's infant daughter, all the unwanted children burning together. . . .

Old Mrs. Chani leaned in and squeezed Rahvey's shoulder encouragingly, so that my sister turned on her a brief, sad smile of thanks.

The moment the official part of the funeral ended and the crowd began to break up, I pushed my way toward Rahvey, keen to get the child to its next feeding. But something was happening behind me, and everyone had stopped moving, turning to look back toward the temple entrance. There was a commotion in the crowd, a rush of muttering and the craning of necks followed by a steady parting, like waves blown by a powerful wind. Through the resultant gap I saw a curtained sedan chair borne by five black men in navy robes and crimson turbans. They wore sabers and pistols at their belts.

The men stooped and the curtains parted, revealing a slender ankle and a foot in a sandal of fine strapwork. The foot found the earth, steadied itself, and an extraordinarily beautiful woman emerged. She wore a deep blue sari shot through with silver filigree and a veil of black mesh that masked her face, but there was no doubt as to her identity.

Vestris!

My heart leapt. It had been two years since I last saw my eldest sister, but her appearance now, after everything that had happened, felt like a lifeline.

Rahvey, sitting alone by the pyre, was transformed by the vision moving so gracefully toward her, and all her stoic solemnity fell away. Vestris slipped back the veil as she reached our sister, resting it around her shoulders like a shawl, and even this simple motion was effortlessly elegant. Her face—delicately, expertly made up—was serious, her fine, almost patrician features showing no emotion. She stooped to Rahvey and kissed her lightly on the forehead, and the younger woman flushed with undisguisable delight.

Vestris held her sister's hand and whispered into her ear, so that for a moment Rahvey seemed to bask in the radiance of her attention. Then the elder was straightening up, a motion I recognized for its deliberation and finality. Rahvey tried to keep the conversation going, but Vestris was politely firm. She had to go.

I hovered, desperate to drag Vestris's gaze away from the buzzing watchers. I shifted on the balls of my feet as if poised to step over the gap between two high ledges, and I felt the thrill of childish delight as my sister's eyes found me. She approached and, without a word, enfolded me in a formal but tender embrace. I held on to her, swallowing back childish tears of joy and relief.

Vestris will make it all right—Morlak, the baby, even Berrit. Somehow.

Over her shoulder I saw Rahvey watching, jealous.

"How are you, Ang?" said Vestris. "It has been too long."

I found myself tongue-tied and acutely aware of the crowd looking enviously on. "I'm well, thank you, Vestris," I said. "Though not, perhaps, so well as you." I grinned.

Ang and Vestris together again.

"Little Anglet," said Vestris, smiling. "You always had such spirit under all that shyness."

"You came to Papa's grave," I said.

"How do you know that?"

"Tsuli flowers," I said. "Who else could afford them?"

She smiled once more. It was a complicated smile: knowing, amused, sad, but still strangely radiant. I felt it again, that sense of sitting in a shaft of sunlight. If she were not my sister, I would have fallen in love with her. Anyone would.

"Where is Rahvey's baby?" she asked.

"Here," I added, the words low and rushed, feeling the weight of the sleeping baby in the satchel. "I have a lot to tell you, much of it bad. I'm in danger and . . ." I risked a look at Rahvey, who shook her fierce head once. "I need to talk to you in private," I concluded.

"I can't, Ang," she said. "Not tonight."

"When?" I pressed. "I really want to see you again soon."

And that was the truth of it. Whether Vestris could actually help, I had no idea. I just wanted to be with her again, like we used to be.

Vestris considered me seriously, then reached into her sari and drew out a silk purse with a silver clasp and a single pearl of luxorite that shone like a gas lamp as she unveiled it. The stone was shaded with smoked glass to soften its brilliance but still cast hard shadows for several feet all around, and in its light, my already beautiful sister became ethereal, angelic.

She handed me an embossed card with gold trim. "You can send me word at this address," she said. "You can still write, I hope?"

She beamed at me, and I nodded enthusiastically.

"Don't come," she said. "They won't let you in. But write to me and we will arrange a meeting. Till then—" She took my hand and emptied the contents of the purse—three silver coins—into it, smiling again softly.

"Thank you," I said, not looking at the money. "There's food—"

Vestris's smile shaded a little, became kindly but also sad. "I cannot stay, little Anglet," she said. "This is not my world. But write to me."

"I will," I said. "I can walk with you now for a moment—"

But she shook her head. "Remember, little sister," she said, "that I love you." She leaned forward and kissed me softly on the cheek, bringing with the motion a delicate aroma of violets and sandalwood—and then the unearthly light was gone with the empty purse and she was making her way back to the sedan chair and whatever version of the world awaited her elsewhere.

I gazed after her wordlessly, unable to think, almost overwhelmed by the impulse to run crying after her, to beg that she take me with her. . . .

The crowd parted silently before her once more, as if she were a benevolent queen visiting her subjects, and some of them peered at me, the nondescript girl who had been so unexpectedly touched by her beneficence.

I pressed her card to my chest.

She had said I could write to her. We would meet. We would talk. Everything would be all right.

I watched her leave as the various well-wishers paid their respects to Berrit's grandmother, though the old woman was probably wishing they were paying her with something more tangible. When it was my turn I pressed one of Vestris's silver coins into the old woman's hand as if I were my sister, elegant and wealthy.

She didn't thank me, but as I was turning away, she plucked me by the sleeve and pulled me back. "Let me see that!" she said. She stabbed with her bony index finger and I winced, expecting it to find my midriff, but it connected instead with the folded newspaper that was sticking out of my satchel.

Baffled, I pulled the paper out and she ripped it from my hands, holding it so close to her face that it almost touched her nose.

"That's him," she said matter-of-factly, thrusting the paper back at me. "That's the chalker who came looking for Berrit. The one with the fancy shoes."

I looked at the image in the paper. It was the photograph accompanying the obituary for Ansveld, the luxorite dealer. I stared at it.

So there is a connection.

"Ang, sister mine," said Rahvey. A summons.

Berrit's grandmother was already beetling away toward the barbecue fires. I turned to my sister.

Rahvey waited for me to approach, her lips thin as she gazed out to where the pyre blazed and the sun set. "What did she give you?" Rahvey demanded.

"Who?"

"Vestris, of course!" she snapped. "What did she give you?"

I showed her the remaining coins that I still had tight in my fist.

She snatched my wrist and helped herself to one of the silver crowns. I tried to wrench away, but she dug in with her nails and hissed, "Call it back payment for services rendered."

I snatched my hand away, my fist tight around what was left of Vestris's gift, then pocketed it. I drew the sleeping child carefully from my satchel and handed it to her. Rahvey swept it hastily under her mourning black and moved it to her breast with a cautious glance around, as if she didn't want people to see. That bothered me.

"What did the elders say?" I asked.

"We have not spoken to the elders," said Rahvey, eyes on the flames still.

"What?" I demanded, incredulity raising my voice so that Rahvey gave me a sharp look. "Why not?"

"Florihn said it was best we didn't," said Rahvey.

"This isn't Florihn's decision!"

"You are right. It's mine."

"So what are you going to do?" I asked in a hoarse whisper.

"Nothing," said Rahvey, looking away again. "It is already done."

I stared at her, aghast.

"You will raise the child yourself, or you will take it to the nuns at Pancaris," she said flatly. "I will help feed her when I can," she continued, as if she were being more gracious than I deserved.

"It's *your* child!" I shot back.

"Not anymore," she said. "You took the oath. Sinchon says you are to do your sisterly duty."

I looked over to where Sinchon was talking to one of his tinker friends. He was holding a chicken leg in his hand, and as I watched, he laughed suddenly, then took a bite.

Rahvey read the anger in my eyes.

"So delicate, sister mine," she said. "So unready for the world."

* * *

RAHVEY, AS IF TO make a point, refused to take the baby with her. I looked for Tanish, but he had slipped away before the funeral ended. I did not know when I would see him again. The thought pained me.

One by one, people drifted away, and the sun vanished beneath the silhouettes of distant towers and chimneys that were the city proper, until the only light remaining in the old temple came from the embers of the two fires. A few days ago I would have been able to see the Beacon like a star riding low over the city.

Strange.

If the government couldn't recover it they would probably put a gas lamp in its place, which wouldn't be the same at all. Without the Beacon, I felt more than usually lost, stuck in this remnant of my past like a character in a discarded book, unable to move any further through the story. I wandered around the temple, cradling the baby, and found a newly carved statue of Cenu, the Lani goddess of prosperity. It had been cut from soft wood and had yet to be painted, but I knew exactly what it would look like when it was done because I had been looking at this image all my life: it would be brightly colored, an overflowing basket of yellow wheat on one arm, an infant in the other, and the woman herself—ample breasted and broad hipped—would have her head tipped slightly to one side, beaming stupidly at the world. The expression gave her the look of someone who had been smoking servitt through a water pipe, but she hadn't been, because only the men of the village did that. She was drunk on her own beauty, on her usefulness to her family, on the Lani way.

I felt the rising red tide I had managed to suppress as it burst the hinges of one of the doors in my heart. All the injustice and frustration I had been wrestling with streamed out like a jet of molten steel. I seized a rock and smashed it into the statue's saintly face over and over till its features splintered into nothing.

CHAPTER
13

THE CHICKEN WAS CHARRED on the outside but sweet and tender within. I had eaten nothing so good since Willinghouse's goat curry, and I devoured it hungrily, the pleasurable relief of it momentarily quelling all my other frustrations and anxieties. I was still in the temple grounds, sitting close to the barbecue hearth, watching the dwindling flames as they shifted from orange and yellow to blue and green. I had moved away from the defaced statue of Cenu, feeling so stupid and ashamed that I left a few coins at its feet: more than enough to repay the carver for the work he would have to do over. Vestris's coin I kept like a talisman.

Down by the river a male hippo bellowed in the dark, and the females of the pod answered in turn. They wouldn't come up into the temple grounds, but I would need to be careful when I returned to the Drowning in case they had left the water to browse. Their teeth were a foot and a half long and the power of their jaws could break a crocodile in half. . . . I touched the sleeping child and it stirred, animal-like, without waking, so that I smiled. I had spent so much time wondering about the baby's fragility that I had not allowed myself to register how beautiful she was, how much a thoughtless part of me was glad to be close to her.

Was this how Papa had looked at me, with the same wondering joy? Or had he seen in me the death of his wife? If ever the latter, he got past it or concealed it utterly, and I was grateful for that. Deliberate or otherwise, it was an act of love. I wondered if Berrit had experienced anything similar, or if his hawkish, grasping grandmother had set the tone for the whole family.

I could make no sense of Berrit's death. Why had Ansveld been to see the boy? If the luxorite dealer had wanted to steal the Beacon, it made a kind of sense that he would contract with steeplejacks, but Berrit just didn't have the skills. The boy could have been part of a team, but if so, why was he the only one to die, and who had killed him? Ansveld was unlikely to have been the one hanging from a brace on the chimney ledge, assuming he had still been alive at that point.

It had to involve Morlak. He would have been the go-between, the agent and manager, though I felt sure I would have heard if the gang leader had ever been seen with a gentleman as elevated as Ansveld. They could have met secretly, of course, but Ansveld had taken a rickshaw into the Drowning: not the action of a man who was trying to be inconspicuous.

Something wasn't right.

I wished I could sit down with Willinghouse and talk it through, but as soon as I thought of it, the memory of the pale man with the scar and the fierce green eyes unsettled me. I was no Vestris, shaking the shanty's mud from her immaculate sandals as she made her escape—confident, exquisite, free of the place where she had grown up. She probably spent her life at balls and soirees, exchanging easy banter with the likes of Willinghouse, meeting those piercing eyes of his and holding them, confident, like an equal. . . .

I would write to her in the morning. She would know what to do. Maybe I could learn something from her about how to deal with men like Willinghouse.

Meaning how to impress them? said an insidious voice in my head.

No. That was stupid.

I thrust a branch into the heart of the fire. The remaining wood flared and spat sparks into the night. In the flickering light, something in the underbrush to my left shifted.

I froze.

Hyena, I thought, getting quickly to my feet and edging even closer to the remains of the fire and the satchel where the baby slept. Once when I was a child and the summer had been particularly dry, a rogue hyena entered a hut on the edge of the Drowning where a mother and her three children slept—

The snap of a twig, and my memories were blown away like smoke.

I stared into the shadows where I had glimpsed the movement. There was a roughly plastered shrine, crumbling with age and overgrown with vines, little more than an altar within a miniature apse, wreathed by day in the smoke of a dozen incense sticks. The more I looked, the more sure I was that there was something beside it. Something that had not been there before.

It moved fractionally again, though the trees behind it stayed quite still and I could feel no breeze. Whatever it was, it was alive and watching. I could feel its eyes upon me.

But the darkness was the wrong shape for a hyena.

The figure rose from its crouch and stepped forward, slowly, letting what was left of the firelight fall upon him.

It was the Mahweni boy with the spear I had spotted when I went to see Berrit's grandmother.

He was young, close to my own age, clad in a simple drape that hung from one shoulder. He held the slender spear casually in one strong hand. His skin was black as the night itself.

My eyes flashed to the satchel, but otherwise I kept very still. The Lani and the Mahweni weren't enemies. The two peoples overlapped very little in culture, language, geography, work, or religion. Inside the city, the Mahweni were factory workers, laborers, market vendors, and street hawkers, like the newspaper girl. They dressed like white people, more or less, and did the same kinds of work, though usually for less money. They were what were called the Assimilated Tribes. But outside the city, the Mahweni were different. They were herders, hunters, and occasional traders, as they had been long before the whites came down from the north or the Lani from across the Eastern Sea. They were fiercely independent, a loose convocation of frequently squabbling tribes who held to ancient ways.

The Mahweni and the Lani kept themselves to themselves, speaking little, sharing less. We weren't enemies, but we weren't friends either.

The boy seemed to hesitate, feeling my eyes upon him. He looked at me, then bent at the waist, a graceful and stately bow that lowered his eyes for a moment.

I couldn't help smiling at the dignity of the gesture, and the smile moved through my body, relaxing the tension I had barely been aware of. The Mahweni nodded toward the fire, and his eyes widened a little in request. At this time of year, it could get quite chilly when the sun went down.

"You want to sit here?" I asked in Lani, checking the satchel. It was quite still. "I suppose so. Yes."

I returned my gaze to the fire, marveling at the strangeness of my composure. Would I have done such a thing two days ago? No. I would have fled. But two days ago, I had not been a detective sitting in an abandoned temple outside the city to avoid a man who meant to kill me. It wasn't that I was braver now. I just had bigger things to worry about.

The Mahweni boy settled beside me, nodding and smiling but saying nothing. He had high cheekbones, and his head was shaved. He almost certainly spoke no words of Lani, but that didn't matter; I was in no mood to talk.

The boy unslung a pouch from round his neck and tipped some sorrel nuts into his hand. He offered them to me and I, more out of politeness than hunger, took one. He smiled broadly and watched me eat it. The nut was sweet and slightly fragrant, which meant it was fresh.

"It's good," I said in Feldish.

The Mahweni boy's face lit up. "Yes," he said in Feldish. "Good." He considered me, still smiling, then added, "I am Mnenga."

"Anglet," I said.

He rehearsed the word in his mouth, enunciating it carefully till I smiled and nodded. There was a single chicken thigh left. I proffered it to him.

"Yes?" he said.

"Yes."

He took it and bit into the flesh, his eyes closing in the ecstasy of the moment. When he was done, he thanked me extravagantly. "Much better than nuts," he said.

I grinned in spite of myself. Normally around boys of my own age I got tense and silent, uncomfortable, as if my skin suddenly didn't fit right. But his presence was strangely calming, and all the fears and anxieties of the day seemed to have curled up by the fire and gone to sleep.

"What are you doing here?" I asked.

He frowned, trying to make sense of the question.

"I mean," I said, "why are you in this place?"

"Oh," he said, the brilliant smile snapping back into position. He had large black eyes, bright with curiosity and seemingly always on the point of laughing. "I have a . . ." He hesitated, looking for the word. "A *flock*? . . . Yes, a flock of nbezu, that way."

Nbezu are something between a goat and an antelope, with tall straight horns that spiral to a point like the cone-shaped shells I sometimes found by the docks.

"Two of them came this way."

"I haven't seen them," I said. "You left the flock alone?"

He laughed at that, a delighted bark that threw his head back like a shout into the sky. "No, no," he said. "My brothers are there. Otherwise—" He gestured with his hands, fingers splayed, palms pushing quickly away from his chest: *They would scatter.*

"I see," I said, shielding the satchel with my body and surreptitiously checking to make sure the baby was still asleep. I didn't want him to see it. "I hope you find them. There are hyenas here."

He considered that and sniffed the air, tipping his head onto one side as he said, "Not tonight, I think. Not unless they are very clever."

He grinned at the idea, then blew out a breath so long that I wasn't sure if he was joking.

"I don't worry about hyenas," he said, overenunciating so that his lips flexed. "I worry about the sun. We have to find water and shade. Even my people, who should know this, stay in the light too long and get burned. Three days ago, an old man, half-crazy from the heat, came down from the cliffs so badly sunburned, he could barely stand up! Sixty years old! Lived every day of his life out in the bush."

I grunted my agreement, and silence crept over us for a long moment. We watched the last of the fire, the ashen branches forming smoldering, shifting caves that throbbed with orange light, then dulled to gray and crumbled. I couldn't decide if I wanted him to leave me alone or not.

"I saw you in the . . . the Lani village," said Mnenga.

"The Drowning," I said.

"Drowning, yes. I was up here."

"I saw."

He smiled, pleased, as if this meant more than the literal meaning of the words.

"Will you move on tomorrow?" I asked, deliberately changing the subject.

"The nbezu are stubborn creatures," he said. "When they find the grass they like and a little water, they do not move. Also, soon we may not be able to come here, so we use it while we can."

"Why not?" I asked, surprised by how much his inconsequential words soothed me.

Mnenga shook his head. He was still smiling with his mouth, but his eyes were troubled. "We have always been able to use this land," he said. "But our leaders say it will perhaps be traded."

"To who?"

"White men in the city. I do not know their names."

"For what?"

"I do not know. 'Development,' they say," he added, poking the dusty earth with a stick.

"Out here? Development of what?"

He shrugged. "Not just here," he said. "All over. Pieces of land our families have shared for generations. They will be fenced. We will not be allowed in."

"Does this involve the Grappoli?" I asked.

He pulled a quizzical face. "Why the Grappoli?" he asked.

"I don't know," I said, shrugging with a sudden sense of defeat. "Just something I heard. Are you being paid for the land?"

He smiled mirthlessly. "Some people will be paid," he said. "Some of our elders say we will get iron tools from the factories. They say it is good for us, that most of the land is useless mountain slopes, not good for grazing. Perhaps they are right. But no one is asking us. The tribal leaders make deals in the city and then tell us afterwards. It is not good."

"You have representatives in the government," I said. "You can't talk to them?"

"We talk through our leaders, but in the end, we must go through Sohwetti, and he wants to sell."

Farrstanga Sohwetti was the chief of the Unassimilated Tribes, the most powerful Mahweni in the country.

"He won't talk to your elders?"

"Oh, he will talk," said Mnenga knowingly. "He is very good at talking. But I do not think he will listen."

"Why not?"

"You know where he lives?"

I shook my head.

"Not in my village," he said. "Not in any village. I have a beehive hut," he added proudly. "One day, I will have a family there."

I smiled but pushed the conversation forward. "Sohwetti does not live in a beehive hut?" I said.

Mnenga shook his head. "He has a big house in the city. His friends are white people. Government people. Rich people. He meets with our council, but he is not one of us. Not anymore. He likes his new life. I think that if he was paid enough, he would sell away all our homeland. And for a handful of nails and hinges and belt buckles, maybe a few guns and some money, my people will say yes. And you know what? I cannot blame them. We are tired of being poor."

His smile was gone now, but he looked more sad than angry, lost, so that I was suddenly sorry for him and, without thinking, took his hand.

He smiled with surprise and gratitude but said nothing.

I don't know how long we would have sat there in silence, as I felt the polished smoothness of his fingers in mine, but at that moment, the satchel at my feet moved.

Mnenga leapt to his feet, startled, and his right hand reached for the spear he had laid on the ground. He raised the weapon to shoulder height as a mewing sound came from the basket.

Horrified, I seized the spear point, and the young man's brow creased.

"Cat?" he said.

"Yes," I answered, my heart beating fast. "A kitten."

"I thought snake," he said, lowering the spear. "Can I see?"

I shook my head, but as I did so, the baby began to cry.

Mnenga's eyes widened. "Not cat," he said.

I looked down, ashamed of the stupid lie. "Not cat," I admitted, stricken once more by a sense of failure.

"Boy or girl?" said Mnenga.

"Girl," I said miserably.

"She is yours?"

"No," I replied, adding a little desperately, "a friend's. But no one can know."

"I see," said Mnenga, nodding.

"I cannot feed her," I said. "I have to wait for her mother."

He looked at me, and his smile was grim, understanding, but when he reached for the basket, probing with one finger as if he was going to give it to the child to suck, I felt a sudden panic and flinched, half reaching to stop him.

He froze, looking at me, then withdrew his hand, nodding again. "I should go," he said.

"I'm sorry," I repeated. "It's just . . ." But I could not explain because I did not understand myself. Instead I just said, "Please tell no one."

He inclined his head seriously, then stood up, but he did not walk away. "You will be here again? Tomorrow, perhaps?"

"I . . . I don't know," I said, my former anxieties crouching hyena-like in the dark places of my head. "I suppose. I have to bring the child back to be fed."

He seemed to sense my mood, and his smile was tempered with something like concern.

"Bye," I said before he could add anything that might embarrass me further.

He began his bow, and I turned away. When I looked round again, he was gone.

I PICKED MY WAY to the city gates, endured the contempt of the guards when they saw the sleeping bundle in my satchel, and made my way toward Old Town, glad of the firm sidewalk and gas lamps after the darkness and rutted tracks of the Drowning. I could smell the ocean now, a clear, salt tang unlike the stagnant sourness of the river edge near Rahvey's hut. Down by the water a few blocks away stood the pillar surmounted by the bronze of Captain Franzen. Tanish would be arriving to start work within the hour. I needed to see someone who would smile at me, someone who would tell me that taking Rahvey's child had been the right thing to do.

Because it didn't feel like the right thing. It felt stupid. *I* felt stupid, and the fact that I was responding to the Lani way that was at least as stupid, maybe more so, didn't help at all. So I walked with the sleeping child slung against my chest, eyes on the ground, lost in misery and humiliation, and I didn't see Morlak in the alley. I saw nothing till he lunged out at me, knife in one hand, the other grasping my hair, and everything went out of my head save one shrill, terrified thought:

The baby. Oh gods, the baby.

CHAPTER

14

I COULD NOT FIGHT back. My right arm flung out for balance as he pulled me into the alley, while my left clamped protectively over the satchel. He assumed I was going for a weapon—the dog I had stabbed him with before—and his knife went to my throat. I splayed my fingers in surrender and gave in as he yanked my hair, spun me around, and thrust me up against the wall.

My head hit the brick, but the pain was nothing to the panic, the dread.

Not the baby, I thought again. *Gods, not the baby.*

The thought shrieked through my raging, thumping heart, my shallow, ragged breathing.

"Put the bag down," he snarled into my ear. He smelled of stale sweat and madness that had once been hate. "Came to see the boy, huh, little Anglet? So predictable."

I hesitated and he pressed the knife once more, so that I craned my neck up like a giraffe. Then, very carefully, I began to lift the satchel strap over my head with my left hand. I could feel the weight of the baby within, could almost hear her breathing, and in my mind, I saw what would happen next: The bag would reach the pavement and, assuming my tools were in it, he would kick it away. . . .

I froze, overcome with a new and desperate horror.

"I said, put it down!" he spat, teeth bared.

I extended my arm as far as I could and slowly, carefully set the satchel on the ground, shrinking away from it as best I could inside his savage grip. His breath was sour, and his lank, greasy hair trailed into my face.

"Take whatever you want!" I gasped.

"All in good time," he muttered, and his grin was dirty, cruel.

He was going to kill me. I knew it as sure as I knew the sun would rise. He would do what he wanted with me, and then he would cut my throat. Nothing else was worth the risk.

"Just don't touch the bag," I said. It wasn't really a plea, and it certainly wasn't a trick. It just came out.

His brow furrowed. Skeptical ideas chased themselves through his eyes, which flashed momentarily to the discarded satchel. He kneed me hard in the stomach, and I doubled over, wheezing.

"How stupid do you think I am?" he rasped. "We will not be making any deals. There is nothing you have that I can't take for myself, and you have nothing worth having anyway. You have nothing, you are nothing, and that is what I'm going to teach you before you die."

I kept very still. His hand was not on my mouth, but if I cried out for help, he would stab me where I stood, and there was no one to hear anyway—not here, not now.

And then, with the softest of sounds, and just as it had done when I was sitting by the fire with the Mahweni boy, the satchel moved.

If he had been looking directly at it, he might have been less surprised, but he caught the shifting of the fabric out of the corner of his eye and jumped. For the briefest of seconds, his knife hand was forgotten. I was forgotten.

I was still half doubled over, my head level with his stomach, with the bandaged hole in his side. I butted the spot hard as I could and he staggered back in pain, releasing my hand. I stepped between him and the satchel and, as he raised his hands to grapple, went low. I kicked him in the groin, then scythed at his left leg, catching him hard on the knee.

He crumpled, but I had bought myself only a few seconds. He

was bigger than me, stronger. Stay a moment longer, and he would kill me. There would be no talk. Just the blade of his knife.

I had one advantage, and that was speed. I stooped to the satchel, snatched it up, and was running before I had it slung safely over my head.

Astonishingly, the baby never truly woke. I ran, taking a thoughtlessly direct route along the dirty side streets between Pancaris and the north wall to Morgessa and eventually out through the West Gate to the Drowning, and as the wind turned, I caught the familiar stench of filth and refuse on the air. Watching me as I approached the edge of the shanty was a huddle of heavyset baboons, so I doubled my pace and arrived at Rahvey's hut breathless and trembling. Baboons are strong, fearless creatures with almost human cleverness, and they bite. I had always been more comfortable in the city than in the wilder places at its edges, but now it seemed that nowhere was safe.

My sister answered my knock with drowsy irritation, anxiously glancing back to where her husband lay snoring. She took the child from me without a word, seeming not to notice my mood and closing the door in my face.

I looked around for the baboons and then curled up on the porch. I did not, could not, sleep.

I WAS UP AT first light for my Kathahry exercises as soon as I had washed and changed, Rahvey watching, bleary eyed, as the child nursed.

"What are you doing?" she asked, her face skeptical, even contemptuous. "Not the exercises. Your life. Job. Are you still working for Morlak?"

I hesitated. "No," I said. "I have a new position. I was going to talk to you about it. I was wondering . . ."

I faltered, and she framed a brittle smile.

"If I could keep the baby here," she said.

"Well, yes," I said. "Just for today. I can pay."

Her eyes narrowed. "How much?"

Reluctantly, I showed her the last of Vestris's silver coins. It was a week's wages for anyone in the Drowning.

Rahvey took it, sensing what it cost me to give it up. "Trying to make a good impression?" she said, and this time the smile was less bitter, more knowing. "At work, I mean. Yes, all right. But don't tell Sinchon, and be sure to get back here tomorrow."

"Yes," I said. "Thanks."

"This changes nothing," she said, in case I might get ideas. "You took the oath. The child is still your responsibility."

"I know."

She considered the baby at her breast, and her smile—a tiny pocket of joy glimpsed through the crack in a wall—betrayed her. She looked at me and closed the crack, but at the same moment, the door of the hut juddered open and Jadary, her youngest, shuffled out and gave me a sleepy wave. She drifted to her mother's side, all eyes on the baby.

"You can help me with her today," said Rahvey.

"We're keeping her?" exclaimed the girl, her face lighting up.

"Just today," said Rahvey sternly.

The girl crumpled but recovered quickly. "I'll wash my hands," she said, knowing that completing this tedious duty would get her to the baby faster.

Rahvey watched her go and the crack reopened, though this time the joy was mixed with sadness and regret, so that for a moment, and for the first time in many years, I almost threw my arms around her. She was afraid of Florihn and did not know how to be anything other than a Lani of the Drowning, but giving up the child was, I realized with shock, tearing her quietly apart.

She caught me looking and fought to get her face under control. When she spoke, it was to change the subject, and her voice had to shrug off a tremor. "You seem . . . different," she said. "These last two days. Worried, but more confident. Why? What kind of work are you doing?" When I didn't answer right away, she considered the coin and said, "How can you afford to give me this?"

"Let's just say I have friends in high places," I said.

I was almost out of the Drowning when it struck me that Berrit had used the exact same phrase mere hours before he died.

CHAPTER

15

I BOUGHT A PAPER from the Mahweni girl because I could, and then made my way to Crommerty Street, where the luxorite shops had not yet opened for the day. There was no sign of Billy, but that didn't matter. I walked past Ansveld's place twice, moving quickly, as if intent on getting somewhere else, not pausing to look into the barred windows. I noted the position of number 23, the Macinnes place, then crossed the street, took a left at the corner of Sufferance Avenue, and looked for a way down the backs of the shops.

The Macinnes store was across the street from Ansveld's. If a Lani boy had visited the dead trader, there was a good chance someone inside would have seen him.

The buildings formed an imposing terrace, all three-story structures of rich sandstone. They had gated backyards—locked—with outhouses and storage sheds, all surrounded by high walls topped with wrought iron spikes, fair deterrents against casual thieving but no obstacle to serious burglars.

Or steeplejacks.

I chose a point in the shade of a sisal currant tree, startling a pink roller from its perch, and climbed up, over, and in.

One flight of stone steps went up to the back door of the shop and main residence while another led down to the servants' quarters below ground level. There was a hand pump and trough beside the outhouse, but neither looked well used.

Indoor plumbing, then.

That meant I couldn't count on Billy's lady friend coming outside anytime soon. I tried to remember what he had told me about her and realized I had forgotten the woman's name. She was a scullery maid, the lowest of the household servants, and would be responsible for unskilled chores: fetching and carrying, scrubbing floors and washing dishes, boiling water, disposing of kitchen refuse. That would have to be my way in. I steeled myself to talk, even to act, then descended the steps and rapped on the door.

It was opened by a harried-looking white woman in her forties, too old and plump to be Billy the pickpocket's belle.

"Yes?" she said, looking past me to the locked gate.

"I was wondering if I could speak to whoever is responsible for your trash collection," I said.

"That would be the butler, but he doesn't talk to tradespeople without an appointment," said the woman. She had opened the door only wide enough to squeeze her florid face through it, and she was already starting to close it again.

"Actually, I would prefer to speak to the person who actually handles the refuse," I said, improvising. "We have a new line of pails and crates specifically for trash that are lighter and stronger than what most people have access to."

"I don't think we're interested," said the woman I took to be the housekeeper.

"Enables the carrying of twice as much in considerably fewer trips," I pressed, wondering where this newfound confidence came from. "Our clients say the kitchen operates far more efficiently for their use."

The closing door hesitated. "Wait here," said the woman.

The door closed. Somewhere inside, pots clanged. I heard voices, distant and muffled, one of them low and masculine. There was another silence, and then the door flew open.

It wasn't the housekeeper or the scullery maid. It was a man in formal black and white, and his face was flushed with an anger that made his eyes flash. "How did you get in here?" he demanded.

"The gate was unlocked," I lied, taking a step backwards.

"No, it wasn't," he shot back. "Reporters!"

"Not a reporter, sir," I said, fighting the urge to run, all my usual diffidence returning like a blanket thrown over my head. He was a big man, and for all his civilized attire, he looked capable of taking a swing at me. "I'm a consultant working with a governmental office—"

"Ha!" he sneered. "Badge? Warrant?"

"I don't carry any formal identification—" I began.

"I'll bet you don't, you Lani whore," he said, taking another step toward me. "Now, get out of here before you feel the back of my hand *and* I have you arrested for trespass."

I did not need telling twice.

"I HAVE NO AUTHORITY!" I protested. "I'm not police. I'm not army or government. I'm not even a licensed private investigator. No one will talk to me!"

Driven by frustrated humiliation, I had taken a cab all the way to Willinghouse's town house, insisting that I be reimbursed for the expense the moment I arrived. This was my one day away from the baby. I had to achieve something with the time I had bought.

"Pretending to be a salesman?" Willinghouse shot back, his scar reddening. "You are supposed to be using your abilities to investigate. No one hired you because of your people skills. I must say that I had hoped you would have made more progress by now. Now, I have to get to Parliament, so if you don't mind—"

"I do mind!" I exclaimed, surprising us both. I stood in front of him, face hot, fists clenched, but when he gave me a long, thoughtful look, I managed to calm down enough to say what I meant. "I can't do what you want me to without earning people's trust. The police can demand that people tell what they know. I can't."

"But that is the point!" Willinghouse shot back, returning his gaze from the cuff link he was trying to fasten. "You are supposed to use *unofficial* channels. I can combine those with the *official* channels in order to get to the truth."

"Then I need to partner with the police."

"Unacceptable."

"Then how can I do my job?"

"The police will not share information with a private investigator," said Willinghouse.

"So they can tell you and you can tell me."

"You don't understand."

"Then explain it to me," I said, snatching his shirtsleeve and deftly fitting the cuff link in place. Morlak wore cuff links; he thought they made him look sophisticated.

Now Willinghouse gave me a fierce look, but when I held his gaze, he sighed and glanced away. When he turned back to me, it was with eyes and voice lowered.

"I am not entirely sure that the police can be trusted," he said. "That is why I need someone to investigate independently."

I hesitated, taken aback. "I don't know that I can," I said, mentally sidestepping the implications of what he had just told me. "Can you at least protect me if I am arrested?"

"Probably," he replied.

"Probably?"

"I don't suppose we'll know for sure till we have to try," he said.

"Not good enough," I said.

"It is the best I can do," he replied. "Listen, Miss Sutonga, I came to you because I thought you a person of talent, ingenuity, and dedication to the truth. If my faith was misplaced, you should let me know so that I can seek someone more suitable."

I felt stung, as I had when Florihn said I wasn't a real Lani. For a moment, I wanted to run away and climb the highest chimney I could find and stay there. But I also felt that this was a defining moment, that if I said the wrong thing, I would not be able to take it back.

I drew myself up. "There is no one more suitable for the job than me," I said.

"Then I do not know why we are having this conversation," he replied. "Do your job in the ways that seem best suited to your abilities, and I will get you what information I can from the police investigation. And please, try to act with a little discretion."

I produced a folded paper on which I had written an address and a few short sentences in pencil. "Could you see that this gets mailed?" I said.

He glanced at it, and his gaze seemed to linger over Vestris's name. "What is it?" he asked.

"Just . . . catching up," I said. "Family stuff."

He considered me, and I sensed both his desire to read what I had written and the certainty that he would not. "Again," he said, "I hope you will act with discretion."

"Of course," I said. I had shared with Vestris nothing beyond the fact that she should write to me at Willinghouse's town house.

For a moment he looked as if he was going to say something significant, but thought better of it. "Now, if you will excuse me," he said.

I was waiting to be driven back to Crommerty Street when I caught the unexpected sound of music drifting down the hall: not the raucous, folksy music of the Drowning or the sensual, drum-heavy music of the Mahweni. This was music from countries north of Feldesland—precise, layered, and complex music played on a keyboard and a tenor viol, over which came the voice of a woman, high and exquisite, touched with melancholy so piercing that it stopped me in my tracks and made me strain to catch the words. It was music like Willinghouse's porcelain through which you can see the sun, music like filigree or finely cut crystal, like luxorite. It sounded like longing, and I who was not born to such elegant sophistication, such poignant and heavenly reach, was suddenly overcome by images of

Berrit, of the child I had left with my sister, of Papa, whom I needed now more than I ever had. I moved quietly to the door through which the sound was coming, fighting an urge to weep.

The song—if that was not too inadequate a word—ended in a patter of polite applause. Suddenly there was animated conversation from within, women's voices, though I could not catch what they were saying.

As I leaned closer to the door, it opened.

It was Dahria, Willinghouse's rude and haughty sister. The sight of her burned off all my tender feelings in a heartbeat.

Her hazel eyes were large and surprised, and as she took a startled step backwards, the conversation in the room behind her ceased abruptly. There were two musicians, young, white, and male, and the woman I took to be the singer, who was older and fuller in the body. Seated on a sculpted couch were two other girls, both white and blond, who, with Dahria, I took to be the audience. All three of them wore pale tea gowns with bustles and low necklines in delicate fabrics with ornamental trim, and they looked less like people than like elegant confections made of spun sugar.

Their eyes raked my drab and dirty appearance, and one of the seated blondes put a hand to her lips as if alarmed, but Dahria recovered her composure quickly.

"Is there something I can help you with?" she demanded, chin elevated so that she looked down her nose at me. She gave no suggestion she had ever laid eyes on me before.

It was a withering look, and I, badly out of my element, flushed and shook my head. I took a couple of hurried steps back along the hall, and the girl watched me before going back into the room and closing the door. There was a momentary rush of whispers and then the unmistakable sound of badly stifled giggling.

I moved as far away from the room as I could, feeling stupid and awkward, and was relieved when another door opened and Stefan

Von Strahden appeared in the hallway, his arms full of papers. The politician gave me his decidedly unpolitical smile, blue eyes flashing with unabashed delight.

"Miss Sutonga!" he said amiably. "You do have a way of cropping up, don't you? How wonderful! Is Josiah keeping you busy?"

"Yes, sir," I said.

"Please don't call me sir," he said with a mock grimace. "Call me Stefan. We are all equals under the skin."

It could have been patronizing, but his manner was welcoming. After my run-in with Dahria and her society friends, I was glad of it, though I could manage only a nod.

"Here to work?" he asked.

"Waiting for the carriage."

"Then our plans align perfectly!" he exclaimed delightedly. "I have to be at Parliament in an hour. You shall ride with me. Give me ten minutes to gather my fusty, bureaucratic nonsense, and we shall be on our way. I don't mind telling you that Willinghouse's coach was refurbished last month. Unlike mine, which makes one sore in ways I cannot, with propriety, describe, it's like sitting on a drawing room sofa all the way. You'll barely know you are moving. What do you say?"

He gave me that expansive smile, so direct and hearty, so unlike Willinghouse's shrewd, shadow-play caution, and I couldn't help smiling back.

"Thank you," I said. "Yes."

He tucked the papers under his arm and held up both hands, fingers splayed. "Ten minutes," he said. "Less if I can find Josiah's seal without having to summon the undead butler. Wait for me in the kitchen and we'll sneak out the back."

I grinned, and he bounded off down the hall. I followed slowly, moving to an open area with a staircase and on down a plain corridor to the kitchen, where a servant was washing dishes noisily at one of the great sinks.

I had been there only a minute when the kitchen door opened and Dahria entered, alone. She stood there, considering me, and when the servant at the sink caught her eye, she gave the tiniest nod, causing the girl to shut the water off, dry her hands, and bustle out with a speedy curtsy.

"I do not think my brother would want you seen by everyone who visits the house," she said. "A little discretion goes a long way."

"That is how you spend your time?" I answered, made bold by anger. "Drinking tea and listening to music?"

My defiance amused her. "There are worse ways to pass the time," she said.

"Before what?" I asked.

She gave me a quizzical frown. "I'm afraid I don't follow," she said.

"Passing the time suggests you are occupying yourself between events," I clarified. "What are the events?"

"Balls, dinners, galas of one kind or another," she said without much enthusiasm.

"More time passing," I said.

"You think like my brother," she said, sitting at the notched kitchen table, turned slightly sideways to avoid wrinkling her dress. "He would have me do Great Things with my time. I don't think I am cut out to be a steeplejack, do you?"

"Are you cut out to be a socialite?" I asked.

Her elegant eyebrows rose and the corner of her mouth twitched. "You are a feisty one, aren't you?" she said. "I can't recall the last time a purebred Lani even looked me in the face, let alone reprimanded me for my lifestyle, excepting Grandmamma, of course."

Her grandmother was Lani! That explained Willinghouse's coloring, his impeccable accent, his knowledge of the Lani way. And now he was a politician, a man of prestige and power. It was remarkable. I wondered why he had not told me at our first meeting, but

Dahria was watching my expression shrewdly, so I went on the offensive.

"Purebred?" I said.

"Oh, don't take offense," she remarked with a casual flick of her wrist. "That's ever so tiresome. You know what I mean."

"I'm not a racehorse."

"Not, I assure you, what I meant," she said with a half bow of mock apology.

I considered her pale face, which was much lighter than her brother's. I would never have guessed she was part Lani. The thought prompted an idea. I had no government seal, no detective papers, no police badge. But there was more than one kind of authority.

"I am going into the city in a moment," I said. "With Mr. Von Strahden. Just waiting for the carriage to be ready."

"And I hope you have a fine day of it," she answered with a slight smile.

"Come with me."

"I *beg* your pardon?" she said, caught between amusement and actual shock.

"Come with me."

"Why?" she said, still dryly amused. "I think Mr. Von Strahden can be trusted to travel with you unchaperoned."

"I don't need an escort," I said, waving away her sly innuendo.

"So, again, why?"

"Better than sitting here all day," I said. "You might have fun."

"With you?"

"With what we will be doing."

"Which would be what?" She was trying to sound disdainful but there was something in her eye she couldn't keep out. Curiosity.

"I'll explain as we ride," I said. "On one condition."

"Which is?"

"We don't tell your brother," I said.

And with that, I had her. Her eyes flashed and something passed between us, the thrill of adventure stripped of consequences, so that for a moment I forgot the woman's snide superiority.

"What are we going to do?" she asked, very slightly breathless.

"We're going to solve a murder," I said.

CHAPTER

16

I HAD DAHRIA PUT me hurriedly into one of her maid's outfits, the kind with a demure coal-scuttle bonnet that shaded my face from all sides, so that I had to turn my head to look at anything not right in front of me, something Dahria found unreasonably amusing. Under the frock I wore a long chemise, drawers, and wool stockings with tightly laced high-heeled shoes on which I wobbled precariously. For her part, Dahria replaced her tea gown with a corset and crinoline that supported a vast frippery of a dress trimmed with lace and ribbon that she thought was more appropriate for outdoors, and I was conscripted into helping her get into it all. I scowled and sneered throughout the process of lacing her into the rigid, formal attire, and told her that she looked like a walking lampshade, but a tiny, idiotic part of me was envious. She could barely sit down, but that just reminded me that her birthright was to be a kind of butterfly, while mine was to hang by my boots and fingernails from chimneys. She donned a broad-brimmed hat with a gauzy white veil and a parasol, and was done, a vision in mauve.

"Walk behind me," she said as we went downstairs to the kitchen. "And speak only when you are spoken to."

It had been my idea, but she was already in charge.

Von Strahden was waiting for us, checking his pocket watch. He turned with a look of comic exasperation, but it stalled abruptly as he took us in. "I was about to berate you for making me late," he said, "but beauty, I see, cannot be hurried. Lady Dahria, you will be joining us, I take it?"

"If my presence doesn't make you too uncomfortable," she said, smiling icily. "We could pick up a bootblack along the way if it would help redress the balance."

Von Strahden beamed good-humoredly and turned to me, speaking in a mock whisper as I walked unsteadily out to the carriage. "Lady Dahria is making fun of my egalitarian principles," he said.

"And what are your plans for today, Mr. Von Strahden?" I asked, mustering what confidence I could and putting on a demeanor I thought matched my costume.

"Dull stuff, I'm afraid," he said. "Survey teams to dispatch, results to examine, more teams to dispatch, more results to examine. Endless, and undeserving of our conversation."

Willinghouse's driver paused when he saw us emerge from the house. "Miss Dahria," he said. "I didn't know you planned to go into town today. Your brother must have forgotten to tell me."

"Quite," she answered. "And you will forget to tell him too."

I loitered in her shadow, offering an arm when she climbed up into the carriage. The driver did not give me a second look, and I don't think he realized who I was. Von Strahden watched her, eyebrows raised.

"Miss Sutonga thinks I should have more adventure in my life," she remarked.

"Quite right too," said Von Strahden as the carriage rolled off. The seats were, as he had said, remarkably comfortable. "It isn't good to stay cooped up in the house with those insubstantial friends of yours."

"My friends have as much substance as you or I," she returned.

Von Strahden snorted derisively. "Gossip and fashion and which spoon to use on the grapefruit," he said dismissively. "Not exactly the stuff of life, is it?"

"I just don't understand why some people are embarrassed to acknowledge their own class," Dahria purred.

"Embarrassment has nothing to do with it," said Von Strahden. "I just don't happen to think it healthy to mix exclusively with people of your own social standing. Sometimes our *betters* have less than we do."

"I will agree," Dahria said, still smiling dryly, "that class is not entirely about income."

Von Strahden gave me a knowing look and spoke sotto voce. "A dig, I fear, at my humble origins. Unlike the lady here and her brother, I was not born to wealth and fortune. My father, when he was my age, was a factory worker in a flax mill on Deans Gate. Worked his way up to foreman and eventually to shareholder. Spent what he had on my education. I was never dirt poor," he confessed, returning Dahria's smile, "but I know what it is to work, to want, even to go hungry, and I don't intend to forget those things now that I have a little power and influence. Indeed, it's because of those things and those people that I sought that power, and I intend to use it for their benefit."

"Hear! Hear!" said Dahria, parodying the voice of an elderly backbencher.

"Yes, yes!" said Von Strahden with a self-deprecating smile. "I'm an absurd and naïve political windbag, but I am at least sincere."

"And you would have my vote if I was allowed to cast one," I said, emboldened by his speech.

"And that will happen in your lifetime," said Von Strahden, earnest again. "When we are in power—"

Dahria cut him off, speaking through a theatrical yawn. "If you are going to discuss politics all the way there," she said, "I will throw myself under the wheels. I swear, Von Strahden, you are worse than my pious brother."

"I will take that as a compliment," he said.

"And while Mr. Von Strahden luxuriates in that," she said, turning deliberately to me, "perhaps it's time you told me exactly what you plan to do with me today."

* * *

VON STRAHDEN DROPPED US on the corner of Crommerty Street and drove off with a smiling nod and a "ladies" addressed equally to us both.

"It seems you have made a friend," said Dahria. "But don't get your hopes up. Mr. Von Strahden has love in his life already."

I bristled. "I'm not here to hunt for a husband," I said.

Dahria smirked and said nothing. It struck me as strange that someone with more than a drop of Lani blood in her should be so much more at home as an aristocrat than a white, male politician who might one day have a hand in leading the country.

Crommerty Street, which had been largely deserted when I last visited it, was now a fashionable pedestrian bustle: white ladies of all ages promenading from shop to shop, pausing to admire the window displays and to gossip. It seemed that everyone knew each other, though those who recognized Dahria were surprised to see her "out and about at this time." The shops themselves were quieter, and very little money was changing hands, but the prices were so high that the establishments might stay comfortably afloat if they made a sale only once or twice a month.

I was anxious about being recognized in Ansveld's shop, but I needn't have been, and not only because the bonnet almost completely concealed my face. I was a servant, and as such, I was as close to invisible as it was possible to be. So long as I kept still and quiet, all eyes would stay on Dahria. The idea was somehow both a relief and an annoyance.

Ansveld's son was behind the counter, wearing a pair of heavily smoked lenses through which he was studying a tiny piece of aging luxorite set into a gold ring. He nodded to Dahria as we came in, but said nothing. The shop was full of an oppressive and musty silence, broken only by the stentorian ticking of a grandfather clock. Those luxorite pieces that were unshaded produced a hard, constant light that made the barred window on the street look dim in comparison. At the end of the counter, now under a shroud, was the great typewriter. It looked not so much discarded as dead.

I wasn't used to shops, doing most of my purchasing at stalls in markets and in street-corner deals, but the extent to which we were left to browse at our leisure seemed unusual and deliberate. I didn't know if it was because people couldn't be harassed into spending vast amounts or because in such a place, discussing money was considered vulgar. But no one spoke to us for ten minutes, and when they did, it was a primly dressed maid offering tea.

Dahria declined for both of us, and began a desultory conversation about the standard of workmanship in the jewelry settings and how tastes had changed over the last decade. Ansveld Jr. was polite but bored and just this side of irritated. Dahria changed that by asking for a hand mirror so that she could try out some earrings. The luxorite grains set in their crystal pendants were small but bright, an almost white light that, with a matching pin to be worn in the hair, gave her a halo. It would have been an arresting effect on anyone. On Dahria, it created an angel. Even Ansveld Jr. stopped what he was doing to admire her.

"How much?" she asked simply.

Most of the merchandise was not priced. If you needed to ask, you couldn't afford it.

"Eleven thousand for the set," said Ansveld Jr.

No one flinched, but for my part, that took an effort.

"I could sell the pieces individually," said the proprietor, "but it would be a shame to break up so unified a collection, so the cost would be higher."

"Of course," said Dahria. "Eleven thousand seems more than fair."

This was a barefaced lie, but she carried it off with aplomb, and Ansveld Jr.'s eyes got hungry.

"One sees so little luxorite that isn't overly familiar these days," she added, still considering her reflection critically. "The same recycled pieces moving from house to house. I find their circulating so unpleasantly common, don't you? Like they are stocks, or servants, or sacks of coal moving around a marketplace. Quite distasteful."

"Indeed, madam," said the proprietor, "the material deserves better."

"I heard of a Lani boy, no more than a street brat, going from shop to shop only last week."

"He came in here!" exclaimed Ansveld Jr., startled out of his professional decorum by outrage. "Ratty little creature with burned fingers. Insisted on waiting to see my father. Said he had luxorite to sell!"

"You sent him packing, I hope," said Dahria, showing nothing.

"Twice! He loitered in front of the store until I had the police move him on. Can you believe the cheek?"

I turned fractionally away so there was even less chance of him seeing my face, but inside, I was burning with anger and questions I wanted Dahria to ask.

"Did he have any?" Dahria asked. "Luxorite, I mean."

"Well, that was what was so extraordinary!" said the proprietor, leaning in conspiratorially. "He did. I saw it with my own eyes. A small piece, no more than a few grains, but quite brilliant."

"You mean . . . new?" Dahria asked, and the excitement in her voice was real.

"I've never seen newer," he said. "It was, I assume, stolen."

Dahria shot me a glance and I risked a nod.

Press him.

"What did it look like?"

"Well, as I said, the crystal itself was barely larger than a pinhead, but its light was hard and pure, as close to a factor zero as I have ever seen. Even at only a few grains, it was quite brilliant. I'll never forget watching that scruffy little boy open his hands—" He mimed the gesture wistfully, remembering. "You could almost *hear* the light, it was so clean and clear!"

"A single stone?"

"Yes."

"Would you have heard if someone in town had been robbed?" Dahria asked.

"The luxorite community is quite small, madam," said Ansveld Jr. "It is the nature of things in a market with a static amount of tradable product. As you so shrewdly observed, much of what is for sale has been circulating for years, and most of it I know by sight. Given time and access to my records, I could produce a listing of the current location of ninety percent of the luxorite sold in the last thirty years. Some has been kept quietly in old families, but it is the glory of the mineral that it attracts attention. What the boy had, I would swear, was unknown to any dealer in the city."

"He wanted it appraised?" asked Dahria, rapt.

"He said he was prepared to sell it," huffed Ansveld Jr., "but without papers of provenance and certification of ownership, that was impossible. I told the police to take him in for questioning, but the brat escaped."

Dahria hesitated, unsure what to ask next, and I, balancing on those absurd heels, gestured quickly toward the clock.

"When was this?" asked Dahria.

"Waterday of last week."

The day before Ansveld Sr. showed up in the Drowning, looking for Berrit.

She considered this, and her gaze strayed once more to me, hovering unnoticed by the door. I nodded sequentially toward the other luxorite dealers in the street outside, then turned my attention to a silver-topped cane in a stand, so Ansveld wouldn't see how hard I was listening.

"And did he try to sell the piece to any of your competitors?" Dahria asked, managing to sound merely intrigued.

"Well, that's the curious thing," said Ansveld Jr. reflectively. "So far as I know, he did not venture into any shop but ours. I spoke to my neighbors. Several saw him hanging around, but he made no attempt to enter. Most peculiar."

"Indeed," said Dahria.

"That's not for sale," he said suddenly, addressing me.

"I'm sorry?" I said, half turning toward him but trying to shield my face.

"That cane," he explained. "The one with the fussy little one-horn emblem on the top. It's not for sale. Someone left it here. I assume my father was supposed to be setting a stone in it. The handle is quite intricate."

I nodded, mute, and moved away from the cane.

"So," said Dahria, carefully steering his attention back to her. "Forgive my gossiping, but has anyone bought anything new lately? I long to know what everyone will be talking about."

"Well," he said with a hint of glee. "You didn't hear it from me, but I've heard that Dowager Eileen Hamilton will be unveiling a new necklace this evening at the opera. I hear it is very fine, bought the moment it went on sale at one of my less salubrious competitors over the road. *Macinnes*," he said with sour astonishment. "If you can believe that. When times are hard, people don't always ask too many questions. Anyway, the dowager must have snapped it up in an instant because I never even got a whiff of it. I'm agog to see it."

He was momentarily transformed, shifting from a rather stuffy little shopkeeper to a delighted enthusiast.

"Assuming I haven't already," he added slyly.

"You think it's the same piece the boy had?" Dahria asked. "That she got it from him?"

"Not directly, I'm sure," said Ansveld Jr. "But Macinnes may have lied about not dealing with the boy. If not, it's a remarkable coincidence. *Two* previously unknown pieces in the Bar-Selehm market!" He clapped his hands together with rapture.

"Sounds delicious," said Dahria. "I'll keep my eyes peeled for more. These, I will, I'm afraid, have to think about," she said, unhooking the earrings. "But you have such a charming emporium that I will not be able to keep away for long."

She said it with such grace, with such beatific elegance born as much from wealth, beauty, and privilege as from the luxorite glow around her face, that he did not even seem disappointed.

"It's a lovely thing, luxorite," he said musingly. "I work with it every day but it never loses its appeal, somehow. My father understood that." He tried to smile, but some other powerful feeling, a deep sorrow, ambushed it, contorted it into a grimace that was hard to look at. His jaw set and his eyes, which had been laughing only moments before, shone with unshed tears.

"I'm sorry for your loss," said Dahria, surprised and uncomfortable.

"We did not see eye to eye on many things, my father and I," said Ansveld Jr. "We argued a great deal. I wish now . . . But he loved luxorite, and not only because selling it had made him a very wealthy man. It's funny, isn't it?" he added thoughtfully. "Everyone knows that if they live long enough, they will see their parents die, but it still comes as a surprise. Turns you into a child again." He blinked and tried to smile. "I expect the feeling passes."

"It doesn't," I said, the words coming out without anything like deliberation.

He gave me a look that was surprised, even indignant, but he couldn't keep it up. "No," he said, managing the saddest smile I had ever seen. "I didn't really think it would."

CHAPTER
17

"YOU WERE RIGHT," GASPED Dahria as soon as we had gotten a safe distance from the shop. "This is fun!"

She fanned herself extravagantly. She had given me a shrewd look at my strange connection with the shopkeeper over his absent father, but said nothing, and if I had seen something like understanding in her face, she had pushed it down and laced it up tight as her corset. Now she was beaming, and I, far from clear about our relationship, let the moment go, turning instead to the mystery at hand.

"So Berrit had a fragment of luxorite," I mused, "but the Beacon hadn't been stolen yet, and no one reported any thefts, so where did he get it?"

"The boy must have had connections to dealers or thieves," said Dahria.

"If so, they were new connections," I said. "He was nobody in the Westside gang. He said he had friends in high places, but if so, he made those friends recently, right around the time he was traded to Morlak."

"So we talk to this Morlak fellow," said Dahria.

"No," I said.

"Why not?" she demanded.

So Willinghouse hadn't told her. I thought for a moment, took a breath, and related what Morlak had tried to do. She stared at me, horrified, disgusted by a version of the world she had barely known existed. When I was done she said nothing, but I thought her sense of me had changed.

"I could speak to this Morlak without you," she said at last.

"I don't think so," I said.

"I'm capable of thinking for myself, you know!" she snapped. "I don't need you spoon-feeding me."

"I just don't think he will respond to someone of your breeding," I said carefully.

"And I think you just like being in charge for once," she shot back.

"You're proposing to walk over to the headquarters of a street gang in the Numbers District dressed like that?" I demanded, my exasperation getting the better of me. "If you got out with merely a mugging, you'd be lucky."

"So what would you have us do?"

I considered the street. I thought of Billy the pickpocket, and nodded toward Macinnes's place, where Dowager Hamilton had purchased her mysterious necklace. "Get me a half hour with the scullery maid in there."

"How?"

"Any way you like," I said. "You're in charge. And when we're done there, I suggest we get tickets for tonight's opera. It turns out I'm available."

MACINNES'S SHOP, THOUGH ACROSS the road from Ansveld's, was an entirely different kind of establishment. Though it justified its position on Crommerty Street through the sale of luxorite, it was clear that most of its trade was more mundane. Inside, it was less the elegant showroom we had just left and more a glorified pawnshop, dealing in watches and knives, firearms and pewter, porcelain and assorted statues, mostly plaster. Everything was kept inside metal cages, and though the merchandise was not so rich as at Ansveld's, the security measures were more conspicuous. A guard with a pistol and truncheon at his belt considered us closely as we entered. Despite the presence of luxorite—much of it amber and fading—parts of the shop stood in deep gloom, and large candles had been positioned around the store to make up for the absence of windows. A NO COLOREDS sign on the counter matched one in the shop window, but when I gave it a querulous nod, Dahria shook her head minutely.

A short man in shirtsleeves and a bowler hat, attracted by the ringing of the bell over the door, sauntered out from a back room and watched us appraisingly.

Dahria drew herself up, staring down the security guard, and led me to a corner cabinet, pulling me in close by my sleeve with one hand as she reached for the oversized candle with the other. To my astonishment, she proceeded to tip the candle toward me, spilling hot wax all down the front of my dress.

"Good gods!" she exclaimed contemptuously. "You clumsy wretch! Look at your pinafore! Why can't you watch what you are doing?"

The man in the hat began to bustle toward us. "Now, ladies," he was saying. "Is there something I can do to help?"

"You can get the wax off this dress immediately!" Dahria announced with breathtaking arrogance.

"Not really my department," said the man, who I took to be Macinnes himself. "I'm sure when you get home—"

"You think I'm going to walk through the street with a maid looking like this?" Dahria exclaimed, gesturing up and down my spattered pinafore. "See to it, man!"

"I'm sorry, but I don't really see how this is my problem," he began warily.

"They are your candles, are they not?" Dahria demanded at her most imperious.

"Well, yes," said Macinnes, quailing.

"Then see to it!"

For my part, I had shrunken somewhat, my face half in my hands, and as close to tears as I could realistically suggest. In truth, it wasn't hard. Faced with Dahria's aristocratic contempt, it was all too easy to imagine myself less than the dirt beneath her heel.

Macinnes faltered, shooting a look at the security guard, and Dahria took the opportunity to step close to him. She snarled into his face, "I assume you have a scullery maid?"

I WAS PROPELLED—UNSTEADILY in those ridiculous shoes—through a stockroom and into a hallway where stairs descended to the servants' quarters and kitchen. I descended cautiously, the security guard at my back, listening to the fading sound of Dahria's rant about candles, shoddy service, and the inadequacies of personal staff. I kept my eyes open for the butler who had turned me out on my ear before, but there was no sign of him, and the housekeeper who had opened the door to me called the scullery maid without giving me a second glance. I blubbered through a handkerchief, hiding my face as best I could, until a girl of my own age entered, looking flustered.

This was surely Billy's lady friend. She was white, pretty in an ordinary sort of way, with rough hands and a round, kindly face.

When she spoke, it was with the accent of the city's working poor. "Oh my, you 'ave made a mess of yourself, 'aven't you?" she said. "Let's 'ave a look in the light."

She shunted me close to a patch of sun that streamed in from one of the high windows I had seen from the backyard.

"'Old on," she said. "Let me get my iron and some brown paper."

"Thanks," I said. "You're Billy's friend, aren't you?"

She looked up at that, startled and, judging by the way she checked over her shoulder to make sure the housekeeper was not in earshot, afraid.

I couldn't blame her. I doubted Billy would be considered an especially suitable catch for someone who worked—albeit menially—on Crommerty Street.

She risked a smile as she put the iron on the stove. "Let's get you out of that pinafore," she said. "'Ave a seat."

I did so, relieved to take the weight off my aching feet. How Dahria walked around in shoes like those all day, I had no idea.

"How do you know Billy?"

"Mutual friends," I said with an apologetic shrug. "I'm Ang, by the way."

"Bessie," said the girl. "You and Billy work together?"

"Nah," I said, handing her the dress and watching as she picked the wax off before applying the iron. "A little overlap, but different circles."

"Well, yes," said the girl, as if that were obvious.

My hackles rose. "What do you mean?" I asked.

"With you being a lady's maid and all," she said, momentarily baffled by my look. "You thought I meant because you are . . ." She hesitated.

"Lani," I completed for her. "Yes. Sorry."

"No need," said Bessie, relieved to get that over. "And to tell you the truth, we don't see many of your sort around here."

That was my chance.

"No?" I said. "What about a boy? Last week."

The maid shook her head.

"Are you sure?" I asked.

"Positive. Why?"

"Someone said there was a Lani boy going from door to door all down the street," I tried.

She shook her head again. Her face was guileless, innocent. I would lay everything I had that she was telling the truth. "I think there was a boy at Ansveld's," she said. "Across the street. Mr. Savil, the security guard, commented on it, but he never came here."

"You're sure?"

"I'd have seen him. I'm never off duty when the shop is open. Mr. Macinnes doesn't like to be understaffed."

I nodded. "Fancy district," I said.

Bessie grinned. "Too fancy for the likes of me," the maid agreed. "Or 'is Lordship, truth be told." She said the last in a low voice.

"His Lordship?" I asked.

"Macinnes," she said, her smile souring. "Jumped-up little nobody, he is. Amazed they 'aven't drummed him out."

"It's a nice house," I said. "Seems successful."

"Oh, he makes his money, all right," she agreed. "But this classy-gent routine is all an act. Why do you think he has the butler and the mahogany sideboard? So no one looks too closely at 'im."

I matched her grin. "Bit shady, is he?" I asked.

"Oh we get all sorts in 'ere," she said. "Especially after hours, when the posh folk 'ave gone 'ome."

"Like who?" I asked, trying not to sound too interested.

"Oh, I don't get to see them," said Bessie. "If he knows they're coming, we're kept out of the way. They usually show up in the house anyway, not in the shop. Couple of weeks ago, some black fella came in. That was a first. Just wandered in from the street, big as life! And not a local black either. One of them 'unter types from the plains. Old bloke. Scared me 'alf to death, he did. Macinnes kept 'im talking for like a hour as well! I thought they'd just throw 'im out, but he was still 'ere when it came time to close."

"But no Lani," I said, guiding her back to the original question.

She shook her head definitely. "There," she said, looking up from the dress and smiling, proud of herself. "That looks like it's got it."

"Very nice," I said. "No wonder Billy is so keen."

She laughed at that, but her question—"You think he's keen?"—was real enough.

"Absolutely," I said, thinking of Billy's two purses and his sweet and silly notion of not soiling Bessie's ring with stolen money.

"Well, that's nice," said Bessie, pretending she didn't really care and smoothing my pinafore. "Just launder it as usual when you get 'ome and Her Ladyship shouldn't give you any more trouble."

"Oh," I said, "she'll find an excuse."

"Don't they always," said Bessie.

CHAPTER

18

I HAD NEVER BEEN to the opera house. I had passed it many times, knew it as a landmark, an icon of the city, but it represented a version of the world in which I had no place. The prospect of going there now both thrilled me and so stirred my guts that I had to pretend to tie my boot just to sit down for a moment and breathe.

The building itself was a vast domed oval, every door and window ornamented with carved patterns and theatrical masks, every area of wall decorated with heraldic animals and coats of arms from the north. This was white Feldesland, and the carved beasts adorning its elegant and imposing exterior were as far from the creatures that roamed the bush only a few miles to our west as I could imagine.

Outside was cool, polished stone the color of pale sand, but inside were darker, richer colors: cobalt blues, emerald greens, and coral reds, all lavishly gilded. There were soft couches in grottoes, upholstered in thick velvet and trimmed with gold braid. Rich mosaics and bold statues filled every alcove, and they were executed not in the elegant northern style but as if they were copies of Mahweni and Lani subjects described to a sculptor who had never seen the originals. Here was a golden fountain in a turquoise pool decorated with Mahweni river spirits. There was a Lani monkey god covered in gold leaf, dancing on top of an elephant. It was luxuriant, even seductive, but strange, dreamlike.

I stood quite still, jostled by the crowd of ticket holders, blinking at the bizarre sumptuousness of the place, and feeling more than usually isolated. I kept my bonneted face turned down like a threatened tortoise.

"Isn't it just darling!" whispered Dahria. "The music is mostly a bore, but the place is so much fun that I come from time to time anyway."

I said nothing.

At one end of the great curved lobby, between a pair of gilded columns, was a bar where fastidiously dressed ladies and gentlemen were congregating before going in to the performance. We drifted in that direction, surrounded by the cream of Bar-Selehm's high society. I saw faces I recognized from the newspapers—aristocrats, businessmen, and politicians—but the biggest shock came rather closer to home.

A man was reporting that the government had withdrawn its ambassador from Grappoli in the ongoing spat over the theft of the Beacon and that street protests were expected tonight in the largely black Morgessa District, which had always been a hotbed of political activism.

I turned, curious why the Mahweni would care about a diplomatic row with the Grappoli, and found myself inches from my sister Vestris. She looked radiant in wine-red silks trimmed with silver that evoked her Lani past while blending perfectly with her newfound status. She was in a circle of white men and women, one of whom, laughing loudly, was Stefan Von Strahden. I stared for a second, shocked and confused, and in that moment, Vestris turned absently to him and plucked a thread or hair from the lapel of his jacket without a word. He said nothing in response, and if he even looked her in the face, I did not see it.

I turned away before she saw me, my mind racing as fast as my pulse. I had to speak to her.

You are a servant, said a haughty, irritating voice in my head that could have been Dahria's. *You will embarrass her. If people realize she is related to the likes of you . . .*

But I had to at least let her see me. If we could just make eye contact, she would find a way to talk to me.

"You turned your back on me," Dahria muttered into my ear. "May I remind you in what capacity you are here?"

"Sorry," I whispered, though I did not turn.

"What is the matter with you?" Dahria hissed, her irritation mounting. "Turn around, girl! Why can't you—?" She hesitated, as if she had just seen or realized something. And then cooed, "I see. You *do* aim high, don't you? But I told you that the Right Honorable Mr. Von Strahden already has a lady in his life."

It took a moment for me to realize what she was saying, and another moment not to correct her. I liked Von Strahden well enough because he was kind to me and treated me like a person, but that was all. What Dahria's remark also revealed was that she didn't know Vestris was my sister.

In the instant I decided that it was better that way.

At my back, the group laughed politely and I felt again the glow of Vestris's presence and the annoyance of being outside it. I turned abruptly and raised my bonneted face just enough that my sister's eyes fell upon me.

They widened, and her glossy lips parted in the smallest gasp.

Something flashed through her face, something more than surprise, and then she was excusing herself and moving quickly away from the group so that Von Strahden looked after her, his brow furrowed.

I lowered my head and followed, muttering apologies.

Vestris left the busiest part of the lobby and vanished behind one of the massive ornamental columns by an empty tea salon. As soon as I rounded the column, she was whispering feverishly into my ear. "What are you doing here, Anglet?"

"I'm working as a lady's maid," I said, barely suppressing a giggle, like this was a game we were playing while we waited for Papa to come home from work.

"A maid?" Vestris demanded. "To whom?"

"Dahria Willinghouse," I said, still grinning.

Her eyes narrowed.

"It's just a bit of fun," I said. "Not like a real job."

"We can't be seen together," she said. "Not here."

"Oh," I said. She was right, but I was still a little crestfallen.

"I'm sorry, Ang, I really am, but reputation is everything with these people. If they knew . . . If they even thought . . ."

I saw the anxiety in her face and realized just how fragile her position was in this strange, elevated society, the Lani girl who made good. It was like being up on the chimneys. One false move . . .

"I know," I said, meaning it. "I'm sorry. I just saw you and had to talk to you."

"I understand," she said, relaxing fractionally.

"I sent you a message, but you won't have got it yet," I said.

"What?" she asked, still flustered.

"Just a note," I said, "so you could contact me. I sent it to the address on the card you gave me."

"Yes," she said. "Right. Ang, I'm sorry, but I really have to—"

"I know," I said. "Go."

She relented a little at that. "Are you all right?" she asked. "Do you need money? Is there anything I can do?"

And that was all I needed, that look of concern, that willingness to help. I was in the glow again, and for a moment, nothing else mattered. "I'm fine," I said, smiling. "I don't need anything. Go back to your friends."

She leaned quickly under my bonnet and kissed me on the cheek, leaving once more the aroma of sandalwood and violets, and then she was gone.

I just stood there, cherishing the memory of her presence, her desire to help; then I took a breath and returned to Dahria, head bowed.

"There you are!" she said as I slid back to her side. "Where have you been, you maddening creature?"

I was about to mutter something about the toilet when I became aware of someone making a speech behind me. There was a patter of applause, and then the light changed, producing a soft intake of awe-inspired breath from the assembly.

I turned and glimpsed a large blond woman, middle aged and dressed in yards of pleated green taffeta that made her look like the prow ornament of a ship, beaming at the crowd, her arms open. At her throat she wore a pendant so bright that, even at this distance, it was hard to look directly at it.

"I think we just found the Dowager Lady Hamilton," said Dahria.

There was more applause, heartfelt this time, and then the dowager adjusted something around the necklace, reducing its brilliance by two-thirds or more, and permitting closer inspection by her admirers. There was no sign of Vestris or Van Strahden.

"We need to get a closer look at that necklace," I whispered.

"My area of expertise, I believe," said Dahria, drawing herself up and slicing through the crowd like a clipper.

I followed, head down, one hand touching the trailing fabric of her dress so I didn't lose her in the throng, but we had gone only a few steps when a bell rang. Dahria hesitated and I almost walked into her, stepping back as the crowd began moving en masse. The performance was about to begin.

Dahria made one last push to reach the dowager, but we were swimming upstream. I got a look at the great lady as she drained her glass, looking flushed and slightly ill at ease in spite of her expansive smile, and then she was steaming into the auditorium.

Dahria scowled after her. "We'll have to catch her between acts," she said. "I have a feeling she'll want to bask as publicly as possible."

We took our seats in the center of the dress circle. As I massaged my throbbing feet as best I could through the cramped shoes, Dahria scanned the gilded hall and eventually located the dowager in a side box. She had muted the brilliance of her necklace still further, and I could no longer see it at all. Around us, those wearing luxorite jewelry were doing the same, closing tiny shutters around their pendants, placing earrings in cases or rotating finger rings till the stone could be placed safely in laps. When the gaslights were turned down, there were only a few pools of light that had to be hastily doused, and only one that required the intervention of a deferential but firm usher. When the stage was bathed only in the pearly glow of the gas-fueled footlights and the above-stage chandeliers, an orchestral prelude swelled from the pit. Then the warmer ambience of aging luxorite torches shone through directional lenses flooded the stage, and with the entrance of the actors, the opera began.

Dahria was only partly right. For all the spectacle; the lavish, spangled costumes; and the opulent glow of the performers, the performance was wooden, dull.

But the music!

Where Lani music is all heart and gut, this was head and soul, and it sounded like the voices of angels, barely within the realm of human possibility. It was high and carefully fitted together like the workings of a pocket watch, but it was also air and spirit and water, remote and beautiful so that tears started to my eyes because I knew that like all good and wonderful things, the sound would eventually stop. In that remote and unearthly music, I felt all that made me different from the people who now employed me, and I felt it like sorrow, like loss. Again, my thoughts went to Rahvey's baby, to Berrit, and to Papa, and I had to dig my fingernails into my palms to keep from weeping.

So I was almost relieved when, after twenty minutes, Dahria nudged me with her leg. Up in the curtained box, the dowager had risen from her seat and seemed to be ducking out.

"Too much wine," Dahria whispered.

I got hurriedly to my aching feet and, ignoring Dahria's hissing protests, excused myself and pushed through a dozen pairs of outraged, well-dressed legs until I was in the aisle and making for the exit, leaving behind a ripple of indignant muttering.

It was strange to be in the lobby now that it was deserted, and with the lights dimmed the looming statues had a new air of menace. I moved to the stairs closest to where the dowager had been seated, pushing past the red velvet rope and climbing a flight of wide, carpeted stairs to the upper gallery. There was no evidence of movement, but there were signs to the LADIES' FACILITIES. I followed them.

Another flight of steps, marble this time, and the sound of echoing movement ahead of me.

I moved lightly, trying to decide what I would do or say when I met the dowager. I could hardly play the society lady merely interested in the necklace, dressed as I was. I would need to be direct and trust that she would want to help solve the death of a Lani boy. It didn't feel promising, and I hesitated on the stairs, catching the slightly fusty aroma of perfume in the stale air. Perhaps it would be better, less intrusive, if I didn't corner her in the bathroom itself. . .? I dithered. Everything about the place and the people in it crowded in on me, made me feel like a rat in an elegant kitchen, or a siltroach frozen in the light of a lamp.

You do not belong here. You cannot do this.

I balled my fists and tried to think, and in that instant, I heard something from the restroom below, a kind of strangled gasp that was almost a cry.

My body took over. In three vaulting strides, I had reached the foot of the stairs and was bursting into the well-appointed sitting area, which gave on to the bathroom itself. There was no sign of anybody here, and I kept moving, slamming through the swinging door into a bright, white-tiled room of sinks and toilet stalls. One of the doors was wobbling on its hinges. On the floor beside it, purple-faced and wheezing, was the dowager, sprawled on her belly like a stricken rhino, panting, her eyes wide with shock and terror.

I grabbed hold of her and tried to roll her onto her back, but she was too heavy. I took her right arm and pulled till she shook off some of her paralysis and pushed herself over and up on one elbow.

The pendant was gone, and the spot where it had hung at her throat was pink and inflamed.

"Came from above," she managed, her eyes flashing back to the toilet stall with something like horror.

I looked, but there was no one there.

She shook her head violently and gasped, one hand at the wattle of her throat. "That way!"

At the far end of the row of stalls a panel was missing from the ceiling: a ventilation shaft. I bounded over and looked up. There was a broad corrugated duct that turned in on itself. I couldn't see round the bend, but it was certainly wide enough for a man to climb through, and now that I was directly beneath it, I could hear the unmistakable sounds of effort.

He was still in there.

As the dowager coughed and sobbed, I stepped onto the toilet seat, cursing my voluminous skirts and the absurd bonnet, and tried boosting myself into the ceiling opening, but it was impossible. I tore off the bonnet and shrugged my way roughly out of the dress, leaving it where it fell. The action had cost me valuable seconds, but it felt good to feel the air on my arms. Clad only in my chemise, drawers, stockings, and those infernal high-heeled shoes, I hoisted myself into the vent.

It smelled faintly of rust, and as I pulled myself inside, it shook, scattering black-and-orange flakes of old metal and dried insect parts. I spat, clawed my way around the corner, and crawled till the tube opened into a dark shaft, which went straight up. There were ladder rungs set into the wall, so I began to climb. I don't believe I had had an actual thought since I heard the dowager's strangled cry from the stairwell.

I could see him above me. A man in close-fitting dark gray clothes with a bag slung across his chest. I could not see his face, and my sense that it was a man came solely from the speed and strength of his ascent.

Though my heart was pounding, this was the first moment since arriving at the opera house that I did not feel alien and inadequate. The shaft was brick, not sooty like chimneys, but scarred, dusty, and irregular: my environment, even if these weren't my clothes. I didn't know what I would do if I caught up with him, but I felt no fear, no uncertainty as I snatched rung after rung, pulling myself up.

When you are used to ladders, they provide a kind of rhythm, your body becoming a machine swinging from side to side like a swimmer. I felt rather than saw my quarry pause for a fraction of a second, looking down at me, and I could almost smell his surprise. I was gaining on him.

The shaft went far higher than I had expected, and it occurred to me as I powered on that we must be moving up through the concert hall's external walls. The higher I climbed, the more I became aware of music, distant at first, but swelling strangely as I neared the top. Another twenty or thirty feet and I was out, standing on a narrow metal gantry, the music from the opera stage below, all around me. I peered into the gloom, my hair falling in my face. There was no sign of the thief, but there were lots of places he could have hid. Ropes and pulleys and great wood-framed canvas flats were suspended in front of me. I was in the rigging for the scenery. Below the gantry I could see nothing but the front lip of the stage and the first rows of orchestra seating, fifty feet below. I took a steadying breath and grabbed hold of a cool brass pipe.

The action saved my life because I didn't see the kick arcing out of the darkness till it made contact with my jaw.

My legs gave, and I sagged, head spinning, but somehow my right hand remembered to hold on as I began to fall. For a moment, the world swam, the darkness above the stage switching places with the brightness and color below. My attacker moved toward me, but all I could do, hanging by one hand, was watch with horror as he turned and looked down into my face.

He wore slim-fitting gloves and was—I was chilled to see—masked. His head was wrapped with dark fabric, but the centerpiece was rigid, shaped out of what looked like gray leather and molded so closely to the face that I could see nothing of its features. The eyes looked hard and dark, but I could not be sure of their color, and my head was full of what he might do as he reached me.

I hung there, dimly aware that the music below had sputtered to a halt and there were cries of consternation from the actors, the only people who could see me clearly. I did not look down. I had seconds of strength left. The masked figure above me paused, staring into my desperate face, and raised a single index finger.

One chance.

Then he was gone, moving along the gantry and farther upstage.

I snatched a breath, flung my other hand up, and caught desperately at the pipe. For a moment, I just hung there, taking the weight off my exhausted right arm, and then I hauled myself up, panting like the dowager I had left on the bathroom floor.

I got unsteadily to my feet. My attacker had raced coolly across the catwalk and now stood above the wings. He seemed to be staring over the stage to the far side, and I followed his gaze up to where a ladder led to an access hatch in the roof. There was no way across but the pipes and ropes from which the lights and scenic flats were suspended, but I knew what he planned to do.

I shook off my daze and watched, amazed, as he ventured out onto one of the long girders. It could be no more than two inches wide, and he spread his arms like a high-wire artist as he took a step out over the void.

He was mad.

But even as I thought it, I found my feet were following him, along the gantry by the theater wall, then up to the same impossibly narrow beam that led out and across the stage so far below. On either side were ropes and cables, some weighted with what looked like sandbags, moored to cleats set into the roofing struts, but they were all impossibly far away. The only way after him was the way he had gone.

I glanced down and saw them now, the upturned, horrified faces of the actors, dreamlike in their makeup. The masked man was already halfway across, perfectly poised, head level. I couldn't see his eyes, but I knew they were set on some fixed point in front of him. That's what you do when you are up high. You pick a spot and focus on it as if you've anchored cable there. . . .

I put my right foot onto the girder, wishing to all the gods that I were wearing my own work boots and not those wretched heels. Then my left. I extended my arms as he had done and took my first step out into space.

I heard a groan from below, and movement, as if other people were coming onstage now to see what was going on above them, but I could not look down. He was in front of me, blocking the fixed point I would have focused on, and for a second, I felt the unfamiliar swell of vertigo, a dizzying sickness in my head and stomach. I wobbled, instinctively taking another step, and another.

The movement restored my equilibrium, but he had reached the end of the girder now, and as he leapt clear, he paused to look back. He raised his hand, two fingers raised this time.

A second chance?

I focused on them, wondering what he meant, but then his other hand came up and I saw the dull gleam of a pistol. He lowered one finger so that only the index was raised, and wagged it back and forth.

No second chance. You should have known.

I flinched as the shot was fired, catching the flash of the thing before the plume of smoke, even before the bang. It missed me, but the shock had distracted me, and now I was falling. Slowly at first, just tipping to the side, but the movement was unstoppable.

One of the ropes hung just above my head. With what little

momentum I could manage, I leapt straight up, grabbing wildly for the rope, reaching back as I failed to compensate for my lean.

The rope's knotted end brushed my forearm and swung agonizingly away. I started to drop just as it swung back. I grabbed it. The jolt threatened to tear my shoulder from its socket, but I hung there. Just for a second. Then rusted staples were popping from the beam above and the rope tore free.

Someone below screamed, and I plummeted toward the stage.

CHAPTER
19

BUT I DIDN'T JUST fall. Halfway down, all the slack went out of the rope. The abrupt halt in my momentum almost tore it from my hands. I felt my palms burn, but I clung on, eyes watering, body shrieking its defiance. And then I was dropping to earth once more, my weight insufficient to match the sandbag counterbalance that shot up the far wall toward the pulley in the roof.

I hit the stage hard, but landed feet first, knees bent and rolling out of the impact. The shock was immense, a juddering crash that ran through every joint and left me breathless, but I thanked the gods I had landed on the sprung timber of the stage and not on concrete or cobbles.

For a long moment, I just lay there, not unconscious, but processing the pain in my legs and shoulder, unwilling even to try to move till I was sure nothing was broken.

Around me, it was chaos: screaming and shouting coming from all over the theater. The ring immediately around me was all actors in their finery and surreal, painted faces. I stayed where I was, cautiously testing each muscle and bone with fractional flexes, managing to focus so precisely that I was oblivious to what those peering at me were saying.

Then a man in uniform pushed his way through the crowd. Firm hands seized my arms and dragged me roughly up from the stage. I tried to protest, but his voice silenced me.

"I'm arresting you for the theft of a necklace, property of the Dowager Lady Hamilton."

* * *

I WAS SITTING ON the wooden bench on which I had spent the night, my ankles chained together, my feet bare. The brick cell was painted in off-white gloss and smelled of sawdust, urine, and vomit. There was a single narrow window high in the wall, barred. The blue door was reinforced with steel bands and plates. At head height was a hatch, about six inches long. It opened and someone looked in.

"Remain seated as we enter," said a man's voice, "or you will be subdued."

I drew the solitary blanket tight about me but otherwise did not move a single, aching muscle as the lock clunked over and, with a juddering thud, the door swung heavily open.

The speaker was a uniformed white officer with a barrel chest and a broad mustache. He was perspiring heavily. As he stepped to the side, two more white men came in, both in suits. One was, I assumed, another policeman. The other was Willinghouse. His scarred face, always unsettling, was rigid, and I felt his anger. He did not look at me.

The plainclothes officer addressed me. "I am Detective Sergeant Andrews. You are Anglet Sutonga, former steeplejack?"

"Yes," I managed. The look on Willinghouse's face had hit me with the full weight of my predicament.

"And you are in the employ of Dahria Willinghouse as a maidservant?" said Andrews.

I started to look at Willinghouse in surprise but caught myself. "Yes, sir," I said.

"And can you explain what you were doing in the opera house this evening?"

I thought fast. Insofar as I had prepared a defense, it was predicated on telling the truth, something Willinghouse apparently did not want me to do.

"I went with Lady Dahria to the opera," I began cautiously. "I had to go to the bathroom. When I got there, I found a lady. She said she had been attacked. Robbed. The man was getting away. I went after him. I couldn't catch up with him and fell."

"So you went to the rest facilities with no sense that the Dowager Lady Hamilton would be there?" said Andrews. He was hawkish, with keen eyes and an almost unnatural stillness.

"That was the lady on the bathroom floor?" I asked.

"Yes."

"No," I said. "I just . . ."

"Needed to use the facilities," said Andrews.

"Well, partly," I said.

Andrews leaned forward. "Yes?" he prompted.

"I'd never been to an opera before," I confided. "I was kind of bored. Needed a break."

A tense watchfulness in his face seemed to unwind, and he took a breath. "I see," he said, drawing a fold of paper from his pocket. "So you have never seen this before?" He handed it to me.

It was not written by hand, but typed on one of those machines like the one in Ansveld's shop. It read,

> Lady Hamilton,
> We have your nefew, Arnold. If you want
> to see his safe return, go to the end
> stall in the lady's toilets half an hour
> after the opera has begun. Bring your
> necklace. Tell no one and come alone or
> the consiquences will be dyre.

I looked up.

"Well?" said Andrews. "What can you tell me about this?"

"It's badly spelled?" I said.

"I mean," he persisted, with an effort at composure, "did you write it?"

"No."

"Do you know who did?"

"No."

"Have you seen it before or heard anyone refer to it?"

"No."

He stared me down for another second, then glanced at Willinghouse. My employer, if he still was that, said nothing. "The man you pursued," said Andrews. "Did he say or do anything that might suggest he was . . . foreign?"

"Are you asking if he was black?" I asked, genuinely confused.

"He's asking if he was Grappoli," said Willinghouse. He sounded annoyed.

I shook my head. "He never spoke," I said.

Andrews frowned. "What happened to the necklace?" he asked.

"I didn't see it," I answered.

"Not at all?"

"It was gone when I got there," I said.

"And you didn't see it on the person of the man you say took it?"

"Well, he wasn't *wearing* it, if that's what you mean," I said, looking up for the first time.

"Well, no," he said, irritated. "But you didn't see him pocket it or something?"

"He could have had it in his hand the whole time and I wouldn't have seen it."

"You saw no sign of its light?"

"Light?"

"It had a luxorite stone in it," he said, clearly disappointed.

"No. Where is my mistress?" I asked, trying to sound concerned. "Is she angry with me?"

"Well," said Willinghouse, his voice low and hard, his eyes flashing green fire. "At very least, you disrupted a major society event, causing her great personal embarrassment and leading to her being escorted from the building—in front of Bar-Selehm's elite—in the company of a police officer. Whether you stole anything or not, your conduct was rash and unseemly."

"Will she—?" I began, then retooled the question, acutely aware of sitting in no more than a blanket and borrowed underwear. "Am I to be dismissed? From her service, I mean."

Willinghouse pursed his lips. His scarred cheek flexed as he clamped his teeth together for a moment, as if he was seriously considering the possibility; then he breathed out and shook his head briefly. "Not this time," he said.

I relaxed—doubly so when, after a nod from Andrews, the uniformed officer squatted at my feet and unlocked my shackles.

"The lady's nephew," I said. "Is he all right?"

"Always was," said Andrews. "There was no kidnapping. The young man lives in Harrisberg. Officers were dispatched on the first available train and found him enjoying a champagne breakfast at home with friends. A simple ruse, but an effective one."

WILLINGHOUSE MARCHED ME OUT of the station without a word, waiting until we were a block away before turning on me. I was dressed in my own—freshly laundered—clothes and boots, which he had brought from the house, and felt, insofar as was possible, more like my old self.

"Do you understand the meaning of the word 'discretion'?" he snapped. "This will make the papers. Apart from the embarrassment you have caused my family, the professional difficulties I will face at work, you have blown any secrecy surrounding our investigation wide open!"

"*Our* investigation?" I replied. I had just tied my hair back as if I were going to work on a chimney, and the action made me feel confident, defiant. "What has your contribution been to this investigation so far?"

"Other than getting you out of jail, you mean?" he returned. "Without me, you would be languishing in there for days. Weeks, maybe."

"And without me, you would have learned nothing!"

"And what, pray, have we learned from your being arrested?" he demanded.

I raised a single finger. If I didn't talk, I would hit him.

"First," I said. "We know that Berrit had access to luxorite before the theft of the Beacon and that he tried to sell it to Ansveld. I don't know what the connection between them was, but there was one, and that was why he died." I raised another finger. "Second, we know that the source of that luxorite was unknown to the trading community, and that when a piece found its way into the Dowager Hamilton's necklace, the people responsible were determined to get it back. Third, we know that those people were connected to Ansveld through more than the boy. They almost certainly used his typewriter to print up the letter claiming to have abducted the dowager's nephew."

"Anything else?" he demanded, still defiant.

"Yes," I said, raising a fourth finger. "We know that whoever stole the dowager's necklace needed no help from an inexperienced apprentice steeplejack to steal the Beacon. He climbs as well as me. Maybe better."

The admission deflated us both a little, and for a moment, we just stood there as the city's morning began around us. Though I saw my investigation into Berrit's death as a personal mission rather than a professional engagement, I needed Willinghouse's money and protection. If there was more to it than that, if I also needed his respect, his admiration, I chose not to think about that too closely.

"I have to go to Parliament," he said, glancing into the street for a cab. "This business over the Grappoli ambassador is escalating badly.

If the Beacon isn't found soon, we could be looking at a major inter-national incident."

"What kind of incident?" I asked. The chatter I had heard about the diplomatic breakdown had been little more than rumor and jokes at the Grappoli's oversensitivity.

"There are powerful people in Bar-Selehm who would like nothing more than open war with the Grappoli," said Willinghouse. "There was a rally last night in Morgessa. What they call a 'demonstra-tion.'" He said the word like it tasted foul. "The second of the week. Except that this time there was fighting: blacks on one side, whites on the other."

"Why?" I asked.

He shrugged the question off. "Because it's what happens in Bar-Selehm when tensions run high. Everyone wants someone to blame."

"This is what you meant when you said we were on the brink of disaster," I said.

"Not yet," he said. "Not quite. But we are getting there. I don't really know how or why, but we are."

"Surely it can't be that bad," I said, scared of his earnestness.

He glowered into the street, then gave me a searching look. "If a shred of evidence, however flimsy, however dubious, links the Grap-poli to the theft of the Beacon, the people who want war will get their wish. Do you know what that would do to this city?"

I shook my head.

"Pray to whatever gods you worship that you never do," he said.

IF I HAD THOUGHT that was the end of the matter, I was sorely mistaken, as I discovered the moment I entered the Drowning. A girl, perhaps Tanish's age, paused in her laundry to give me a long look, after which she hurried inside the tent she called home. A few minutes later, as I strode to Rahvey's hut, I found I had accumulated a straggling tail of onlookers, not all of them children.

Florihn intercepted me before I could reach my sister. "Did you think we wouldn't know?" she yelled, stomping up the dirt track with her head lowered like a one-horn. "Did you think we were too unsophisticated to find out what you had done?" She slapped a newspaper into my hands.

I took the paper and flipped it open. I had made the front page, and the paper was particularly shrill on the scandal of my falling to the stage in my underwear. It was almost laughable, but not quite. There was no picture, and the headline called me only a former steeplejack, but my name was in the small print. So were Dahria's and Willinghouse's. I squeezed my eyes shut and tried to lock out Florihn's babbling outrage.

"And you with a child to raise!" she sputtered.

I stared at her, feeling once more the rising anger that had led to my smashing the statue of Cenu. "It was a misunderstanding!" I gasped. "The police already released me. It has no bearing on my ability to look after the child."

I marched away before she could say anything else, my face hot, arms trembling. At Rahvey's hut, I took the child without speaking, ignoring her indignant questions, feeling stupid, furious, and above all, lost.

"Don't come back till two o'clock," she said.

"She'll need to eat before then."

"Two o'clock," Rahvey repeated. "Not a moment earlier."

And she went to work.

IN NEED OF CALM and a chance to plan my next move, I took the child to the temple yard and performed the Kathahry exercises under the vague eyes of the nameless baby and a ring-tailed genet that watched from the branches of a coral tree. I had just finished and was sponging my arms and face when I saw the Mahweni boy I had met on the night of Berrit's funeral. Mnenga.

"Anglet," he said, beaming. "I am glad you came. I brought you something."

I was taken aback. My thoughts had been too crowded for me to reflect much on our last meeting, and I was surprised to find how much his reappearance pleased me.

From behind his back he produced two corked earthenware bottles.

"What is it?" I asked.

"Milk," he answered, proud. "And look."

From the pouch around his neck he produced a rubbery object, which he proceeded to squeeze onto the mouth of one of the bottles. It was an artificial nipple.

"For the little girl," he said in a comic stage whisper.

"Where did you get this?" I asked, marveling.

"We carry them for the young nbezu. Sometimes their mothers do not feed them, and we have to do it by hand. I have cleaned it."

"And the milk is . . ."

"From the nbezu, yes. It is very rich and sweet. Good for human babies."

"She's actually just eaten," I said, "but thank you. I will try it."

He made no move to go. "I am very good at this," he said. "I can help."

He took the bottle and placed the rubber nipple against the baby's mouth. At first, the child did not respond, but when he teased her lips open, she began to suck.

"She's taking it!" I exclaimed, delighted.

Mnenga chuckled happily. "What is her name?" he asked.

I hesitated. "We have not had the naming yet," I said.

He looked troubled. Naming had even more potent associations for the Mahweni than it did for the Lani. A child with no name was like a ghost or an animal, a soul without proper human form.

"I think she looks like a kalla," I said on impulse. "The flower over there."

He glanced at the rich and fragrant blooms that hung from a gnarled tree on the edge of the temple grounds and beamed. "*Hlengiwe* in my language," he said, adding "Kalla," trying the feel of the word and liking it. "Yes."

"I will suggest it to her mother," I said, taking the bottle from him and continuing to feed her.

"Good," he said. "I helped."

"Yes," I said. "Thanks."

I remembered what he had said the last time we met and added, "You did not tell your brothers?"

"No," he said. "They notice nothing. I could have taken half the flock and they would not see."

"Did you find the two that were missing?"

"Yes!" he said, glad that I had asked. "They had not come this far. But we are still looking for the old man."

I gave him a puzzled look. "Old man?" I said.

"The one I told you about who came from the cliffs."

"Oh," I said. "The one with the sunburn."

"Yes," he said. "He is still lost, and some of the tribe are worried, so we have to look. It is very foolish. I am glad I found you instead," he said.

"So am I," I answered. The child was still drinking, the habbit forgotten by her side.

"I will come again tomorrow with more," he said.

"I may not be here," I said. "I have work to do."

He shrugged and smiled that broad, infectious smile of his, then got to his feet. "I will come tomorrow," he said. "In case. And I will get more nbezu milk. I think it is sweeter than her mother's."

"I DON'T SEE WHAT you think I can do to help," said Dahria. I had arrived at the town house unannounced, and she had reacted coolly, as if merely speaking to me was endangering her reputation.

I showed her the baby I had already begun to think of as Kalla, and she took a step back, her face an almost comic mask of astonishment.

"I'm in danger," I said.

"If you are going to ask me to look after *that*—," she began, appalled.

"I'm not," I said. "But if I am going to continue my investigation, we need protection. Perhaps I could borrow one of your brother's men."

"I thought you were supposed to be working in secret?" she asked. "I hardly think being accompanied by henchmen *and* an infant is going to lower your profile."

My face fell. For a moment, she just looked at me; then she made a decision and opened a desk drawer with an intricate key. She produced a long, hexagonal-barreled revolver and a velvet bag of ammunition.

"Do not tell my brother or, for that matter, anyone else in the world, that you got this from me," she said.

"Can you teach me to use it?" I asked.

"You point it and pull the trigger," said Dahria wryly. "Pull the hammer back after each shot, like this, and hold it tight. It will kick. There's little more to it. That's the great and terrible thing about guns. You don't need a lot of skill with them to be lethal."

"Then that should work out," I said, taking the heavy weapon from her and hefting it less comfortably than I pretended.

"Just . . ." She faltered, eyeing both me and Kalla. "Be careful."

CHAPTER
20

I SAW FEVEL ON my way to the Drowning. He was loping down the center of the road by the Westside Gasworks, gazing about him like a weancat, hunting.

For me, I thought, shrinking against the wall of the post office on the corner and peering between the drainpipe and the wall as he walked on, scanning. Less weancat, I decided, more hyena. I hugged the child to my chest, glad that she was sleeping.

When I arrived, Rahvey snatched the child from my arms so that she woke with a start and began to cry, silencing only when she found my sister's breast. "It's starving," said Rahvey, shooting me an accusatory look.

It wasn't, in fact. Mnenga's nbezu milk had kept the child satisfied.

"What are you doing all the time?" she demanded. "You look terrible."

I thought of telling her about Berrit, but Rahvey was the kind of person who thought that the difficulties of her own life—which were undeniable—rendered everyone else undeserving of sympathy.

"Does it matter?" I said.

Rahvey turned to look at the baby she was nursing, and suddenly it was like we were girls again, waiting for Papa to come home. I think I always knew that Rahvey resented the attention I got from Papa, attention she saw as stolen from her. I remember one time when Vestris was reading the tale of Shantali the hunter as we all ate together, and Papa was so caught up in it that his food went cold as he listened, spellbound. The next day I made a clay model of Shan-tali and the elephant he killed by mistake as a gift for him, but Rah-vey broke it. She said it was an accident, but I didn't believe her, and I was still crying when Papa got home. Vestris took him out of the hut to tell him what had happened, and when he came back, his face was tight with anger. He never shouted except in delight, so his silence was terrible. He told Rahvey she had done a disgraceful thing, and Rahvey wept, protesting her innocence till even I wasn't sure whether she meant it, or whether she had just started to believe her own lie. Children do that sometimes.

That night as we lay quiet in our beds I had seen Rahvey's face in the lamplight as Vestris stroked her hair, and she had looked beyond anger and grief. She looked lost and without hope. And then it was like I was seeing myself from her bunk, and I was an interloper, someone who had appeared when no one expected it, stolen her father's love from her, and captivated her beautiful elder sister.

Had I given her cause to hate me? I didn't think so, but maybe what I thought didn't really matter. It occurred to me that the soup my father had allowed to go cold while listening to Vestris's story would have taken Rahvey most of the afternoon to make.

"Morlak's boys came for you, Anglet," Rahvey said now, without looking up from Kalla's face. "Found Sinchon at his work. What did you do?"

And that was also Rahvey. No concern for me. Just the assumption that her idiot sister had messed up in ways that would incur a punishment she probably deserved. If there was any other emotion, it was irritation that my problems had somehow involved her.

"Please just feed Kalla," I said, weary.

"Kalla?" said Rahvey. "Who is Kalla?"

I flushed a little. "It's what I call her," I said. "The baby."

Rahvey drew herself up still farther, like some bush lizard flexing its crest to ward off predators. "There has been no naming," she said in a leaden voice. "When there is, I will name the child, not you. And it will not be called Kalla."

"She," I corrected. "Not it."

Rahvey glared at me, but I held her eyes, and for once, it was my sister who turned away first. "And I would appreciate it if you didn't bring your sordid city friends out here," she added.

I tensed. "Believe me," I said, "I have no interest in talking to Morlak."

"Not just Morlak!" she snapped. "There was another. Said his name was Jennings."

"Billy?" I said. "What did he want?"

"Says he has to tell you something. Something he saw. Wants you to meet him tonight under the statue of Captain Franzen at eleven."

I frowned. Cleaning that statue had been one of Tanish's jobs, and though it was in the heart of Mahweni Old Town, it was only a stone's throw from the Martel Court. It was also where Morlak had attacked me. The coincidence made me uneasy. If Morlak had gotten to Billy, this was a trap.

"How did he seem?" I asked.

"What?" said Rahvey, as if I were speaking another language.

"Did he seem like he was hiding something?" I said. "Or like he was scared, nervous? Did he mention Morlak?"

She shook her head. "Morlak," she sneered. "These city Lani. You can't trust any of them."

I RETURNED TO BAR-SELEHM before the lighting of the streetlamps and got the baby safely tucked into her basket in the clock tower before making the cautious climb down. I had the pistol in my belt under my charcoal gray jacket. I did not know what to make of Billy's sudden decision to be helpful, and I wanted to be ready for anything.

Old Town was the most respectable black district in the city, made venerable by age if not by space. The houses were small, the streets smaller, though their inhabitants kept them meticulously clean. In the square at the end of Range Street, under a pair of blue-tiled minarets that rose like lighthouses above the uneven rooftops, a group of Mahweni protesters were clearing up what was left of their rally, gathering up handbills so they couldn't be done for littering. I thought of Mnenga's stories of suspicious land deals, and the image of his face and his gift of the nbezu milk made me smile. I remembered the touch of his hand, the surprise in his face, and the pleasure that had followed it.

And then, as if the memory had conjured him, he was there. He was huddled among the remaining protesters in his Unassimilated garb, so he stood out among the coats and collared shirts. With the spear in one hand, he looked fierce and out of place. He was talking animatedly to one of the protesters, his face earnest, angry even, and as I watched, he gestured dramatically, his forefinger stabbing from his clenched fist so that the other man, who was dressed as a factory worker, shook his head and took a step back. I did not call to Mnenga, and not only because seeing him here in the city was so jarringly strange. He suddenly seemed quite different, his manner, his very presence here hinting at something I had not seen in him before, something he had kept from me.

What was he doing here? There was clearly more to him than the humble nbezu herder he had claimed to be. Were there even any nbezu? He could have bought that milk anywhere. . . .

Whatever the truth was, however innocent it might be, it was clear as luxorite that while I had trusted him with my private thoughts, I did not know him, and his appearance in my life suddenly seemed more than convenient. It was suspicious. I turned quickly away, so he would not see me, and kept walking. A policeman gave me a look as I rounded the corner, but—since I was neither friend nor obvious foe—went back to monitoring the protesters in the soft glow of a gas lamp, Mnenga among them.

I picked up my pace.

This time of year, the night came early, and as the temperature fell, the city became an entirely different place. The district around the Martel Court, where I had left the baby and which thronged with people in daylight, was deserted now, and its statues of old justices, brushed with the pearly light of the streetlamps, became ghosts of a forgotten world. It was only a couple of blocks to where the statue of Captain Franzen stood on his triumphal column, gazing forever out toward the coast with his bronze telescope.

A sound behind me. Footfalls, or just the echo of my own feet on the stone?

I faltered and they continued for a moment, then stopped. I turned and looked back the way I had come, but the mist that blew in from the river on cold nights had blended with the city's persistent pall of smog, and I could see no more than twenty yards, even where the street was open and well lit.

I began walking and almost immediately, I heard the steps behind me start up again. They were uneven and punctuated with a rhythmic tap, like someone using a cane, someone very slightly off balance. . . .

Morlak.

I quickened my pace, dimly aware of Captain Franzen's column looming out of the fog ahead, its shape cluttered with the scaffolding Tanish had been using. My pursuer matched my speed.

I reached for the pistol in my waistband but did not draw it. Not yet.

As the square opened up, I could see the base of the column clearly, with its four massive bronze rhinos turned outward as if guarding. A figure was sitting on the steps at the foot of the column itself.

He was slumped over sideways. Unmoving.

A puddle of blood was thickening around him. There was a wound in his chest. One I had seen before.

It was Billy.

CHAPTER
21

HIS EYES WERE OPEN, but when I stooped and touched his throat, I felt no pulse, though the body was still quite warm. I closed his eyes with one hand and sat on the stone flags in front of him in numb shock. I adjusted his jacket, which had rumpled, smoothing the front as I thought he would have liked, and I felt the bulge in his breast pocket.

Two purses and a quarter sheet of newspaper, carefully folded.

I took it all, but did not read the cutting. My mind would not process what had happened. I had doubted him, but he was true, and in trying to help me, he had died. Shock and grief and guilt threatened to overcome me, and I stuffed the newspaper into my pocket without another glance.

Two purses, one for the ring he will never buy . . .

I heard the footsteps. I don't know how I had forgotten them, but I had. They were closer now, more careful, but they were the same ones I had heard earlier. I heard the tap of the cane, and suddenly I was sure that whoever was following me had been here already. He had known I was coming and who I was to meet. One half of his job was done. I was the other half.

Morlak hobbling on his stick.

Or Mnenga with his spear?

The thought horrified me, but would not go away. I had seen the Mahweni boy only a few blocks away, in a place he should not be, and armed. . . .

I spun around, trying to locate the source of the sound in the eerie glow of the gaslit fog, and as I did so, I snatched the heavy pistol from my belt and pointed it into the shadows.

Another careful footstep.

"Who's there?" I demanded. "Step into the light. I'm armed!"

Silence. Then the distinctive ring of steel: a long knife or sword sliding from its sheath.

I cocked the gun's hammer and aimed the long barrel into the gently swirling mist, but there was nothing to see. How close might he get before presenting me with a target? Ten yards? Five? The fog seemed to confuse the sound so that I wasn't sure which way I was facing, and when a distant train blew its whistle, the sound seemed to bounce from all directions.

My gun hand trembled. I had just enough presence of mind not to shoot blindly. Some of the buildings around me were residences. A stray bullet could go through a window. . . .

I pointed the revolver's barrel into a patch of exposed dirt where a fractured flagstone had been removed, and fired once.

In the silence, the sound was a cannon blast, and its reverberation slapped around the facades of the square like thunder. My ears rang, and for a moment the world seemed muffled. I heard a window open somewhere to my left, and then the distant but unmistakable shriek of a police whistle.

From my attacker, the man I assumed had already killed Billy before turning his attention on me, there was no sound.

Then there were footsteps again, coming toward me. I turned, seized the lowest bar of the scaffolding, which crisscrossed its uneven way up the column to the bronze pirate on the top, and began to climb, my hair swinging in my face. The pistol was still in my hand, but the last I saw before the fog swallowed the ground beneath me was the shape of a man moving to Billy's body, hesitating, and looking around as the shrill blast of the police whistle sounded once more.

I could not see who it was.

I climbed higher, faster, hoping against hope that I would not be trapped at the top of the column. The earth fell away beneath me. The fog swallowed me up. And still I climbed. At the top, a set of four gas lamps gave a faint opalescent aura to the bronze figure, but the column itself was utterly dark, so that the statue seemed to float like a specter above the city. It was not till I reached the top that I found what I had hoped for: a slim and rickety bridge made of ladders and cable, which the cleaning crew used to bring supplies from the roof of a nearby building.

It sloped downward, creaking when I put my feet on it, and it had never been designed to be used in the dark, but I could hear voices below, muffled by the fog. The police? Billy's killer? Perhaps both. I took my first unsteady step onto the slim bridge and felt it wobble under my weight.

There was a single cable at waist height, which served as a handrail, on the right. There should have been one on the left too, but it was missing. I pocketed the gun, gripped the cable with one hand, and holding the other out for balance, pressed on, eyes front, feeling my way with the soles of my boots. The fog was too dense to see where the bridge ended.

The voices from the square were louder now but less distinct, and for a moment everything seemed to fall away, even my horror of Billy's death, so that it was just me up there in the night sky, trusting to hands and feet and instinct.

Below me, someone screamed. It was a strange, disembodied sound, and for a split second, I wondered if it was me, if the feelings I kept locked behind the dam had somehow broken out without me realizing. . . .

The bridge ended on the ornamental roof of an office building. I used a discarded ladder to cross onto the Merchant Marine headquarters next door, and then dropped onto the fire escape of the Dragon's Head. I covered the next block and a half on rooftops and one decorative ledge, reaching the League of Magistrates' chambers, and finally the south entrance to the Martel Court.

I scaled the clock tower as quickly as I could, shut myself in, and rushed to the child I had left there. The only good thing about the night was that she had not been with me, and the idea that being near me was likely to get her killed settled in my gut like a stone.

The baby was sleeping soundly. The strangeness of her peace after what had happened first shocked, then calmed me, and I lay with her, feeling her breathing, her heart, as I stared wide eyed into the blackness, the habbit clutched tight in my hands. Her safety was, I saw now, an illusion—something I had wanted to believe in but which was clearly impossible to achieve. I could maintain the pretense no longer.

I MOVED BEFORE DAWN, giving Captain Franzen's square a wide berth and reaching the orphanage called Pancaris, the place I had vowed never to revisit, just as the city came to life. I laid the basket on the steps. In it, the girl I called Kalla slept. The nuns would give her a new name, I thought, as I rapped hard with the knocker three times, walking quickly away before the door opened. If I saw her again years from now, I could be introduced to her and still not know her. She would, of course, not know me either.

The morning breeze chilled my tear-streaked face, but no one pointed or shouted or seemed to see me at all, in spite of the guilt and failure, the terrible, exquisite sadness that seemed to burn in my heart like the lost Beacon.

It was the only choice, I told myself over and over as I walked, but though I believed it, the mantra did not help at all.

I STUDIED THE NEWSPAPER cutting I had recovered from Billy's body. It was stained with his blood, but still legible. The headline read, ICONIC RED FORT TOWER TO COME DOWN BEFORE HANDOFF. It meant nothing to me. I felt weary in ways that went far beyond my lack of sleep and food.

For the first time in months, I thought of going out to that bit of the Drowning where Papa had lived, as if there was a chance that he might be there, sitting on the porch, watching the sunrise. I could tell him about Kalla, about my doomed investigation, and it would all be better for saying it. I thought of how his face would light up when he saw me, and the pain was suddenly as sharp, as paralyzing as the day he died.

But Papa was gone and I was alone. I didn't know what I was doing. A man had died because of me. That seemed unavoidable. Whether I had made any kind of progress, what he might have told me, and if I was any closer to bringing justice or clarity to what was going on in Bar-Selehm, I had no idea.

"WHAT DO YOU KNOW about the Old Red Fort?" I asked the newspaper girl on the corner of Winckley Street.

She looked amazed to see me. "You're famous, you are," she said. There was a wariness in her face I hadn't seen before. "Made the paper and everything," said the Mahweni girl. "And here you are, walking around, big as life."

"What makes you think that's me?" I said, bluffing badly. "There's no picture."

"'Former Lani steeplejack of marriageable age, Anglet Su-tonga—'" she read aloud.

"Yes, all right," I interrupted. "It's me. But if you read the whole thing, you'll see I wasn't charged. The police don't think I stole any-thing."

The girl tipped her head on one side, and her eyes narrowed. "Stole?" the girl said.

"At the opera house," I replied.

She hesitated, watching me, her eyes narrow. "You don't know, do you?" she said.

"Don't know what?"

She flipped over the paper and pushed it across her crate toward me. "You're wanted for murder," she said.

I stared, first at the photograph of Billy Jennings's lifeless face, then back at her. My mouth moved, but nothing came out.

"Practically the only headline in the paper that doesn't include the words 'Beacon,' 'Grappoli,' or 'Protest,'" she mused.

I continued to gape, and for a moment the world swam so that I took hold of the edge of her crate to steady myself.

She considered me and came to a decision. "You know the alley that connects the back of the Hunter's Arms to Smithy Row?"

I nodded, mute.

"There's a storage shed behind the bins. Meet me there in twenty minutes. And stay out of sight."

I WALKED, UNSEEING, STARING straight ahead, moving as if in a dream. The shock muted everything but my own horrified thoughts. I pieced it together: the cop who had seen me near the Mahweni rally; Billy's girlfriend, Bessie, who would have been interviewed as soon as they realized who he was, and who would have mentioned my visit to Macinnes's shop.

Gods, Bessie.

I felt the two purses in my pocket. Somehow I would have to get them to her. The emptiness of the gesture, the stupid pointlessness of trying to make right what I had done, kicked in my chest like an orlek.

The alley behind the metal workers' shops was heaped with coal ash and rusting iron. It smelled like blood. I paced, waiting, beside the shed.

"I told you to go inside," said the newspaper girl when she arrived. "Stand around out here, and they'll get you for sure."

"I didn't kill him," I said.

"For the likes of us," she said, pushing the shed door open and ushering me inside, "that's not always relevant."

"I have friends in the police," I said, talking as much to calm my nerves as to convince her.

"What were you doing out there at that time?"

"Meeting him," I said. "He had something to tell me. He was dead when I got there. There was another man there. Morlak, I thought. Or . . ."

Mnenga.

"Someone," I continued. "He had a cane. Maybe some kind of blade too," I added, managing not to say "spear," though the word floated up in my mind like driftwood dislodged by an unseen crocodile. "That was what he used. . . ."

Billy. This was my fault. I hadn't stabbed him myself, but if it wasn't for me . . .

"And he told you nothing?"

"I told you. He was dead when I got there. He had this in his pocket," I said, producing the newspaper clipping.

She considered me for a moment and then stuck out her hand. "Sarah," she said. "That's my street name anyway."

I nodded vaguely, still stunned.

She shrugged like it didn't really matter. "And you are Anglet," she said.

"Ang. Why are you helping me?"

"Haven't done anything yet." She shrugged again.

"You have," I said. "And you aren't going to turn me in."

It wasn't a question.

"We have to stick together," said Sarah.

"Who?"

"I don't know. People."

I put my hands to my temples and squeezed my eyes shut.

It was all too much. But Billy had died to bring me information. I owed it to him to follow whatever trail he had left me.

"Please," I said, eyes still closed. "I'm in trouble, real trouble, and I don't know what to do. Tell me about the Old Red Fort."

"You really ought to read the whole paper," she said, very dry, "not just the bits about you."

I couldn't manage a smile, but I opened my eyes.

She nodded at the newspaper article. "It's part of a deal negotiated last year," said Sarah. "The fort is being turned over to the Unassimilated Tribes, a goodwill gesture from the government."

I thought of Mnenga again, his talk of land deals, and nodded, letting her talk in that strange way of hers, calling up what she had read and interspersing those fragments with her own editorial commentary.

"It was built out on the Sour Ridge Road during the occupation three hundred years ago and was the battalion headquarters for the so-called Glorious Third—the King's Third Feldesland Infantry Regiment—stationed to guard the city from the Grappoli and the tribesmen to the west. It was besieged by Mahweni warriors several times but was always repaired and became a symbol of northern military power. It hasn't been used as a serious military facility for several years, and it's starting to fall into disrepair. Since they don't want to pay for the upkeep anymore, the military—very magnanimously—agreed to turn it over to the Mahweni for use as a cultural center, museum, and tribal meeting venue. It's a token, a gesture, but not everyone in the government is in favor, and some of the Mahweni think it will be more expensive to run than it's worth."

"A white elephant," I said.

She grinned bleakly at that. "White is right," she said. "That's why the tower is coming down next week. It was used as a holding pen for prisoners of war. A lot of my people—well, kind of—died there. It has the regimental badge on it, and some military types thought it should be preserved for that alone, but the government voted to demolish the tower and hand over the rest of the structure intact. The plan is to leave it as rubble until it gets naturally overgrown; turning back into the land is the idea. Responsibility for the demolition went to—"

"The Seventh Street gang," I guessed. I don't know why, but somehow I sensed that was coming. Everything was connected.

"Under the direction of Mr. Morlak," she added. "Yes. But you can't be considering going out there now. You're on the run. The police will find you."

"Probably."

"So why do I get the feeling you're going to go anyway?" asked Sarah.

"I suppose you are just a naturally intuitive person," I said.

CHAPTER
22

I RODE TWO STOPS on the underground to save time, head down so that no one would recognize me, getting off the train when I saw a policeman board at Wallend. I walked the rest of the way to the Drowning, and made my way down to the river, where the massive hippos wallowed and huddled, backs to the water. I loitered high on the bank, watching them uneasily till one of the girls saw me and alerted Rahvey.

My sister came up from the laundry, eyes flashing. "You're late," she said as soon as she was out of earshot of the other girls. "And I don't have break for another hour."

Word of the morning newspaper report clearly hadn't reached the Drowning, and that was all to the good.

"I don't have her," I said.

"What?" said Rahvey, irritable.

"I gave her up," I said, knowing I couldn't speak more fully without losing control.

"What?" said Rahvey again.

I took a breath. "Pancaris," I said. "I just couldn't . . ."

Rahvey just looked at me, stunned, and the wrongness of what I had done coursed through me like cold, bright water. Then she was nodding woodenly, her face set, and turning quickly away. She said nothing as she walked, and I did not pursue her.

THE POLICE SEEMED TO be everywhere. It may have been because of the rallies and protests that were cropping up all over the city, or it might have been because of me. It was hard to believe that the death of Billy Jennings would generate such a manhunt, but it was clear that Billy, as well as Ansveld and Berrit, was part of something much larger, a tiny wheel in a great mechanism that, as Willing-house had warned, was ticking toward disaster.

And now I am at its heart.

I traveled almost a quarter of a mile over rooftops and fire escapes and scaffolding—the best way to stay unseen, since ordinary people never look up—before dropping from a signal gantry into the yard behind the Great Orphan Street railway station. I bought a ticket on the western line, which arrowed its way right across the continent to Gronmar and the bronze coast: Grappoli territory. The local trains went nothing like so far, and the long-distance services had been suspended pending the resolution of the current diplomatic dispute.

The train I boarded was a Blesbok class locomotive with four coaches that served the farms, homesteads, and mines forming a narrow corridor of land bought or stolen in war from the Mahweni. I curled up under my coat, pulling it over my face and leaving the ticket sticking out of the pocket, so that the conductor wouldn't feel the need to "wake" me.

I climbed down from the train at Coldsveldt, a rural halt not far from the pit where Papa had died, and got off the road as soon as I was out of sight of the station. So far I was as sure as I could be that no one had recognized me.

Leaving crowds behind should have been a relief, but out here, there were other perils. There wasn't much cover, and what trees grew there were low and stunted, giving little or no shade from the hot sun. My best chance of reaching the fort unnoticed was to skirt the main defenses, trekking through the tall savannah grass, and circling round to the north side. I swallowed. If I came upon a wean-cat or clavtar, the revolver in my belt would not be enough to stop it.

And it wasn't just predators that were dangerous. A spooked one-horn or nervous buffalo would be just as lethal.

It was a long, hot walk. My skin glowed under the relentless beat of the sun, and the thin, dry grass scratched my hands and face as I pushed through. From time to time I heard the rattle of mice scurrying through the stalks to get away from me, and once I startled a flight of franklins, which rose up, beating their wings and circling, so that I forced myself to keep still for several minutes, in case anyone was watching from the fort. As I knelt there in the grass, I heard something very large moving close by, a crunching, tearing sound. I rose cautiously and was horrified to see a solitary elephant emerging from a copse of marula trees, stripping bark from one of them not thirty yards away. It had not seen me. I kept agonizingly still for several minutes, trying to determine if I was up- or downwind of it, and in the process, it saw me.

It did not trumpet or charge, but it turned to face me, becoming motionless as stone, its ears spread wide, its brown eyes fixed on mine. I knew nothing of elephants and had no idea how you would gauge how old they were, but the eyes gave the impression of age and, beneath the caution, thoughtfulness. For a long moment, we watched each other, and I had the strangest sensation that she could see through to my heart, my soul. For reasons I couldn't explain, I found myself thinking of the baby I had left on the orphanage steps.

You could offer her nothing. She's better where she is.

Familiar ideas that I did and did not believe, though under the elephant's gaze, I felt a kind of peace with my decision. It might not have been the right thing to do, but I had done it for the right reasons, and that, for now, would have to be enough.

The elephant kept looking at me as it began to graze again, its trunk feeling for the leaves before tearing them off and gathering them into its mouth, but I felt no mounting sense of danger, and when I eventually stood up, it did no more than watch. Eventually, heart hammering, I walked slowly away. The elephant did not come after me.

The walls of the fort were only a hundred yards away, and though I could see no sign of movement, I could hear the steady, uneven clatter of tools on stone. After another ten minutes, with my sand-colored tunic and leggings dark with sweat, I cut west, approaching a half-collapsed turret. Reaching the foot of the escarpment, I began to climb.

I would be visible here, so I moved quickly and carefully, pausing only to check my handholds for scorpions and spiders. Once I saw a long, dark snake, spangled with aquamarine, sleeping away the winter in a hole, and kept watch for similar openings thereafter. I had assumed the pinkish color of the wall was paint, but it turned out to be the brick itself. It had crumbled over the years, and there were plenty of places to put my fingers and toes, but I was careful not to send telltale runnels of grit and chippings in my wake. The wall angled like a long-sided pyramid with a narrow battlement at the top, and in seconds, I was up and sliding cautiously over the parapet.

I could see them now, the huddle of Seventh Street boys gathered at the foot of the tower in the center, wielding their picks and shovels. They had a wagon, and one who was taller than the rest—Fevel, I thought—was unloading wooden beams. I was familiar with the process, one we used to bring down unwanted chimneys in confined spaces. It is precision work because the chimney has to fall just where you want it. In this case, the courtyard had several two-story buildings that were, presumably, to remain intact. That meant the tower had to drop eastward, losing some of its sixty-foot length as it fell if it wasn't to demolish the main gate in the process. The team would cut away the bricks from a corner of the tower's base, replacing them with pit props, till the timber struts were bearing much of the tower's weight, then set a fire. As the wood burned up, the whole stack would fall. The kids loved it.

But miscalculate the cutting point, the wooden joists, or the wind direction, and it could go all manner of wrong. I hoped they knew what they were doing. Morlak didn't do much in the way of real work anymore, but he generally oversaw this kind of thing personally.

Not this time.

I dropped into a crouch and moved slowly around the walls to get a better view. *No sign of him.*

Tanish was using a hammer and bolster chisel to break up the mortar lines. He wielded them well, positioning, striking, and clearing like a professional.

"Nice work, hummingbird," I muttered to myself.

I crept along till I came to a set of weathered steps down, and moments later I was watching the boys from the shadow of a long, narrow chamber only yards from where they were working.

It took ten maddening minutes to safely attract Tanish's attention. He made a great show of dropping his tools and checking with Fevel before trudging over, as if he just needed a break from the sun. I hugged him once, and we moved deeper into the dark chamber.

"They're saying you killed that Jennings bloke," he said. It wasn't a question.

"Billy," I answered. "I didn't, but I think someone wants it to look like I did." He nodded seriously, satisfied, and I hugged him again gratefully. He tried not to look pleased, and when I let him go, he leaned against the wall as the older boys did.

"No Morlak?" I asked.

Tanish shook his head fervently. "Says he has better things to do," he said.

"Such as?"

"Mostly sitting," said Tanish. "He hasn't been able to get upstairs since you . . . you know."

"Stabbed him," I said.

"Right," said Tanish, grinning again.

"Was he out last night?" I asked, thinking of the sound of the cane on the street where Billy Jennings had died.

Tanish shrugged. "He can walk around a bit, but not far, and no stairs. Mostly he sits in the old machine room on this box he had delivered by some Mahweni a few days ago. Barely takes his eyes off it. Smacks your knuckles with his stick if you so much as touch it. Like we care. Probably full of spades and brushes. He wants us to think he's the big crime lord when he's really just a hired man. Pathetic."

This was as much a part of his pose as his careful leaning against the wall, but I didn't call him on it. He wasn't as safe now that I wasn't around to watch out for him, and if pretending he wasn't afraid of Morlak helped, that was fine by me.

"A box?" I asked. "How big?"

Tanish motioned with his hands: about a yard long and almost as high. Big enough for the Beacon.

"And he's just sitting on it?"

"Waiting to make 'the trade of his career,'" he said mockingly.

"Who is he selling to?" I asked.

Tanish shrugged. "He's talking to Deveril, but he's just a whatchacallit: 'third party,'" he said. "The buyer won't show till he makes the handoff." He eyed the pendant round my neck. "Wasn't that Berrit's?"

I nodded.

"Why are you wearing it?"

Now I shrugged, uncertain. "Someone has to remember him," I said.

He gave me a shrewd look. "Why do you care about him so much?" he asked.

"Because nobody else does," I said, light as I could, keeping the doors barred, the dam bolstered.

"But you didn't even know him," he replied.

I took a breath and tried again. "It could have been you, Tanish," I said. "Or me, or any of us, and no one cares. That's not right. It can't be." He frowned and I redirected the conversation. "These men Morlak is trading that box to, what do they look like?"

He shrugged again. "Black fellas," he said.

My stomach turned. "Not Grappoli?" I asked, pushing the image of Mnenga's face from my mind.

He shook his head. "Could be working for them, I s'pose," he said, liking the idea. "You think there'll be a war? Fevel says it's time we gave the Grappoli what's coming to them. Says they killed some Feldeslanders last week. A crowd of Grappoli tore them to pieces. Some of the killers are friends with Mahweni right here in Bar-Selehm!"

"Fevel doesn't know what he's talking about," I said.

"Do you?" he asked, giving me a sour look. "Everyone knows you can't trust the Grappoli or the blacks."

"You work with Mahweni all the time," I said.

"Those are city blacks," he said. "The others—the Unassimilated who dress in skins and carry spears—those are the ones you have to watch out for. They aren't like us. Sell us to the Grappoli in a heart-beat if they had the chance."

The remark annoyed and unsettled me, but I didn't want to fight with him, so I changed the subject. "Who is paying for the demoli-tion?" I asked.

"Our first government contract," said Tanish proudly.

"Did they send an overseer?"

"Nope," said Tanish. "It's just us."

I frowned.

"What?" he asked, as if I were taking some of the shine off their achievement.

"Nothing," I said. "Just seems odd that they'd give you a big job when Morlak can't be here and not send someone to make sure it goes smoothly."

"Why?" said Tanish, getting irritable now. "What's the big deal? It's just a job."

"I know. I'm sorry."

"We can manage without you, you know," he blurted.

"What's that supposed to mean?" I asked. "I didn't say you couldn't do it."

He looked sulky and glanced back to the bright, weed-strewn square as if he wanted to leave.

"Hey," I pushed, nudging him and smiling. "I know you can do it. You are the most destructive hummingbird I know."

"Don't call me that," he said. "Makes me sound like a kid."

"All right," I said. "I won't."

"I should go. Fevel will be . . . I should go."

I nodded, biting back my sadness, patting him awkwardly on the shoulder as he pulled away.

I WATCHED HIM LEAVE, and the farther away he got, the stranger it all seemed. The newspaper had definitely said that the tower would come down next week, not today, so either someone had changed their mind, or the city had been deliberately misled.

Why?

The same reason that there was no official presence at a government-funded demolition, no representative from the military who had once run a historically significant base, nor any spokesperson from the Mahweni who had so wanted the tower destroyed? Bringing a tower down was a grand spectacle, but there was no press photographer to capture the moment, no one—in fact—of any kind to see anything.

Someone wants this done quietly.

I needed to get a look inside before it came down. What better place to hide something than in a building destined for demolition, one that would be left as rubble to be overgrown, a semisacred monument to an ancient and troubled past?

I waited another half hour, thinking uneasily about Mnenga, and what Tanish had said about the Mahweni, not knowing what to believe and wary of my own instincts. It was almost a relief when the boys dragged their wagon into the shade to eat, and I could break into a skulking run, careful to keep the tower between me and them. As soon as I got close, I could smell the paraffin and oil with which the timber supports had been doused, and I winced away from it, eyes watering. I tried the tower door. Locked.

Why seal a building destined for demolition?

The tower windows were little more than rifle ports and far too tight to squeeze through. But the top of the tower was open, with only a timber frame remaining of what had once been a roof. There would be a way in from there.

The tower was vertical and considerably higher than the perimeter wall, but its brickwork was no better maintained. I fished in my satchel for a chisel on a loop of cord, which I hung round my neck. I pulled my hair back and began to climb carefully, using the lintels and sills of the gun ports where I could.

It was slow going. Twice I had to stop to work my chisel into the mortar line to give me a handhold, and by the time I reached the top, my shoulders ached and my hands were unsteady from the exertion. I was rewarded with a trapdoor in the floor. Unlocked.

The boys had finished their break and were coming back across the square. Staying low, I unlatched the trap cover and folded it carefully back, revealing an ancient iron ladder set rusting into the wall below. I shinned down into a guardroom with an alcove containing a stained and fractured toilet bowl. The door, which was hanging open, gave onto a tight spiral of concrete steps, the only part of the structure not constructed from brick. I descended onto a landing with another solid door, this one locked.

There was a screen in the upper portion, not unlike the one in the police cell, but it was stuck. I worked it with my chisel but didn't want to use the hammer in case the sound carried to the boys outside. I strained at it, then tried cutting away the doorjamb around the hinges.

But it was hard work and I was tiring. Partly it was the heat which—far from being less intense in the tower's shady interior—seemed to be mounting, and I slumped against the door, trying to get my breath back, fighting the urge to cough. It was only then that I caught the acrid tang of woodsmoke on the air. The boys had set the fire.

I had minutes before the tower became unstable.

I jammed the chisel into the shutter groove, cursing, slamming the heel of my hand against it, and felt it shift a fraction. Gasping in the thickening air, I adjusted the chisel and tried again. Part of the rusted groove popped out. The shutter moved, and with three sharp blows from my hammer, I drove it open.

The room inside was bare save for a heavy wooden chair with a high back and leather straps fastened to the arms. Restraints. Sprawled against the far wall was the body of a man.

CHAPTER
23

HE WAS DEAD, AND probably had been for some time. Even through the smoke, it smelled sour in there. The corpse lay on its back, one arm twisted beneath it, the other splayed, hand open. He was black, elderly, his hair gray and unkempt, and he wore nothing but a loincloth and sandals, one of which had been kicked off. A bottle lay empty beside him. The floor was stained, and in one moist patch, something like fungus seemed to be growing pale pink tubes, delicate and foul.

I pulled my face away, tried to gasp fresh air and got only smoke, which left me wheezing and hacking.

I followed the concrete spiral down, but it was clear before I saw the flames that I would not be able to reach the door in the intense heat. The skin on my face was starting to shrink, and a wisp of hair stuck to my sweaty forearm curled and smoked. I would have to leave the way I had come in.

I ran up the stairs, past the torture cell, and up to the ladder, breaking out into the hot, dry air with a cry of relief. There was nothing to be gained now by staying hidden, and I moved to the parapet and began to wave and shout to the boys below. They had retreated from the fire and were watching from a safe distance. For a moment I feared they wouldn't hear me, but then one of them was pointing, and Tanish was jogging forward, shouting and gesticulating.

"Put it out!" I yelled. "Put the fire out!"

Tanish stopped, ran back to the building where they had been eating, and dragged out the water barrel, but he had made it only a few yards when someone stopped him. Fevel. I couldn't hear what they said, but they were arguing, and when Tanish tried to push past him, Fevel knocked him down. Two of the other boys came to help him up, but they did not let him return to the barrel. I could just see the anguish in his upturned face.

No, I thought. *They wouldn't.*

But as I stood there shouting and waving stupidly, it was increasingly clear that they would. They were going to let me burn.

Except that the tower itself, being brick and stone and concrete, would fall rather than burn. I considered climbing down the outside wall, but as I took a step toward the far parapet, something gave beneath me. One of the pit props had collapsed in the inferno, and the tower shuddered. I didn't have long. I took another step, but before my right foot had come down properly, the world shifted sideways. A terrible sound came from the base of the structure, a creaking that swelled, turning into an animal bellow, as the tower began to split.

The floor beneath my feet tipped toward the boys, and realizing I had no other option, I turned and ran down the sudden slope to the parapet and stepped up onto it as the tower began to fall. I had one foot up, one back, arms spread, like I was riding a great wave. For a moment, I seemed to hang there in the hot air, almost motionless but tipping fractionally earthward, and then I was hurtling toward the ground in a long, deadly arc that threw up dust and hunks of brick as the tower collapsed.

I timed my jump, waiting for the last possible moment, springing forward and rolling as the top of the tower broke against the square below.

The swelling roar ended in a deafening explosion and I tumbled head over heels, knees and elbows tucked tight into my body as bricks rained down around me. I felt the skin strip from my arms and legs, the impact of the debris on my back and shoulders. Eyes and mouth shut, head buried in my hands, I rolled, then I stopped, and pain boiled over my body like fire.

It took all my concentration to reach into my belt and pull the revolver out, and by the time I had rolled onto my back and raised the weapon, Fevel was almost on me.

He had a chisel in one hand, and his eyes were mad and vengeful, but he felt the black eye of the gun on his heart and he stopped as I snapped the hammer back.

For a long moment, he fought with his own survival instinct, and then, at last, he spat and took a step backwards. He turned as Tanish came running past him, slashing at him with the chisel, but the younger boy danced away and came skidding to my side.

I had not moved. Every bone and muscle seemed to cry out in agony. The fall had reopened Florihn's slashes across my face, but I was still training the gun on Fevel's retreating back, my finger curled around the trigger.

"Ang," whispered Tanish. "It's all right. You're safe now."

But I barely heard him over the furious roaring of the blood in my veins. It was a long time before I lowered the gun and got clumsily, painfully to my feet.

I leaned on Tanish, staring back to where the dust still swirled over the fractured heap of rubble that had been the tower. Fevel recovered his swagger as he neared the other boys, and then, very slowly, I limped away.

IT TOOK TANISH AND me two hours to get back to the city. It would have taken me twice that without him. My right ankle had twisted in the fall, and I could put no weight on it, but while I didn't think I had broken anything, it felt like I had been beaten head to foot, and the longer we walked, the more the aching stiffness blossomed into torment. At least we encountered no animals. We would have been easy prey for a clavtar or hyena pack, gun or no gun.

At the city walls I approached the nearest dragoon and gave him my name. "I should be in your records," I said. "I'm wanted for murder. You are going to want to find Detective Sergeant Andrews."

I said it coolly. The police had no terrors for me worse than what I had already gone through, and I felt, however misguidedly, the confidence of innocence. I had, after all, not killed Billy. Even so, my composure was unexpected, and I realized how much the last few days had changed me. Not so very long ago I would have been hesitant and tongue-tied in the presence of the authorities. Now, at least in my own head, I had some authority of my own. I had earned it.

The police response was almost comically excessive. Three armed men chained my hands and feet and bundled me into an armored carriage, watching me as if I were a wild animal, though I was mild and compliant throughout.

At the jail I was grilled by the duty officer about my relationship with Billy, and my movements the previous evening. He was openly scornful of my version of events, the "cloak and dagger nonsense" of messages and secret meetings, and particularly of my claim to have heard another man in the fog, a man I took to be Billy's killer. I told him about Morlak, but not Mnenga, though I wasn't sure why. After I had recounted my story twice, I said I would not speak again till Andrews arrived. This might have earned me a beating, but the command with which I spoke of Andrews gave the duty officer pause, and they decided to save their more physical response till my claims had been debunked.

"Two death-defying falls in as many days," said Detective Sergeant Andrews as he walked in a half hour later. "You do live on the edge, don't you, Miss Sutonga?"

The duty officer stared at him, gaping like a fish astonished to find it had leapt onto dry land.

While a nurse dressed my wounds and plied me with grilled sausages and vegetable soup, I told Andrews what I had seen, saying what they would find in the rubble of the tower. He watched in silence as I ate, then called for a uniformed officer to "ready a vehicle" for the Red Fort.

"We can discuss Billy Jennings on the way," he said.

The carriage's route took us past the bleak high railings and blank windows of Pancaris, and I had to force myself to look away.

AS THE SUN BEGAN its slow drop into the horizon over the city, I returned to the walls I had scaled only a few hours before. Sitting opposite Andrews in the police carriage, I said nothing.

Tanish had returned to Seventh Street, insisting that the gang was still his home and that it was better he returned of his own volition than be found by Fevel and the others, having turned his back on them. They might even respect him for it, and in the end, he said, their fight was with me. I had expected the gang's attempt on my life to jar Tanish out of the belligerence he had shown me before I went into the tower, but it had only increased his confusion and resentment. When I asked him to keep me informed as to anything unusual happening at the weaving shed, he gave a noncommittal grunt.

"Not betraying my friends, Ang," he said. "I'll help to keep you safe if I can, and I already told you about the box Morlak's going to trade, but I'm not turning on my own kind."

I wasn't sure what to say to that or what he meant by "kind." Lani, I supposed, though not all the gang were. Poor? Bound to work in danger with only the fear of Morlak's cruelty to keep them going? What kind of identity was that to cling to?

But they did. I had done it myself, making pride and honor out of shared misery and deprivation. It was how you lived with yourself, how you survived.

"I'm just trying to find out what happened to Berrit," I said.

"This has nothing to do with Berrit," Tanish said. "This stuff at the fort. You want it to be about Berrit because you want it to be about Morlak, but it's not."

I had nothing to say to that, so I just nodded and told him that if he ever wanted to get word to me, to speak to the newspaper girl on Winckley Street and I'd come find him.

"Bye, Ang," he said. It felt sad. Final. But I didn't know what else to say, so I let him go.

Andrews and I entered the fort through the main gate, which was surmounted by what I took to be the regimental crest: the head of a one-horn inside a laurel wreath. Two other vehicles were already there: a horse-drawn ambulance and another wagon from which two men got down with sleek, tan-colored dogs on leashes, their noses low to the ground. It took them no more than a few minutes to start barking at a particular area of the tower's shattered remains, but it was almost an hour before the policemen had painstakingly picked the rubble clean.

"There is indeed a body," said Officer Andrews, returning to me.

"I know," I said. "I told you."

"But you don't know who he is?" Andrews asked.

"You've asked me this twice," I said. I wanted to crawl into a real bed and lie very still for a long time. "No. I don't know who he was."

"An elderly Mahweni tribesman, by the looks of things. Unassimilated. He has been dead several days."

"Yes," I said. I turned at the sound of another carriage arriving at speed. The crest on the door was all too familiar. Willinghouse and Von Strahden clambered out and strode over, demanding to know what was going on. The detective moved to greet the two politicians, and I got a second to compose myself.

But only a second.

"You're hurt," remarked Von Strahden, striding toward me and turning my face into the light.

"A little bruising is all," I said, embarrassed, avoiding Willinghouse's unreadable gaze.

"We should take you to the hospital," said Von Strahden.

"I'm fine," I said. "Really."

That was, apparently, enough for Willinghouse. He turned to Andrews, all business, and I felt a prickle of annoyance.

"The officers at the gate said you'd found a body?" he said.

"Damaged in the tower's collapse," said Andrews delicately. "Yes. Broken and burned."

"Burned?" I said. "No. That's not possible. The smoke came up the tower, but the fire stayed at the bottom."

"The corpse shows signs of burning, particularly on the hands and chest," said Andrews.

"Then he was tortured," said Willinghouse.

Andrews's brows contracted, but he did not dispute the point.

"By whom?" asked Von Strahden. "The garrison hasn't been occupied for months."

"That," said Andrews, "is the good news."

"Why?"

"Because the last thing the city wants is a scandal involving the Glorious Third," said Willinghouse.

I gave Andrews a quizzical look.

"The King's Third Feldesland Infantry Regiment," he said, "is the oldest and most storied outfit in the region. Instrumental in the initial conquest and the prime defense force over the next two hundred years, a breeding ground for diplomats, civil servants, and politicians, including a few prime ministers. Benjamin Tavestock himself was a junior officer for the regiment during the Mahweni rebellion. The Glorious Third are an institution in Bar-Selehm, and their roots go long and deep. Why do you think the Red Fort was demolished on the quiet like this? A lot of people didn't want to see it come down at all: powerful people, some of them. We're going to need to keep this business with the body quiet until we have a clearer sense of what happened here. The boys in the demolition gang didn't know it was there?"

"I don't think so," I said. "My friend didn't."

"A stray herder looking for work and sleeping rough out here?" said Willinghouse. "Stole from someone, or fell in with the wrong sort?"

Von Strahden thought for a moment before reluctantly adding, "Or someone just didn't like the look of him."

"You mean the color," I said.

"Could do without that," Andrews said. "Racial tensions are high enough as it is with these rumors of land deals and the blacks working with the Grappoli to steal the Beacon. Better hope this fellow was just in the wrong place at the wrong time."

This fellow. The phrase struck a chord in my memory. Except that it hadn't been "fellow," it had been "fella."

" 'This black fella came in,' " I said.

"What?" asked Andrews.

I tried to remember the whole conversation that one word had triggered.

This black fella came in. . . .

Bessie. The maid at Macinnes's place who had hoped to settle down with poor Billy Jennings. That was what she had said. *A first,* she had said. *Just wandered in from the street, big as life!* And he hadn't been one of what the policeman had called "the city blacks," either. *One of them 'unter types from the plains. Old bloke. Scared me 'alf to death, he did. . . .*

It could have been another man. Of course it could. But it wasn't. And it suddenly seemed likely that this was also the old tribesman Mnenga was looking for. The elderly herder had come here, or he had been brought here. Which meant that there was a connection between the dead Mahweni in the tower and the luxorite dealers on Crommerty Street, possibly to Ansveld himself, and therefore to Berrit as well, a connection that—almost certainly—went through Morlak. It could be no coincidence that the gang Berrit had joined days before he died was the one employed to quietly pull down the evidence of another murder.

It also meant that Mnenga was involved, that his interest in me was not what it appeared, so that what had been a hunch solidified into something familiar, like disappointment. I told them everything and felt a thrill of vindication, even though it was mostly supposition and conjecture. Willinghouse nodded approvingly, and I fought to hide my smile.

"What?" asked Von Strahden, reading something in my face.

"One more thing," I said, covering. "Morlak has a box he's planning to trade. He has it at the weaving shed on Seventh Street, but he's looking to move it soon. I suggest you keep an eye on the building."

"Wait," said Willinghouse. "You think it's the Beacon?"

"Yes," I said.

"Then we need to go in and get it now," said Von Strahden.

"If you do you won't catch whoever set the thing up," I said.

"We'll get it out of him," said Andrews.

I shook my head. "He may not even know," I said. "Not if it goes high up."

"But we are on the edge of a major international incident," said Von Strahden. "The Beacon is the heart of the city! If we can recover it, show progress, stability—"

"Miss Sutonga is right," said Willinghouse, shaking his head. "Without proof of where the Beacon is going, the rumors about the Mahweni and the Grappoli will continue. They'll escalate. Wait till he tries to move it, and you'll learn more."

"And if we miss it?" asked Andrews.

Willinghouse turned to me. "You are sure of your contact within the gang?"

I thought of Tanish, of the way the boy's attitude to me had wavered, but I nodded. "I'll tell you when to move," I said, hoping beyond hope that I could keep my word.

Willinghouse said nothing. Once more I found myself wishing that he would show more . . . what? Pride in me? Admiration?

Don't be absurd.

Andrews kicked the dirt at his feet. "You had better make it fast," he said. "The city is on a knife edge."

Willinghouse turned to me. "Will you return to the house with me?" he asked. "Looks like you could use a decent night's sleep."

The prospect of falling into one of Willinghouse's inevitably sumptuous feather beds was impossible to resist, but I pretended to think about it before shrugging.

"I suppose so," I said, like I was doing him a favor.

CHAPTER

24

I OPENED THE DOOR to Ansveld's shop and eased myself inside, trying to look inconspicuous.

"I'll be right with you," said Ansveld Jr. He was sitting at the counter, studying a piece of luxorite under a set of smoked, folding lenses. I took the opportunity to move in close so that even if he chased me from the shop, I'd have a few yards to try to change his mind.

He finished what he was doing, snapped the velvet-lined lid on the presentation box closed, and looked up. His smile died immediately and his eyes narrowed, but he did not shout. "You!" he said. "The maid who wasn't. The woman from the opera!"

"You were there?" I said quietly.

"Of course I was there," he returned. "Everyone was there. I went to see the dowager's necklace, remember?"

"Oh, yes, I remember," I said. "You went to see if the luxorite in her necklace was the same piece the Lani boy showed your father."

He said nothing.

"And was it?" I said.

"The paper said you killed a man," he said.

"I didn't, and the police believe me," I answered. "But the man who died had wanted to tell me something. I'm trying to make sure he did not die in vain."

Ansveld considered me seriously, and I took his silence as acceptance.

"So," I continued. "The dowager's necklace. Did it contain the luxorite the Lani boy showed to your father?"

"No, but it came from the same source."

"How can you be so sure?" I asked.

"Who are you really?" he said. "The boy's mother?"

"Gods no," I said. "That's one disguise I couldn't pull off."

Which is why Kalla is at Pancaris. . . .

"But you are also not a thief, unless the police are even less competent than I thought."

I gave him a rueful smile and shook my head. "I may have snagged the occasional crust when times were hard—well, harder than usual—but no, I'm not a thief. I really do work for the Willinghouse family, but not as a maid."

"I thought as much. You are a private investigator, are you not?"

"Yes," I said.

He clapped his hands together, pleased with himself. "I knew it!" he announced to the empty shop. "And this is somehow all about the Beacon?"

"I think so," I said.

Ansveld smiled, satisfied.

I pressed my advantage. "In the days before your father died," I said, "did an elderly black man, a bush herder, come here?"

The question seemed to surprise him. He pulled a face of utter bafflement and shook his head.

I rubbed my temples, feeling the tenderness of my fall from the tower.

"Sorry," he said. "That was clearly the wrong answer."

I tried a different tack. "Am I the only Lani, other than the boy, who has been in your shop in the last few weeks?"

He screwed up his face in thought as he cast his mind back. "I can't think of any others, why?" he said. "Do you have someone in mind?"

"A gang leader by the name of Morlak," I said. "Big man. Wears his hair long and tied back. You'd know him if you saw him."

"Never been in here," he said at last and with finality.

"Or visiting any of your competitors? Mr. Macinnes, for instance?"

Again the comically furrowed brow followed by a head shake. "I'm afraid not," he said with a sigh. "Much as I would like to incriminate that old fraud across the street, I fear I can tell you nothing."

"Or Billy Jennings," I tried. "The man who died. Did he ever come in here?"

"I recognized him from his picture in the paper," said Ansveld. "I used to see him in the street from time to time, and I believe I saw him with one of the girls who works for Macinnes, but he never came in here."

Bessie.

This was getting me nowhere. I changed course. "So. The luxorite in the dowager's necklace . . ."

"Yes!" he said, slapping his hand on the counter. "The reason I think it was a sister to your young friend's piece is not just because the light was unusually bright. It was—and pay very close attention to this because it is most singular—the same *color.*" He said the last word like he was unveiling something magical, then stepping back to let me see it in all its glory.

"Is that unusual?" I asked, baffled.

"The color," he said, touching the side of his nose, "was. Very."

"I don't follow," I said.

"When I saw the boy's piece, something about it struck me not just as impressive, but as very slightly odd too. I couldn't put my finger on it at the time, but it nagged at me. So when I went to see the dowager flaunting her pendant at the opera, I went prepared."

"Prepared? How so?"

"You are familiar with these?" he said, showing me a selection of goggles and spectacles with smoked-glass lenses.

"Of course," I said. "They protect your eyes from the glare."

"In part," he said, "but they are subtly shaded to screen out different colors of light as well. Combining these lenses helps me to get a precise sense of the luxorite's color and therefore its age. Here. Try these." He handed me a pair of wire-rimmed glasses with an array of lenses and produced a tray of tiny luxorite fragments from a drawer in the counter.

"Now," he said as I scanned each piece, "luxorite when first mined blazes with a hard, white light whose heart, if properly screened, shows distinctly bluish. See?"

He flicked a couple of lenses into place, and in one of the jewels, I saw a chill blue, like summer lightning.

"As luxorite ages, the mineral's light follows the same pattern as metal taken from a hot fire. White heat gives way to yellow, then to gold and amber, then red, and finally dulls to black as the piece spends the last of its energy. This takes decades, of course. Sometimes even centuries."

I took the spectacles off because they felt strange on my nose, and considered him. He was clearly preparing another magical revelation.

"So, imagine my surprise," he said, his face full of boyish excitement. "Out swans the Dowager Lady Hamilton with her precious necklace, and I put on my special spectacles, and lo and behold, I find that at its heart, the light of her pendant—though seeming brilliant and as white as any luxorite I have ever seen—is very slightly—" he paused dramatically, "—*green*."

I stared at him. "Are you sure?" I asked.

"On my father's grave," he said. "I have never seen its like before except in the hands of that Lani boy."

"What does this mean?" I asked.

"I do not know," he said, "but it is all very mysterious and very exciting." His eyes got wide, and he grinned broad and mad as a doll.

"You think your father made the same discovery?"

His smiled faded. "I do," he said. "I think he realized he had seen something unique and tried to find where the boy had gotten it."

"You think that is why the dowager's necklace was stolen?" I asked. "Because it was unique?"

"Or because the thief didn't want anyone to see just how unique it was, yes," he said. "Thievery," he added wonderingly. "It is everywhere these days. It did not use to be so. I had one—a thief, I mean—right here in the shop two days ago. And he didn't look the type at all. A white gentleman in a frock coat. Very civilized."

"And he stole from you?"

"While I was helping another customer," he said, nodding.

"Did you report it?"

"I did not," he said. "Because what he stole was not mine to begin with." He peered past me toward where I had been standing when I visited with Dahria, so that I turned and my eyes fell on an empty umbrella stand.

"The cane," I said.

"You remembered!" he exclaimed, pleased.

"A cane with a silver top," I said.

"Not just a cane, as it turned out," he said. "A sword stick. I took the liberty of looking at it more closely after you had gone."

A sword stick.

I heard it again, the slight metallic tapping between footfalls in the fog, the silken swish of steel coming out of a sheath, and now I saw the wound in Billy's chest. . . .

I pictured the cane that had been in the umbrella stand, and something clicked into place like the tumbler of a lock. "It had a design on the handle," I said. "An emblem containing the head of a one-horn," I said.

"I did a little research, you know," said Ansveld Jr., "and guess what I found out? That little emblem is actually the badge of—"

"The Glorious Third," I said. "The King's Third Feldesland Infantry Regiment."

"Whose headquarters were, until very recently—" said Ansveld.

"In the Old Red Fort," I concluded.

Another lock tumbler snapped into place. This was what Billy had seen, or part of it: someone from the Glorious Third in Ansveld's shop. And he had known this was strange or important.

"The man who took it," I said. "You said he was white, a gentleman?"

"Yes."

"But you had never seen him before?"

"Never."

"Could you describe him? How old would you say he was?"

"Well," said Ansveld Jr, "I didn't really get a good look at him. Sixty, perhaps, but virile. The shop was unusually busy that day."

"And you were helping another customer," I said.

"Exactly."

"And did that customer make a purchase?"

"No. He browsed some illuminated clock faces—" he began, and then his eyes grew wide once more. "Oh, I see. You think the customer was a ruse to keep me busy while his accomplice stole the cane. Seems a lot of trouble to go to just to recover a sword stick."

"Yes," I said, thinking of the wound in Billy's chest. "It does. This customer was also an older gentleman?"

"Oh no," said Ansveld. "He was quite—what's the word?—strapping. Yes. Perhaps thirty. Athletic. A virile young black man with a pale scar just above one eye. An old cut."

"He was black?" I said, taken off guard.

"It's not unusual," said Ansveld, very slightly defensive. "We do not discriminate here."

"Not if they can pay," I said.

Ansveld's face clouded with indignation, but I cut in before he could say anything.

"I'm sorry," I said. "I didn't mean that to sound . . . Of course you don't discriminate, and of course your customers—all your customers—have to be able to pay. Luxorite is an expensive commodity."

Ansveld's hauteur had drained a little, but he was still standing on his dignity. "My father was not an easy man," he said. "Very strict in his ways. Conservative. But he did not believe in the old Feldesland lie about the hierarchy of peoples, and he had some feeling for what was taken from the Mahweni when our ancestors came here. In his own small way, he did what he could to restore balance, and in this, at least, I try to emulate him."

"Of course," I said. "I apologize. This is not my world, Mr. Ansveld," I said, gesturing around the shop, with its beautiful, elegant merchandise, sparkling in its own light. "I am in it because it is my job to be so. But I am not *of* it, and at times it seems quite . . ."

"Hostile?"

"Let's say foreign," I said with a half smile.

He considered me, then conceded the point. "I can see how it would," he said.

"So this young Mahweni," I said, regrouping. "You called him strapping."

"Athletic," he said thoughtfully, and it struck me that he had a connoisseur's eye for more than luxorite. "But it was more than that. He had a certain bearing, a poise . . ."

"Military?" I asked.

The word struck him with the force of inspiration. "Exactly!" he said.

"And the white man?"

Ansveld wobbled his head uncertainly. "Perhaps," he said. "I really didn't get a good look at him, and his movement was less—" Something dawned in his face. "He had a limp! I had forgotten, but I'm sure of it. Not too pronounced, but a kind of stiffness down one side that made him shuffle. I remember wondering if he might break something."

"One more question," I said.

Ansveld smiled, pleased to show how useful he could be.

"When did the cane appear?" I asked.

"I didn't see the person who brought it," said Ansveld Jr. "It wasn't there the day my father went to see the Lani boy, I'd swear to it, and I closed the shop that night."

"So someone brought it the following day?" I asked. "The day your father died."

"Well, that's the odd thing," said Ansveld, his face contorted with the effort of remembering. "I'd swear it was already there. I opened the shop before I heard about my father's death, and I remember seeing it there in the umbrella stand. But that would mean someone put it there overnight, or the previous evening after I had closed up. Whoever it was must have broken in."

"And left his cane in an umbrella stand?" I said doubtfully. "That doesn't sound right. Was there sign of forced entry?"

"None."

"Was there anything else unusual when you opened the shop that morning?"

"Cigar ash," said Ansveld, staring at nothing and clearly unnerved. "Over there beside that chair. I spoke to the maid about it, but she said my father had told her not to bother cleaning the shop that evening."

"Was that unusual?"

"Yes."

"And you did not mention this to the police?"

"I was told my father had died by his own hand. There was no reason to think . . . But, now . . ." His face, which had been clouded by doubt, became suddenly focused and intense. "You think he was killed by someone. That's why you are here asking questions. You think he met with someone here the night before he died, someone who left his cane behind, and that that person typed a suicide note on that infernal machine of his, and then killed him. *Murdered* him." He sat down abruptly, face slack as his mind put the pieces together.

"Yes," I said. "I do. And that person has killed others as well. Billy

Jennings was the most recent, but not the youngest. That was the boy called Berrit, who also met your father. There was an old Mahweni as well, though that never made the papers. And me," I added. "He tried to kill me the night he got Billy, and I am certain that he is going to try again."

CHAPTER
25

THE DUTY OFFICER TOLD me—somewhat skeptically—that I would find Sergeant Andrews near Szenga Square, where a pair of protests had broken out. One of the protests was largely white and in carnival mood, singing raucous patriotic songs, waving flags, and burning an effigy of the Grappoli king on a bonfire outside their empty embassy. The other was quieter, angrier, a swelling horde of black men and women who chanted antiwar and antigovernment slogans. Mnenga may have been with them, but I couldn't see him, and as soon as Andrews caught sight of me, he shepherded me around the corner.

I thought of Kalla, wondering how she would weather whatever turmoil was coming to the city, and reminded myself that she would fare no worse for being at Pancaris.

Almost certainly better.

I cared about the child, but I could not care for her. For all the dourness of the orphanage, she was safe there, and I was free to do my job, my duty to my friends and the city. Without her, my mind was clearer, like gazing through clear glass into a blue, empty sky.

I watched the Mahweni demonstrators. You could almost taste their fury and frustration. It was like some great penned beast that had been starved and tormented for years, outrage and injustice heaped on it day after day, till it exploded with lethal, snapping fury. It had just been a matter of when. Mounted dragoons had been called in to Acacia Road, and they waited there, rank upon silent rank, steaming in the heat.

Andrews gave them a long look.

"Will they be sent in?" I asked.

"Let's hope not," he answered, avoiding my eyes.

MACINNES'S FACE FELL THE moment I walked in, and that was before he saw the uniformed policemen and realized who Andrews was. He tried for righteous indignation first, exclaiming on the barbarism of storming into a respectable place of business in ways that might tarnish his reputation, but Andrews blew through that as if it were steam from a kettle.

"I am Detective Sergeant Andrews of the Bar-Selehm police department," he said. "And you are Elmsly Macinnes, shined-up lowlife."

"I have always been most cooperative with our fine friends in law enforcement," said Macinnes. "I see no reason for besmirching my good name."

"Your good name," said Andrews, "smells like what comes out the back end of a warthog."

"I don't have to stand here and listen to you casting aspersions on—"

"In fact," said Andrews, "that's exactly what you have to do. So. Mr. Macinnes, are you aware that trading in stolen luxorite is a crime punishable with a thousand-pound fine and three years in prison?"

"I did, actually," said Macinnes at his most cherubic, "though I can't image why you think that might pertain to me. You ought to be protecting the likes of me from looters."

"Is that right?" said Andrews. His three uniformed officers had eased themselves around the store, and they projected an aura of regimented menace, like dogs ready to break the leash. One of them, truncheon already out, was watching the bullish security guard closely, and though the guard was both imposing and armed, he looked very unsure of his role. "Then perhaps," Andrews continued, "you would like to explain why the Dowager Lady Hamilton told me not one hour ago that she purchased a luxorite pendant with some very shaky-looking documentation from this very establishment."

Macinnes must have considered his options earlier. He was the kind of man who kept his ear close to the ground, and news of what happened at the opera house had surely reached him. He had been expecting us.

"I did indeed sell the good lady a piece of fine jewelry," said Macinnes evenly, "but I am shocked to hear that you think the paperwork not entirely in order. I assure you that when I acquired the piece—"

"Who from?" Andrews cut in.

"What? Well, I'm not sure I can remember. It was so long ago—"

"No," I interjected. "It wasn't. The stone was new, but judging by what you have in this case, the setting wasn't. You mounted it yourself, yes?"

"I'm sorry," he said, stiffening. "I don't believe I've seen your badge."

"Miss Sutonga is a consultant," said Andrews, daring him to argue. "She is assisting the police with their inquiries."

"Sutonga?" he echoed. "You're the one what did for young Billy Jennings!"

"Miss Sutonga has been cleared of those charges," said Andrews.

"Did you get the stone from a Lani boy?" I pressed.

"A Lani boy?" he repeated, still hostile.

It was the first time since we had come in that he seemed off script. He looked surprised, confused even, as if he might have misheard.

"Did you get the luxorite from a Lani boy?" I pressed.

"No," he said.

"Then who?" Andrews demanded.

"I have many associates—" Macinnes began, acting again.

"Three years in prison," said Andrews, "and a thousand-pound fine. Both of which I can make go away if you are as cooperative as you say you are."

The color drained from Macinnes's cheeks. He opened his mouth to protest, but Andrews just stared him down. No one else in the shop made a sound.

"How do I know you'll be as good as your word?" he ventured. "If I had, indeed, anything less than strictly legal to report, which I'm not saying I have."

"You don't," said Andrews. "But I'll tell you this. I don't actually care about tracking stolen goods. This is a murder inquiry."

Macinnes looked taken aback, but before he could say anything, a door into the rear of the shop opened and a woman came in.

It was Bessie.

She had been about to speak to Macinnes, but hesitated when she took in the sight of the police. Then she noticed me.

Her face flushed, her eyes—already red rimmed from crying— shone, and she took two decisive steps toward me before anyone could stop her. She slapped me hard across the face, and though I turned fractionally, I did not try to evade the blow.

One of the officers seized her from behind before she could strike me again, and for a moment she struggled before sagging into their arms, face averted, sobbing.

Macinnes looked embarrassed, and Andrews merely turned his eyes down. Through my confused horror I felt an urge to go to her, to whisper my apologies, but this was not the time. It probably never would be.

"Perhaps we should step outside," said Andrews, motioning Macinnes toward the door.

We moved into the street, and the terrible sound of Bessie's furious grieving was lost to us. It felt like an evasion, and for what felt like a very long time I stared off down the road, seeing nothing.

"I got it from this black fella," Macinnes said. "The dowager's pendant. I'd never seen him before. Hand to god. He just came in and showed me what he had."

"He wanted you to sell it for him?" asked Andrews.

"Kind of," said Macinnes.

"What does that mean?"

"He wanted to know what it was worth, how much I could get for it, how much I thought I could sell if he brought more."

"He said he had more?"

Macinnes nodded. "Showed me another piece about the same size and shape," he said, "but said he could get more."

"Did he say where he had gotten it from?"

"I asked, but he wouldn't tell me. Said he would bring me more and we would talk then. Was supposed to be here three nights ago with more merchandise. I waited up, but he never showed. That's all I know. Certainly nothing about no murder."

"This black man," Andrews said. "Young or old? Local or Unassimilated?"

"Old," said Macinnes, relieved to be able to answer something definitively. "And not local. Tribal herder type, by the look of him. Didn't speak Feldish too good either."

"Name?" asked Andrews.

"Didn't give one. Said he'd find me."

"And he said nothing about where he had come from?" asked the detective.

"Nothing. And, to be honest, he seemed a bit, well, not entirely right in the head. Looked like he'd been out in the sun too long. Even his hands were burned up."

"Wait," I said, speaking for the first time since we had fled from Bessie's awful sorrow. "His hands were burned when he came to see you?"

"On the insides, yes. Blistered and pink. None too steady on his feet either."

"Did he visit any of your neighbors?" Andrews asked.

"He got thrown out of a couple places," said Macinnes. "Saw it myself. Not all my competitors have my eye for a bargain."

"Or your flexible ethics," said Andrews.

Macinnes scowled but said nothing.

"Did he go in there?" I asked, nodding across the street.

"To Ansveld's?" said Macinnes. "That he did."

"And was thrown out?"

"Not so far as I saw," said Macinnes, grinning now. "Was in there at least a half hour, then came out and wandered off down the street. I wouldn't be surprised to find that the high-and-mighty Mr. Ansveld, who thought he was too good to walk on the same cobbles as the likes of yours truly, made a little purchase that day."

"LET ME GO IN by myself," I said to Andrews.

"This is a police matter, Miss Sutonga," said the detective. "I'm letting you tag along. That's all."

"I was talking to him earlier," I said. "We don't want to alarm him."

" 'We'?" said Andrews, lowering his voice and turning his shoulder so that the uniforms wouldn't be able to see his face. "There is no 'we.' I represent the police. You—"

"Have helped."

"That may be true," said Andrews. "But you have also been, shall we say, an instigator. Trouble follows you like weancats after a wounded gazelle."

"Just give me a minute alone with him," I said. "If he doesn't tell me what we need to know, you can question him."

"And if he lies?"

"I'll know," I said.

"Really! And how does that work exactly?" said Andrews, his eyes starting to bulge.

"I'm a good judge of people. Of their moods," I said.

"Are you getting anything right now?" said Andrews.

I gave him a wan smile.

"Fine," he said. "One minute, then we come in."

I turned, but he stopped me, and there was something different in his eyes that was almost compassionate. "Are you all right?" he asked. He was talking about Bessie.

"Fine," I said.

"It wasn't your fault, you know," he said. "Billy Jennings, I mean."

"I know," I said, only half believing it. "Make sure she gets this, will you?" I said, handing him Billy's two purses.

ANSVELD JR.'S EYES LIT up as I stepped in. "I see the police paid a visit to the honorable Mr. Macinnes," he said, not bothering to contain his glee. "What has the little scamp been up to this time?"

"They are coming here next," I said.

His smile stalled, as much at my manner as at my words. "Here? Why?"

"Macinnes had dealings with an elderly black man," I said, "an Unassimilated herder who came offering undocumented luxorite for sale. Macinnes sold one of his pieces to Dowager Hamilton. But the man also came here and had another stone."

"You already asked me about this, and I told you I didn't know what you were talking about."

"I know," I said, "and I believe you. But it seems certain that the Mahweni herder did come here and spoke to your father."

"My father would not have bought from him. An undocumented piece is a stolen piece. Simple as that." He thought for a moment. "You think the boy got the piece from the herder?"

"Not directly," I said, "but yes. When you first mentioned the boy, you said his fingers were burned. Is that right?"

He blinked, casting his mind back, then nodded. "A little, yes," he said. "Why? Is that important?"

"I'm not sure," I said honestly. "Luxorite can be broken up, right? Cut like diamonds?"

"Of course."

"So one way to disguise stolen stones would be to recut them into new shapes?"

"Yes."

"And does that process change the quality of the light that the stone produces?"

"It can," said Ansveld Jr. "At the microscopic level, the stone is made up of crystals which are at their brightest when they are first cut. Over time, they dim. Nothing you do to the stone can reverse that process, but recutting the stone will rejuvenate it, though—of course—at the expense of its size."

"Might it alter the color of the core light?" I asked. "From blue to green, say?"

Ansveld Jr. shook his head.

"Nothing can change the essential nature of the mineral," he said.

I nodded, feeling disappointed, conscious of Andrews waiting outside. "And your father didn't speak to you about his meeting with the old man?" I asked.

"I was away on business in Thremsburg until two days before he died," said Ansveld. "We barely talked."

"Who might he have spoken to?" I asked. "If he thought there was something strange going on involving the illegal trade of luxorite."

"The police, I suppose." He shrugged. "My father was not what you would call the talkative type."

"And if it was a delicate matter? One that had larger implications for the industry?"

Ansveld was shaking his head, but then his features brightened. "He might talk to Archie," he said. "If it was a matter of trade interests or something. They have known each other for years."

"Archie?"

"Sorry"—he grinned—"Archibald Mandel. Secretary for Trade and Industry. All very respectable. Used to be a colonel in the army. Technically, I believe he was still in charge of the Red Fort until a few months ago."

I stared at him. Another tumbler of the lock turned over.

CHAPTER

26

I DID NOT TELL Andrews or Willinghouse about the link between Ansveld, Mandel, and the Glorious Third. I probably should have done, but I didn't, because I didn't know who I could trust. Mandel was a powerful man.

And I wanted to act.

I didn't want instincts and possibilities, but facts. If there was a hard link between Mandel and the dead Mahweni herder, I planned to find it and hand it to Willinghouse, confident that it was watertight.

That night I did not go to the Drowning or to the temple grounds, though I guessed that Mnenga would be there, waiting for me. Instead I curled up in my blankets above the Martel Court clock, trying to keep my mind from turning over the questions in my head or from noticing the slightly sour odor of spilled milk.

THE NEXT MORNING, I bought spiced meat and vegetable pasties with Alawi juice for Sarah and me, and we sat in Ruetta Park, watching doves and gray ibis squabble over crumbs.

"Where can I find out about the Glorious Third?" I asked.

Sarah gave me a cautious look. "What do you want to know?" she asked.

"Personnel," I said. "Current and recently discharged."

"Some of that would make the papers," said Sarah. "Officers, war heroes, men who go on to become politicians or public servants. But the list would be incomplete. You might be better in the regimental museum."

I raised a quizzical eyebrow.

"There's always a regimental museum," she said. "Usually in a castle or training facility."

"And for the Glorious Third?"

"It was at the Old Red Fort," said Sarah, gazing through the trees toward the minarets of Old Town, "but it was dismantled when the garrison moved out. It is currently in storage facilities at the public library pending the identification of a suitable future home. It is not, at this time, open to the general public, and all correspondence concerning requests to view materials should be addressed to the office of Colonel Archibald Mandel, Secretary of Trade."

I stared at her, unnerved as before by the command of her recall and the way it seemed to shelve her personality as it worked. She blinked and frowned, as if just now processing what she had said.

"As Secretary of Trade," I said, "would Mandel know Willinghouse?"

"For sure," said Sarah, "though they are on opposite sides of the aisle. They may not be friends, but they work in the same area. What?"

I shrugged.

"Willinghouse has never mentioned him," I said.

"Should he have?"

"Probably not," I conceded. "But then there's a lot of things he hasn't mentioned."

"Is he just naturally taciturn?" asked Sarah. "One of the strong, silent types?"

I gave her a sharp look. She was grinning at me.

"He's my employer," I said. "I don't spend much time thinking about his personality."

"Oh," she answered, still grinning. "I see."

I blinked, pushing away the thought of whatever she was implying. For a moment, I felt a strange and swelling sense of vertigo, as if

I had put a foot wrong and was a heartbeat away from falling off a tall chimney.

"Does Willinghouse have ties to the Glorious Third?" I asked, my face carefully neutral.

"Not that I ever heard," she answered. "And if he had a military background, I doubt it would be with them."

A flicker of something in her manner caught my attention. "Why?" I asked.

"You said he's mixed, right? Racially, I mean."

"His grandmother is Lani," I said, "though you might not know that to look at him. Does it make a difference?"

"To the Glorious Third? I'd say so."

I gave her a quizzical look.

She munched on her pasty for a moment, then shrugged. "Every Feldesland regiment was racially integrated within forty years of the Settlement War."

"So?"

"Not the Glorious Third," she said. "It took them another one hundred and fifty, and when they did, it was through the creation of a *colored* company—Lani and Mahweni—that was kept separate from the rest of the regiment. Effectively, they were a separate unit created to appease the tribal council and the likes of your boss man's father."

"Willinghouse?"

"Willinghouse senior, yes. Led the charge to break up the region's last whites-only regiment after reports of racially motivated beatings and imprisonments during citywide police actions."

There it was again, that sense of the girl accessing some unthinking storage region of her brain. But it was different this time. Her voice was edged with bitterness.

"This was all in the papers?" I said.

She shook her head. "Bits of it, cleaned and polished for polite society reading, perhaps, but the guts of it, no."

"So how do you—?"

"My uncle was one of the first enlisted into the *colored* unit," she said, framing the word in a way both snide and a little sad. "Thought he was doing his part for Bar-Selehm's race relations."

"And?"

"He wouldn't talk about it," she said. "Equal parts discretion, pride, and fear, I'd say. But I'll tell you this: they made his life a misery. I don't know the details. I think my mum knew more, but she wouldn't say anything."

"Could I talk to him?" I asked.

"You got some special Lani way of crossing over the River of Souls for a cup of chai and a chat?" she asked.

"He's dead?"

"Two years now," she said. "Took a head wound during—wait for it—peacekeeping operations during a Mahweni protest over food prices. One of his own people threw a paving stone at him. Didn't seem bad at the time. Had it all bandaged up, and he was walking around. Making jokes about it. Two days later, he collapsed. Never regained consciousness."

"I'm sorry," I said.

"To the stars we are as flies, and they do not note our fall," she intoned, one of the bleaker Mahweni phrases. She smiled mirthlessly and turned to watch a vervet monkey squabbling with the ibis. "Well," she concluded, "this was cheerful."

I grinned. "Has anyone ever written about it?" I asked.

"Like a newspaper piece?" she asked. "No. Some things are still too hot to touch."

"For some people, perhaps," I said. "Maybe one day, you could do it."

"When I'm living off my column inches instead of how many papers I can flog?" she said, unable to keep the grin out of her face.

"Why not?"

"Well, the *Bar-Selehm Standard* isn't the Glorious Third," said Sarah, "but you won't find many of my color—or yours, for that matter—turning in stories to delight and inform our ever-expanding readership. One day, perhaps, if we survive whatever the Grappoli have in store for us."

"You think there might be war?"

"Wars have been fought over less," she said. "I think the disappearance of the Beacon is unlike any other kind of theft we've ever experienced. It's like our heart. And it's spectacularly valuable, which makes things dangerous. Whenever you have an international dispute over something valuable, things get dangerous. But in this case, you've also got a potential war over a commodity that most of the people who will do the actual fighting could never afford."

People like her father, she meant, and all the other Mahweni who would be conscripted to protect the Crommerty Street merchants with their NO COLOREDS signs.

"Fight for Bar-Selehm? Sure," she said. "For liberty, for principle. But for luxorite and those who trade it? I think we'd tear ourselves to pieces long before a shot was fired at the Grappoli."

I stared at her, registering for the first time the depths of our divisions and the peril Willinghouse had glimpsed on the horizon, barreling toward us like a rogue bull elephant.

"I suggest you find that Beacon," she said. "And fast."

"I think I know where it is," I said, "but I don't know who paid to get it. What if it really is the Grappoli?"

"Then run," she said grimly. "And don't stop till you reach people who have never heard of luxorite or Bar-Selehm."

"Agreed," I said. "Now, how do I get into the library's storage facilities?"

"That," she said, getting to her feet and brushing crumbs from her dress so that one of the nearby ibis came strutting over, "is your department. Thanks for the pasty."

* * *

MNENGA SMILED WHEN HE saw me climbing up through the cemetery. He wanted to talk, and brandished the little milk bottles with the rubber teats as if they were a special prize I had won. He started telling me about a dream he had had, in which I was standing down by the river like some water spirit risen from the depths—

I was rude. Brusque, at very least, and I caught the hurt in his eyes, so that I wondered for a moment if my suspicions about him were mistaken. But in one respect at least, it was too late.

"I don't have the baby," I said. "That's what I came to say. I left it at an orphanage." I had forced myself not to call her Kalla, as if that would make me seem more sure of my actions.

Mnenga looked stung, his big black eyes wide with shock, as if I had slapped him. "Orphanage?" he repeated.

"It's a place where you take children, who . . . ," I began, angry that I was having to explain myself. "It doesn't matter. It's not my business anymore."

"Anglet . . . ," he said, taking my hand, but I cut him off.

"I'm sorry," I said. "I have to go."

"Yes," he said, letting go of my hand with slow deliberation as if he were releasing a bird. "I understand."

He didn't, of course. How could he? But I believed that he wanted me to feel better about the terrible thing I had done, and in that moment it felt like the kindest thing anyone had said to me in a long time.

Without thinking, I kissed him quickly on the cheek. His disappointed smile turned into something else entirely.

I fled, feeling guilty and harried.

As I walked, those feelings swelled till they seemed to trail behind me like the great anchor chains wrapped around the massive cleats of the dockside. I tried to shake them off, but the more I struggled, the tighter they became, so that in spite of my haste, I had to pause and be still.

I didn't know why Mnenga's care for me bothered me so much. I had liked him. I really had. And had trusted him, which was rare for me and exquisite as the ruby-petaled sunset flowers that sometimes grow from the fractured bricks atop Bar-Selehm's tallest chimneys. But I didn't trust him now. He was altogether too convenient, too supportive, too quick with his dreams and his kindness. They couldn't be real, and if they were, I did not deserve them.

I began walking again, wondering about Sarah's teasing hints so that for a moment I saw in my mind's eye Willinghouse watching me shrewdly with his sharp green eyes.

THE BAR-SELEHM PUBLIC LIBRARY was one of the city's gems, a domed and colonnaded monument to egalitarian principles the region remembered only partially. It had wide doors, and though from time to time, powerful people had tried to make them narrow, they had survived the attempt, rooted as they were in what had once been so obviously right that they had come to stand for both progress and tradition. It was, perhaps, the only place in the city where you might see whites, blacks, and Lani, irrespective of class or gender, in the same room.

They knew me in the library. Vestris had gotten me my first library card when I was seven, and my record was immaculate. No lost books. No fines. Nothing overdue. It was amazing how disciplined you could be when you knew that there was no one to bail you out of trouble. But my addiction was to novels, not history, and certainly not military records. I spent a long moment studying an unhelpful floor plan and then scanned for someone familiar.

Miss Fischer was an elderly white lady who had worked there longer than I could remember. She was thin, austere-looking, her hair in a tight silver bun, her eyes peering over gold-rimmed reading glasses that she wore on a chain around her neck. Her dress was vaguely funereal, and she was the kind of person you could not imagine anywhere but inside the library's strictly maintained silence. She watched my approach with the stillness of a heron in the reeds where frogs abounded.

"Good morning," I said.

"Miss Sutonga," said Miss Fischer, taking in my slashed and bruised face, "so nice to see you are out of jail." She said it without inflection, and I colored under her fixed gaze.

"You saw the paper," I said. "They got the wrong end of the stick."

"It would not be the first time," said the librarian. "I assume you have come to read rather than practice your climbing."

"Yes, Miss Fischer," I said.

"And you were looking for a recommendation?"

"Actually," I said, "I am looking for two things. First, where can I see details of recent real estate transactions?"

The heron stirred fractionally, as if something unexpected had swum into view. "We have listings of house sales by county—" she began, but I cut her off.

"I was thinking more of land outside the city," I said.

The Mahweni didn't want to go to war with the Grappoli, I reasoned, but that wasn't all they were protesting. There were rumors of land deals, ancestral territory sold off to the highest bidder. But sold off to who? And was the Beacon somehow a factor in the trade? Were the Grappoli? I had been treating all these things as separate issues, but what if they weren't? What if this was finally about something ordinary but important: something that fell squarely under the control of Colonel Archibald Mandel, Secretary of Trade? What if the Beacon was the center of something much larger, something people were prepared not just to commit murder over, but which would drive us to war and annihilation?

Again, Miss Fischer's movement was fractional, a contracting of her eyebrows. She was intrigued but would not dream of asking.

"Fourth floor," she said. "Cartography. What some of our less erudite visitors call 'the map room.' The Regional Transactions card catalog there cross lists sales by date and region."

"Thank you," I said. "You have been most helpful."

"It is the nature of my job, Miss Sutonga, if not my personality. Is there any other assistance I can offer?"

"I'll need to look at regimental memorabilia as well," I said. "But I'll cross that bridge when I come to it."

Miss Fischer maintained her level stare. "So long as crossing bridges doesn't lead to you scaling the masonry or falling through the ceiling," she said.

"You can't believe everything you read, Miss Fischer," I said.

"Yes, thank you for that," she answered. "Being a librarian, I had no idea that print was not always reliable. Do come back if you find you need books on flower arranging or how to assemble a steam engine, won't you? Your interests have become so diverse of late."

It was, I think, as close to a joke as Miss Fischer ever came, and I shot her a quick, if slightly abashed, smile before heading upstairs.

I HAD NEVER BEEN on the fourth floor. It smelled different from the books I was used to, though perhaps that was some kind of olfactory hallucination brought on by the places the room evoked. There were racks of rolled-up charts in tubes bound with ribbon, and high ceiling hangers of vast maps drawn on parchment, vellum, and leather. It made me think of standing down by the docks and watching the ships bound for strange and foreign parts.

I studied the various maps and associated deeds and bills of sale, monitoring the way the borders fluctuated by date. Those shifting dotted lines told a tale of steady conquest, a military snatching beginning quickly and dramatically, then turning into the slow rolling sprawl of the last century and a half. The Mahweni territory shrank and pushed into the dry west under the gaze of the watchful Grappoli, while Bar-Selehm swelled like a gorging leech. I saw the Lani's token independence from the whites who had brought them from their homeland dry up entirely as they became absorbed by the city, and the fracturing of the old Mahweni kingdoms as some tribes assimilated, and others did not.

And then, about forty years ago, it all stopped. The borders solidified, the military incursions and rebellions evaporated as diplomacy, politics, and institutionalized tolerance became the watchwords of the day. Unrest persisted in pockets, and there were occasional demonstrations that turned into riots and police actions, but for the most part the maps grew quiet, even the restless and expanding city growing sleepy with all it had consumed.

But then, a week ago, something had happened. In fact, it looked like *somethings*, since all the trades were separate and apparently unconnected, but the coincidences could not be ignored, though the map refused to explain them. This was a single event. It had to be. But, I thought, as I hastily scribbled down some notes and rough charts, the sales made no sense.

One was a patch of lush mudflat on the edge of one of the river's tributaries, while another was a square of rocky crag in the mountains overlooking the city. One raggedly shaped parcel included a piece of coastline, while another was an arid bit of semidesert. There were eight deals in all, totaling no more than a hundred square miles, scattered around the land to the north and west of the city, none of them connecting, all of them traded within the last week by the Mahweni council to an independent development company calling itself Future Holdings. The deals were all signed by the man Mnenga had dismissed as a profiteer, Farrstanga Sohwetti, head of the tribal council.

I was on the brink of a realization. I could feel it. But I did not know what it would be and knew that to find it I needed to learn more about the Glorious Third. I wasn't sure why, but the prospect frightened me.

CHAPTER
27

THE LIBRARY'S BASEMENT WAS a warren of narrow corridors between floor-to-ceiling cages. The silence was oppressive, so that my footsteps on the varnished hardwood made me feel clumsy and obvious, but as I neared the storage hold for the Glorious Third, I heard something beyond my own movement: the grunting of incautious exertion and the dull thud of something falling. There was a muttered curse, and then what sounded like the shuffling of papers.

I moved quickly and, rounding the corner, saw a man with his back to me, bent at the waist and muttering irritably. He was black, and broad shouldered. On the opposite wall of the cage where he was working was a navy blue jacket trimmed with gold and crimson. A soldier's jacket.

I straightened up, ignoring the ache of my battered back and shoulders as I took on the stance of a corseted lady. "Excuse me," I said.

He turned hurriedly, startled, dropping some of the papers he had gathered into his arms, and struggled to his feet. "Yes?" he said, looking me up and down, his gaze lingering on my bruised face. "Can I help you with something?"

He had a tiny scar above his right eye.

"I'm sorry," I said, all bashful smiles and a voice I had borrowed as best I could from Dahria. "I realize you are not employed here, but I wonder if you might be of assistance."

He looked momentarily puzzled by the juxtaposition of my aristocratic Feldish and my Lani appearance, then recovered something of his gallantry. "If I can," he said.

"That's sweet of you," I replied, dropping my eyes and pressing my hands together at my waist girlishly. "I'm looking for the storage records of the Glorious Third."

He blinked and smiled, albeit a slightly baffled smile, and said, "You've found them. They're here. But they aren't open to the public at the moment, I'm afraid."

"Oh, that is a nuisance," I said with a petulant scowl. "Not sure what I'm going to do now."

"What is it exactly that you were hoping to find?" he asked.

I put my hands to my face. "It's my senior project!" I exclaimed.

"Your . . . ?"

"Senior project!" I shot back, as if it should be obvious, my voice rising and developing an emotional crack.

"You're in school?" he asked, unable to keep the surprise out of his voice.

"Clock Street Girls'," I said, dropping the name of one of the city's most exclusive preparatory schools as if it were an old apple core.

"Oh," he managed. "I didn't realize they took . . ." He blundered to a halt, and I gave him a sharp look.

"I'm adopted," I said crisply. "Not that it's any of your business."

"I'm sorry," he said, cowed. "I didn't mean to suggest—"

I pressed my advantage. "We're supposed to be sewing banners in support of local institutions for the Settlement Day parade," I said with earnest hauteur. It was amazing how easily the words came when I wasn't being myself. "I was assigned the Glorious Third by Miss Foster—who is an absolute beast to her pupils, I don't mind saying—but she flatly refuses to help, and when I told her the museum was gone, she told me to 'use my resourcefulness,' and frankly, I'm not sure I have any, and now the deadline for our research is almost here and I have nothing to show for it, and Miss Foster will report me to my parents, who have devoted every penny they can spare to making sure I get a good education so that I can be a useful member of society, especially if I can't find a suitable husband, but who would marry a Lani girl who failed out of prep school . . .?"

This may have been the longest sentence I have ever uttered, and as it wended its way toward its strangled ending, it got higher, shriller, more desperate, so that the poor soldier looked positively alarmed, saying, "There, there," and, "I have a spare moment. Let's see what we can do."

I apologized for my shameful outburst, thanked him for indulging my weakness, and joined him in the little storage carrel. He clearly had no idea what to make of this strange young woman who looked so unlike the things she was saying and how she was saying them, but he didn't dare offend me in case it was all true. On the battlefield, he would be sure of his authority, but in here, he was as out of place as I was.

As he dutifully showed me racks of medals won in old campaigns, I wrestled with how to ask a Mahweni why he was serving in a famously white regiment, then realized that embarrassment about such things was my old Lani self speaking. Society ladies had no such compunction.

"I had no idea there were blacks in the King's Third," I said flatly. "It must be terribly exciting for you."

He seemed caught off guard again, as if I had revealed that I outranked him. "Yes," he said. "It is. It's an honor to be a member of such a fine old regiment."

"And your family don't mind?" I asked, unabashed.

"Miss?"

"I mean, the Glorious Third have fought your people for a long time," I said matter-of-factly.

"In the past," he said, his jaw tight. "That is true. But I am a citizen of Bar-Selehm. So are my parents. The regiment defends the city against threats foreign and domestic, and I am proud to serve."

"Are there many black members of the regiment?"

"I am Corporal Emtezu, commander of a twenty-five-man company," he said, his polite smile rigid.

"Really?" I exclaimed, willfully missing the tension. "How extraordinary. I had no idea. And do the black soldiers perform the same duties as the other men, or are they more like servants and cooks?"

This time his hesitation, and the way his knuckles blanched on the edges of the box he was holding, seemed impossible to ignore, but I held his eyes, my chin tipped up.

"The Mahweni company," he replied carefully, "is as well trained and equipped as the rest of the men, and we function in exactly the same capacity."

"Oh," I said. "Well, jolly good for you, Corporal Emtezu. Could I see some photographs of the current regiment?"

Another hesitation. He took a breath. "Certainly," he said. "Are you looking for anything in particular?"

"Not really," I said, shrugging. "Why don't you show me your friends?"

He opened a wooden filing cabinet and drew out a folder of posed sepia photographs showing a company of black soldiers in dress uniforms standing on what looked to be the central square of the Old Red Fort. They were arranged in a horseshoe around a brass cannon on a carriage, the men at the front kneeling, their rifles augmented with sword bayonets. Standing on the far right, beside the men at the back, was Corporal Emtezu himself, and on the other side were two older white men.

One of them had a handlebar mustache and a monocle. The other, draped in a heavy cape and staring down the photographer beadily, was leaning on a cane. I couldn't see much of the cane's handle, but it had the stiff, glossy look that might well have housed a long, slender blade.

It was my turn to hesitate and breathe. "Who are these gentlemen?" I asked.

The corporal indicated the man with the monocle. "This is Colonel Archibald Mandel," he said, "the former regimental commander."

"The politician?" I asked.

He gave me a sharp look, and to cover my interest, I said, "His granddaughter goes to our school."

"He retired last year, when it was determined that the regiment would be restructured."

"And the fort closed," I supplied.

"Yes," he said, clearly not wanting to talk about it.

"And this one?" I asked, putting my fingertip on the image of the glowering man with the cane.

"That would be Sergeant Major Claus Gritt," said Emtezu. "Colonel Mandel's granddaughter goes to your school?"

I felt a chill of caution, but opted for defiance. "I believe so, why?" I said.

"That's curious," he said, rising.

"How so?"

"It was my understanding that the colonel was a lifelong bachelor. Never married. No children."

"It must be his goddaughter, or perhaps his niece," I said. "Between us, I don't much like the girl, so I haven't paid attention to her family tree."

He held my gaze, looming, and I knew he didn't believe me. "How did you get those cuts on your face?" he asked. "Unusual in a lady of your class, wouldn't you say?"

"I should be going," I said.

"So soon?" His eyes were hard now.

I got to my feet. "Can't be helped, I'm afraid," I said, taking a half step toward the cage door.

He reached for me, seizing my wrist in a powerful grip. "Who are you?" he said. "What are you really doing here?"

"I told you—" I began, but he squeezed deliberately, expertly, and the pain drove the words out of me.

He pulled me in close and his face was implacable. I could feel the cold pressure of the holstered revolver at his belt. When he spoke, it was in a voice low enough to be a whisper. "You're press," he said. "Aren't you?"

I thought quickly. Being a reporter meant I had some coverage under the law. It meant I wasn't alone.

"Yes," I said.

"Why are you writing about the Third?"

It was a forceful question, but it was—I'd swear—a real one, and underneath it was something else: anxiety, even curiosity.

"It's just a feature," I said, improvising. "A history of the Red Fort and the handoff."

He shook his head, and with the speed and precision of a striking snake, he snatched up my satchel and opened the flap. "If that were all it was," he said, "you'd have said so. And," he added, showing me the inside of the satchel with a raised eyebrow, "you wouldn't be armed. So what is really going on?"

I couldn't mention Berrit or Ansveld. I had to think of something that might plausibly interest an undercover reporter but wouldn't make him panic.

"Land deals," I said. "Real estate trade with the Mahweni. Might have something to do with the Grappoli."

His eyes narrowed, but I was sure his grip on my wrist lessened slightly. "You mean the withdrawal of the garrison and conversion of the fort?" he asked.

"Partly," I said. "But there have been other deals—quieter deals—which have given up Mahweni land to a development company, land your people have fought to hold on to for decades, centuries even. I want to know what's changed."

Emtezu shook his head. "Ancestral land being traded out of Mahweni control?" he said. "No. I know there have been rumors, possibilities, but nothing has happened yet. Someone has been telling you stories."

"It's true," I replied. "I've seen the legal briefs and the maps. It's all gone through quietly, kept out of the papers, and it looks like the trail has been partly covered by multiple retrades. But it has happened, and quickly."

"That can't be right," he said, still shaking his head.

"I have notes. Copies of the documents."

"Where?"

I nodded at the satchel and he reopened it, taking out some of my scribblings and staring at them. For a moment it was like he had forgotten I was even there, and when he remembered, it was with something like shock. He stuffed the papers back into the bag and pulled me close again.

His face, inches from mine, was studiously blank, but he couldn't keep that flicker of curiosity out of his eyes.

I gambled. "And I want to know why the body of an elderly Mahweni tribesman was found in the ruins of the Red Fort's central tower."

"What?" he gasped. "When?"

"Yesterday," I said. "I saw it myself. Looks like he was imprisoned and tortured over several days."

He looked drawn, stricken with a horror that left him rigid and bloodless.

"I want to know if it was a revenge attack," I said.

"Revenge?" he echoed blankly. "Against who?"

"*Coloreds,*" I said, choosing the word with care. "The people responsible for the Glorious Third handing over their famous bastion to be turned into a black community center."

He stared at me, and suddenly the blood, the life, was back, and his eyes flashed. "Come with me," he said, shrugging the satchel strap over his head and shoulder.

"What? Where to?" I gasped, the fear that had stilled for a moment rearing and plunging again in my head. I should have told Andrews and Willinghouse what I was doing. How could I have been so stupid?

"Not where to, *who* to," he said, marching me out into the narrow corridor and slamming the wire door to the carrel behind him.

"I'm not going anywhere with you," I said.

"Yes," he said, moving his right hand to his belt and unbuttoning the flap of his pistol holster so that the heel of his palm rested almost idly against the curve of the revolver's handle. "You are."

CHAPTER
28

WE LEFT THE LIBRARY at a brisk walk, and as we crossed the great central lobby on the main floor, he even let go of my wrist, though his eyes held me almost as tight. As we passed the main desk, I caught sight of Miss Fischer, stamping cards methodically. I could call out to her, I thought, say something innocuous sounding but out of character that would make her suspicious, and then . . .

What? She'd summon the police to say a Lani girl had been seen leaving the building with a well-built Mahweni?

No help there. I kept walking, feeling the big man's presence at my shoulder, and as I did so, a strange calm descended on me. Before Emtezu had led me up from the basement, there was a moment when he had looked me in the face and said, "Ready?"

It might have been a half threat that was supposed to drive away any thoughts of stunts involving Miss Fischer, just a caution with a chill core of menace, but it didn't feel like that. It felt more like a pair of actors about to step into a scene together, an act not so much of warning as of solidarity. Whatever we were doing, we were in it together.

"Where are we going?" I asked as we went clattering down the library stairs.

He said nothing but hailed a two-seater and barked an address to the driver, who gave him a quizzical look.

"You sure about that address, sir?" said the cabbie.

"Just go," said Emtezu.

We sat in the back and he looked out the side. His hand was still near his gun, but his attention seemed elsewhere and he looked troubled.

If you bolt now, leap down to the street, and break into a flat sprint as you come out of your roll, you might find an alley, a fire escape, a maintenance ladder. You might find freedom and safety. . . .

I could see it all in my head. It could go wrong, of course. It could always go wrong. I could be caught under the wheels of the cab or trampled by a horse going in the other direction. Emtezu might stand and draw and shoot me down with military precision before I made it across the street. But then again, maybe not. Maybe it would all work perfectly and I would vanish into Bar-Selehm as easy as winking.

I stayed where I was. Yes, I might get away. But I had looked into Corporal Emtezu's eyes, and what I had seen there was not the henchman's murderous chill, the sadist's amused anticipation, or the drilled soldier's unthinking and potentially brutal sense of duty. There was something going through the head of the man beside me, something complex and uncertain, and I wanted to know what it was.

I didn't know this part of the city, a wealthy enclave on the northside shore of the ocean, where the port traffic gave way to highwalled mansions and opulent oceanfront hotels. The railway had brought holidaymakers from all over Feldesland, though such visitors were almost exclusively white, so I was taken aback by the florid animal gateposts at the head of a long drive.

A uniformed Mahweni approached the cab, another a few paces behind, his rifle unslung and ready.

He spoke first in one of the tribal languages, as if on principle, then translated.

"You can go no farther," said the officer. His uniform was unlike any I had ever seen, heavily decorated with gold braid and topped with a pith helmet sporting ostrich feathers. On other men the uniforms might have looked foppish, silly, but the earnestness of the soldiers themselves, their no-nonsense scowls and the ease with which they wielded their weapons, suggested it would be dangerous to underestimate them.

Emtezu pulled a sheaf of papers from an inside pocket and thrust it toward the guard, who considered it, then stepped back to allow us room to climb down. I did so as Emtezu paid and waved the cab away. The driver gave me a look, then wheeled the horse, glad to be leaving.

I shot Emtezu a similar look, but he shook his head fractionally. He was telling me to keep quiet, to let him do the talking.

We were escorted up the long drive by the rifleman, the outer gate closing and locking behind us with a clang that reverberated through the hot air, the metal ringing. The finality of the sound, the way it seemed at odds with the bright sky and manicured grounds, gave me a chill, though Emtezu kept walking, eyes locked on the house ahead, saying nothing.

I had expected a formal mansion, but this was more a vast and luxuriant villa sprawling like a great cat on the undulating grounds. The core of the house was brick, three stories high and sprouting a single broad chimney stack, but the rest was a pastiche of traditional Mahweni architecture with dense, sloping thatched roofs and wooden verandas. There was a swimming pool ringed with a grove of what looked to be patanga fruit trees, and svengalene bushes buzzing with hummingbirds. Statues of orlek and giraffes erupted out of the lawn, huge and stylized, the marbled stone dressed with garlands of flowers and feathers. The steps up to the house itself boasted a balustrade that combined classic urns with a handrail carved to resemble a massive python, all glass and semiprecious stones. As I turned back to consider the way we had come, a black weancat wearing a studded collar paced evenly across the gravel and on through the garden.

"What is this place?" I asked.

In answer, a young black man in impeccable livery appeared at the head of the steps and stood quite still, waiting till we reached the top before saying, "Welcome to the home of Farrstanga Sohwetti, head of the Unassimilated Tribes of the Mahweni Nation. Please follow me. His Excellency will see you shortly."

THE INSIDE OF SOHWETTI'S lavish villa reminded me of the opera house. Though every surface was decorated with Mahweni images and artifacts—large pots and masks, ceremonial skirts and headdresses, ancient spears and hide shields—it was all somehow bigger, shinier, richer than normal, and I remembered what Mnenga had said about its owner. This was not the stuff of the life Mnenga led, nor the culture of his village. This was a gilded memory of something no longer lived, like the glass eyes of a stuffed weancat. Somewhere between the performance of heritage and its rejection was this strange house that felt, in fact, less like a home and more like the souvenir shop in a museum.

We had been shown through a long hallway, through two separate open areas, and into a formal room with a great cold fireplace and no windows, deep in the heart of the house. I perched on a bench upholstered in zebra hide and stuffed with hair. Emtezu stayed standing, his face closed, and he looked at me only when he returned my satchel to me. The pistol Dahria had given me was still inside, but Emtezu had confiscated the ammunition.

At last a pair of double doors opened and Sohwetti himself strode in. I had seen his picture in newspapers, but I was unprepared for the scale of the man. He was tall and wide, heavyset but strong, and clad in cream-colored robes that flattered his bulk. His graying hair was worn in tight braids, and he wielded a stick like a riding crop, short and with a head of orlek hair that he might flick to keep flies away. At his broad leather belt he wore a curved knife with an elaborate gold knuckle guard.

And he smiled wide as the ocean, wide as the plains, wide as the sky itself, so that you felt his power and benevolence like heat. "Emtezu, my friend," he said in Feldish, reaching for the corporal's hand with both of his, clasping it in the Mahweni way and looking him squarely in the eye. "It is good to see you."

"Excellency," said Emtezu with a nod that was almost a bow.

"And you have brought a guest," he added, turning to me. "And such a pretty one. What is your name, child?"

"I am Anglet Sutonga," I said. I almost added "Excellency," as Emtezu had done, but the word felt strange in my mouth, so I simply lowered my eyes.

"Perhaps we should converse alone," said Sohwetti to Emtezu. "If the lady would not mind. For a moment."

"That is not necessary," said Emtezu. "It's her you need to speak to."

Sohwetti hesitated, and for a moment I was sure he was displeased, but the smile never went away, and when he turned it upon me, it seemed genuine again. He took a couple of long, ponderous steps, lowered himself into a thronelike chair beside a desk and nodded. "Very well, child," he said, his voice low but still booming, like barrels rolling in a cellar. "What have you to tell me?"

I was confused and embarrassed. What I had to say, insofar as I had anything to say, concerned land deals on which this man had signed off. Unless the signature was forged, I had nothing to tell him that he did not already know. I gave Emtezu an appealing look, but he just nodded encouragingly.

So I told him about the body in the tower and my idea that it might be spite at the handoff of the fort, and he listened gravely as Emtezu nodded along, as if in time to a tune he already knew.

When I was done he added, as if it were an afterthought, "And tell him about the land deals."

Sohwetti looked up, and his eyes moved from the corporal to me very slowly. His hands became unnaturally still.

"It's all public record," I ventured in a small voice. "I've seen nothing that isn't open to anyone who looks in the right places and connects the pieces."

"What have you seen, child?" asked Sohwetti. His voice was calm, even soothing, but it didn't make me feel better.

"Maps," I said dully. "Charts of land parcels. Letters of agreement. Contracts issued by Future Holdings and signed—"

"I see," said Sohwetti, interrupting. "Yes."

He rose and turned to the desk so that for a moment I could not see his face. I felt a curious, thoughtful stillness about the man, although when he turned round again, he was his usual, beaming self.

"I know what you are referring to," he said. "A small matter we did not think worthy of attention, but your curiosity—and your dedication, Corporal Emtezu—suggest that we may have miscalculated, and for that I thank you. We can resolve the matter publicly before anyone gets, as they say, the wrong idea." The smile bloomed again, showing white, even teeth.

"And the dead herder?" asked Emtezu.

"That is most serious," said Sohwetti. "I will follow the police investigation closely, publicly if necessary, and if it seems that it is being swept under the Glorious Third's rug, as it were, I will bring the matter to the council itself. Times have changed. Some of our northern brethren have been reluctant to accept this fact, but if they think they can torture and kill our citizens because they have lost a thimbleful of their power, they are deeply and tragically mistaken. We will bring the wrath of eight hells down upon them."

His voice had swelled and his face darkened as he spoke, but now he breathed again, shrugging off his stately passion. When he smiled, he seemed ordinary.

"This has been most helpful to me and to the Mahweni Nation," he said. "I am in your debt, Corporal." He took the younger man's hand once more, clasped it, then made a fractional turn, which presented Emtezu with the door.

"And there is nothing else I can do, Excellency?" he asked.

"Nothing at all," said Sohwetti genially. "I will see that my carriage gets you back into the city."

Emtezu bowed, took a step toward the door, then glanced back to where I had begun to get to my feet.

"But Miss Sutonga has not enjoyed my hospitality before," said Sohwetti. "She should stay here awhile."

"I need to get back to work," I said.

"Nonsense." Sohwetti smiled, flicking the notion away with his fly stick. "I won't hear of it. I will treat you to a true Mahweni banquet. You have never had the like, I guarantee it. I will show you the estate personally and see to it that you get back home safely this evening."

I hesitated. Emtezu was lingering in the doorway, one hand on the knob, looking back at me unreadably.

"I really can't stay, Your Excellency," I said, trying for politeness. "My employers will be worried."

"I will send word of your whereabouts to assuage their anxieties," he said, magnanimous in his certainty. "I would take it as an affront if you were to decline." He made a mock show of offense, though the smile crept back into place like a jackal stealing into an untended kitchen.

I gave Emtezu a last, uncertain look, but knew he could do nothing without upsetting the great man for no real reason. A moment later, he was bowing his way out, leaving me alone with Sohwetti.

"Sit," he said, doing so himself. He said it almost casually, but the smile was gone. He took a long breath and reached for a silver box on the desk beside him. He opened it, took something, and pushed the box toward me.

"Help yourself," he said. "Dried cadmium grapes. Sweet and tart. They are a small addiction of mine. Quite harmless, I believe, but it bothers me nonetheless, feeling like a slave to my body's cravings. Do you ever feel that, Miss Sutonga, that you are not completely in control of your own life?"

"I've never felt otherwise," I said.

He nodded thoughtfully. "I used to feel that way," he said, as if we were old friends at the end of a long evening's catching up. "Long ago. I used to feel powerless in the face of all I could not do because the world had taken from me what should have been mine. And not just mine. My whole people's. Robbed by diplomats whose friends had better weapons."

He smiled again as broad as before, but bleak now. He chewed one of the dried grapes reflectively.

"It is a terrible thing, not to be in control of your own life," he concluded.

"It's just how things are," I said.

"Really?" he said, genuinely interested. "You think so? And yet here I am, in this house, a man of power and influence because I chose to make it so, while you are . . . what? Not a reporter, that is for sure. Those cuts on your face are recent. So you are . . . what? A detective? A spy? Working for who? The Grappoli?"

His confusion seemed real, but his manner was somber, and it made me uneasy. I thought of Emtezu, wishing—despite the manner in which he had brought me here—that he had not gone, and I realized his mistake. The news he had wanted me to bring was about the outrage represented by the dead Mahweni herder in the ruins of the tower. He had wanted me to bring this to Sohwetti as evidence of racial atrocity perpetrated by men in the Glorious Third, something to be exposed and punished. But Sohwetti wasn't interested in that. Not really. He was interested in the land deals, and not because he hadn't known about them.

The house was utterly silent. I could hear no voices, no distant birdcalls. We were deep in the heart of the building. If I were to run, I would have to go through a labyrinth of rooms and corridors before I made it outside, where armed men and big cats with spiked collars patrolled the grounds. . . .

Sohwetti was still watching me, waiting for me to answer his question about who I was working for. His eyes were attentive, almost predatory in their focus, and I understood that whatever danger I was in could be held off so long as he thought I had important information. How he might opt to extract it, I did not dare consider.

"I have . . . connections," I said. "But I am working for myself."

"Doing what?"

"Investigating."

"Come now, Miss Sutonga," he said, suddenly brusque. "Do not play games with me. I do not have time for such things. *What* are you investigating?"

"Partly," I said, watching him carefully, "the disappearance of the Beacon."

He leaned forward fractionally, and his eyes contracted. "A strange occurrence indeed," he said, giving nothing away. "Was it the Grappoli?"

"I have found nothing to suggest so."

"That is my feeling too," he said. "Though I fear that truth alone will not save us. But you said 'partly.' What else are you exploring?"

"The death of a Lani boy called Berrit," I said simply.

His confusion seemed to deepen. He was either a skillful actor or had no knowledge of either matter. It was unsettling.

"Who is this boy?" he asked.

"Nobody," I said, and even here, when things might go so very badly, the sadness of that truth pained me. "Just a boy who got in the way of other people's plans and got killed."

"I know nothing of any dead Lani boy," he said.

"But you know about the land deals with Future Holdings," I said. "You signed the deeds yourself."

He smiled again, smaller this time, and there was something in the look that spoke of weariness and regret. "Yes," he said. "Those I know about. I wish to the gods that you did not. I wish that our worthy corporal had not thought to bring you to me."

"Why did he?" I asked, pressing for time to think. "He didn't know about the land deals. He didn't know you were involved. I expect he thought you had been cheated or deceived by enemies of the Mahweni people."

He nodded sadly. "Corporal Emtezu is alert to enemies of the Mahweni," he said. "It is his passion and his secondary occupation."

I gave a sigh of understanding. "You pay him to inform on race issues within the military," I said.

"Actually, he does it for free," said Sohwetti. "I offered him money, but he declined it, said it was a matter of principle. He considers himself a"—he smiled at the word—"'watchdog.' And there is a great deal to watch. We say we are all equal in Bar-Selehm, but you know as well as I do that that is not even close to being true. You cannot simply take people's land, property, freedom from them and then, a couple of hundred years later, when you have built up your industries and your schools and your armies, pronounce them equals. And even when you pretend it is true, you do not change the hearts of men, and a great deal of small horrors have to be ignored, hidden, if the myth of equality is to be sustained."

It was, I suspected, a familiar speech for him, though he believed it still.

"I know," I said.

"I am sure you do. The Lani have never organized as we have and they never had anything to barter, being themselves outsiders. So yes, I am sure you understand. Corporal Emtezu is, for the most part, focused on the smaller crimes, those little lingering uglinesses that people perpetrate when the world around them changes faster than they would like."

"Like the imprisonment, torture, and murder of a Mahweni herder who had the misfortune to meet up with some old-fashioned soldiers?" I said carefully.

He sat back then, looking me up and down with something like respect, though it was colored by a resignation that drained him of the energy he normally conveyed. "Precisely like that," he said, "yes."

"So he gathers evidence against his superiors," I said, "channeling it through you and the council you represent."

"I have a voice in government," said Sohwetti, drawing himself up. "I may not have the ear of the prime minister like some of my white colleagues, but I am a man of influence and I do my best to use it for my people."

"But you also feather your own nest at your people's expense," I said, once more amazed by my own self-possession. "Secretly selling off their land, their birthright, despite the fact that they have clung to that land against the very men Emtezu is trying to expose."

"The two matters are unrelated," said Sohwetti, flicking his fly stick, color rising in his cheeks. "The casual murder of a stray Mahweni is a tragedy that has been played month after hellish month in and around this city since before your grandparents were born! The selling of land, land which—for the most part—my people cannot use, is a completely separate matter. The tribes will benefit directly from those sales. They will see profits they would never have gotten from grazing on that worthless scrub. It is no more than a few square miles of dirt and rock. If the truth were known, the only reason the white men did not take it from us before was because it has no value!"

"So why the sudden interest?"

"I do not know," he said, "and it does not matter."

"Is it about the Grappoli?" I asked, desperate to keep him talking.

He shook his head. "If we go to war with the Grappoli, the city will be in ruins long before they get here," he said sadly. "I will have no hand in that. My duty to my people will be to keep all possible peaces. To do so, there must, alas, be sacrifices. You should not have come here. You have forced my hand most unfortunately."

"It will all come out sooner or later anyway," I said. "Silencing me won't make any difference. The Unassimilated Tribes already know about the sales. What does keeping it quiet in the city for a few more days buy you?"

"The Unassimilated Tribes know we are *discussing* land transactions," said Sohwetti carefully. "They do not know that they have already happened."

I stared at him, horrified, and very slowly, he nodded.

"Yes," he said. "I am sorry. I thought I would be able to change the council's minds, and in time I am sure I would, but my buyers were impatient. Insistent. They wanted the land now or not at all. I just need a few more days of silence, time to talk the council 'round, after which we will announce the sale and no one will be any the wiser. The results would be the same. Only the date on some paper no one will ever look at will be wrong, and not by much. A clerical error, perhaps. Or it would have been, before you."

"I'll say nothing," I said, fear taking hold. "I promise. I'll tell no one."

"I'm sorry," he said again. "I am weary of this conversation and must take time to consider my choices. Excuse me, Miss Sutonga," he said, getting to his feet. "You seem like an intelligent and interesting young lady. I wish with all my heart that we had never met."

And with that he left, locking the door behind him.

CHAPTER

29

I BLINKED, AND THE tears that had clung to my eyes broke through and ran down my face. He wouldn't come back. Not Sohwetti himself. I was sure of it. Some nameless guard would come to get me, bind my hands, and shuttle me somewhere quiet and removed. Maybe they would just do it here, then dump my body in the ocean. There was a spot not far from here—Tanuga Point—famed for the yellow-finned sharks that haunted the bay. It had been, in the old days, a place of execution, first for some of the Mahweni tribes, then for the northern Feldeslanders, because it was safe to assume that corpses tossed into the water there would be shredded in minutes. No grave, no inconvenient bodies washing ashore to be venerated as political martyrs. To enter the water at Tanuga Point was to go through the great meat grinder of the world, and what emerged was as close to nothing as made no difference.

I could brandish Willinghouse's name. Or Vestris's. Both had power and influence, albeit of different kinds, and both would come to my aid if I could reach them. But their worlds were not Sohwetti's, and their names alone would not save me here.

You have to get out.

That meant forcing the door, since we were in the core of the house and there were no windows . . . or using the chimney. I considered the fireplace, wiping my tears away and tying my hair back. I doubted it would take Sohwetti long to wrestle with his conscience and find a willing henchman. It didn't sound like the dead herder in the remains of the Red Fort tower was anything to do with him, but I would be a fool to think he had never been responsible for bloodshed.

His manner when he left was downcast, sad even, but not horrified, not appalled by what he was considering. Sohwetti, like many a politician before him, was resigned to expediency.

I snatched up the satchel Emtezu had left behind, pulled its strap over my head, and climbed into the hearth, which showed no sign of recent use. Leaning against the sooty black wall, I looked up. There was an iron damper in the shaft, and I pulled the lever to open it. The opening was narrow and the chimney beyond it utterly lightless, which meant it twisted and turned on its way up.

I remembered my first days in the Seventh Street gang, when I had still been small enough to serve as a chimney sweep for the big houses. Sometimes it was just a matter of shoving a long-handled pole with a brush on the top up the shaft, but in the older houses, especially where there were multiple fireplaces, the chimneys would meander and intersect, narrowing as their walls got caked with old bird nests, masonry shards, and accumulated soot. If the house used a lot of wood, there would be resinous tar that could burn for hours if ignited, and which had to be scraped off with chisels. Angles were tight and the shafts contracted unexpectedly in the blackness, so that getting stuck was a real danger. That had happened once to a boy called Micah. They say he died of fear, and because the owner didn't want to cut half the wall away to get the body out, they lit all the fires in the house, even though it was the middle of summer. I don't know if it was true, but I heard that for months afterwards, the remains of his blackened bones continued to tumble down into the grate every time the south wind blew.

Lani children everywhere I turned. Kalla and Berrit, Tanish and me, crammed into the darkness, out of sight, forgotten, burned up like so much trash. . . .

Stop it.

I squeezed the doors in my head closed again, locking out the rising tide.

At least inside the chimney I would be safe for a while from Soh-wetti and his men, none of whom would be able to follow me up.

I worked my hands in through the damper, then my head. It was funny how it all came back, the childish thrill, the dread of the dark and the spiders. I was used to high places, out there in the sky where you could breathe, where you could see what you were doing, but this, the blackness, the closeness and cinder reek of the air, the tightness of the space where the bricks pressed in on shoulders, arms, legs, belly, chest, and head all at the same time, like you were in a long, upright coffin, this was different.

I inhaled raggedly, then stood tall as I could, reaching above me for handholds in the brick. I could feel where the shaft—about a yard across in the fireplace—stepped in. If it got much tighter, I wouldn't be able to get through. There was nothing to hold on to, so I drew my knees up to my chest, one at a time, and managed to put my boots on the damper. I straightened again, boosting myself another three feet to where the chimney tightened like a python squeezing a springbok. I could see nothing. I could hear nothing beyond the thumping of my heart and the laboring of my breath.

I reached higher and this time felt a ledge on the right-hand side, where the passage seemed to open. There was only one chimney stack on the roof, I reminded myself. That meant that every fireplace in the house connected inside and ran up to the top. Moving sideways might give me the option of dropping into another room, one that was unlocked, or that had windows. . . .

I dragged myself up and found the shaft angling up and to the right, forming a square, uneven tunnel through which I could crawl. One of the sides of the shaft was now a roof, but one that dipped erratically so that I had to stay low to avoid skinning my forehead. I inched forward, brick after brick moving under my gritty palms.

Stay focused. Keep going.

Something moved in my hair, and I brushed at it with revolted feverishness, which banged my head against the shaft wall. For a moment, the darkness was flecked with light and color, and I had to fight not to lose a sense of where I was, which way was up. It was only noise from below that brought me to my senses.

A click, like a door. Then hurried footsteps and the clank of the damper as someone tried to see up. I had left that shaft now and would be invisible to them, even if they had a light source, but it wouldn't matter. They knew where I was.

I picked up the pace, my bruised knees, back, and hands aching from the effort, and now I could hear raised voices, not just back the way I had come, but from all over the house, as every fireplace bore their voices up through the labyrinth of flues.

Faster.

Going down to one of the other fireplaces and slipping out of the house unnoticed was not an option anymore. I had to make it to the roof.

The shaft stank, as chimneys always did, of carbonized wood and bitumen and old smoke. New smoke, fresh and sharp enough to set you coughing, was an entirely different thing, and I recognized it with a new thrill of horror.

They couldn't come up after me, so they were lighting the fires.

I crawled another yard, moving so fast that I almost fell when the floor of my awful tunnel simply stopped. I reached blindly into the space in front of me and, finding only air, had to swallow down a sob of panic as I reached around and up. I was at an intersection, perhaps the biggest in the house, and as I decided whether to try to cross the abyss that had opened up in front of me, I caught the distinct movement of the smoke coiling up from below, thick and gray, smeared with a sulfurous yellow.

I blinked. I could see the smoke. And that meant . . .

Above me, the chimney flue narrowed to a square of bluish light. *Sky.*

I reached across, testing for the far wall, then braced my feet against it and scrabbled for handholds in the brick. For a moment I was hanging over the emptiness of the shaft below like an insect, and then I was climbing, the smoke billowing about me, thick and hot. I coughed again, but knew that hesitation meant death. I fixed my eyes on that square of light and hauled myself up. Where there were no handholds, I used the strength of my knees and back, bracing myself across the shaft and walking up the flue as I had done at the cement works the day we found Berrit's body.

The temperature was rising fast. Too fast. I glanced back down and saw not merely the dense swirl of gray smoke, but flashes of orange too. Part of the unswept chimney had caught fire.

Great, I thought. *I'm going to die ironically.*

I swallowed hard and pushed my way up to where the breeze from outside was dragging the smoke and flames upward. I pushed the clay chimney pot clear, seized the mortar cap, and dragged myself up and out onto the roof. I had barely moved more than a couple of yards over the tile when the smoking chimney became a jet of fire, shrieking up out of the flue and scattering sparks. I moved as far away as I could, but my coughing doubled me up and I spat soot.

I could hear voices, people running around outside. They would have guns, so I stayed low. But as I looked cautiously about, trying to find a safe way down, I realized that the smoke wasn't all coming from the chimney. The sparks from the blaze were scattering all over the house, and in at least two places the lower thatch, Sohwetti's concession to his Mahweni roots, was already ablaze.

I moved upwind, toward the front of the house, going quicker than I would like, banking that the fire would take more of their attention than hunting for me. I reached the edge of the roof, found an ornamental buttress carved to resemble a buffalo head, climbed the first ten feet down, and dropped the last five onto a portion of thatch that wasn't yet ablaze. I loped along, bent over like a monkey, then slid down a snake-shaped column, spiraling as I went, and hit the ground at a staggering run.

I didn't go down the road to the gate, but through the wooded parkland to the high wall of the estate, where—still coughing, still holding off my smoldering exhaustion—I pulled myself up. As I sat on top of the wall and risked a last look back at the house through the shrubbery and the great tower of yellowish smoke rising from it, a black weancat with a collar, its spots just visible in the sheen of its coat, gave me a long look with bright yellow eyes.

I felt no fear, and was sure that even on the ground only feet from the beast, I would be in no danger, and not because it was a pet that looked dangerous only to people who didn't know the truth. This, in spite of its collar, was a wild and powerful hunter, a creature of speed and stealth that would kill without hesitation. But it was also somehow, and in ways that made no literal sense, me, and I felt only an uncanny kinship with the creature.

It was an animal out of place, separate from its kind, fatherless, uncertain of who it was, who it could trust, knowing the collar was there but knowing also that it was a collar of the mind: when the moment was right, you could refuse to believe in the collar and it would go away. And that was essential, because all the cat had was itself: muscle and sinew, claw, tooth and bone, senses, experience, skill, instinct and roaring, blood-pumping animal need. Nothing else, not the wall, not the strange people, not the food and water meted out at regular times daily, and not—most certainly not—the collar, none of it mattered one iota.

I dropped onto the other side of the wall and ran.

CHAPTER
30

"WHAT'S THIS?" ASKED SARAH, considering the sheaf of papers I had pushed into her hands.

"Your first story," I said.

It had taken me over an hour to get back into Bar-Selehm through the orchards and gardens behind the oceanfront mansions, twice as long as it had then taken me to cover the familiar streets to the newspaper stand on the corner of Winckley and Javisha. I had paused only once at a fountain just south of Tanuga Point to wash the worst of the soot and smoke from my clothes and hair.

Sarah scanned the scribbled notes and charts. "You're sure about this?" she said. "You can prove it?"

"The original documents are sitting in the library, where anyone can check them," I said. "Or they are at the moment. I would move quickly if I were you."

She thought, but quickly, and then she was packing up her stall, hands quick and efficient, eyes wide with the thrill of risk and the gleam of determination.

"Why are you doing this?" she asked as she finished and stood ready to go into whatever adventure awaited.

There were lots of answers I could have given. I could have said she was my friend and I was trying to help her, or that a great wrong had been perpetrated on her people and it should be brought to light. Both were true, and there were other things—things to do with Berrit, and with Billy, and with the collared weancat—that I couldn't put into words but that were also true.

"Until this gets printed," I said, "I'm a target."

She nodded, turned, and broke into a run.

I FOUND MNENGA SLEEPING in the old Lani cemetery beside a weather-beaten shrine decorated with clumsily carved monkeys. He opened his eyes, one hand flashing toward the short-shafted spear on the ground beside him, but he knew me before his long fingers had closed around it. He blinked, then smiled his radiant and uncomplicated smile. He sat up. He did not reproach me for how long I had been gone.

Before the conversation could go somewhere that made me uncomfortable, I asked the question I had been mulling since I left Sohwetti's house in flames.

"Why are you in Bar-Selehm, Mnenga?"

"I told you," he began, "the nbezu—"

"Forget the nbezu," I said. "Tell me about the old man."

He grew still, his face setting. "Ulwazi," he said at last.

He read the confusion in my face.

"The old man," he said. "The one who is—" He gestured with his hands: *Gone, like smoke blowing away.*

"He is why you are here, and you fear he has come to harm at someone else's hands."

For a long moment he said nothing, and I wondered if I should clarify my phrasing, but he understood me perfectly and eventually nodded. "I *am* herding nbezu," he said. "But that is not all of the truth. The elders of my village sent me. Ulwazi said white men wanted to buy land from us, but he did not know why. He said he would find out, but then he disappeared. I have been trying to find him or learn what happened to him, but I do not know how to be in the city. My own kind—the ones who live here, the Assimilated—do not want to talk about old men from the bush. I did not mean to lie to you." He shrugged, and his smile became bleak and knowing.

"Mnenga," I said, deciding on impulse to trust him as I once had. "I'm sorry, but I don't think you will find him."

His face tightened with doubt and wariness.

"I think he is dead," I said. "I think I saw him."

"Where?"

"At the Old Red Fort," I said. "He may have been imprisoned there."

For the first time since I had known him, the Mahweni boy's face hardened and his smile vanished entirely.

"You know the place?" I asked.

He nodded slowly and emphatically twice, and at the end of the second, he hung his head, teeth gritted and eyes closed.

"What have you heard about it?" I asked.

For a while, he said nothing. Then he opened his eyes and shook his head. "Bad things," he said in a low voice, thick as the darkness gathered around us. "Old things about the war, but also new things. There is a man there, or there *was*. My people call him Tchanka, an old name for a kind of devil. He has the head of a jackal. Comes to your hut at the darkest part of the night, when the moon is down. Gets down very low on his belly and comes in under the door. He takes your children. Eats their souls."

I swallowed. "Do you know the man's real name?" I asked.

Mnenga shook his head. "Only Tchanka. He was a soldier, perhaps still is."

I thought for a moment, and an idea that had never occurred to me before spilled out. "If there is a war with the Grappoli, Mnenga," I said, "would you fight?"

He frowned. "The bush tribes would not be forced," he said. "Not at first. But we would be stupid to think that war between the Grappoli and the Bar-Selehm would not come to our villages in the end, and I think I would probably fight sooner than that."

Something in his eyes gave me pause.

"How much sooner?" I asked.

"They say Mahweni stole your Beacon to sell to the Grappoli," he said bitterly.

"They?"

"The white people in the city," he clarified. "They say if there is a war, my black brothers in the city will have to decide which side they are on. They say it like the choice should be easy, but I do not think it is, and I think for the bush villagers, the herders, the *Unassimilated,*" he added, pulling a sour face, "people like me and my brothers, who the city ignores till they want our land, we will also have to make a choice."

"You will stand with the city Mahweni even if they rise up against Bar-Selehm?"

"Rise up," he echoed, liking the sound of it. "Yes. But not against Bar-Selehm. The city is many things. We would rise up only against parts of it."

"You'd be killed," I said. "They have better weapons, trained soldiers . . . . You wouldn't stand a chance."

He nodded thoughtfully. "That is possible," he said. "But the Grappoli also have better weapons and soldiers. If we are going to die, better it be for what we believe is right."

The weight of the previous week pressed down on me, and I suddenly felt weary and sad beyond measure.

Again he shook his head, this time like a whinnying orlek, as if to clear it. "I am sorry about Kalla," he said. "You would have made a good mother."

"If you actually think that," I said, "you haven't been paying attention."

"Paying?" he echoed.

His confusion annoyed me. Even in the moment, I was ashamed of the feeling. "I wouldn't make a good mother," I said. "I'd make a terrible mother. If I've learned nothing else over the last few days, I've learned that."

"No!" he said. "You cared for her. You kept her safe. When things are calm and you have a good husband—"

"No," I said, my voice louder and harsher than I meant it. "I climb chimneys. I hurt people. I put the lives of everyone I know at risk."

"No," he said. "You are a good person, Anglet. A beautiful person—"

He extended a hand to mine but I ignored it, getting quickly to my feet. I knew he was trying to be helpful, supportive, and though I could see something else in the way he looked at me that I didn't have time to reflect upon, I appreciated it. But the extent of my failure crowded in on me and made me bitter.

"I'm grateful for your help, Mnenga," I said in a voice that showed no gratitude at all, "but don't think you know me. You don't, and it's better for you that way."

He blinked as if I had slapped him, and though I was struck with sudden remorse, I could think of no way to mend the moment except by leaving it.

"I'm sorry," I said, turning and walking away before I could change my mind.

THAT NIGHT AS I was making my way back to the Martel Court for a few hours' sleep, I heard the sound of chanting and followed it to look. In Unification Square, a crowd of Mahweni had gathered, and I saw that among the Assimilated majority were men and women in the homespun weavings and animal skins of the tribal herders. They all sang, rocked back and forth like a basin of unsettled water, their voices full of suffering and anger. Earlier in the day, one of the white rallies had replaced the effigy of the Grappoli ambassador with the puppet of a black man with wild hair, broad lips, and staring eyes. They had burned it in a metal drum, but some of the Mahweni had recovered the remains and it was now the repurposed focus of their own protest. A company of white dragoons was watching the writhing, boiling fury of the crowd with growing unease, and when I saw one young officer nervously unbuttoning the flap of his pistol holster, Willinghouse's words came back to me.

The very brink of disaster . . .

CHAPTER
31

CORPORAL TSANWE EMTEZU LIVED in Morgessa, the largely black area on the northeast side of the city, close to the Ramsblood temple, an orderly neighborhood of small, well-maintained terraced houses with tiny front gardens where roses and the sandalwood-scented heylas grew. Most of the people who lived there were factory workers and tradesmen. Their children went to Hillstreet School or, if they were religious, to Truth Mountain, which was run by Pancaris nuns. Most left at twelve, going on to apprenticeships or, like Sarah, straight into employment.

Emtezu's wife opened the door, cradling an infant only a couple of months older than the one I had left at Pancaris. She was black, though I had seen other wives and husbands in the neighborhood who weren't, and she looked me over, her face carefully empty. When she led me through into the back, she moved with unstudied economy, graceful as a dancer, and as we passed the foot of the stairs, she called up, stilling the movement and childish laughter that came from above without raising her voice.

"When I come up there I expect you to be ready for school," she said.

She led me into the kitchen, where her husband was sitting at the table, staring at a newspaper. He did not seem surprised to see me.

"I suppose I should be glad I'm not being arrested for the way I took you to see Sohwetti," he said. He glanced at his wife, who was fussing by the sink, and I could tell his casualness was feigned. "Am I likely to be?"

"No," I said. "You didn't know what you were leading me into."

"It seems I had our leader's priorities wrong," he said bitterly.

The front page of the *Morning Star* on the table in front of him blared, SOHWETTI SIGNS SECRET LAND DEAL!

"What will happen to him?" I asked.

He sat back and folded his arms. "It's not yet clear whether what he did was illegal or not," said Emtezu. "It will cost him his political position, of course, and probably a lot of money, not least of which will be in refurbishing the state residence for his successor. It seems there was a fire there after I left."

He said it carefully; a statement, not a question.

"Apparently so," I said, considering the competing images on the front page, a formal portrait of Sohwetti and a rushed, blurry image of the burning villa. "I was lucky to get away unhurt."

His eyes held mine for a moment, then he nodded. "So yes," he said. "Sohwetti is finished, and rightly so, though his fall will please some a good deal more than the Mahweni he represented, and that is less good. He was not a great man. He had his weaknesses, but he served my people as well as himself, and his disgrace reflects badly upon us."

"He will be replaced," I said.

"Yes. In time. And after a good deal of squabbling, all of which will allow our political enemies to regroup and consolidate. Until then, the unrest will build. Bloodily. If we are forced into a war with the Grappoli over the stolen Beacon, men like me will have to play riot policeman to thousands of my people who do not want to fight and die for a mineral they could never afford to buy and are not allowed to touch. Then I will have to decide which way to turn my rifle, and that is not a day I look forward to. I am glad to see you well, Miss Sutonga, and I mean you no harm, but your appearance has not been good for me or my people."

"I understand that," I said.

Emtezu's wife pushed a ceramic mug across the table toward me, then returned to the sink. The baby she was cradling in one hand was asleep. I sampled the drink. It was cool and fragrant, a sweet wine made from flowers.

"So what can I do for you, Miss Sutonga?" asked her husband. "I assumed matters were concluded, but your presence here suggests otherwise."

"The missing Beacon has not yet been recovered," I said. "And I don't think the Grappoli have it."

Emtezu just sat there, head tipped slightly on one side. When I matched his silence, he eventually shrugged. "I'm sorry," he said, "are you accusing me of something?"

"No," I said. "I'm trying to make a connection."

"Between what?"

"Between the disappearance of the world's largest piece of luxorite and the death of an old Mahweni in the Red Fort."

He waited for more, then just shook his head. "I can't help you," he concluded.

"What do you know about Archibald Mandel?" I asked.

He sighed, then shrugged. "Not much more than you, I imagine," he said. "His command was only nominal, particularly since he became a politician. I barely saw him."

"So the running of the fort fell to . . .?"

"Sergeant Major Gritt," he said.

He spoke the words carefully, without inflection, but I felt the sudden stillness of Emtezu's wife. It was as if a cloud had crept across the sun.

"That's the man with the cane," I said. "The sword stick."

He said nothing, but looked away for a second. His wife had still not moved a muscle.

"What are you driving at, Miss Sutonga?" he asked, unfolding his arms. "You come into my house with no authority—"

"Exactly," I said. "I have no authority. Nothing you say to me has any legal weight. Everything is off the record."

He stared at me, and there was doubt in his eyes.

"Have you heard the term 'Tchanka'?" I asked.

The static charge in the room seemed to leap. Emtezu's eyes widened, but he shook his head.

A lie.

"Tell her."

His wife had not turned around. Not yet. But then she said it again, and this time she did.

"Tell her, Tsanwe," she said.

"I don't know what you—" the Corporal began.

"If you don't, I will," she cut in. "He is a monster. A tyrant to our people. A killer, and not only in war."

"Hearsay," said Emtezu. "Hearsay that could cost me a dishonorable discharge at very least."

"This will not go to the papers," I said. "Or, if I can help it, the police. I am a private investigator exploring a separate crime."

There was a moment of silence, and the walls of the kitchen, so different from the extravagant opulence of the Sohwetti estate, felt like they were closing in like the jaws of a vise.

"What do you want to know?" asked Emtezu.

"Several days ago you went to a luxorite dealer's shop on Crommerty Street," I said.

Whatever he had been steeling himself for, it was not this. He looked utterly baffled. "Yes," he said. "So? Gritt said he had something to collect."

"His cane."

"Yes."

"Why did he need you to go with him?"

"There had been some minor disagreement over the price of a piece he had been looking at," said Emtezu dismissively. "He didn't want to make a fuss. Just take his cane and leave while I talked to the shopkeeper. He seemed to think that a black man in a luxorite shop would attract so much attention that he would be able to do what he wanted unnoticed. Thought it was funny. Why? What is this about?"

"You didn't think that strange?"

"Gritt sometimes . . ." He sought for the words.

His wife supplied them. "The sergeant major thinks his corporal is his personal servant," she said. "The man uses his authority to make my husband, a good man, a strong man, run errands like a child, a slave." Her face was hot, her eyes wide.

Emtezu bowed his head and, feeling his weary humiliation, I tried to refocus the conversation.

"You are sure it was his cane?" I asked.

"Absolutely," said the Corporal. "He's had it for years. It was a gift from the prime minister himself when he left the regiment."

"Benjamin Tavestock gave him the cane?" I repeated.

"Yes. So?"

"And how did it come to be in the shop?"

"It had been stolen a few nights before," said Emtezu. "These things sometimes show up in pawnbrokers' very quickly."

"Ansveld's shop isn't a pawnbroker's," I said. "Luxorite only. Other shops on the street are less singular in their focus. Macinnes's, for instance. Does that name mean anything to you?"

Emtezu shook his head.

"Did Gritt know a Lani gang leader called Morlak? Big man, wears his hair long and tied back."

"If he does, I've never seen them together," he said.

"Do you think him capable of torturing a man to death?" I asked.

There was a long, loaded pause. Under the hard stare of his wife, Emtezu finally nodded.

"He's done it before?" I asked.

"During the food riots, we took Mahweni prisoners," said Emtezu. "They were locked up in the tower and interrogated. Some of

them were there for days, and the black soldiers—my company—
were kept at a distance, sent on maneuvers, patrols, or crowd control."

I thought of Sarah's uncle, who had died of his wounds after one
of those riots.

"One day when we came back, the cells were empty," said Emtezu. "They had been rinsed out, but you could still smell the blood
and filth, so my men were ordered to scrub them clean." He said the
last words as if they were barbed and tore his throat on the way out.

"And the prisoners?"

"Never heard from them again," said Emtezu. "At least a couple
wandered home a day or two later, barely able to stand and reeking
of alcohol. Getting people drunk was one of Gritt's favorite methods
of making them talk, but it also makes sure no one believes them if
they tell tales of imprisonment and torture. One man's body was
found not far from the fort, killed, it was said, by weancats or hyenas. Two others were never found. An internal investigation found
no evidence of wrongdoing against anyone stationed at the Red
Fort."

I nodded. There was a finality in his voice that said quite clearly
what he thought would come of any poking around on my part. The
likes of Gritt were immune to prosecution, and any attempt to bring
them to justice would probably result only in collateral damage.

"Is this why you were going through the archive in the library?" I
asked. "Searching for evidence of Gritt's activities that you could
feed to Sohwetti?"

He smiled sadly. "You are very clever," he said. "But I found nothing. And with Sohwetti humiliated . . ." He shrugged. "I'm sorry I
can't help."

"You have," I said. "And I'm grateful." I turned to his wife. "And
for the wine. It was delicious. I hope . . ." I faltered, unsure of what
to say. "I hope tomorrow is a better day."

"We all do," she answered, showing me out. "Every day. These are bad days in which to raise children."

I nodded, thinking of Kalla so that my eyes fell on her infant and my heart was suddenly filled with sadness and regret.

"Miss Sutonga," added Emtezu.

I turned and found him brooding, watching me. "Yes?"

"Do not go near Claus Gritt," he said. "He may not actually be the devil the Mahweni think him, but he is close to it. Very close indeed."

CHAPTER

32

SARAH WAS CARRYING A bundle of newspapers to sell, but her entire demeanor had changed. She seemed taller, more buoyant, as if success had inflated something within her. Possibility, perhaps.

"Still selling papers?" I remarked. "I thought you'd be editor in chief by now."

"As of next week," she said, unable to keep the furious joy out of her eyes, "I'm going to be an apprentice reporter."

"Congratulations, Sarah," I said. "And thanks. That story may have saved my life."

"You're welcome," she said. "And it's Sureyna from now on."

I hesitated for only a second. "Your birth name?" I said.

She nodded. "Now would seem to be the time," she said, caught between pride and embarrassment. "Did you see this?" She thrust a newspaper into my hands and indicated a block of text.

> The Right Honorable Thomas DeKlepp, Secretary of National Security, responding to recent Mahweni protests said, "It is unfortunate that elements of the black community do not show an appropriate level of patriotism. It makes one wonder where their true loyalties lie." When pressed as to whether he thought Mahweni elements may have been involved in the theft of the Beacon and may be in league with the Grappoli, the secretary said that he could not comment at present but that investigations were ongoing and that "nothing would surprise" him, particularly given the recent "failures of leadership within the black community."

I winced.

"I don't know what you are doing exactly," said Sureyna, "but whatever it is, do it well and do it fast. You don't have very long. None of us do." As she spoke, she fished something from her pocket. "I hope this helps."

She handed me a scrap of paper penciled in Tanish's untidy scrawl.

Morlak handing off box tonite. Pier 7, Ware house 3.
Midnite. Westsiders will be there too.

I stared at the note.

Finally, I thought.

This was where we took a step back from the brink.

"What's in the box?" asked Sureyna.

"Not sure," I said.

"But you suspect."

"I suspect," I agreed, my eyes wandering up and over the rooftops to where, not so many days ago, the Beacon had once blazed for all to see. "Can you meet me before you start work tomorrow?"

"Where?"

"Here," I said. "First light. I will have something for the apprentice reporter. Something special."

"**THAT PART OF THE** docks serves ships using the Cape shipping lanes," said Willinghouse, considering Tanish's note.

He was sitting beside me in the police carriage. Von Strahden was next to Andrews.

For a moment, as the full implication of this settled upon us, no one spoke.

"The Grappoli," said Andrews.

"That seems likely, yes," said Willinghouse.

"Then we're going to war," said Andrews, "unless we recover the Beacon and find a way for the Grappoli to save face."

"How?" asked Von Strahden. "If anyone finds out, and I mean *anyone*—"

"If we recover it, it's a victory," said Willinghouse. "We can make the rest go away. We may even emerge with some bargaining power against the Grappoli."

Von Strahden conceded the point. "We'll have to time our entrance very carefully," he said. "We need to catch them in the act of the handoff."

"My men are ready," said Andrews, taking a revolver from his pocket and slotting bullets into its cylinder. I had loaded mine too, helping myself to ammunition from a supply bin back at the station when no one was looking, but Andrews didn't know I was armed.

"The Westsiders," said Willinghouse, rereading Tanish's note. "Who are they?"

"A minor gang who work the south-bank docks," said Andrews. "Led by a man called Deveril."

"Wears a top hat," I added. "They've been dealing with the Seventh Street gang for weeks, swapping merchandise, even personnel."

Berrit another commodity to be traded, this one disposable.

There was a thoughtful silence. I could smell the tang of the sea through the city's constant eddies of sulfurous industrial fog. In the distance, I could hear chanting. One of the protests downtown was going late. I wondered if troops had been sent in yet.

"Well," said Von Strahden to break the tension, "this is all jolly exciting!"

"Makes a change from dispatching survey crews and reading reports, I imagine," I agreed, remembering the day he had driven me into town with Dahria.

"Survey crews?" said Willinghouse blankly.

"She just means government work," said Von Strahden heartily. "Oh yes, this is much more thrilling."

Willinghouse still looked fogged, but Andrews cut them off with a sober look.

"When we get to Dock Street," he said, "I want you three well clear. This is a police operation. I want no civilian casualties, and I sure as hell don't want amateurs messing things up. The department is being watched very closely on this one. I have to report to the prime minister's personal secretary before returning home tonight."

"In a few hours, you will be able to hand him the Beacon personally," I said.

Von Strahden gave me an encouraging smile, but Andrews merely frowned.

WE CROSSED THE RIVER by the fish wharf and reached the Warehouse District an hour early. Pier 7 was on the outer edge of the south-side harbor: strictly cargo served by a single railway siding. Even in daylight it was unsavory, its corridors of stacked containers, squalid shipping offices, and looming, faceless warehouses permanently hung with the stench of the river and the engines that worked it. The worst slums in the city were on this side of the river, and after dark, only those who truly had to go there walked the streets.

The police presence numbered a dozen, not including Andrews, and they bristled with shotguns and breech-loading carbines. I had never seen such firepower outside the dragoons and it made me uneasy.

Andrews arranged his men around the perimeter of the warehouse, dispatching Willinghouse and Von Strahden to a storage facility some distance away. I was supposed to go with them, but I slipped away as soon as we got there, working my way back to Warehouse 3 by way of the corrugated roofs, service gantries, and freight cranes that made it possible to cover almost the entire distance without ever touching the ground.

A series of long ventilation shutters ran along the warehouse's ridgeline, and I was able to jimmy one open and squeeze through, dropping silently onto a maintenance catwalk. It ran to a shuttered observation booth suspended from the roof, but otherwise, there was nothing up there. Below, the warehouse was spread out; a mass of heaped crates, pallets, and sacks lost in shadow save where a single gas lamp glowed. The place smelled of the sea, rusting metal, and the warm, dry pine of the crates. I lay on my back, trying to get glimpses of the stars through the vents, listening.

It was nearly done. In an hour, we would have the Beacon, answers, and—shortly thereafter—peace. It was about time.

For a long while, nothing stirred in the warehouse, and some of my excitement began to drain away as I put all my effort into keeping still. When a door somewhere finally creaked open, it did so loudly, clumsily, and with it came the sound of conversation and a bark of laughter. They were either very confident or out of their depth.

I rolled slowly onto my stomach, feeling the slight sway of the catwalk as I shifted, staring through the welded footplates to the little pool of bluish light below. I recognized Fevel, the black man who had chased me the night I was taken to Willinghouse's place, and two others whose faces I couldn't see from above.

It was those two who were carrying the crate. When they set it down, Fevel sat on it, as if to prove his nonchalance, and lit a cigar. I saw the yellow flare of his match, and the tiny red glow as he drew on it. My mouth was dry. Fevel had sentenced me to die in the tower and was prepared to finish the job when I'd survived.

I felt the weight of the loaded revolver in my satchel, as I watched him from above like a perching eagle. He was no more than fifty or sixty feet away, and after a few moments, I could smell the smoke from his cigar, but I was invisible to him in the shadows of the roof. I thought of the Lani myth of the angel of death, who swoops unseen to carry off the departed, then of Gritt, the devil-man the Mahweni called Tchanka. Would he make an appearance tonight? It would be tidy if he did, and would make his conviction easier, but I had no desire to see him. The man's reputation had worked itself into the dark places of my head.

I thought of the tap of the cane between the footsteps in the fog the night Billy had died. Had that been him, or Morlak? I was as sure as I could be that it hadn't been Mnenga, and that was a bigger relief than I had expected.

On the warehouse floor, the big Mahweni had a shotgun, which he cracked and checked. Fevel produced a pistol and toyed with it. The other boys had crowbars and knives, and they fidgeted with them, putting on a show of strength they didn't quite believe.

The Westsiders arrived five minutes later, led by Deveril himself, complete with his feathered top hat. He had another four with him, big men armed with rifles and boat hooks. They looked to be Lani, and they moved with the splayed, rolling gait of men used to being on-board ship. Fevel and the boys instinctively clustered, outgunned and outmanned in every sense of the term.

Up there in the roof, I could feel the tension, the menace, as if it were drifting up to me on the cigar smoke.

The Westsiders spread out, creating a wide circle around Fevel and the box, but the conversation, when it started, was so low that I couldn't catch what was said. One of them threw a bag of coins to the floor at Fevel's feet, but he did not move from his seat, waiting instead for one of the boys to stoop to it, check it, and pronounce it acceptable. It was only when the boy tipped his face up to speak that I realized who it was.

Tanish.

I gasped and began, against all reason, all judgment, to get to my feet. A sudden hollowness gripped my stomach, and my chest and throat tightened, as if some great vise were crushing the air from my body. I hadn't thought they would involve him in this, hadn't thought they trusted him. He had probably asked for the job to prove his loyalty.

Stupid, I thought. *Both of us. I should have seen this coming.*

And in that instant, I caught a flicker of movement, not down on the warehouse floor but from the observation booth in the roof. Someone had raised the blind carefully, and I could see two figures working by the light of a dim oil lamp: two uniformed figures and a piece of equipment with a hopper and a long, hefty barrel like a sawn log.

I stared, trying to make sense of what I was seeing, catching the chink of metal as one of the men in the booth upended a bag into the hopper and the other took hold of a pair of handles, so that he sat like a mantis, aiming the barrel down in the warehouse.

It can't be.

I had never seen one before, but I recognized the machine gun for what it was moments before it opened up with a blaze of flame and a stream of deafening bangs.

I leapt to my feet, shouting at Tanish to get down, that it was a trap, but my words were lost in the chaos as the bullets rained down. All the muted panic and anxiety were swept away as everyone down below ran for cover and returned fire. The machine gun didn't stop, its huge barrel revolving with each shot, each yard-long spurt of fire, and I knew what I had to do.

No one down below could stop it. I drew my pistol and ran toward the shuttered window.

Bam-bam-bam-bam-bam-bam went the relentless machine gun, splintering crates, carving up the concrete, punching through corrugated metal. And flesh.

I heard the screams.

Tanish . . .

I sighted along the hexagonal barrel of my revolver toward the shadowy figure who was turning the machine gun's crank, and fired. The gun almost kicked out of my hand, but I held on to it, drew back the hammer, and fired again. The report was deafening and fire seemed to flash out of the side of the cylinder as well as from the muzzle, but I had just enough composure to move through the smoke, cocking the pistol and aim afresh before squeezing the trigger a third time.

The gunner—who was wearing the silver and navy of a policeman—slumped to one side, clutching his shoulder, and his companion snatched the handle from him, dragging the barrel of the weapon up and around toward me, still spewing fire and noise all along its deadly arc, perforating the metal walls and roof as he tried to get me in his sights.

I fired twice more, pulling the hammer feverishly back after each shot, then again, and again, shooting blindly into the smoke, driven by fear and horror until I realized the empty pistol was clicking over and over.

But the machine gun had fallen silent.

For a moment, I clung to the rail as the gantry swam. My stomach felt like iron but was somehow moving—cold but molten—and I sank to my knees, sweat running down my face, unable to breathe.

Below me, Andrews and his men cannoned in, weapons raised, hunched over as they advanced into the warehouse. Andrews shouted orders, but the sound echoed oddly, and I could not hear the words. Then came the blare and flash of a shotgun, and suddenly, it was a chaos of running and shouting and gunfire.

There were bodies on the ground.

One of the Westsiders drew a pistol and fired twice at the policemen before rushing toward the back door. He reached it as it blew open, crashing against the wall, and more police came through. He fired again, and I heard a shout of pain before a barrage of gunfire cut him down where he stood.

I forced myself to get to my feet, fighting back nausea and dizziness, staggering along the catwalk to the metal stairs, wincing as bullets sang and whined through the stuffy, smoke-laden air. Somewhere a shower of shotgun pellets rained down on metal, and up ahead, the gantry sparked as a stray round skipped off it.

But I had to get to Tanish, who was down there in the middle of it all. There was more shouting, another cannonade back and forth, and the slap of bullets into wood, then two more shots, and suddenly, amazingly, nothing.

My ears rang, but I kept moving, half falling down the metal steps and into the cover of the stacked crates, where one of the policemen was sitting on the ground, nursing his bleeding arm. Andrews was shouting again, and in the unearthly glow of the gas lamp and the fog of gunsmoke, I could see people with their hands raised as the police closed in, weapons still up and level.

I ran drunkenly to the light, hands shaking, almost blind with the horror of what had happened, what I had done, and what I might find.

Tanish was sitting on the ground, his back to the trunk. Ignoring Andrews's shout to stay back, I ran to him, dropped, and folded him in a crushing embrace, pressing his cheek to mine.

"It's all right, Tanish," I babbled, pulling him to me. "It's over now."

Police officers were swarming all over the place. Two of Deveril's men were dead or badly hurt. Fevel too. Whoever had been operating that machine gun hadn't cared which gang they hit.

"What the hell was that?" exclaimed Andrews, who was dragging a wounded Deveril—his top hat battered but still on his head—out into the light.

"Ambush, sir," said one of the officers. "Someone wanted them all wiped out."

"And with military-grade hardware and police uniforms," spat Andrews. "When I study that machine gun, am I going to find that it's gone missing from storage belonging to the Glorious Third?"

Deveril shrugged, wincing at the wound in his right arm as he did so. "What can I tell you?" he said. "Seems I have enemies in high places." He chose the words carefully, and for a moment, his gaze fell on me.

"Well, gentlemen," said Willinghouse, appearing beside the crate with Von Strahden. I guess I wasn't the only one who hadn't obeyed Andrews's orders to keep clear. Both men were wearing the smoked glasses worn by luxorite dealers. "Shall we see what someone was so desperate to recover?"

Andrews stepped back, and one of the policemen flipped the hasps on the crate and pulled the lid open.

I flinched instinctively, and I don't think I was the only one, but there was no explosion of light from within, just a large and shapeless mass wrapped in oilskin. Andrews stooped to help, and together they lifted the package out and onto the warehouse floor. The policeman unfastened some lacing, then flapped the fabric open so that it spilled its contents.

Still no luxorite glare, and for a moment, I could only stare in baffled dismay. The oilskin contained perhaps twenty roughly conical objects that curved toward the tip. They were about two feet long and hard, the bases ragged and stained with what looked like blood. I continued to gape, but could make no sense of what I was seeing till Andrews, his head in his hands so that his mouth was muffled and the words came out low and indistinct, spoke.

"Rhino horn."

There was a stunned silence.

Overcome with a new wave of nausea, I started to get to my feet, but as Tanish began to slump, I caught him in my arms again.

"Hey," I said. "Come on, Tanish. Stand up."

He did not respond. He felt unnaturally heavy.

"Tanish?" I said.

But the boy did not move. Had not moved.

No.

One of my hands was wet and sticky.

"Hummingbird?"

Still nothing.

No.

I pulled back to look at him properly, and it was only then that I saw the dark pool beneath him, silvery in the eerie glow of the gas lamp. I stared, speechless, feeling his blood run through my fingers, and then I was rocking him again, violently now, desperately, and someone was screaming.

The doors to my heart, the dam I had fought so hard to keep closed, had broken at last.

CHAPTER
33

POACHING THE GREAT BEASTS of the savannah was an old Feldesland problem, but it was only recently that it had become a major business concern, ivory and horn commanding astronomical prices on the Grappoli market and elsewhere where the great beasts were exotic, even magical. Once last year, some kids had come upon a one-horn stumbling about on the edge of the Drowning. She was blind and crippled by rifle fire but had somehow got back on her feet even after the poachers had sawed off her horn. She blundered around for a while, bleeding heavily, mad from the pain, and eventually collapsed down by the river. It took another two hours for her to die.

What the poachers took was sold as trophy art or ground into "medicine" overseas. The barbarism of it all, the pointlessness, sickened me, but then, in the stony silence of the police carriage, I had other reasons for that.

The dam had burst, and I was swept away by what came through.

I held Tanish's body for a long time, and crying seemed to drain me of strength and will, so that I was only partly in the world. The rest of me was nowhere, was nothing, and my sense of what was happening around me was muted, my vision blurred by more than tears, sound echoing faintly, as if coming through fog from a great distance.

Andrews had roared and cursed and said he had been a fool for listening to some slip of a Lani girl, and how was he supposed to look the prime minister in the eye after this fiasco? Von Strahden tried to say that the smuggling bust was a significant achievement, but Andrews told him that no one cared about a few one-horns. We had nothing on Morlak, on Mandel, on Gritt. Nothing at all. It had all been a waste of time.

"I was sure it would be the Beacon," said Von Strahden, speaking as if in a daze.

"The Beacon!" sneered Andrews darkly. "I suspect that the next people to see the Beacon will be Grappoli troops who dig it out of the rubble of what was Bar-Selehm."

The two machine gunners were not merely costumed gang members. They were junior police officers from the Fourth Precinct, though who had ordered them to join the operation—if anyone—no one knew. Someone had, presumably, given them the hardware and told them to cut down whoever showed up in the warehouse. They had no interest in the crate and were there—Andrews said—to clean up loose ends. We would never know who hired them because both gunners were dead.

I had done that. I had killed two men whose names I didn't know, whose faces I never saw. I had done it to save Tanish, and I had failed.

Willinghouse said nothing, just watched me, his eyes hooded, even when the stretcher bearers came to take Tanish away from me. I leaned into his shoulder, staining his clothes with Tanish's blood, crying as I have never cried for anything before, not even Papa, so that I was not Anglet Sutonga anymore. I was a screaming, writhing, desperate animal of grief and guilt and horror, and it was only Willinghouse's grip on my shoulders that stopped me from flying into madness.

"Shh," he whispered. "I will see that he gets the best doctors in the city. He is not dead yet. We will do everything we can. You have my word."

THE POLICE WENT TO PICK up Morlak, but he denied any knowledge of the deal, suggesting this was a sideline operated by Fevel and some of the other boys. There was nothing to connect him to either the poachers or the smugglers for whom he had been the middleman, and Andrews—already humbled by his shamefaced report to the prime minister—said they did not have enough even for a search warrant. If Morlak had the Beacon hidden away in the shed, it would likely stay there for the foreseeable future.

Not that I cared. They told me, and I heard, but that was all. I sat at Tanish's bedside, holding his hand, reading him the story of the cloud forest, the one we always read together, the one Vestris had once read to me, and I spoke to no one else. He just lay there, small and frail, still and silent.

"Sorry," I whispered through tears. "I'm so sorry, hummingbird. I would have taken you with me."

Willinghouse said I should go home and rest, that he would sit with Tanish in my place, but I didn't respond.

Home.

What did that even mean? His home, I suppose he meant, as if I were living there now, their pet steeplejack. No. That was not my home. But then neither was the Drowning. I hated to admit it, but in my heart, home was the weaving shed on Seventh Street, bleak and miserable though it was, because for the better part of a decade, it had been mine, though I could never go back there again.

Morlak. Everything came back to Morlak. I couldn't connect all the pieces, but he was at the heart of everything, like a spider in his web, and somehow, in spite of the stolen Beacon, and the fort, in spite of Berrit, Ansveld, and the Mahweni herder, in spite even of Tanish, who lay huddled on the bed in front of me inches from death, Morlak was free and likely to stay that way. The police wouldn't even search his place because he was, in the eyes of the law, a fine, upstanding citizen. . . .

I stared at Tanish, tears streaming down my hot face.

"I have to go now, hummingbird," I whispered, squeezing his tiny hand. "I'll come back. Unless they kill me, I'll come back. I promise. But there's something I have to do."

The police couldn't do it, but I, as Andrews and Willinghouse had pointed out so many times, was not police.

I STUDIED THE LINE of the shed roof where it met the tower and chimney stack. It was a smooth red brick that gave no climbing purchase, but there were drainpipes, and in places there were rungs set into the wall. Two of the lower windows had been bricked up years ago, but the top one was shuttered, and I could see how to get to it, though it would take nerve.

Nerve, I had. Nerve and fire. When the dam broke, more than grief gushed out, and some of what came slicing through those awful waters had teeth.

I watched a jackal prowl along the street, its sleek body low to the ground, its ears pricked, and as it rounded the corner and trotted out of sight, I moved.

After shinning up the downspout to the roof of the shed, I picked my way softly over the slates, moving almost on all fours, low and swift like the jackal. At the point where the blockish tower reared up from the shed, I squatted, listening. The city was as quiet as it would ever get. Somewhere down Bell Street, I could hear the distant clank of machinery as the night shift worked on, and there was an occasional boom from the foghorn at the river mouth, but otherwise the night was still.

There were rungs set into the tower wall, though they had probably not been used since the weavers left, and they were rusted and flaking. I took hold of one, tested it, and pulled myself up. I climbed swiftly till I was forty feet above the roof of the shed, then paused. Higher up, the rungs led to the roof, where the old winding gear had been, but the shuttered window to Morlak's treasure house was on the other side of the tower. A ledge ran around to the window. It was a single brick wide.

I took a breath, then stepped out onto the ledge, my back to the tower and all my weight on my heels. I kept my arms beside me, palms flat to the wall, back slightly arched so that my shoulders brushed up against the brick. I did not look down, not because I was afraid of the height, but because tipping my head might throw off my equilibrium. Right now, I was afraid of nothing. I edged a few inches at a time, out into the night.

I hesitated at the corner, feeling my way around, thinking of nothing but Tanish's face.

Three more feet and I was at the window aperture. I felt the timber of the shutter and the simple iron hook hinges and taking hold of them, pivoted briskly to face the wall. Death waited, hard and hungry on the cobbles below, but I disappointed him. My mind and fingers probed for the crack between the shutters, then I reached into the satchel, which had lately doubled as a cradle but was now just a tool bag again. I produced a slim and serrated metal blade on a wooden handle. I slipped it through the crack near the top, guiding it down till I found the restraining bolt.

But there was no need. The shutters were not closed properly, and the haft for the bolt had been cut. Puzzled, I put the saw away, wrenched the uneven shutters apart, and climbed through.

The night was moonless, and if there were stars, you could not see them through the smog, so the room was utterly dark even with the window open. I paused, feeling my heart starting to thud against my ribs. I had felt no fear perching birdlike on the tower ledge, but being inside it stirred an old dread.

Morlak.

He would be downstairs, sleeping, perhaps still incapable of coming up to catch me, but I felt his presence like a foul and poisonous odor.

I closed my eyes and took a deep breath, filling my chest, holding it in my lungs for a moment, before blowing it softly out. I did it again, and felt my heart steady a little. I dragged the shutters closed so that anyone who happened to look up from the street would see nothing amiss. They snagged and squeaked, as if out of alignment, but I got them shut.

I took a stick of candle and a metal box with a close-fitting lid from my satchel, drawing from it a single phosphorous match, which I struck on the brick of the windowsill. The match popped and flared white then yellow as the wooden stick took hold. I lit the candle and shook the match out, taking in the room by the uneven light.

It was a cramped space, the walls crudely plastered, just big enough for an untidy bed, a chair, and in the corner, a chest with a heavy padlock.

Easy.

I squatted down, set the candle in a hardening puddle of its own wax, and got to work with the hacksaw.

But this too had been cut. I dragged the lid open and peered in.

The inside of the trunk was divided into two latched compartments. I opened the one on the left and rummaged through books, ledgers, and files before reaching a bundle of pound notes, a bag of coins, and several small pouches of gold and rough-cut stones.

No luxorite.

I opened the second compartment. It contained a single hessian bag twice the size of my satchel. I pulled on the drawstring neck and opened it. Inside was something shapeless and wrinkled, cool to the touch like metal but yielding to pressure: a dull gray foil. I lifted it out onto the chamber floor and began to unwrap the stiff folds. The object inside was roughly spherical, no bigger than a couple of loaves of bread, but heavy as stone.

I peeled back the metal foil and recoiled from a light more brilliant than anything I had ever seen.

For a second, it was as if the tower room had exploded, but silently, the blaze of yellow-white glare causing every object in the chamber, every splinter of the floor, and every irregularity of the plastered walls to cast hard, leaping shadows. Even with my eyes closed and head twisted away, I felt its pale burning presence, and the inside of my eyelids glowed red.

At last, I thought as I fumbled blindly to re-cover it.

My mind reeled with dizzying exhilaration. I had always known it had been Morlak, and if I acted fast, I could lead Andrews right to him. My heart thrilled to the idea, though I knew it was a poor revenge for Berrit and Tanish even if it was justice as far as the law allowed.

But even there in my one moment of glory, doubt leached my certainty. I thought of the old Mahweni, of Gritt, and the strange, greenish luxorite that had appeared *before* the Beacon went missing.

Stop, I told myself. *Morlak is guilty. You've seen the proof. The rest will make sense later. . . .*

I stood there, immobile, paralyzed by a sudden uncertainty, and my eyes fell on the crack between the shutters whose lock had been so expertly cut. I thought of Morlak's wound, the injury I gave him that had kept him largely immobilized. He could not have brought the Beacon here himself the night it was stolen because he was out drinking and didn't roll in till morning. And from the moment I fought with him, he had been able to walk—just—but not to climb the tower. Tanish had said so.

And now the voice in my head shifted, became not the mouth-piece of surety and decision, but of doubt and unease.

So what if he didn't bring it here? What if someone else, someone with the climbing skills to take it in the first place, scaled the tower after you had so conveniently wounded him, forced their way in, planted it here to impli-cate him? He hasn't been up since. He might not even know it is here. . . .

Why would anyone do that, though? Why would someone steal something of such value only to point the finger at someone else?

Because they hated him so deeply? Or because they wanted the city looking in the wrong direction while an entirely different crime was perpetrated, a crime that would lead to war, devastation, and the restructuring of the entire continent?

I considered this, and suddenly it felt as if I were sinking into deep cold water. I had been sure it was all about Morlak because I hated him and wanted him to be responsible so that he could be punished for all he was, but now I was not so sure. The Beacon was so big, so bright, it had seemed that it must be the center of everything that had happened, but in the chill, dark hollow of my gut, I knew this wasn't true.

It wasn't about the Beacon. It never had been. I had been wrong. Again. I thought of Berrit; of Billy Jennings, the incompetent pick-pocket who had made the mistake of trying to help me; of Tanish, my hummingbird apprentice—and the scale of my failure closed over me like drowning.

Not now. You have to go.

Clumsily, I thrust the Beacon back into the hessian sack and latched the compartment. After the brightness of the light, I could see almost nothing. Hands unsteady, I closed the trunk and scraped up the spilled candle wax. I had just gotten to my feet, ready to make my exit, when I heard the tower stairs creak.

It seemed I had not been so quiet as I thought.

I froze, heart in my throat, listening as the sound came again. This time it was accompanied by something between a grunt and a sigh. A human noise. A big man laboring.

Morlak.

I moved for the window, shoving at the shutters, but one would open only a few inches, and the other wouldn't move at all. Something I had done when I forced them open—or something that was done by whoever had broken in last time—had jammed them.

I couldn't get out.

CHAPTER

34

I MOVED QUICKLY TO the corner with my satchel of tools, flattening myself against the cracked plaster as the door flew open.

The floor was suddenly lit by a soft, filtered glow. An oil lamp. Morlak was holding it out in front of him. He came in, pushing the door so wide that it actually hit my shoulder, where it stopped, but he did not seem to notice.

The moment he cleared the doorway, I would slip behind him and out, down the stairs to freedom.

I waited, poised.

Morlak hesitated in the doorway.

I listened, my heart starting to race again, and I realized what he was doing. He was sniffing the air.

The phosphorous match.

The room still held the ghost of its acrid tang. I stifled a gasp, and in that moment, Morlak stepped into the room and slammed the door behind him. It latched, and we were alone together again.

But he had not seen me.

The gang leader made directly for the trunk, lowering himself with difficulty and muttering curses as he saw the broken half of the padlock.

In seconds he would find it. Then he would panic and turn to the door, where he would see me cowering, with nowhere to run. Noiselessly I reached into my satchel, ignored the empty pistol, and took hold of the next thing my fingers found.

The hacksaw.

I could move up behind him, silent as sleep, and sweep the blade across his throat. For years of torment. For his attempted rape. For Berrit. For Billy. And, most of all, for Tanish.

I took a step out into the room, the saw held out from my side like a talisman, a magical thing in which death strained to get out.

And I hesitated. For the torment and what he had tried to do to me, he was certainly guilty, but for the rest? I had thought so. I had wanted to believe so. But now? I was not so sure.

And then the room went white and glaring, as if I had been dropped onto the surface of the sun, as Morlak dragged the Beacon from its foil wrapping, cursing amazedly, and I stepped back, blinded.

I collided with the door and, sightless, fought for the latch. I heard him behind me, shouting and stumbling about, but I had the door open and he was—I was almost sure—at least as surprised by what he had uncovered as I was. I ran. On the second step, I missed my footing, and fell headlong, the satchel spilling open beneath me. Pain burned bright as the Beacon in my head, but I fought to right myself and my already bruised legs felt unbroken. I half ran, half fell down the stairs.

I could still see nothing.

I blundered into a doorjamb, dimly aware of another male voice, dull and confused by sleep, at my elbow, but I kept moving. Eyes squeezed shut, I recognized the smell of the weavers' shed, the edge of oil and unwashed bodies, and I made for it, feeling rather than seeing the cavernous space open up around me. I faltered for a moment, trying to get my bearings in the unnatural darkness, then plunged on. Somewhere a door opened and a boy cried out, "Who's there?"

I adjusted, then picked up speed, heedless of the damage I might do to myself if I ran into something, or somebody. Farther back, still on the stairs, I could hear Morlak bellowing curses.

I ran into the wall, taking most of the impact on my outstretched arms. I felt the brick and, gazing into the blackness, caught the merest shadow of difference two yards to my left. I made for it, and my hands found wood and the metal fittings of the alley door.

I pressed the latch and shouldered it open.

Instantly, the darkness grayed a little, which was enough. I could have walked these streets blindfolded.

I burst into a hard run, feeling nothing because to feel anything would have made me stop. They would come after me, but I had a head start, and they would not know where I was going.

As I ran, I replayed the one thing I felt sure of in my head.

It's not about the Beacon. It never was.

It was about money, of course, and about the deaths of a boy and an old man who no one thought worthy of attention. These were what really mattered, and I felt suddenly ashamed that it had taken me so long to recognize as much.

SUREYNA WAS WAITING FOR me at her spot on Winckley Street. The lamps were still lit, and the dawn was, for the moment, cool and fresh, but there was broken glass in the street, burned-out carriages on the corner, and shops with their windows shattered and shelves ransacked. And blood. Not a lot. Not yet. But there would be more. "Unrest," the papers would call it, if there still were papers. The protests were souring, the city splintering along lines of race and faction, and Willinghouse's dire prophecies were coming true. We were falling over the brink, and the blood would run in rivers through the streets long before the Grappoli ever got here.

Mnenga's among them.

The idea shocked me, but a part of me was sure it was true. The city blacks would revolt against the rich whites who were leading them into war, and the Unassimilated would come to their aid, bringing spears and hide shields to fight men with machine guns. For a second, I could see his face in the crowd, proud and open and strong even as the gunfire rang out. . . .

Sureyna looked anxious and checked over her shoulder as I approached. I spoke urgently, telling her what had happened at the warehouse, all I knew and suspected, so that she took out her pencil and started scribbling.

"You need to go to the police," she said.

"That's your job," I answered. "There are some things I have to do first, and not all of them are strictly legal."

"Why am I not surprised?" said Sureyna.

I gave her a bleak smile. "I have no choice," I said. "I have to end this before anyone else gets hurt. And, Sureyna?"

"What?"

"This is not about the Grappoli. It never was. Say so. Say it clearly."

She nodded with grim understanding, then—as if remembering something important—snatched one of the newspapers from her stack and thrust it into my hands. "There's a follow-up piece in there you are going to want to read."

I looked at the cover story. For a long moment, the headline stopped my breath and closed my eyes. It read:

SECRET LAND DEAL COALITION CROSSES PARTY LINES

And there were photographs.

BREAKING INTO THE HOUSE on Canal Street was no harder than finding it. I entered through a third-floor window accessed via a downspout, emerging in a well-appointed bathroom. The house was empty of people, as I had expected it would be, and though I moved silently from room to room, I felt no sense of danger. The Lani decorations in the bedroom gave me pause, but I swallowed back any feelings of sadness and remorse as I rifled the office cabinets till I found the charts I had been looking for. The locations were scattered, but I knew what connected them because I had seen the same locations in the land deal records in the library. Each one was marked, the same topographical symbols circled on each map: a broken, wavy line that might have been a stream intersected by a slash mark, over crowded contours. The locations, however, were miles apart, scattered all around the bush north and west of the city. I needed to narrow my search.

In my heart I had suspected it would come to this, though I had hoped to find another way, and I climbed out of the windows and down as if carrying a great load.

Outside, a squad of dragoons was clearing the road. A curfew had been imposed on the city. The streets would be silent until I either unearthed the truth at last, or Bar-Selehm devoured itself in blood and fire.

IT TOOK ME ALMOST an hour to reach the Lani temple on the edge of the Drowning. I did not think Mnenga would be there, would not blame him if he wasn't. And if he was, I had no time to discuss what was on his mind. So though I ran every step of the way, I dreaded getting there, and feared finding him almost as much as not.

He was there. He stood up when he saw me, and his smile was lit by relief, by hope. It broke my heart to see it, to know that I was breaking his, but I had no time to soften the blow.

"I did not come to take back what I said before," I said. "I'm sorry. I came to ask you about something."

"You do not treat me well, Ang," he said, sad rather than angry. "Do you know this?"

"I know," I said. "You are right. I know and I'm sorry. But I must ask you this."

He looked away, his eyes squeezed shut as if he did not want me to see his face.

"Please," I said. "I will ask nothing more of you after today."

He turned back to me then, his face hot as if I had slapped him. "What about me?" he said desperately, hating to have to put it into words. "After today, what about me?"

I looked down and tried to find something to say.

"I see," he said in a hollow voice. "Very well. Ask your question."

"Mnenga," I said, "it's not that I don't—"

"Ask your question," he repeated.

I took a breath. "The old man," I said.

"Ulwazi," he said. "It is important that you call him by his name."

"Ulwazi," I said. "Yes. I'm sorry."

"You said he was dead."

"He is," I said. "Where did he come from? Before he came to the city, where had he been?"

"The bush," he said. "The mountains."

"Yes," I said. "But where. Show me." I rolled out the maps.

He peered at them, then me. "What is this about?" he said.

"I will tell you everything," I said. "I promise. But right now, I just need to know where he was before he came to Bar-Selehm. Your people saw him after he had been sunburned and before he came to the city. Where was that?"

Mnenga scanned one map and shook his head, then considered another. "I do not understand these," he said. "I cannot read them."

"Look," I said, trying not to sound impatient. "Here is the city. These are the mountains. The ocean is here. See? We are here, so the bush goes this way, away from the river." I turned the map and pointed.

He nodded thoughtfully, then leaned over the map and put one dark hand over it. "Here," he said. "There are . . . high walls of stone."

"Cliffs?" I said.

"Cliffs, yes. And streams when the rains come with—" He gestured vaguely with his hands: something rolling down.

I gently pushed his palm aside and put the tip of my index finger on one of the circled topographical symbols, the stream, broken by a short line.

"Waterfall," I said.

I TOLD HIM HOW to find Sureyna and—on impulse—gave him the address of Pancaris. Perhaps with Willinghouse's help, the nuns would let him return Kalla to Rahvey so she could make one last appeal to the elders. I had to try. The orphanage was a terrible place, and I couldn't set off for the old freight line that snaked out of the Riverbend sidings without feeling like I had at least tried to save the girl from it. I may never get the chance again.

So I hopped on the back of a locomotive hauling a mixed cargo of coal and grain, knowing that I was asking too much of Mnenga, but that there was no one else I could trust.

Trust.

I reflected on the word miserably as the train slid its slow way north, leaving behind the weedy, soot-blackened brick of the railway yards, the signal boxes, and gravel access roads as we circled the city like an aging lion, then began the climb toward the mountains.

And who do you trust now, Anglet? Who, apart from the Mahweni boy you have rejected, will stand by you now?

I rode on the footplate because cargo can shift with the movement of the train, crushing those unwise enough to be sleeping between pallets. Not that I would be sleeping. The sun beat on my arms and face, sweat ran down my neck, and the noise and smoke from the rattling engine overwhelmed my other senses, but I had never been more awake in my life. I watched the increasingly wild and ragged bush, catching sight of a herd of black wildebeests and a loping group of rinx giraffes—the ones with the gray and yellow mottling—but no people.

I had never been comfortable outside the city.

Suddenly, strangely, I found myself missing Papa again, and I wondered if the day he died had been the day I stopped trusting anyone.

They would be ahead of me. I knew that the moment I saw the empty house. The police, and maybe a reporter or two, would be following, but my enemies were ahead of me.

Curious that people I barely knew could be my enemies, but they were, and not merely because they wanted me dead, something they would feel more strongly with every step I took toward the point marked on that map. I was more than an inconvenience to them, someone who would upset their plans. I stood for something. Or they did. I wasn't sure what those things were exactly, but I knew they were opposites, and that was why we were enemies.

The collared weancat prowled my mind.

I didn't study the map, but as soon as I saw the water tower, I started looking for a place to jump down where I was least likely to turn an ankle. There was no cover to speak of, just elephant grass and the occasional thorn tree, and no way to go but to follow the streambed till the slope became a cliff. If they were expecting me, they might pick me off with a rifle long before I got there, but I was trusting their arrogance and condescension. They didn't think me worth watching for.

I was fairly sure of my destination now, the only spot where Ulwazi's wanderings overlapped with the parcels of land sold by Sohwetti. The rest, I was sure, added up to little more than a ruse, a screen so that no one would notice the one location that mattered.

Well, I had noticed, and as soon as I was certain of all the details, they would answer for their crimes.

At the edge of the dried river, the grass had been beaten flat, and I could see the prints of work boots. Lots of them. Deep wheel ruts and hoof marks crossed the riverbed back toward the city, and under a wizened marula tree I found an abandoned water cooler and a helmet. A work team had been here recently.

I wanted to believe that they were all gone, but I knew they weren't. My enemies were here to bury their traces for the time being, and if I didn't find them quickly, they might still walk away rich and free. I couldn't wait for assistance—if it would ever come—from the police. I was on my own.

But then, you always are, aren't you? However much you pretend that isn't true, you will always be alone. You are the blind and blundering rhino, hornless, staggering about alone, lost, waiting for death, incapable of protecting those dearest to you. . . .

I thought of Tanish and for a moment my body tightened, eyes clenching and stomach cramping so that I bent my knees and hunched my shoulders against the sun, hands drawn to my chest like a nun in prayer. A scream of anguish fought to come out, but I bit it down and shut it back inside the dam.

I inhaled, opened my eyes, and straightened up. There would be time for such feelings later. Perhaps.

The rhino had been mutilated. I was whole. I was strong. And the collar was a collar of the mind.

I tied my hair back.

There was a thin trickle of water in the base of the creek bed, but the torn-up grass on its banks thirty yards apart suggested that not so very long ago, it had been a torrent. Then it would have hummed with insects, but now it was silent, and I saw nothing but a pair of dassie watching me absently from the rocks. Nevertheless, I walked carefully, eyes down for hibernating snakes and the giant crab spiders that lived in these parts, picking my way between boulders strewn by the flood the river barely remembered. As the climb became steeper, the river divided like the fingers of a hand, each digit pointing a different route to the high ridge above. I considered it, caught sight of startled crows circling, but could not see what might have dislodged them. I checked the map, squinted into the sun, and chose the middle tributary.

Within ten minutes, I was using my hands occasionally, and within twenty, I was climbing, being careful not to dislodge the scree, which would crash into the valley below. It was hot work, and I cursed myself for bringing no more than my usual water flask, which was already half empty. Sweat ran in my eyes, making them sting, but I could not pause. Not yet.

I have never been so ill at ease climbing. I'm used to smooth brick and concrete, iron and stone, and I know their textures and their natures, what will yield to pressure, what will crack or splinter, how much weight they can bear, and where I might find places to hook fingers or toe caps. For the most part, the rule of these materials is regularity, and it is the breaks in that regularity—the chinks and nooks and crevices—that I know how to find and that keep me up. But cliffs are all irregularity, and while that means more handholds, more places where I can brace myself with knee or foot, the materials are unknown to me. I found that I had no idea what would crumble in my grasp, what might dislodge and fall beneath me, what might tear out as soon as I put weight on it.

I stopped, nestled in a crevice, and shrank into the shade, where I could breathe and slow my heart. Every joint and muscle seemed to ache. If I survived the day, I decided, I would lay my battered and exhausted body down and not move for a week. One way or another, it would all soon be over.

A breeze I had not noticed seemed to funnel up the cliff wall, and I turned into it so that it chilled the sweat that streamed down my face. As I did so, my eyes fell upon a darkness in the cliff above and to my right, no more than twenty yards as the crow flies.

An opening.

It wasn't the source of the dried-up waterfall, which came from higher, but it had probably been screened by that cascade throughout the rainy season. Now it was dry, a curtain had been lifted, and what it showed was a cave—and a new one, at that. There were others in the cliffs, mere natural apses, little more than hollow pocks cut by wind and spray over time, but this was different. Its edges were hard and bright, and below, I could see shards of fractured stone the size of a one-horn. The waterfall had eroded the cliff till part of it had given way, but no one had seen the opening till the torrent dried up.

No one, that is, except an elderly and eccentric Mahweni herder, who had then come down the mountain with tales to tell and fortunes to make.

I flattened myself into my alcove still further. If they were keeping any kind of watch, they would be close by. I checked my satchel. I had a knife with a long blade, as well as assorted chisels and a hammer, but my revolver was still empty.

Which isn't necessarily a bad thing.

I shook the thought off, but before it had faded from my mind, I thought of the machine gunners I had cut down, and of Tanish, bleeding in the warehouse. It hadn't been my enemies who shot him, not directly, but his blood was on their hands nonetheless. I tucked the pistol into my belt in the small of my back. Then, once more, and with a sense of looming finality, I did what I always did.

I began to climb.

CHAPTER
35

THERE WAS NO ONE in the cave mouth, but there was a coil of long rope, which had been fastened to a spike driven through a crack in the uneven floor.

They aren't all climbers, then.

I had guessed as much, but it was as close to good news as I was likely to get, so I stored the thought away for future use and crept soundlessly inside. A jagged rock like a huge fractured canine, part of the cliff face itself that hadn't come free when the surrounding stone collapsed, dominated the cave. I squeezed past it and found myself in an open area with a single narrow access point that burrowed back into the mountain. I peered cautiously in, but the passage turned, and no light came from around the corner.

I swallowed, touched the empty gun at my back, and inched my way into the dark.

I heard them before I saw them, grunting, gasping, and cursing. Flattening myself against the rock wall, I listened.

"It's too big," said a gruff, male voice in Feldish. "We'll never shift it by ourselves. We should send back for the survey team, get a couple of the biggest of them up here. Topple it across the entrance, then pile rubble on it."

"We're trying to keep the place secret!" said another voice, a voice I knew, and my heart sank a little, though I was not surprised. "Are you mad, man? We can't lead people to the very spot we don't want them to find."

"We have them do the work, and then we make sure they don't leave," said the gruff voice, darkly.

"That's your solution to everything," said the other. "And look where it's gotten us. If you leave bodies behind, people come looking for them. Have you not even learned that much?"

"No one will come for a couple of damned fuzzies. They didn't come for the last one."

"Yes," said the other voice. "As a matter of fact, they did, and he was an old man with no children, a bush wanderer. The men on my team are citizens of the city. They have wives and families, and you will not treat them as disposable labor to bury your mistakes. God, you disgust me!"

There was a chill silence, and then the gruff voice I had never heard before but which I knew in my bones came from Sergeant Major Claus Gritt, the devil-man Mnenga called Tchanka, the man who had stalked me in the street and run his sword stick through Billy Jennings's chest, spoke again.

"Now, you listen to me, *politician*. This is *our* mistake, not mine, and if you address me in that tone again, I'll be strewing your joints out there with the fuzzies, for the vultures. Do you hear me?" There was a muffled sound, which I took to be assent, and then Gritt added, "Now, fetch me that crowbar, the long one, and we'll try levering this onto its side. Maybe we can roll it into place."

"Give me a moment. I don't feel well."

I kept very still, breathing shallowly, listening as they worked, trying to decide how much more I needed to see and hear.

Over the next few minutes, they tried different ways of shifting the rock, but eventually they gave up, cursing, and there was a long, ragged silence while the two men fought to get their breath back.

"If Mandel hadn't gotten cold feet we'd be able to do it," said the smoother voice.

"That's neither here nor there," said Gritt.

"You said he was in all the way," said the other. "You said he'd protect us, that he'd make sure no one looked too closely till it had all blown over."

"Leave the colonel out of this," said Gritt. "He has to be more careful than us. He has more to lose."

"And always has had."

"Meaning what?" Gritt demanded.

"We weren't all born with silver spoons in our mouths. If we had, we wouldn't be in this mess."

"There is no mess. Our investment will take a little longer to mature, is all, and when it does, our profits will be greater since we have the colonel's shares."

"And if someone finds it before then?"

"They won't if we can block the cave, so I suggest you get off your fancy trousered behind and get to work."

I thought furiously. Surely, I had enough. I had names, I had the location, and I had a complete sense of the story. I couldn't prove all of it, but I wouldn't get that evidence standing here. It was time to go for help.

I turned, but found the passage behind me blocked. Silhouetted at the corner of the tunnel was a figure in gray, a bright but purposeful-looking pistol in her raised hand.

"Greetings, sister mine," said Vestris.

CHAPTER
36

I DID NOT PLEAD for her to let me go. I did not remind her of old times or sisterly bonds. I did not ask her why. I did not tell her we could all walk away from this if only we kept our heads and didn't do anything rash. That's what people in books did, and that was where it worked. Not here, not now, and I would not humiliate myself by trying.

But I felt it all. I had known that she was almost certainly involved, but a part of me was sure she would be able to explain, that it had been some strange misunderstanding, that she had been caught up in something driven by other people. But in the seconds after she had spoken in the passage, I looked into her eyes as well as into the muzzle of her gun, and I knew the truth in my heart. She was not the person I had thought her, and she did not care for me at all. I didn't know why, would never know why, but it felt like a part of me had been cut away, torn out like the rhino's horn, so that life was pouring out of me through the ragged hole.

Not just life. It was the way I had thought the world was, the things that I loved and valued. That was what was gushing out of the wound Vestris's betrayal had made. I gazed at her, the beautiful woman who had once been half sister, half mother to me and Rahvey, so graceful, still smelling faintly of sandalwood and violets. But the glow I had always felt around her, the light and warmth that made you feel special when it touched you—that was gone.

"Sergeant Major!" she called. "Come out here, please, and relieve my sister of her gun. She is strong. She may be the third pair of hands you need to do your job."

I heard him move into the crevice behind me, smelled his sweat, felt his strong hands snatch the revolver from my belt; then he turned me around and looked into my face, smiling without humor.

"Miss Sutonga," he said in a voice cold as the steel of his sword stick. "You have been in the wars, haven't you? I *am* glad to see you again. We have unfinished business." His eyes were hard and bright, and inside them was nothing at all.

The Tchanka, I thought. *The jackal-headed devil-man who slinks under the door and eats your children. Berrit and Tanish—even, somehow, Kalla.*

Then he was pulling me roughly around the corner and into the cave.

It wasn't, of course, the actual cave, the cave that mattered. That was beyond an uneven hole where the rock had collapsed, the hole they were working to plug. This was a mere antechamber, roughly circular, like a bubble in the rock, scattered with weapons, tools, and chunks of stone which they were using to block the way through.

Stefan Von Strahden was inside, lit by the soft glow of an oil lamp. He had just enough dignity to look down, shamefaced, when my eyes fell upon him. I had known as much, but I still felt a strange and sapping misery that was about far more than this one disappointing man.

"You turned on everything you believed," I said. "Everyone."

"We aren't all born onto estates like Willinghouse," he said, mustering a little defiance, so that his normally open, welcoming face—a face I had instantly liked—looked petulant. "You of all people should know that."

"I do," I said. "And that's why I know that excuse isn't good enough."

"You're dazzled by him," said Von Strahden, who looked sick and sweaty. "By his elegance and good looks and money."

"And you are dazzled by my sister," I said, managing a thin and hopeless smile. "We all were."

"I didn't know you were sisters," he said, as if that made a difference. He sounded weary and a little defeated, even sad. "Not till a few days ago. Vestris never . . . I didn't know."

I turned to face her. She was staring at him, her face hard and unreadable.

"You were a steeplejack?" I said. "Before you became . . . whatever you are now?"

Her face flashed with anger for a second, and I braced myself for her to slash the pistol across my face, but she recovered her composure and framed a smile, though I saw the sweat glistening on her forehead. Like Van Strahden, she looked greenish, unwell, and there was a spot above her left ear where the scalp showed through her hair.

"That was a long time ago," she said. "I have moved up in the world, and not by climbing chimneys."

"Climbing into people's beds—" I began, but did not finish.

The inevitable blow made the chamber spin, and I went down for a moment. I tasted blood in my mouth, and the raging throb of my already battered cheek, but I felt only vindication and a strange, savage joy.

"All my life I have looked up to you," I said from the ground. "Everyone back home does. But now that I know you for what you are, I pity you."

"Home?" snapped Vestris. "You think that stinking shanty was home to someone like me? I'm above it. I always was, and in your heart, you think that you are too."

I blinked, trying to keep the truth of her remark from my face, but she saw it anyway and smiled.

"What a strange and self-deluding person you are!" she said. "You thought you could be a mother to Rahvey's brat? You thought you could escape your past by working as an aristocrat's hired help? Poor, sad little Ang. I once thought us so similar. It's really rather disappointing."

"We were," I said, unable to keep the sadness out of my voice. "Once, when it was just Papa and the three of us—you, me, and Rahvey. We were similar. Did you forget?"

She made to hit me again, and I flinched away. "As for pity," said Vestris, as if I hadn't spoken, "save it for those who need it. Yourself, of course. And your apprentice, Tanish."

She read the flicker of puzzled anxiety in my eyes.

"Oh, you won't have heard!" she said. "I'm so sorry to be the bearer of bad news. Your little friend died this morning."

No.

I said nothing as they got on with their work. I felt the cool stone beneath my hands, heard the breathing of my enemies, and saw the brutal cascade of images in my head, things I had done, things I had failed to do, but I said nothing. There was nothing left to say. My eyes had flooded, and though I fought to keep them open, I blinked at last, and tears ran down my face.

I'm not sure how long I stayed there like that, but after a while, as if bored by my silence, the woman who had been my sister spoke again.

"You want to see, little Anglet?" she said. "You might as well. It is, after all, what you will die for."

I looked up at that, searching her face for a glimmer of doubt or remorse, but there was nothing. I knew she had tried to kill me at the opera house, but I was still surprised. She was implacable, determined, and it was as if I had never seen her before, or if in pursuit of what she most wanted, she had gone through some appalling transformation, a nightmare butterfly. The Vestris who had read to me when Papa could not was gone.

"No," I said.

"Ah"—she smiled—"a little spirit yet. But there are times when you should do as you are told."

"You're going to kill me anyway," I said.

"True," she said. "but I haven't decided what to do about Rahvey's brat."

I stared at her. "Why would you harm Kalla?" I asked. "She's not even Rahvey's anymore."

"Because it would hurt you," she said, as if it were obvious. "You see, Anglet, how much better it is to be truly independent? Too late now. Climb through there, or I will find the child and kill it."

I did as I was told.

The passage was already half packed with rubble, and I had to squeeze my way through, stooping so as not to hit my head on the low ceiling. Vestris followed, moving more awkwardly than usual and breathing heavily, but the pistol stayed leveled at my back. I wondered if she could really shoot me down, or murder her sister's infant out of nothing more than spite.

Family is family, said the vestiges of the Lani way in my head.

No, I decided, and not just for Vestris. Willinghouse was right. Some things were more important. Or you made your own family. Tanish was family. So, I decided, was Mnenga. It couldn't just be about blood.

We walked and the corridor turned, swelled, then clenched again, turning twice more before I was sure. It should have been dark as the inside of a chimney, but it wasn't, and with each step, the light ahead grew stronger. I rounded the final corner and had to turn away.

I was standing in a vaulted cavern, but the details were impossible to see because it blazed with a hard, white light that pulsed from every inch of the rock surface, a blinding, constant wall of energy so intense, you could almost hear it.

The chamber was made entirely out of luxorite. Even in my despair, I quailed at the enormity of the thing.

"You knew, didn't you?" said Vestris, who had stayed in the mouth of the passage so she could see me better.

"Yes," I said, my voice low and flat, eyes shaded from the glare. "This is where the dowager's necklace came from. That was why you had to get it from her. Couldn't have people asking too many questions about its origins till you had secured the source for your-self. I assume that's why Ansveld had to die too, yes? He wanted to know what had happened to the old Mahweni who showed him the stone. Went to his old friend Archie Mandel, which was unfortu-nate. Gritt met with him in his shop, tried to scare him off, but that didn't work, so you killed him. I assume it was you. Climbing in through the upper story to cut a man's throat isn't really Gritt's style, is it?"

Vestris said nothing. The light was unbearably intense, and my head was starting to hurt.

"You killed him," I persisted, determined to say it all just to prove I knew, "but not before you risked a massive diversion. You wanted to suggest Ansveld was involved in some shady dealing with Morlak and the Grappoli, so you paid one of the boys to take a piece you got off the old Mahweni to lure him out. You stole the Beacon and planted it in Morlak's tower. Then you killed Berrit, like he was just so much trash to be tossed away."

I paused. It wasn't just my head that was swimming. My stomach was starting to churn as well, but I saw the blankness in her eyes.

"The boy on the chimney," I said. "Berrit Samar. You went to his funeral! But first you killed him and left him, as if no one would even notice. I noticed. I wear this in his memory."

I showed her the pendant, and she considered it with scorn.

"So you are, what? An avenging angel?" she said, grinning with disdain. "I came to the funeral to see if anyone cared about him, anyone who might ask questions. I never thought it would be you. You didn't even know him."

I swallowed back my outrage, took a steadying breath, and found, for once, the kind of calm that comes from clarity. "Why does every-one keep saying that?" I remarked, realizing the importance of the question as I said it. "Why does whether I knew him or not matter? He was a child, a boy you murdered. I have to avenge him *because* I didn't know him. Because he will never have what other boys his age look forward to. He was snuffed out, all his possibilities ended by your knife, and I am not supposed to care because I didn't *know* him? Who are we if we care only for our own, Vestris? What are we? What separates us from the hyenas and the weancats is that we care for those we *don't* know, those who have nothing and nobody they can rely on."

Vestris actually smirked.

"I didn't know him," I exclaimed, "but I knew you, and you betrayed me and anything I ever believed in! Berrit called you his friend in high places, but that was a lie. To you, he was just a tool to be thrown away when you had used it. Not to me. No, I didn't know him, but I will fight for him and people like him because I have to or the world makes no sense, and in that sense, yes, I am his avenger."

"When did you become so talkative?" said Vestris icily. "You were always such a quiet, secretive child."

"You killed Berrit," I said again. "But that was where things started to go wrong, wasn't it? Morlak never made it up to his tower room because I hurt him, so he never panicked and tried to get rid of the Beacon in ways bound to get him caught. And Berrit's death, which was supposed to be dismissed as an accident, started to get attention. My attention. You used your friends' connections to get Morlak to bury Ulwazi, the old Mahweni, in the rubble of the Red Fort, but you didn't bank on the body being found. That was me too. And it was I who stopped the gunners you hired to wipe out both gangs."

"You have a smug streak, Anglet, did you know? It's not attractive."

"I wasn't trying to be. Ever," I added. "Which is one of the differences between us."

Her smile curdled further. "The Lani are rarely right about anything, Anglet, but I think there might be something to their ideas about third daughters. You really are cursed."

If there had been any part of me that still thought of her as my sister, it died then, but I felt no pain at the loss. Indeed, it made things clearer, easier. Vestris mistook my silence for doubt or shame and pressed what she assumed to be her advantage.

"What you think you have achieved doesn't add up to anything," she said, barely suppressing what I could only describe as pleasure. "You will still die here, and no one will ever find you or this cave. Do you have any idea what it's worth, sister mine? You can't. The numbers are not big enough. What you are looking at is beyond wealth, beyond price, even beyond power. This cave is worth nations. Empires."

And now, for the first time, I surprised her. She stared at me.

"Why are you laughing?" she demanded.

"Because you are all idiots," I said. "Because you've been blinded by your own greed, which is brighter and hotter than the luxorite of which, sister mine, this cave is *not* built."

"What nonsense is this?" she scoffed.

"Not nonsense," I said. "It's true. You must have noticed the color difference. New luxorite produces a white light tending to blue, but not this. This leans to green. It's not the same mineral."

"Even if that's true," she shot back, "it doesn't matter. A minute color variation you can't even see except under lenses? No one will care."

"They will when they learn what it does," I said, taking a step toward her and smiling. "You say this cave is nations, empires. It's not. It's hell. It's disease and death. How are your fingers, by the way? You notice any burning where you have handled the stone? It's subtle at first, but it's only the first symptom. The dowager had been wearing hers for only a matter of hours, and she was already getting sick. I thought the old Mahweni herder had been tortured to death while Gritt tried to get the location of the cave out of him, but he just died, didn't he?"

"He was ill when we found him," said Vestris, a hint of panic in her voice.

"Yes, I'm sure he was," I said. "From this place and from carrying pieces of it with him."

"No."

"Yes," I pressed. "I see you are starting to lose your hair."

One hand started to move to her head, but she stopped it.

"What you have bought, sister mine," I said, feeling the doors close, the dam setting against the pressure beyond, "what you have killed for, is not just worthless. It's a death trap, and you will never sell an ounce of it."

She lunged for me then, swinging the gun at my head in a wild, desperate cut. I caught it, brought my knee up hard into her stomach, and as she crumpled, jabbed my elbow into the side of her face. She went down heavily and, once she hit the stone, did not move.

I took the gun, made sure I knew how to work it, and went back along the passage till I reached the half-blocked entrance into the circular antechamber. The men were working with their backs to me, so I climbed noiselessly through and stood tall, feet shoulder-width apart. Gritt straightened up slowly, turning, as if stirred by some military instinct that told him he was being sighted along a gun barrel. His eyes were hard with fury. Von Strahden stared with shock and horror, and as he put the pieces together, he took an unsteady step toward me. I swung the gun around on him, but even as I did so, I caught my sister's name on his lips, saw the anguish in his face, and I hesitated.

In that half second, Gritt moved, throwing himself at me. I pulled the gun around, firing once, hitting nothing as the big man slammed into me, almost stunning myself with the deafening report and the muzzle flash in the low light of the cave. I fell hard, losing the gun, Gritt's weight pinning me down.

"Lani bitch," he grunted, swinging his fists at my face.

I kicked and rolled, but could not throw him off, and then when it seemed like he might just take a rock and bash my skull in, he was scrambling to his feet and turning toward the sound of voices.

My head was ringing with the weight of his blows, but I managed to get onto one elbow and looked to where two black men had entered the cave. I had never seen them before, and neither, judging by their astonished and uncertain faces, had Von Strahden or Gritt. They were young men, bare chested and wearing only the belted grass skirts of the Unassimilated Tribes, and at shoulder height, poised to throw, they bore short spears with long, leaf-shaped metal tips.

Gritt's rage was boundless. He did not hesitate, but snatched for the pistol in his belt and swung it round in a low, precise arc.

He pulled the trigger.

It clicked. Empty. It was my revolver. He lunged, snatching up Vestris's fallen pistol, turning, and aiming at the black boys he so despised.

I was still on the ground, half behind him, but I kicked him hard in the ribs with my steeplejack's boots, and his first shot went wide. There was a sudden silence. I did not understand why he had not fired again—not till he slumped beside me, one of the Mahweni spears buried in his chest.

I rolled away in horror and revulsion, remembering only at the last instant to take the gun and train it on Von Strahden, who was motionless, braced like a cornered animal.

It was a long moment before I dared consider the two boys, and I saw the resemblance immediately.

"You are Mnenga's brothers," I said.

One of them nodded. "Mnenga said you might need help," he said. "That you were alone among hyenas."

"Thank you," I gasped. "I was."

CHAPTER
37

ONE OF THE BROTHERS—the elder, whose name was Embiyeh—led Von Strahden out of the cave and down by a hidden path to a point closer to the freight line, and I followed with the pistol while the other brother, Wayell, went back to guard Vestris, remaining in the antechamber so that he would not be exposed to the mineral.

The mineral that is slowly killing my sister, moment by moment.

We had not reached the bottom before we saw the mismatched carriages barreling along the Bar-Selehm road in a column of dust.

Among them were Andrews and a squad of armed officers, Willinghouse in the family coach, and a pair of cabs stuffed with reporters led by a dictatorial Sureyna. The last to emerge was Mnenga, who embraced his brother and spoke to him softly in their own language. Me, he kept his distance from, giving me simply a nod and a bashful, cautious smile when he found me looking at him.

I walked to him, folded him in my arms and held him tight to my breast, breathing my thanks and apologies. I felt the strength of his grip around my shoulders, the shuddering of his breath against my chest, and I was not surprised to see the tears in his eyes when we finally parted, though he immediately took a step back and away. The space between us yawned like a chasm, and for a long moment we just looked at each other. Then Willinghouse was beside me, and Mnenga took three quick strides away.

"Are you all right?" asked Willinghouse, his face pale save for the sickle-shaped scar, which glowed like hot metal. "That looks like a nasty cut."

I unfastened my hair, shook it loose, and considered him.

I wanted to ask him how much he had known or suspected about Von Strahden, how much he had not told me, even though that might have put my life in jeopardy; I wanted to yell at him, to blame him, but I could not.

After a moment, he broke eye contact, gazing out across the bush toward the city, and he nodded. "Good work, Miss Sutonga," he said.

Again, I considered him, and he opened his mouth to say something else, but then looked at his shoes. I had never seen him so ill at ease, and for all his finely cut clothes and air of authority, he looked thoroughly out of place.

"I'm glad that . . ." he said, then hesitated. "Well. Yes. Very good work indeed."

And then he was walking away, and through the space where he had been, I saw Mnenga watching. For a second our eyes locked and something sad and pained passed between us, and then he too turned to face the city and began to walk away.

"Excuse me, Anglet, if it isn't too much trouble!"

The voice came from the Willinghouse coach. The window screen was down, and Dahria was leaning out, her eyes full of exasperated boredom.

"Dahria," I said as I approached.

"First name terms now, is it?" she said.

"I'm not pretending to be your maid anymore," I said.

"Quite," said Dahria. "Well, I have one final duty for you, and I would be obliged if you would take care of it immediately because it is exceedingly tiresome."

"What?" I asked.

She opened the door and leaned back so that I could see inside.

Tanish was sitting in the corner—pale, tired, and bandaged, but very much alive and smiling like the spring.

"No time for children myself," said Dahria, "but I thought it would cheer you up, his not being dead and all."

"Out of the way, you maddening, bloody woman," I muttered,

climbing in and throwing myself on the boy, who laughed, albeit with difficulty.

I gripped Tanish to me, like holding life itself, laughing and crying at the same time till he begged me to stop.

"And there's this," Dahria added, picking up a basket covered by a blanket.

It was Kalla. I lifted her to my heart and kissed her forehead, inhaling the life of her.

I stepped down from the carriage and found Mnenga with my eyes. He hadn't left after all. He was loitering at a distance, but watching so that I did not need to call my thanks. He met my eyes and nodded once, smiling in spite of everything.

"Well, yes," said Dahria, regarding the baby like an unwelcome parcel. "Quite. It's very hot out here. Has anyone noticed? It would be much more pleasant at home. I merely mention it—"

"You have a baby," said Willinghouse, nonplussed. "Whose is it? Why do you have a baby?"

"Oh yes," said Dahria, dry as the desert air. "Master detective, you are."

MNENGA'S BROTHER WAYELL CAME staggering down the path all by himself. After a good deal of heated chatter with his brothers, he told a story of how he had waited for a long time before venturing back into the false-luxorite cave, but found no sign of Vestris. It was so bright up there that I had not seen the other passage, which seemed to turn into the mountain before creeping out into the air.

Embiyeh fumed and said he had let the family down, and Andrews chuffed about the killer's escape, but I was neither surprised nor—in the face of Tanish's survival—as upset as I might have expected. Vestris was sick, sicker than she realized, but there was no point searching the mountain for her. She would climb and she would hide—she was good at both—and eventually the strange illness that came from the false luxorite would overcome her. Animals would get to her body, and we would not see her again.

I was almost sure of it.

TANISH COULD NOT BE dissuaded from rejoining the Seventh Street gang, at least for the short term, but he was escorted back to the weavers' shed by two police officers and a pair of mounted dragoons in dress greens, to make sure Morlak's boys got the message: Tanish was not to be touched. Tanish was to complete his recovery in peace. Tanish was to be happy in his work. If he wasn't, life for the gang would get very difficult indeed.

Morlak was arrested for assault and receipt of stolen goods, Von Strahden for conspiracy and treason. He would hang for the latter. His story was a sidebar in the papers whose headlines blared simply, BEACON FOUND!

Archibald Mandel resigned under a cloud after the papers got hold of the fact that he owned sizable shares in Grappoli munitions factories. Given the war footing we had been on, said Sureyna's report dryly, "this should have been considered a conflict of interest." Meanwhile, diplomatic relations were reestablished with the Grappoli, border troops stood down, and the nightly demonstrations that had threatened to plunge Bar-Selehm into chaos evaporated without a trace. It would be absurd to say that race relations were now harmonious, but with the truth of the Beacon's theft and the Mahweni land deals out in the open, the city took its step back from the brink of disaster at last.

The false-luxorite cave was secretly and reluctantly sealed by the government, but only after they proved that monkeys that were shut in there were dead within two days and that anyone who handled the mineral developed increasingly severe burning, headaches, nausea, and hair loss. Doctors had never seen the like of it before and didn't have the beginnings of an idea how to treat it, so they took a couple of tiny samples, which they protected inside a box alternating lead foil with ceramic and an outer casing of steel that they sealed in a vault, then pumped concrete into the cave mouth. That the substance otherwise looked like luxorite was, astonishingly, kept under wraps, to keep people from trying to dig their way in. Those of us who knew different were instructed not to breathe a word of it or we would face charges of high treason against the state. I felt I had to tell Sureyna after all she had done, but I made her swear she wouldn't print a word of it.

I appeared in the papers myself, though it was made to sound as if I had merely stumbled upon the cave and found the villains at work. I had acted "with honor and courage," though the stories were not specific as to how, and soon the city was awash in rumors about a mysterious Lani woman who had saved the region from some terrible weapon. I told people it wasn't true, but they preferred the heroic version, and tended to just nod and smile when I said otherwise, as if I were being discreet or modest.

TWO DAYS AFTER IT was all done, I returned to the Drowning in Willinghouse's coach, Dahria dressed to the nines at my side, escorted by Mnenga and a liveried driver. I led them wordlessly through the tumbledown huts and faded awnings, through the ripe smells of moldering vegetables, charcoal grills, and foraging warthogs, to Rahvey's house. We accumulated a watchful train, and word of our arrival went ahead of us like fire leaping from bush to bush till it seemed the whole community was out to see the return of their most curious prodigal.

In my arms I carried Kalla, openly for all to see.

Rahvey and her girls were already out on the porch, and Sinchon came running up from the river with a rusty pot in his hands. Dahria lifted her dress above the mud, but for once, said nothing, and her face was impassive, as if she had not noticed the way the crowd stared at her. Indeed, no one spoke, and I did not mount the porch steps, but stood below my sister, whose face was guarded. From the edge of the crowd I saw Florihn, the midwife, bustling imperiously to the front, her face hard. Four of the elders were there too. They looked cautious, watchful. Jadary, Rahvey's youngest, stood on her tiptoes to see the baby in my arms, her hands clasped in front of her chest.

"I have brought you your daughter, Rahvey," I said. "I took her to the orphanage, but I have seen it, and it is a hard, unfeeling place designed not to nurture children but to break them. They should not have your little girl. I cannot keep her myself, for though I have feelings for the child, I have neither the skill nor the patience to be her mother. You do. It is your gift, and I think that in your heart, you love it. I have a job, at least for now, which pays rather better. If you want to take her back, I will bring you money. Every week. More than enough to feed and clothe the child, educate her too, if you don't object."

Florihn snorted with scorn, but Rahvey said quietly, "Why would anyone object to educating a girl?"

I nodded cautiously, and for a moment, we watched each other. My focus was broken by a ripple in the crowd. A cab had arrived. Willinghouse, in tinted glasses and wearing a pale, elegant suit with a cravat, was watching from the road.

As if sensing something in the air, Florihn spoke. "The rule against four daughters is not merely about money," she said, drawing herself up. "It is about what is seemly, what is traditional."

"Traditions evolve," I said. "People move on."

"People leave, you mean," said Florihn. "And when they do, they lose the right to decide what is appropriate for their people. You come here with your fancy friends, your *white* friends—"

"My grandmother was born just over there," inserted Dahria brightly, in flawless Lani, pointing toward the river. "We're quite an astonishingly diverse little band." She smiled as if she had just remarked upon the weather, and the crowd stared at her. "I'm sorry," she added to Florihn, who was blinking but otherwise motionless, as if in the grip of some curious catatonia, "you were saying?"

"It doesn't matter what she was saying," said Rahvey. "She does not speak for me. Or for the Drowning."

Jadary stared wide eyed at her mother, a look of shock and delight.

"How dare you!" Florihn blustered, but the crowd was not on her side.

I don't know if something had happened or if I was merely glimpsing it for the first time, but Rahvey was right. The midwife did not speak for the people, and I saw two of the elders exchange sidelong glances. One of them tipped his head fractionally and raised his eyebrows, the smallest shrug I had ever seen.

And with that infinitesimal gesture, the Lani way buckled and reshaped itself, the curse was dispelled, and the Drowning changed.

"I shall keep the child," said Rahvey, "and her name will be . . ." She hesitated, her eyes still locked on mine. "I was going to name her Cenu, after the goddess, but I think we will call her Kalla."

I smiled then, though tears had started to my eyes, and before I could change my mind, I kissed the baby on her forehead once and handed her to her mother.

"Take this too," I added, fishing the habbit from my satchel.

"But that was yours," said Rahvey, gazing at it with wonder. "Papa gave it you."

I nodded, weeping, and could just manage to say, "She likes it."

"No," said Rahvey. "You may have use for it."

I managed a smile as I put it away, but I saw the sadness in her face and knew something else was coming.

"You have to go now, Ang," she said. "Though I release you from it, you broke your vow. And I think killed our sister. I almost understand, and I am sure you could explain, but you cannot be here. Not now."

"Rahvey!" I said, suddenly breathless. "You know what she did?"

My sister—my sole surviving sister—nodded, tears in her eyes.

"I know," she said. "But in a way, Florihn was right. You are not one of us. Not anymore."

I opened my mouth to protest, but no words came. Tears ran down Rahvey's cheeks, and she smiled sadly when I, after a pause that might have been a lifetime, nodded.

She embraced me then, and as we separated, she hesitated, to trace the thin scars on my cheeks with her fingertip. The wounds had closed, but I suspected the marks would be there forever.

"I'm sorry about your face," she said.

I remembered the day Florihn had made the cuts with her knife so very long ago, and I said now what I had said then. "It doesn't matter."

Then I turned and walked back to the carriage, eyes streaming, parting the crowd before me as Vestris had once done.

I knew then that I would never return, not really, and the pain was deep and exquisite, as if a fine blade had slit a thin, cruel wound in my heart.

AT WILLINGHOUSE'S URGING, MNENGA and his brothers were given the Bar-Selehm Medal of Citizenry, an award by which they were both amused and baffled, but they bowed and thanked the people they were supposed to thank, and pleased the press and other onlookers with how little they cared about the whole thing. Since their activities were deemed related to exposing the theft of the Beacon, they also got a cash reward, some of which they bestowed upon their village as an investment in their community's future; they put the rest toward financing the Red Fort's monument to that community's past. It was, I supposed, a satisfying vengeance on Gritt and people like him. When reporters expressed amazement that they were keeping so little for themselves, Mnenga shrugged.

"There isn't much to buy in the bush," he said.

* ★ ★

TWO NIGHTS LATER, A little after midnight, with the moon a vast and smoky yellow disk in the perennial fog, I scaled the tower of the Trade Exchange. Willinghouse, Andrews, and two armed officers stood guard in the street below, but there were no press, no cheering crowds. Replacing the Beacon was to be as stealthy an act as its removal had been.

Tanish served as my apprentice, lugging tools and ropes, checking fastenings and harnesses. There was a lot he still couldn't do, and he stayed on the top of the tower as I began the steeple climb, but he had insisted on being there. I worked my way up, using a leather loop around the narrowing column of stone to brace myself as I walked the spire, leaning back and out into nothing. It felt quite natural, a relief after all my other activities over the last two weeks, and I smiled to myself as I climbed. This was my life, a part of who I was, and regardless of what else came my way, that would always be true.

At the top, I opened my satchel, removed a hammer and chisel, and opened up four carefully spaced holes in the old mortar before calling to Tanish. As he winched up the pot of moist, fresh mortar, I positioned the brass plate Willinghouse had commissioned two days earlier. It was a simple piece etched with ladder trim, which was the sign of the steeplejack's trade, and in the center it read, BERRIT'S SPIRE.

There would be no announcement, no unveiling, and very few people in the city would ever know the plate was there, but I would know, and that was what mattered right now. Only when I was happy that it was securely in place did I call to Tanish for the larger bag. I opened up the iron gate of the great glass globe that was the steeple's crowning glory and, when the bag reached the pulley beside me, snapped the smoked lenses of my goggles down and opened it.

The goggles made little real difference, and I had to work with my eyes shut, fitting the massive chunk of luxorite into position on little more than memory, fumbling with the new and elaborate lock once I had the door closed. Before I descended, I looked out across the brilliantly lit streets of the city, gazing out over Bar-Selehm from Berrit's Spire as if I were the god who'd brought starlight to the world, as in Papa's story.

Once on the ground, I looked up to where the urban shadows of the night had been driven into nothing by the hard, white light of the Beacon. Bar-Selehm would wake to its comforting glow, and the world would seem a little closer to being as it should be once more. I wasn't sure what I thought of that. Too much had changed for me to believe that things would ever be the way they had, though I suspected that much of that change was in me, and that most people wouldn't notice it.

"Content?" asked Willinghouse as I reached the bottom. He was watching me closely with those penetrating green eyes as I untied my hair, and in the bright light of the Beacon, his scarred face looked strangely tender.

"Content," I said. "Is there anything else to do?"

"Always," he said. For a moment, he gave me a searching look, and I was sure he was going to say more, but then he was turning and leading me back to the carriage and whatever else the city had in store.

ACKNOWLEDGMENTS

This story was long in the telling, and I would like to thank those who encouraged me to complete it when it seemed that it would never find the right home, particularly my agent, Stacey Glick, who believed in it from the start; my editor, Diana Pho; and those who read early drafts, particularly David Coe and a little gathering of writers, including Faith Hunter (who also supplied notes) and Misty Massey, who heard me read the first chapter and liked it. Of such stuff is courage made. Thanks also to my guides and rangers in South Africa and Swaziland, particularly Brilliant Makhubele and Ezakiel Sibuyi, and to my wife and son, always my first readers.

Turn the page for a sneak peek
at the next novel in the Steeplejack series

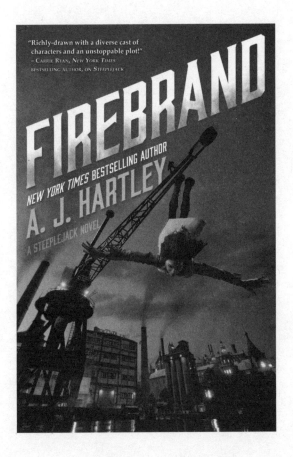

Available now from Tor Teen

CHAPTER

1

THE THIEF HAD BEEN out of the window no more than a minute but had already shaken off the police. The only reason I could still see him was because up here we got the full flat glare of the Beacon two blocks over, because I knew where to look, and because he was doing what I would be doing if our positions were reversed. Moments after the theft had been reported and the building locked down, he had emerged from the sash window on the fourth floor of the War Office on Hanover Street—which was probably how he had gotten in in the first place—and had climbed up to the roof. Then he had danced along the steeply pitched ridgeline and across to the Corn Exchange by way of a cable bridge he had rigged earlier. The uniformed officers in the pearly glow of the gas lamps below blocked the doorways leading to the street, milling around like baffled chickens oblivious to the hawk soaring away above them. If he hadn't shot one of the guards on his way into the strong room, they wouldn't have even known he had been there.

But he had, and he was getting away with a roll of papers bound with what looked like red ribbon. I didn't know what they were, but I had seen Willinghouse's face when the alarm had been raised and knew how badly he needed them back.

Not Willinghouse himself. Bar-Selehm. The city needed them back, and I, Anglet Sutonga, former steeplejack and now . . . something else entirely, worked for the city. In a manner of speaking.

The thief paused to disassemble his cable bridge and, in the act of turning, saw me as I rounded a brick chimney stack. His hand went for the pistol at his belt, the one that had already been fired twice tonight, but he hesitated. There was no clearer way to announce his position to those uniformed chickens below us than by firing his gun. He decided to run, abandoning his dismantling of the bridge, betting that, whoever I was, I wouldn't be able to stay with him up here on the ornamented roofs and towers of the government district.

He was wrong about that, though he climbed expertly. I gave chase, sure-footed in my familiar steel-toed boots, as he skittered down the sloping tiles on the other side and vaulted across the alley onto a metal fire escape. He moved with ease in spite of his formal wear, and the only time he looked away from what he was doing was to check on my progress. As he did, he smiled, intrigued, a wide hyena grin that made me slow just a little. Because despite the half mask he was wearing over his eyes, I knew who he was.

They called him Darius. He was a thief, but because he was also white, famously elegant, and limited his takings to the jewelry of wealthy society ladies—plucked from their nightstands as they slept inches away—he was known by the more romantic name of "cat burglar." I had never been impressed by the title. It seemed to me that anyone whose idea of excitement—and it clearly was exciting for the likes of Darius—involved skulking inside houses full of people was someone you needed to keep at a distance. I've stolen in the past—usually food but sometimes money as well—and I wouldn't trust anyone who did it for sport, for the thrill of standing over you while you slept. For all his dashing reputation and the breathless way in which the newspapers recounted his exploits, it did not surprise me in the least that he had killed a man tonight.

I was, I reminded myself, unarmed. I didn't like guns, even when I was the one holding them. Especially then, in fact.

I too was masked, though inelegantly, a scarf of sooty fabric wrapped around my head so that there was only a slit for my eyes. It was hot and uncomfortable, but essential. I had a job that paid well, which kept me out of the gangs and the factories that would be my only tolerable options if anyone guessed who I really was. That would be easier if anyone realized I was Lani, so my skin stayed covered.

I crossed the wire bridge, slid down the ridged tile, and launched myself across the alley, seventy feet above the cobbled ground, dropping one full story and hitting the fire escape with a bone-rattling jolt. Grasping the handrails, I swung down four steps at a time, listening to Darius's fine shoes on the steps below me. I was still three flights above him when he landed lightly on the elegant balcony on the front of the Victory Street Hotel. I dropped in time to see him swinging around the dividing walls between balconies, vanishing from sight at the fourth one.

He might just have hidden in the shadows, waiting for me to follow him, or he might have forced the window and slipped into the hotel room.

I didn't hesitate, leaping onto the first balcony, hanging for an instant like a vervet monkey in a marulla tree, then reaching for the next and the next with long, sinewy arms. I paused only a half second before scything my legs over the wall and into the balcony where he had disappeared, my left hand straying to the heavy-bladed kukri I wore in a scabbard at my waist.

I didn't need it. Not yet, at least.

He had jimmied the door latch and slipped into a well-appointed bedroom with wood paneling and heavy curtains of damask with braided accents that matched the counterpane.

Fancy.

But then this was Victory Street, so you'd expect that.

I angled my head and peered into the gloom. The bed was, so far as I could see, unoccupied. I stood quite still on the thick dark carpet, breathing shallowly. Unless he was crouching behind the bed or hiding in the en suite, he wasn't there. The door into the hotel's hallway was only thirty feet away, and I was wasting time.

I took four long strides and was halfway to the door when he hit me, surging up from behind the bed like a crocodile bursting from the reeds, jaws agape. He caught me around the waist and dragged me down so that I landed hard on one shoulder and hit my head on a chest of drawers. For a moment the world went white, then black, then a dull throbbing red as I shook off the confusion and grasped at his throat.

He slid free, pausing only long enough to aim a kick squarely into my face before making for the hallway. I saw it coming and turned away from the worst of it, shrinking and twisting so that he connected with my already aching shoulder. He reached for the scarf about my head, but I had the presence of mind to bring the kukri slicing up through the air, its razor edge flashing. He snatched his hand away, swung another kick, which got more of my hip than my belly, and made for the door.

I rolled, groaning and angry, listening to the door snap shut behind him, then flexed the muscles of my neck and shoulder, touching the fabric around my head with fluttering fingers. It was still intact, as was I, but I felt rattled, scared. Darius's cat burglar suaveness was all gone, exposed for the veneer it was, and beneath it there was ugliness and cruelty and the love of having other people in his power. I wasn't surprised, but it gave me pause. I'd been kicked many times before, and I always knew what was behind it, how much force and skill, how much real, venomous desire to hurt, cripple, or kill. His effort had largely gone wide because it was dark and I knew how to dodge, but the kick had been deliberate, cruel. If I caught up with him and he thought he was in real danger, he would kill me without a second's thought. I rolled to a crouch, sucked in a long, steadying breath, and went after him.

The hallway was lit by the amber glow of shaded oil lamps on side tables, so that for all the opulence of the place, the air tasted of acrid smoke, and the darkness pooled around me as I ran. Up ahead, the corridor turned into an open area where a single yellowing bulb of luxorite shone on intricate ceiling moldings and ornamental pilasters.

There were stairs down, and I was aware of voices, lots of them, a sea of confused chatter spiked erratically with waves of laughter.

A party.

More Bar-Selehm elegance and, for me, more danger. I had no official position, no papers allowing me to break into the hotel rooms of the wealthy, nothing that would make my Lani presence among the cream of the city palatable. And in spite of all I had done for Bar-Selehm—for the very people who were sipping wine in the ballroom below—I felt the pressure of this more keenly than I had Darius's malevolent kick. Some blows were harder to roll with.

I sprang down the carpeted stairs, turning the corner into the noise. The hallway became a gallery running around the upper story of the ballroom so that guests might promenade around the festivities, waving their fans at their friends below. Darius was on the far side, moving effortlessly through the formally dressed clusters of startled people. He was still masked, and they knew him on sight, falling away, their mouths little O's of shock. One of the women fainted, or pretended to. Another partygoer, wearing a dragoon's formal blues, took a step toward the masked man, but the pistol in Darius's hand swung round like an accusatory finger and the dragoon thought better of his heroism.

I barreled through the crowd, shoving mercilessly, not breaking stride. The party below had staggered to a halt, and the room was a sea of upturned faces watching us as we swept around the gallery toward another flight of stairs. As I neared the corner, I seized a silver platter from an elegant lady in teal and heaved it at him, so that it slid in a long and menacing arc over the heads of the crowd below and stung him on the shoulder. He turned, angry, and found me elbowing my way through the people as they blew away from him like screws of colored tissue, horrified and delighted by their proximity to the infamous cat burglar. And then his gun came up again and they were just horrified, flinging themselves to the ground.

He fired twice. The gilded plaster cherub curled round the

balustrade in front of me exploded, and the screaming started. Somewhere a glass broke, and in all the shrieking, it wasn't absolutely clear that no one had been seriously hurt, but then someone took a bad step, lost their balance, and went over the balustrade. More screaming, and another shot. I took cover behind a stone pillar, and when I peered round, Darius had already reached the stairs and was gone.

I sprinted after him, knocking a middle-aged woman in layers of black gauzy stuff to the ground as I barged through. My kukri was still in my hand, and the partygoers were at least as spooked by the sweep of its broad, purposeful blade as by Darius's pistol, though it had the advantage of focusing their attention away from my face and onto my gloved hands. A waiter—the only black person in the room that I could see—stepped back from me, staring at the curved knife like it was red-hot. That gave me the opening I needed, and I dashed through to the stairs.

Darius had gone up. I gave chase, focusing on the sound of his expensive shoes. One flight, two, three, then the snap of a door and suddenly I was in a bare hall of parquet floors, dim, hot, and dusty. A single oil lamp showed supply closets overflowing with bed linens and aprons on hooks. The hall ended in a steel ladder up to the roof, the panel closing with a metallic clang as I moved toward it.

He might be waiting, pistol reloaded and aimed. But he had chosen this building for a reason. Its roof gave onto Long Terrace, which ran all the way to the edge of Mahweni Old Town, from where he could reach any part of the northern riverbank or cross over into the warren of warehouses, sheds, and factories on the south side. He wouldn't be waiting. He was looking to get away.

So I scaled the ladder and heaved open the metal shutters as quietly as I could manage. I didn't want to catch him. I wanted to see where he went. It would be best if he thought he'd lost me. I slid out cautiously, dropped into a half crouch and scuttered to the end of the roof like a baboon. Darius was well away, taking leaping strides along the roof of the Long Terrace, and as he slowed to look back, I leaned behind one of the hotel's ornamental gargoyles out of sight. When next I peered round, he was moving again, but slower, secure in the knowledge that he was in the clear.

I waited another second before dropping to the Long Terrace roof, staying low, and sheathing my kukri. The terrace was one of the city's architectural jewels: a mile-long continuous row of elegant, three-story houses with servants' quarters below stairs. They were fashioned from a stone so pale it was almost white and each had the same black door, the same stone urn and bas-relief carving, the same slate roof. Enterprising home owners had lined the front lip of the roof with planters that, at this time of year, trailed fragrant vines of messara flowers. The whole terrace curved fractionally down toward the river like a lock of elegantly braided hair. For Darius it provided a direct route across several blocks of the city away from prying eyes.

The nights were warming as Bar-Selehm abandoned its token spring, and the pursuit had made me sweat. We had left the light of the Beacon behind, and I could barely keep track of Darius in the smoggy gloom, even with my long lens, which I drew from my pocket and unfolded. At the end of the terrace, he paused to look back once more, adjusting the tubular roll of documents he had slung across his back, but I had chosen a spot in the shadow of a great urn sprouting ferns and a dwarf fruit tree, and he saw nothing. Satisfied, he shinned down the angled corner blocks at the end of the terrace and emerged atop the triumphal arch that spanned Broad Street, then descended the steps halfway and sprang onto the landing of the Svengele shrine, whose minaret marked the edge of Old Town. I gave chase and was navigating the slim walkway atop the arch when he happened to look up and see me.

I dropped to the thin ribbon of stone before he could get his pistol sighted, and the shot thrummed overhead like a hummingbird. He clattered up the steps that curled round the minaret and flung himself onto the sand-colored tile of the neighboring house. He was running flat out now, and I had no choice but to do the same. I jumped, snatched a handhold on the minaret, and tore after him, landing clumsily on the roof so that I was almost too late in my roll. Another shot, and one of the tiles shattered in a hail of amber grit that stung my eyes. I sprawled for cover, but Darius was off again, vaulting from roof to roof, scattering tile as he ran, so that they fell, popping and crackling into the street below. Somewhere behind us, an elderly black man emerged shouting, but I had no time for sympathy or apologies.

As the narrow street began to curl in on itself, Darius dropped to the rough cobbles and sprinted off into the labyrinth which was Old Town. The streets were barely wide enough for a cart to squeeze through, and at times I could touch the buildings on either side of the road at the same time. There was a pale gibbous moon glowing like a lamp in Bar-Selehm's perpetual smoky haze, but its light did not reach into the narrow ginnels running between the city's most ancient houses. Down here his footfalls echoed in the dark, which was the only reason I could keep up with him as he turned left, then right, then back, past the Ntenga butchers' row and down to the waterfront, where I lost him.

The river wasn't as high as it had been a couple of weeks before, but it filled the night with a constant susurration like wind in tall grass. As the carefully maintained cobbles gave way to the weedy gravel around the riverside boatyards and mooring quays, any footfalls were lost in the steady background hiss of the river Kalihm. I clambered down the brick embankment that lined the riverbank and revolved on the spot, biting back curses as I tried, eyes half shut, to catch the sound of movement.

There. It may have been no more than a half brick turned by a stray foot, but I heard it, down near the shingle shore only fifty yards away. It came from the narrow alley between a pair of rickety boathouses that straddled a concrete pier. I made for the sound, opting for stealth rather than speed, one hand on the horn butt of my kukri, picking my way over the rounded stones, my back to the city. Even here, in the heart of Bar-Selehm, when you faced the river, you stepped back three hundred years, and there was only water and reeds and the giant herons that stalked among them.

I heard the noise again, different this time, more distinct, but in this narrow wedge of space between the boathouses, almost no light struggled through. The river itself was paler, reflecting the smudge of moon in the night sky and touched with the eerie phosphorescence of glowing things that lived in its depths, but I could see nothing between me and it.

Or almost nothing.

As I crept down the pebbled slope, I saw—or felt—a shape in front of me as it shifted. Something like a large man crouching no more than a few feet ahead. A very large man. I slid the kukri from its sheath, and in that second, the shape moved, black against the waters of the Kalihm. It turned, lengthening improbably as it presented its flank to me. It was, I realized with a pang of terror, no man. It was as big as a cart, and as it continued its slow rotation to face me, a shaft of light splashed across its massive, glistening head. I felt my heart catch.

The hippo rushed at me then, its face splitting open impossibly, eyes rolling back as it bared its immense tusks and bellowed.

ABOUT THE AUTHOR

A. J. HARTLEY is the international bestselling author of a dozen novels, including the YA Steeplejack series with Tor Teen, the Darwen Arkwright middle-grade series, and the Will Hawthorne fantasy adventures for adults. He is the Robinson Distinguished Professor of Shakespeare at UNC Charlotte.